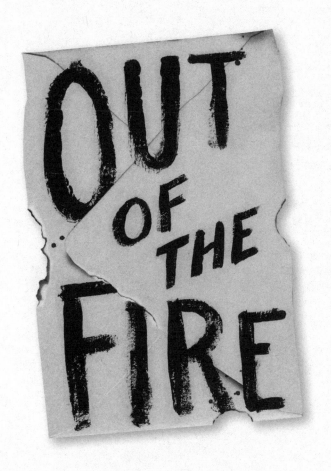

OUT OF THE FIRE

ANDREA CONTOS

SCHOLASTIC PRESS / NEW YORK

Library of Congress Cataloging-in-Publication Data available

ISBN 978-1-338-72616-9

1 2021

Printed in the U.S.A.   23

First edition, October 2021

Book design by Maeve Norton

TO MY DAUGHTERS, EVANGELINE AND JOSEPHINE.
FOREVER AND ALWAYS.

CHAPTER ONE

We were like fire, the four of us. Catching each other's sparks until the flames grew, spread, raged beyond our control.

They told us this would happen. They said it like a warning rather than a promise.

But *we* promised. We promised each other.

We made the flame and gave it life. Stoked it. Let it breathe until it became a thing outside ourselves.

And now we watch as the wind lifts it higher, stretching the fire's orange tongues toward the gray-black sky. The flames destroy everything they touch, snaps and groans piercing the night air, as the walls of the home below grow black and blistered.

The wind shifts and heat caresses my face, tears prickling in my eyes, and the muted wail of sirens grows sharper.

Margot squeezes my hand, and on my other side, Ori shudders.

Nomi is still, quiet. Her hand links to Ori's, but it may as well be mine.

We're all waiting for her, to tell us when she's seen enough. We'll stay all night, perched on the overlook that frames her former stepfather's house below. Mosquitos swarming our ankles and creatures rustling in the trees at our backs.

We'll stay until Nomi's ready to go. That's the deal. The promise. The vow we made that night, deep in the woods where crickets chirped and wolves howled.

"Cass." It's the first word anyone's spoken in fifteen minutes, but none of us are surprised to hear Nomi's voice. "I'm ready."

Our hands unchain, separate now but no less connected, and the flash of lights paints our faces in blues and reds as we fall back from the fire we made.

Tonight is for Nomi. But there are more nights to come.

They warned us bad things would happen.

They didn't know we were just getting started.

Monday, October 4
11 Days Before the End

There was a time I didn't live by the countdown of days. When each month was just another marker of time—not a terrifying reminder of the night that changed everything.

But this is my "new normal," according to my therapist.

There's nothing normal about the pink envelope that'll be waiting for me later today. Envelopes don't appear in any of the self-help books I've been given to read, the online support chats I've searched through, or all the methods I've been given to cope.

That doesn't make the letters any less real. I won't be imagining it when one appears later. Maybe in my car, my locker, my *bedroom*.

Of course, my therapist doesn't know about the envelopes.

No one does.

No one but me, and the man who sends them.

"Adams!"

Coach Pheran screams my name as the volleyball I'm supposed to be spiking sails over my head.

There was a time when I'd have slammed that ball so hard the poor girl on the other side of the net would be afraid to block.

That was before the sound of a ball hitting parquet flooring started to sound like a trunk slamming shut above my prone body.

That means Coach Pheran is just *Ms.* Pheran to me now—from school-related volleyball and rec-league coach to plain old gym teacher—but some part of me can't make the transition.

"Cass!" Coach yells again, because I still haven't responded to the last time. "Do you need to sit out?"

"Yes." It's the truth, but she's not happy to hear it.

She hasn't been happy with me at all since I quit the team last year, right before the junior national championship game.

Our team was already registered, the entry fee paid after a full year of fundraising. All our travel booked and airfare purchased.

Everyone but me got on the plane.

We lost.

Coach sighs. She's almost given up on me. "Take five."

I'm out the door before she changes her mind, breathing in the scent of Pine-Sol that clings to the quiet hallway.

I shudder, because as much as I crave the stillness surrounding me, I need the security of people more. Not people themselves—witnesses. Today is one month since the last envelope. And he's never late.

Lockers swirl by as I rush toward the exit, the harshness of my breathing the only disruption to the steady hum of the school's furnace and low murmurs of teachers that drift from half-open doorways.

Cold shocks my lungs and sunlight rails against my eyes the moment I shove through the exit, goose bumps jumping from my skin.

The boys have gym outside today even though it's October in Michigan. It's too cold, but none of them seem to notice, probably because they're all covered in sweat, their footsteps forming a chaotic rhythm as they follow the curve of the track.

I let them pass before I enter the field—I may want witnesses, but I *do not* want conversation.

The frigid cold of the bleachers soaks into me the second I sit, and I press my elbows into my knees, let my vision go blurry until the boys are a muddled watercolor in motion.

"Care for—"

I scream and jump from the bleacher, except I'm too close to the edge and my back foot hits air instead of metal.

My body tenses for impact, but warm hands wrap around my arms, dragging me back to standing with a surprising amount of strength.

"I'm so sorry," Tyler says for the third time. "I didn't mean to scare you."

Tyler Thorne belongs on a California coast somewhere instead of this Midwest tundra. He's all blond hair, blue eyes, tan skin, lean build that belongs in a wet suit and carrying a surfboard.

He seems as out of place as I feel, and there's something in the way he looks at me that says he knows it too.

He peels his fingers from my arms but hovers inches from my skin, like he's afraid I might fall again.

I mean, he's not wrong.

"It's okay," I lie. I rub my arms to cover how badly I'm shaking. "Just a little jumpy today."

"Sorry. I thought—"

"Shouldn't you be running?"

He breaks into a crooked smile and shoves his swoopy dirty-blond hair from his forehead. "Doctor's note. On account of my asthma."

"Do you even have asthma?"

"I did when I was seven."

The boys run past us, and Noah Rhoades slows his pace to stare at me—and Tyler. I don't know which of us he's glaring at, but honestly it could be either.

Tyler is a bit of a social outcast—the leader of his misfit group of friends but an enemy to the socially acceptable contingent of the school. And I'd bet a lot of someone else's money he was vaping beneath the bleachers a minute ago.

According to rumor, Tyler's family has plenty of money, but there's absolutely nothing about him that shows it, which should be a point in his favor.

And me, well, I'm the girl who kissed Noah Rhoades in the school hallway one early evening, promised to call that night, and four hours later retreated from everything.

No one wants to be the guy whose kiss turned a normal girl into a hermit.

Of course, my hermit-dom has nothing to do with Noah, but it's not like I've ever told him the truth.

I'm supposed to be working on that. The hermit-dom. My therapist tells me very logical things like "you can't go to college if you're too afraid to go anywhere besides home and school."

Of course, *she* doesn't know that it's not fear that's the problem. Not really. I don't think everyone around me is a threat or that some different stranger might toss me in their trunk.

The problem is this: I don't like to go anywhere, because I know I'm never alone.

Noah stutters to a stop, standing his ground even as classmates bump into his shoulders. I doubt any of them could knock him over even if they tried.

He's very . . . sturdy. I remember that, from the way he held me upright while I tried to melt my entire person into him.

The wind tousles his dark hair, and he opens his mouth in this way that tells me my name is perched there.

There's a part of me that wants to hear him say it, exactly the way he did the last time we spoke, when he stood only inches away, the height and breadth of him blocking out every part of the world that wasn't the warm brown of his eyes, the feel of his hand dwarfing mine. But then Coach Bulger yells at him to get his ass moving and he jogs off. But not before shooting one last glare over his shoulder.

"What's his problem?" The sun catches Tyler's eyes, and they shade an inhuman sort of blue, the kind that reminds me of glaciers and the sky at the height of afternoon.

"We used to be friends." My fingers are numb, my body shaking with the cold that's buried into my bones, but I'm not going back to gym, where everyone's waiting with their worried glances and the questions I haven't given them the chance to ask.

Much safer to stay out here. "Safe" being a relative term.

I'm not sure anyone has ever described Tyler as a safe option.

Except me.

Tyler may be the kind of guy my dad's warned me about since I was eight, but he's also the guy that sat at my lunch table—opposite sides and a few spaces down—when I quit the team and stopped returning everyone's calls last year.

He cut off whatever excuse I was about to give and said, "I won't talk, but you looked like maybe you needed to not be alone."

Now we do this. Partake in short conversations whenever our paths cross, which seems to be at increasing frequency.

"Not that it's any of my business, but it seems to me a real friend would've maybe said hello. Or waved."

"*Used* to be friends. My fault we're not anymore. I stopped talking to him."

He leans back, arms spread wide over the bleachers as the boys stampede by again. "Sounds like he deserved it then."

Except he didn't. Neither did Margot. None of them did.

I stare into the sun until my eyes burn from the light instead of tears. "Not really."

"Okay." He pauses, like he's weighing his words. Like he knows this is more than I've told anyone else. "Then it seems to me that a real friend would've tried to find out what happened."

My voice snaps through the air, even though I know he's trying to help.

I'm just so tired of lying, to everyone. I'm tired of being afraid. "What happened is none of their business. And none of yours either."

I jump from the bleachers, my body hot and my breaths uneven, and I ignore every one of the apologies that tumble over my back.

Apologies. Like I didn't just exhibit an extreme overreaction and attack him, completely unprovoked.

"Adams!" It's not Tyler's voice calling me, not Noah's either. Those I could ignore.

I stop and turn slowly, in time to see Coach Bulger lope into view.

His breaths form tiny clouds that match the sprinkle of gray in his dark hair. "Hey, Cass."

"Hey, Coach."

He's not technically my coach. He's the school's conditioning guru though, and Coach Pheran used to use him to kick all our asses in preseason prep.

His favorite saying is that he'll never push anyone harder than he pushes himself, which is a bullshit form of comfort because he's in better shape than nearly every student here.

He crosses his arms over the whistle that dangles at his chest. "Coach Pheran know you're out here?"

"Yes."

He stares and I stare back and we both know I'm lying.

I wait for him to send me to the office, or give me detention, or worse—send me back to Coach Pheran—but instead he says, "We missed you this summer."

I blink, too fast, trying to hold back the tears.

This was all much easier over the summer, when I could avoid everything and everyone. School started a month ago and I'm already cracking, already saying things I shouldn't.

I should've known better. I should've learned by now that conversations only lead to places I'd rather not visit.

Places I *can't* visit, not when the countdown in my head has reached zero.

I don't look at him when I say, "Yeah, I missed everyone too."

"Not too late to come back. I'd even throw in a few extra conditioning days for you."

Despite myself, I laugh. The first day Bulger trained with us, I was so desperate to make a good impression and secure my spot on the team, I sought him out after to tell him I loved it. Then I puked all over my shoes. He's never let me forget it.

I hug myself tight and mumble, "It's too late for *me*," because that's exactly how it feels—like everything has passed me by.

The bell rings, saving me, and I barely say goodbye as I rush past him, the trill of his whistle screaming to round up all the boys as I reach the doors.

I storm through the halls, not even feeling my legs, and head straight into the locker room.

I'm still cursing Noah, Tyler, Coach Bulger, and mostly myself when I fling open my locker.

That's where I find the pink envelope, waiting for me.

CHAPTER THREE

Monday, October 4
11 Days Before the End

I lock myself in a bathroom stall, forehead pressed to cool metal, and let the nausea pass through me.

I run multiplication tables in my head, starting off easy when I'm too panicked to handle more than four times four and nine times nine.

Then it's thirty-six times thirty-six, sixty-three times sixty-three. Seventy-four times twenty-eight and anything else that makes me focus. Makes my brain concentrate on something that's not *him*.

The envelope is like acid in my hands, but I can't let go. And I tell myself I won't look—like I promise every time. But I always do.

It's the not knowing that always undoes me. The wondering if it's *more* this time. More threatening. More terrifying. More personal.

I know one thing though, even without opening it, without looking at the front.

I know it'll be addressed to "The One That Got Away."

That's me. Literally. The girl who got away from him. From his trunk and his blindfold and the duct tape around my wrists.

I got away but that doesn't matter, because he knows who I am. And every month he sends me these notes to remind me.

Sometimes, he sends my own possessions with them.

The bathroom door bangs open, ushering in choked sobs, then the clap of heels on tile floor.

I should probably care more about my fellow student-kind and ask if she's okay, but really I just want her to leave so I can read my stalker letter in peace.

She growls, "That motherfucker!" and kicks the door open. I'm assuming—but it certainly sounds like a kick, and the metal walls around me shudder.

Her door shuts, the lock slides into place, and then there's a thud followed by a slow slide as Margot Pennington slips to the floor.

We sit in silence—well, she sits, I stand—until she says, her voice stuffy, "I can see your feet, Cass."

"Congratulations."

Margot and I used to be friends too. Then I quit the volleyball team and she moved into my spot.

She sniffles. "Why are you standing in the bathroom?"

"Why are you sitting on the floor of the bathroom? That's really gross."

"Cass." She says my name the way she used to, on a sigh that could be amused or exasperated, her head tilted, her dark artfully messy bun lilting to the side.

If I close my eyes, I can picture it.

Her voice whispers through the quiet. "Are you ever going to tell me?"

I'm out of my stall and nearly past hers when she says, "Cass, wait."

I pause, even though I should just keep going, right out the door, farther away from Margot's life.

I press my palm to the door of her stall, as close to reaching out as I'll allow myself. "What happened?"

"Jared." She does *not* say *his* name the way she used to. "We broke up."

"I know." I may not leave the house much, but social media still exists.

"Yeah, well, he's being an asshole about it. And, like, threatening me, I guess?"

My skin goes hot, my thoughts melted into a mass of white-hot fury. Jared always was an asshole. "Margot, open the door."

She slides the lock free, and when the door swings open, her eyes are red and puffy, her face splotchy.

Margot is never splotchy or puffy. She's vintage outfits and effortless style. Pale white skin and bloodred lips. But underneath the aloof art-student facade, she's a huge marshmallow. I know, because when I started school here last year—recruited even though we didn't call it that—Margot was the first girl on the team to say hi. The first to sit by me at lunch. The first to ask me to hang out.

My breaths come too quick, because it's impossible to ignore that I miss her.

And Jared did this to her.

My voice comes out thick. "Threatened you how?"

She looks to the ceiling and blinks once, twice, then gives up and lets the tears fall. "It's my fault."

I slide to the floor across from her, even though I'll have to burn these jeans later and the toilet paper dispenser is wedged against my temple. "I doubt that."

"There are these pictures. Of me. *Picture* pictures. And he said he'd post them if we didn't get back together."

I will kill him.

That's what plays in my head. A continuous loop of all the methods by which I could maim or otherwise injure Jared Bedford.

Pictures. He has to know what that would do to Margot.

She's gorgeous, with pinup model curves. But I don't know how many times I had to coax her from the locker room because she hated how small the shorts in our uniform were.

I amend my head loop to the methods by which I could maim or otherwise injure Jared Bedford in a way that would lead to a horrible, painful death.

"Margot." *Forty-eight times forty-eight is two thousand three hundred four.* "He's blackmailing you into dating him again?"

"Well, he didn't exactly say it like that."

"Who cares how he said it! You—"

"This was a mistake." She jumps from the floor and I follow, holding my hand over the lock.

"You should report him." I regret it the second I say it, and Margot sighs like she knows exactly what I'm thinking.

Sometimes reporting things makes it all worse.

Margot would have to admit she took the pictures. The entire school would see them. Those photos would follow her forever—definitely long enough to be seen by college application committees. Her parents would find out. Her mom would lock her in her room and not let her out—except for games, of course.

I let my hand fall. "Okay, don't report him. But . . . you can't get back together with someone who'd do that to you."

"Yeah. You're so right. Maybe I'll, like, stop talking to him, and then everyone else, and pretend my friends don't exist anymore."

Her words slam into me, stealing the things I want to say.

Her gaze locks on the envelope clutched in my hand. "What's in the pretty pink package, Cass?"

I can't look at her. Can't do anything but fist the envelope tighter, let its sharp edges bite into my skin.

"That's what I thought."

Her heel strikes echo through the room again, fading too fast, and I let myself slip back to the floor.

Knees bent, I drop my head to my arms, and for the first time today, the five-month anniversary of my kidnapping, I let myself cry.

"Hey."

I jump at the sound of the voice, ramming my head against the toilet paper dispenser. "Umm, hey."

Nomi Tanaka stands in my open stall doorway, thick black eyeliner smudged around her eyes, combat boots below fishnet tights and a ripped and wrinkled black dress. "I can't believe you're sitting on the bathroom floor. That's fucking disgusting."

My laugh tumbles out of me without warning, followed by a fresh wave of tears. "I'm not even going to argue."

She nods, the sharp angles of her glossy black hair shifting. I don't know where she came from or how much she heard. Or whether we can trust her with it.

Nomi and I aren't strangers. Once, we were friends. We were both seven, but she was a good person then, and people don't change. She even tried to keep in touch with me after I moved, as only second graders can. But then I moved again, and again after that—and so did she, and now we're both here, our lives intersected.

If she tells anyone what she heard, it'll ruin Margot.

I clear my throat to buy time to figure out how to phrase this. "Listen, I don't know what you—"

She cuts me off with a quick raise of her hand. "If you need help fucking up Jared Bedford, you let me know."

She turns and leaves, not waiting for a response, and when I'm finally alone again, fucking up Jared Bedford sounds like the only way I'd like to spend the remainder of my day.

CHAPTER FOUR
CASS ADAMS

The Events of Monday, October 4
11 Days Before the End

It's not the sights and sounds I remember most. Not the glare of fluorescent lights, the crackle of police radios. Not the stale, sludgy coffee, the hard ledge of the chair that pressed into my thighs. Not even the sting of antiseptic at my wrists.

It's the helplessness.

The off-balance dizziness of a life that didn't feel like mine.

Some other girl went for a run through the woods, down the trail she'd traveled hundreds of times before.

Someone else heard a voice call out, a muffled and distorted yell because her EarPods were playing too loud.

She shouldn't have been running alone, the police said. Shouldn't have played her music so loud. Shouldn't have left her phone in the car and she shouldn't have done so many things and now she's here, there, everywhere, sitting in this hard seat with her stale coffee, apologizing for all the things she did wrong.

She's apologizing like she was the one who put the tape across her mouth. Like she caused the darkness that covered her eyes, her arms held tight.

She was supposed to be stronger than this. She wasn't supposed to let him put her in that trunk. She was supposed to fight and kick and she *did* but none of it mattered because *he* was strong, his hands everywhere at once. Her ankles, her wrists, the rip of duct tape, then her hands, binding them tight.

Then the thump of her body echoing through the trunk, the sparkle of stars in her eyes and the throbbing in her head.

She shouldn't have made her runs so routine—should have varied the routes, the times. She should've known to order her life around this man's desire to hurt.

And she tried—she *tried* to count the turns, the stops. She tried to count the seconds and convert them to miles and listen for the sounds that could be clues, but that music—too loud, she should've known it was too loud—kept screaming in her ears.

She worked it free though, rug burns on her cheeks, her earlobes, until she could hear again. She strained, pulled, against the tape on her wrists until it stretched, just enough to slip her arms beneath her, under her legs, beneath her feet, to the front of her body, where she could rip the gag from her mouth and the blindfold from her eyes and *there*.

The trunk release, glowing in the dark.

She waited. *Two times two is four. Three times three is nine.* Until twenty-four times twenty-four was five hundred seventy-six.

Then the car rolled to a stop, shifted into park. And when the car door opened, she pulled the lever and ran.

She didn't turn around though, to see what kind of car it was. To catch a license plate or the face of the man who put her in that trunk. She should've. That would've helped, to catch him. It would've helped, to wonder why they were in an empty park. To wonder why he didn't give chase.

It would've helped, to give a little more evidence to her story.

Her *story*.

Instead, she ran through the park, faster than she had down the trail. So much faster. Until breathing didn't matter and the burn in her muscles felt like nothing at all and, finally, there was a family.

A woman who tucked her children behind her as the feral girl ran at them from the woods. The girl whispered, "Please help me," because she wanted to scream but couldn't find her voice.

And the woman *did* help. She sheltered the girl and the children with her arms, rounding them like little ducklings into her truck, where she locked them all inside with the sound of her phone ringing and then, "911, what's your emergency?"

That part she got right. She called the police and they rushed to her side. They put her in that room and, for a moment, she thought she was safe. Until their questions felt like accusations, their words like knives.

She sat there with that cup of coffee in her hand, paper against her palm growing cold as she became that stupid girl who did everything wrong.

Her dad tells her she was so brave. So smart.

I want to be that girl. That brave, smart girl who escaped. I want to be the girl that can tell this story out loud instead of words on paper. Who doesn't need the safety of penning them on something you can throw away. I want to be the girl who tells what happened without planning to take it all back.

Maybe I am.

But this is what I know: I may have gotten free, but I haven't gotten very far.

CHAPTER FIVE

Chem lab is a minefield of dread and the threat of teacher-forced partnering.

Ms. Phelps assigns new partners every class, spelling them out in royal-blue dry erase so they're waiting for us the second we walk in.

This kind of interaction is enough to spread anxiety in the normalest of students, and I'm far from normal now.

But I can do this. I can have conversations. No one knows what happened and I don't have to answer any questions. My therapist says so.

Maybe that's where I messed up. I could've gone on like nothing happened, told everyone I was too sick to go to the party and waited until the skin that ripped open from the duct tape healed. If I could've just pretended to be better, life could've gone on.

No big deal, right? I didn't die. The whole thing took less than an hour.

So maybe I could've, if not for the letters that always keep it right there, only a few thoughts away.

Besides, there's no room for regrets. Focus on the present, as my therapist would say.

And for right now, I'm grateful Margot is in this class. For once, I'm hoping to see my name scribbled next to hers.

I should know better than to hope.

Cassandra Adams—Noah Rhoades

Like I said, minefield.

I shuffle to my seat and toss my bag to the ground.

My therapist might say I'm focusing on Margot's problems to avoid my own, and my therapist would be right.

But Margot needs my help. I'm "making meaningful connections with my peers" again. Look at me go.

Noah says, "Why were you talking to Tyler?"

"Hello to you too."

"I see your *laryngitis* has cleared up."

Today is not our first chem lab pairing. The last time, my "laryngitis" prevented any communication. "Feeling much better, thank you."

I'm not. I can't remember the last time I held this many conversations in a single morning.

"I don't mean to sound like your dad, Cass, but of all the people you could deign to grace your presence with, Tyler is the wrong choice."

"You're right."

"You're agreeing with me?"

"Yes. You sound exactly like my dad."

He sighs, and Ms. Phelps instructs us to greet our partners and share something about ourselves, create harmony. Ms. Phelps is the world's only chemistry hippie.

Noah holds out his hand. "Hi. I'm Noah. I used to have a friend named Cass."

The thing I used to love about Noah—and now hate—is that he's obnoxiously forthright.

Always has been.

"I really want to kiss you, Cass. If that's okay with you."

Our eyes lock and the air is too thick, my cheeks too hot, then Noah's breath hitches.

I am *not* shaking his hand.

I bail from my seat and keep low, waddling to Margot's lab table, where Shelly is "sharing" that she's a defensive specialist in volleyball. Like Margot doesn't know that. They're on the same fucking team.

I nudge Shelly and whisper, "Switch me."

"What?" Shelly scowls because she hates me for costing us nationals on the rec team last year. And any chance of a school championship this year. "We can't *switch*."

"Switch me, or I'll rejoin the team and take your spot."

The nice thing about cutting yourself off from high school society is that it doesn't matter if people hate you.

"You wouldn't."

She's obviously right, but she doesn't know that.

She mutters an "ugh," but then she's gone and I slide into her seat.

Margot stares straight ahead. "I can't fail this class."

"Me either."

"I'll get kicked off the team."

Ms. Phelps launches into a safety lecture—we're playing with fire today, so she's extra concerned—and I say, "You need something that's more embarrassing than the pictures. Then you can threaten him back."

"I'm not talking about this."

Ms. Phelps dims the lights, saying something about discovering which substance has been given to us by the color of the flame. We're supposed to light them all at once. Count of three. *"A rainbow of fire!"*

She's entirely too excited about this.

Margot follows along as Ms. Phelps dons her safety gear, and I scramble to keep up while I whisper, "I've been kind of a shitty friend."

"Kind of?"

"I'm sorry."

"Sorry doesn't fix anything, Cass." Her eyes flutter beneath her safety glasses, and she rips off her glove to wipe a tear.

She's right. Sorry doesn't fix anything. But maybe, if I can help her with this Jared thing, I can stop feeling like I'm standing still. Maybe I can be that brave, smart girl I want to be.

For that, I need her to trust me. And there's this part of me—this scared, stupid part of me—that just wants someone else to know.

Ms. Phelps clicks on her safety lighter and reminds us about the count of three. She's barely finished with "one," and I can't hold it in anymore.

"I was abducted."

"You were fucking what?!" Margot's head swivels toward me, her voice shouting over Ms. Phelps's "two." Then Margot's hand drops.

Our substance ignites, dancing green flames flickering in the hazy darkness (we got boron, apparently), and Margot's chest heaves, because Ms. Phelps is a second from throwing peace and love out the window and Margot can't fail this class.

From across the room, Nomi's substance lights, a tower of crimson, and she calls out, "Strontium!"

That's all it takes. Every substance flares to life, none of them on the count of three, and when Nomi winks at me, I feel okay for the first time in a very long time.

The class is a symphony of shouted chemicals and writhing flames and Margot hasn't stopped staring at me.

Her phone buzzes, mercifully dragging her attention away, but then Jared turns from his seat two rows up. He says nothing. Doesn't have to.

Our green flame coats him in a sickly hue, flaring higher just before it goes quiet.

Margot isn't staring anymore; she's frantically texting, and I was wrong.

Margot doesn't need something embarrassing to counter-blackmail Jared. He threatened her. He's trying to force her to be with him, against her will.

She's not locked in a trunk, but she might as well be.

I rub the lines on my wrists, where the duct tape burned while I struggled, where it ripped my flesh apart when I tore it free.

Embarrassment isn't good enough.

It's not good enough for any of them.

Jared Bedford needs to be taught a lesson.

Jared Bedford needs to know what fear feels like.

CHAPTER SIX

Monday, October 4
11 Days Before the End

I have rules about the letters.

I don't react when I first see them, and I don't read them anywhere he might see.

That second one is harder to accomplish than one might think. The first, I've had plenty of practice for.

The first letter came on a Sunday, not even two days after *that night*. After a Saturday spent curled into soft bedding and surrounded by soft lights, I made myself go out.

Dad was already googling therapists and staring at me when he thought I wasn't looking.

All I wanted to do was forget it ever happened. Stick it in that place where all the memories of Mom are, the ones from before we decided it was time to stop making new ones.

So I told myself I was brave and smart, and I made myself walk to the library. No music this time. No running either. Slow. Aware. Taking note of every surrounding. This time, I was determined to do things right.

By the time I made it back home, the world felt warmer. The sun melting into my skin, a steady breeze that tickled the leaves and flowers.

The first second that pink envelope entered my sight, I thought—stupidly, ridiculously—that it could be from Noah.

And so I smiled.

I know I smiled, because he took a picture of it. Not Noah. *Him.*

He took a picture and included it in the letter I got the next day.

Two letters, two days in row, and that was my fault. Because I took the first letter, and the EarPod I'd left in his trunk that he sent alongside it, to the cops.

There were no fingerprints. No DNA. No return address. No clues.

Dad still doesn't know I overheard when one of the cops asked if it were possible I'd sent it myself. Or if maybe, this was all some elaborate jilted-girlfriend setup. If it were possible I'd let things go too far with whatever boy may have been with me that night and regretted it.

And even then, I took the second letter to the cops. The ones who didn't believe me about the first one.

The second letter, the one with the picture of my smiling face, the one with a necklace that had been in my jewelry box the day before, said this:

ARE YOU LOOKING FOR ME, CASSANDRA?

JUST ASK. I'M ALWAYS HERE.

That's what he took from my visit to the police station. That I was trying to find him. I sat there, huddled in the corner of my closet, hands shaking too hard to read until I pressed them between my knees, world spinning because no matter how many breaths I took they couldn't fill my lungs, and he believed I wanted this. Wanted *him*.

And that's when I knew. There was no reaction he wouldn't read wrong, no action he wouldn't twist to fit his world.

So surviving meant giving him as little of myself as I could. I didn't know it would mean throwing away the person I used to be.

But that didn't matter then—the only thing that did was learning. How to live in his world. Understand how he thought. Play his game.

So that's what I did.

I learned and I didn't take the letter that came the next day. The one I found in my school locker after the cops put a watch on my house.

I didn't take the third letter, and when my dad asked, I told him there wasn't one.

I didn't get another letter the next day. When I stopped pushing, when I stopped relying on the people who couldn't help me anyway, *he* stopped too.

And now we have a truce—my kidnapper and I. I don't go to the cops, and the letters only come once a month.

It's a tentative sort of status quo, an equilibrium that's always threatening to tip to the wrong side, but it's better than those first two days. It's better than having to read his words every day of my life. I finally got the courage to stop sleeping in my closet, phone clutched in my hand.

It's better when I can pretend there are moments where he's not there. Those are the only moments I can breathe.

As for the first of my rules—the not-reacting one—I had to practice for that. I spent days watching the scariest movies I could find, with a mirror propped next to me.

I've developed an excellent poker face.

And that's why I can control my reaction when Margot catches me in the hall after fourth period and asks if I want to go to Roasted Beans after school.

No, I do not want to go to Roasted Beans, because he will be there. Today is letter day. He'll be everywhere.

And Margot will want details. I *did* casually drop an abduction bomb in the middle of chem, so the questions are warranted. I'm just not sure I have the words to answer them.

But I can't convince Margot to teach Jared a lesson if I can't even go to a coffee shop. So I say yes.

Except I'm still so rattled about the very idea of public spaces I nearly barrel into the person headed the other way as I turn the hall corner.

Ori Bello gasps, her dark eyes wide with shock—probably because I would've crushed her if we both hadn't pulled up short.

Ori is a full head shorter than me, leaving me full view of someone—a teacher by the looks of the khaki pants—strolling down the hall, headed in the opposite direction.

The sun slants through the windows and across her dark brown skin, highlighting high cheekbones and the small smile she gives me.

Her curls shake around her head as she whispers, "I'm so sorry. I should make more noise when I walk and—"

"No. *No.* It was my fault. I was sort of, running away."

I can't meet her eyes. I barely knew Ori before *that night.* I barely know her now. Still, she's the person at this school I came closest to telling what happened.

It was the Monday after, and I would've skipped it and every one after if truancy laws didn't exist.

Five hours. That's how long I lasted. Ignoring everyone, avoiding every conversation, jamming in my cheap replacement earbuds so I had an excuse for not responding when everyone called my name.

I couldn't turn the volume on though. Every time I did I was back in that trunk.

Ori found me in the stairwell. She wasn't looking for me; she was on her way to class while I stood there, bent over, hyperventilating.

She didn't say a word. Instead, her hand reached out, open, waiting, and I grasped on to it like the lifeline it was. And then I proceeded to sob all over the place while she stood there, holding tight to my hand.

That's when I almost told her, because she didn't ask, because she was someone I barely knew. We'd never had a conversation. We shared no classes—I was in some AP courses, but she was in all of them. One of those kids who can tell you their exact GPA.

But then I imagined saying the words, and I imagined the ones she'd say back. If I let her stay this silent girl, she couldn't tell me she didn't believe me.

I ripped my hand free and raced down the stairs instead.

"Are you okay?" Her quiet voice yanks me to the present, where she's avoiding my gaze as much as I am hers.

"Listen. I never thanked you, for that day."

"I didn't do anything."

My voice comes out thick. "Yes. You did."

I clear my throat and soldier on, because it turns out I'm not any more ready to hear her response now than I was then. "Sorry again, for . . . running you over."

She smiles. "It's okay. I was kind of running away too."

My thoughts come together in a rush. "Running from that teacher? Why—"

"What? Of course not. Anyway, I should get to class, so—"

She ducks around me, flinching when I grasp her arm, even though I barely touched her.

"Ori?"

She turns, and the look in her eyes is far too easy to recognize.

Maybe I'm projecting, too clouded by my own issues. I could be making the biggest mistake. "Were you running from that teacher? Did he do something to you?"

She doesn't ask, just presses her lips together while tears form in her eyes, and just like she did for me, I don't make her say anything.

Instead, I reach for a scrap of paper in my bag, scribbling my number.

I tuck it into her hand and walk away before she has the chance to do what I would do: give all the excuses for why she doesn't need it, will never use it.

The least I can do is make her not alone in whatever she's carrying.

And then she's down the hall before I can say anything else, and I'm left with nothing but the looming threat of Roasted Beans in my future.

I scan the other drivers the whole way there, study every pedestrian.

I haven't read the letter yet, and the longer I go, the larger its presence becomes, until it steals the air from my lungs and crawls inside.

I hate that feeling. Hate feeling naked, stripped of my protections, watched and on display.

I hate our agreement.

It was easy—*so* easy—to insist Jared be taught a lesson. Far too easy to offer myself as the person to deliver justice. And yet here I am, a letter in my backpack that I'm too much of a coward to read. Five months spent hiding in shadows and cowering at even a whisper of wind.

And what I hate more than anything is this person he's turned me into. One who runs from her problems, hides the truth, and loses herself to someone else's. That person isn't me. It's my mother.

I can't be her. I *won't*.

Beans is crowded, patrons spilling onto the outdoor patio even though it's too cold, the wind too brisk. But the waft of buttered croissants and roasted coffee coats the air in the illusion of warmth.

I duck inside, scanning for Margot, but she probably doesn't speed-walk through the school parking lot like I do.

Before I can change my own mind about reading, I head for the bathroom.

I stand there, flickering sconces on the warm brown walls plastered with dancing coffee beans, and I hold my pink letter.

For the first time, it's not the cold tendrils of fear that wrap around me; it's the burn of rage.

The glue pops free as I slide my finger beneath the edge. Carefully. The first one, I ripped open. I shouldn't have done that, they said. Best to preserve evidence as best as one is able. Maybe if I hadn't, they'd have been able to get some sliver of DNA, some hint of a fingerprint. Instead, all it got me was another letter.

There are no trinkets this time. No stolen keepsakes from my home, my room, my locker. There's not even a picture.

But the rush of relief is gone in a single heartbeat.

The slip of paper is thick in my hands, textured, and in deep black text:

ARE YOU READY YET?

Following that, a phone number.

I'm frozen, every fiber of my being immobilized until my head goes dizzy with lack of oxygen.

This is what I've been waiting for—the inevitable moment when notes aren't good enough. When I'm not the only one who grows tired of our agreement.

Equilibrium tipped.

I was wrong. I am *just* like my mother, because all I want to do is hide.

The paper slides from my shaking hands, floats on the air until it skitters along the tile, and my stomach heaves.

I breathe through it, letting the cold porcelain of the sink ground me, remind me I'm safe, *here*. I'm not in that trunk anymore. Not running through the woods. Not even in the police station, waiting for an end I won't get.

A double knock sounds at the door and I call out that someone is in here, and Nomi's voice responds, "I know. I saved us a table."

I scan my brain for the memory of inviting Nomi, but it's not there, because it didn't happen.

I fling open the door. "Did you follow me here?"

"Obviously. You look like shit. You dropped something."

The piece of paper lies on the floor, the pink envelope only a foot away. I need them both, to put with the others.

He gave me a phone number. *Are you ready yet?*

The answer to that, to whatever it means, is an emphatic no.

Nomi shoves past me and ratchets a few paper towels free, using them to pick up the note. "Backpack?"

I nod because I can't speak. I can't touch them, and I think she knows.

"Margot's at our table."

Our table. I don't know how to feel, being part of something, when I've been alone for so long.

The café teems with people, murmured voices, the hisses and bangs from behind the counter. My fingers twitch with the need to cover my ears.

School I'm used to. With its slammed lockers and random shouts. Shoes squeaking on waxed floors and chiming bells that herd us to our next class.

These are different noises, the kind I'm not used to without the comfort of my dad in arm's reach.

Holy shit does that sound pathetic.

Sixty-three times sixty-three is ... three thousand nine hundred sixty-nine.

I stumble into my seat, where Margot has a double mocha waiting for me.

She remembers. And it nearly breaks me.

So much of my life, so much of who I am, is still locked in that trunk.

But Margot's here now, and she ordered my favorite drink for me, and I can almost pretend the last five months never happened.

We may have only met last year, but I spent as many hours at Margot's house as my own until *that night*. Gossiping about our classmates and sitting silently, side by side, puzzling out homework neither of us wanted to do. Celebrating after games and falling asleep to each other's laughter.

I took her position on the team, and she never complained about it. She's the one that got the other girls to accept me when they found out. Part of me assumed she'd be grateful when I quit last year. But then, volleyball was never Margot's end game, even if it's her mother's.

"Cass. Are you okay?" Her tone is soft, soothing, because the last five months *did* happen.

I wish I could take back what I told her today. It's a door opened when I should've kept it slammed shut, where I didn't have to answer all the questions she'll have. Because it's still not a thing I can talk about like it's my own. It's still that "other girl" when I close my eyes and remember.

I can deal with Margot's anger, hers and everyone else's. But not her pity.

Not those looks the cops gave me, their sad eyes and their gentle shoulder squeezes.

And now, being exposed in this packed room, I could swear every pair of ears is tuned in to my voice, every eye drifting toward me, and I scan the room for a face I've never seen.

Nomi says, "So about this Jared motherfucker," and my eyes go as wide as Margot's.

Margot stares at me and I hold up my hands. "I didn't tell her anything. She heard us in the bathroom."

Nomi sips her black coffee. "Apology accepted for the two of you talking about me like I'm not here, but yes. I heard you in the bathroom."

"I'm sorry, but . . ." Margot blinks, twice. "Did you just *show up* here?"

"Technically, I followed Cass."

I can't help laughing, because I wish I had half of Nomi's honesty. "Margot, she wants to help. I think we might need it."

Margot shoves aside her macchiato to lean in close. "We don't even know *what* we're planning to do! Besides, I thought we were going to talk about . . . you know."

The pink envelope, the thick paper, the handwriting, the number, already seared into my brain, and I grip the table so I won't leave, so I don't have to say the words to Nomi like I did to Margot earlier.

Nomi's voice is quiet. "I already know, Cass."

When I gape at her, she adds, "Not details or anything, but . . . my dad's a detective."

I should've realized people would know, even if I couldn't tell them myself. "You never said anything. To anyone." Even I'm not sure if it's a comment or question.

She shrugs. "Not my story to tell."

That night, at the police station, and the nights that came after when I stood in windowless rooms, holding my letters, my story was everyone's to tell. Passed along from person to person and typed into reports for anyone to read and judge.

It still is. Nothing about what happened to me *belongs* to me—except the guilt. The regret. The nightmares.

I give Nomi a nod that I hope says "thank you" and turn to Margot.

But I still owe her an explanation, and she hasn't pushed for me to give it.

Every time I remember it's like living it all over again, the helplessness, and the knowledge that the world isn't always the place you expect it to be. That all the things you thought were guarantees are weightless whispers, slipping through your fingers right when you need them most.

This, right now, is real though. I'm *here* and I'm safe.

Deep breaths.

"The night I didn't show up at the party, when I stopped talking to everyone, I went for a run and there was a guy and a trunk. Then there was an emergency release and, voilà, I'm still here."

Margot's eyes fill with tears, and she whispers, "I wish you would've told me."

"I'm sorry." I am. For both of us. "It messed me up and I couldn't . . . I still can't—I don't like talking about it."

It's wholly inadequate, but Margot mercifully doesn't ask for more. Instead, she reaches across the table and squeezes my hand.

I shouldn't, but I squeeze back, even though it feels like I'm breaking, the armor I've built around myself fracturing. It's dangerous, exposing the only places I have left.

Someone yells Margot's name from across the room, and the spell over our table breaks.

Margot's mom makes it halfway through the café, the duffel Margot needs for practice tonight slung over her shoulder, before she stutters to a stop, eyes narrowing on me, then on Nomi. Margot is smart enough to run to her before she gets to us, and Nomi and I spend their entire five-minute discussion debating which one of us Margot's mom hates more.

Neither, according to Margot when she gets back. "She just . . . I was really upset last year, Cass, when you disappeared. She's afraid I'll get hurt again. And, Nomi, she doesn't know you, but she said you . . ." Her voice trails off. "Sorta look angry."

"Dammit!" Nomi can barely speak through her laughter. "I thought I was pulling off the delicate Asian flower thing so well!"

Margot rolls her eyes. "About as well as I pull off the blond, svelte Swedish bombshell."

It's my turn for genetics sharing, but Mom wasn't exactly the "sit around and talk family tree" type. "I don't even know half of my ancestry, but I'm sure there's some stereotype I'm not living up to."

"Stereotypes are boring anyway." Margot laughs, but it's muted. "My mom said it was dangerous, hanging out with you guys. If she only knew." She swallows hard. "She fucking *loves* Jared. If—if she ever found out, she'd kill *me*, not him."

Dangerous.

I want that to be true.

Dangerous people aren't afraid. They don't live their lives around the rules of someone else. They don't hide and worry. A dangerous girl wouldn't wait for the next letter—she'd end them.

If Dad could hear the things in my head, he'd react just like Margot's mom. That familiar fear would creep into his eyes.

Truth is, the things in my head scare me too. They're not Cass thoughts. They're things my mother would say. And no part of me is like her.

I may not be able to solve my problems, but I can solve Margot's. I owe her that. "So. We're all in?"

It's been a long time since Margot and I could telegraph our thoughts, but everything in me is saying we can trust Nomi. People don't change.

Margot taps her nail against her cup, because I guess my opinion doesn't hold the weight it once did. "No offense, Nomi, but what's in it for you?"

It's a fair question, but Nomi doesn't seem fazed. "Jared is an asshole, and—" Her eyes flicker away, and for a second, all her bravado slips away and there's something there. Something that's *not* Jared-related. "Anyway, I'm tired of assholes never paying the price for being assholes."

Our table falls silent, each of us meeting the others' eyes, and just like that, we're a trio.

The three of us versus Jared Bedford.

I like our odds.

I speak before I can think better of it, my voice low and strained. "It doesn't have to end with Jared."

I'm thinking of whoever hurt Nomi. I'm thinking of Ori's tears when I asked about that teacher today. I'm thinking maybe they all need to learn lessons.

And now it's out there, too late to take back. The spark of flame waiting for the right kindling to catch on.

Nomi says, "What about . . . ?" and gestures to my bag, to the letter inside it, and I want to say yes so badly it burns on my tongue.

Yes, we'll find him. The way he found me. And *yes*, we'll watch him the same way, until I've invaded every part of his life and there is no safe place for him. *Yes*, to seeing the look in his eyes, to watching as he realizes he's paying for what he did.

Instead, I shake my head. I can't ask that of them, and I wouldn't know where to start. "Consider this a pro bono offer."

Margot's smile starts small but doesn't end that way. "I'm in. For whatever. You guys do this for me, and I'll return the favor. Even yours, Cass, if you change your mind."

Nomi pauses, but then she nods, a sharp slash that makes her hair swish. "Yes. Okay, yes. We take them down together."

I raise my double mocha high. "To assholes paying the price for being assholes."

Seconds later, Nomi's coffee and Margot's macchiato meet me in the middle, and we toast to the three of us—the dangerous girls who are going to teach lessons.

CHAPTER SEVEN

Monday, October 4
11 Days Before the End

Dad jumps from the couch the second I swing open the front door. We both freeze, eyes locked—me confused and him guilty.

He says, "You're here!" with cheer that doesn't match the strain on his face.

I check my watch because he shouldn't be home right now. Dad is a doctor. At the hospital. It's not the kind of job where you work from home. He used to be able to take time off whenever he needed. He used to be able to plan his own schedule and work something other than the midnight shift.

That was before we moved, again, and when we'd run out of cities that were close enough to his old hospital, he had to start over, at the bottom of the hierarchy. All because of her.

I search his eyes for clues. "Did something happen?"

To Mom, is what I mean. We may not talk to her anymore, or even know where she is—the last card she sent came from some shitty motel, room 207, return address in someone else's handwriting—but there's still this place inside me that holds on to the wish that, one day, she might be different. That she could go back to the beginning, when it wasn't so bad.

My mother was forever searching for the joy everyone else missed. Spontaneous, exuberant, and just a little bit reckless.

Cordelia Adams was *alive* in a way normal people aren't.

That meant days primed for adventure. Consequences be damned. Like when she pulled me from school for an impromptu trip across the state to see the tulip festival, until we both decided tulips were boring and spent the night watching the sun set over the rocky beach.

Or the days she'd convince Dad to call off work, use one of those "million personal days he'd never take on his own" so we could go on some grand excursion. *The Good Doctor Adams.* That's what Mom always called him.

It wasn't until I was older that I realized she didn't always mean it as a compliment.

Dad puts on his blank face—the one he uses to give reports to families who come through his emergency room when the news is anything less than good. "She's fine, Cassie. Or . . ."

As far as I know is what he doesn't say.

We haven't known for a year now. That's how long it's been since Dad stopped trying to save her and I stopped hoping he could, and we all agreed we were better off without each other. We went our way, and Mom went hers, covering her tracks behind her.

I let out a shaky breath. "Are *you* okay?"

"Yeah!" He's chipper again, and it's still forced. "How was your day?"

I let my backpack thump to the ground. "Dad. Why are you here?"

He lets out a long sigh before squeezing me in a hug so hard my back cracks. He lets me go and stares over my shoulder. "You didn't come home after school."

Oh.

Oh.

Sometimes I forget he's lived the past months with me too. Sometimes, it's all too clear how afraid he is I'll end up like my mother, with trauma she never found a way to work through and a heart that can never belong to anyone. Not her husband. Not even her own child.

Truth is, she never needed us. Not like we needed her. There was always someone else willing to take our place. My mother was the sun. Bathing you in the warmth of her love and affection until any moments outside her presence were cold and empty.

But the more you needed the less she gave, and all of them—me and

Dad too—wanted what they couldn't have. They always do, and Mom was never meant to belong to anyone but herself.

And when she tried, that's when it all went wrong.

I feel so guilty about making him worry I almost don't want to ask one very important question. "Hey, so how did you know I didn't come home?"

"Right. That." His cheeks twinge pink before he shuffles across the room. He still has his doctor clogs on. In the house. He must've been near panic. "I—Well. I asked Mrs. Henderson to keep an eye out for you."

He had me watched.

Every drop of blood drains from my head and the room tilts until I have to squeeze my eyes shut.

It's not his fault. He doesn't know I've spent the last five months with my breath held, tracked by invisible eyes that follow every movement. He doesn't know that hearing someone else has been watching for me, staring out curtained windows, is like that moment on the trail, in the half second it took for my brain to understand what the arms wrapped tight around my waist meant.

Mrs. Henderson has been watching me, and I didn't even realize.

I thought I was paying attention this time. I thought I'd gotten better.

"Cassie, I—"

"It's okay." I open my eyes, force a smile. He didn't know because I didn't tell him. *I'm* the person I should be mad at. "Really."

He wraps me in a hug again, gentler this time, and I breathe in his spicy dad soap beneath the sterile hospital scent that clings to his scrubs.

Even this is tainted. There's nothing that happens—even here, in *my home*—where I don't imagine him watching.

Dad whispers into the top of my head. "I just worry, Cassie. I don't know what I'd do—"

Please don't let him cry. Please don't let him cry. There is literally nothing that can reduce me to a blubbering mess faster than that.

He clears his throat and releases me, ruffles my hair. "Sorry, kiddo."

He doesn't realize, the way he started calling me "kiddo" again after the abduction. That he hasn't called me Cass since that same night.

"It's okay, Dad. I'm not mad." The spots from my tears stretch and feather in his scrubs.

He pulls back and he's beaming, genuine this time. "Tell me about this busy day you had!"

I swallow, clench my hands to stop them from shaking. "I went to get coffee with friends. I should've told—"

"No! No. It's okay. I'm glad you went out! Was it fun? You had a good time?"

Well, Dad, we made plans to meet in the woods later this week and destroy our enemies if that's your idea of fun!

"I had a great time. It was good."

"That's great to hear, Cassie." He hugs me again, and he's so happy—so *relieved*—because he doesn't know.

He doesn't know our lives are still upside down. That I'm still in danger. That there's nothing he can do to protect me.

And it would kill him to discover any of it.

It's the fuel to my fire, another log catching the flame. Five months. Five months of lies and secrets. Five months of fear. Five months of letting *him* make all the rules and hoping for a miracle to make it all disappear.

Maybe there is no miracle. Maybe I'll never know who he is, or why he picked me.

But I'm still alive, and as long as that's true, I can do for Margot, Nomi, and maybe even Ori, what I can't do for myself.

I can help bring a little sliver of justice into the world.

CHAPTER EIGHT
CASS ADAMS

The Events of Thursday, October 7
8 Days Before the End

The three of us entered the woods that night, me, Nomi, and Margot—guarding our secrets beneath the weight of our fear. Beneath our shame and our guilt.

We stumbled over twigs and branches missed by the narrow beams of our flashlights. Our breaths mingled with the crisp night air, every exhale an act of courage.

The woods feel empty. Only me, Margot, and Nomi under the darkness of the forest. And *he* could be here too, a threat to all of us now.

We carry our unspoken thoughts like weapons; we drag our fear like an anchor out to sea.

There is no return from tonight. No taking back the promises we'll make or the plans they'll birth.

But it's an illusion, for all of us, to pretend we have other choices. It's a lie, to believe there's another way, that the world will seek vengeance for us. The world chose sides already, before we were even born.

I try to summon guilt for the things we decide tonight, but there's only emptiness in the place where it should be.

Nomi leads us into a circle where trees give way to trampled grass, a ring of tree stumps lining a pit of sand and gravel. She came here, when she was much younger. Only two years after her parents' divorce and a year after her mom remarried and shattered any naive hopes of a parental reunion.

She came here with her mom and stepdad, she said. She didn't say the memories weren't happy, weren't filled with the kinds of days you'd want to remember, but some things don't need to be said.

I pull the items from my bag—different ones than Tuesday night. Everything is different.

Nomi watches silently, until, "Did you bring *snacks*?"

"Want some?"

"Hell yes." She grabs my bag of pretzels, then the tortilla chips too.

Branches crack deep in the woods, and we all turn to the sound, tensed, wary, ready to protect this thing we've barely started.

But it's me that has the most to fear. Not fear for myself though. I brought the girls into my world—a place *he* inhabits as much as I do.

A sharp light pierces the column of blackness where we came through the woods, then, standing in the middle of it, is Ori Bello.

She waves, barely a raise of her hand. "Sorry."

It takes a second to realize what she's apologizing for. "I invited you."

What I didn't do was tell Margot and Nomi I invited her. Mostly because I didn't think she'd show.

I hate it, but I borrowed a tactic from my stalker and left a note in her locker after she never used the cell number I gave her.

"Cass," Nomi says, an unmistakable edge to her voice. "Care to explain?"

I do care to, but I don't *know* anything about what brought Ori here. Not really. Her history is as much a mystery to me as mine is to her.

Ori's voice is nearly lost to the forest—the skitter of a leaf against the roar of wind through a thousand trees. "You were right."

I fill in the blanks. "We ran into each other in the hall, and Ori was running away from someone. A teacher."

Ori says, "Us meeting like that, then finding out you were all meeting here, it felt . . ." She pauses, then rolls her eyes at herself. "Scripted."

I raise an eyebrow, and I don't have to look at Margot or Nomi to know they're doing the same.

Ori's mouth opens, but no words spring forth, until she finally speaks in rapid fire. "Like a movie is what I mean. Like a superhero movie. A group of misfits that don't belong all happen to find each other and they all unite behind a common goal despite their opposing personalities and then they become . . . like . . . family."

Her whole body deflates. "Never mind. I can go. I'll—"

"No!" My shout makes everyone jump, and Nomi and Margot look to me.

I bristle, because this shouldn't be all my decision—I'm not the girl who makes decisions.

Or at least, not the right ones.

Branches crack and we all swivel toward the sound, and for the first time, I realize Ori's just as afraid as the rest of us.

I can't tell her to leave, not when she was brave enough to ask for help. Not when I would've given anything for someone to have helped me once. Not after she held my hand and didn't breathe a word. "You should stay."

She smiles and scampers to a stump across from me, and Nomi's and Margot's gazes catch mine.

I shrug, because I can't telegraph all my reasonings with a soulful gaze. And bravery should be rewarded. I've barely left the house in months, and Ori walked into the woods alone.

I can't turn her away, questioning whether all her decisions were the wrong ones too. I won't do that to her. I won't make anyone feel as alone as me.

We gather kindling and a few bigger branches, all of us working in silence. This is what we agreed to—telling our stories, nothing held back. No secrets.

We lie to everyone else. To each other, we tell the whole truth.

I drag a Vaseline-coated cotton ball from my plastic bag and tuck it between dried bark and brush, and sparks follow the strike of the match.

Our fire roars to life, wood splitting and cracking while orange flames grow stronger, feeding on the piles we've gathered.

I brush dirt from my palms and claim my stump. "Should we do something to show our allegiance? Like a blood oath or something?"

Nomi's nose wrinkles. "No offense, but how do I know none of you have illnesses or STDs or something?" When Ori's eyes flare wide, Nomi adds, "Not you, Ori. Or—" She points to me. "Not you either, I guess, since you never leave the house."

Margot throws up her hands. "Perfect. So just me then? Because I'm the slut, right?"

Nomi winces. "I didn't call you a slut. I'm just saying I know about bloodborne pathogens—we had to take a whole class at lifeguard school."

"Wait." My brain gets stuck on the idea of Nomi in any public-service job, let alone one that requires a Speedo. "You're a lifeguard?"

"I *was*, yes. And I was good at it, so fuck off."

Ori raises her hand, waiting for me to nod at her before her quiet voice carries over the fire. "Can we maybe, if you all are okay with it, try to be a little less . . . slut-shamey? And a little less self-harmy, with the blood oath thing?"

She stares at her hands, muscles tense like she's waiting for someone to disagree, but she's right.

"Okay. No blood oath. No slut shaming. No . . . *questions*."

The group goes silent, just the snap and rumble of the fire, while I search for the words to explain. "What I mean is, no second-guessing. No judgments. Not now, not ever. We all made the best decisions we could."

It's a selfish request, designed to save me from answering why I hid the letters. Why I didn't tell anyone. Why I didn't look back. Why I did all the wrong things.

But from the looks on everyone's faces, they have their own questions with the wrong answers.

Nomi drags her hands through her hair. "Yeah, okay. And fuck it. I'll go first."

And she does. She tells us about her former stepfather, the one that broke her mother's arm. Then her wrist. And after that, her cheekbone.

Then she stares at each of us, defiant.

I feel it in the deepest part of me, in that place I pulled from lying in that trunk, while sitting in that precinct, explaining the things I did and all the reasons I didn't do them differently.

And Nomi's waiting now, for the questions we're not supposed to ask. Why didn't your mom leave him? Why didn't you tell your dad? He's a cop.

But the questions don't come, and Nomi's voice wavers. Because it wasn't the time her stepdad held her mom against the wall, not the times he threatened to kill her that changed everything.

It was the time his fists found Nomi that her mom found her strength.

They lost everything. The house, her dog, her clothes, her books.

They fled, thieves in the night, from the man who stole their safety.

It was six solid months before Nomi or her mom told anyone where their new home was—including her own dad.

Through the flames, I watch as Ori rises, walks in silent steps to Nomi's side, and lowers next to her, hand outstretched.

And as Nomi slips hers into it, Margot begins.

It wasn't just the pictures. The ones she sent only after weeks of requests and threats.

Threats to end things, but also, to reveal things.

Jared was her first, and she wasn't ready. But he asked, and asked again. He mocked, and when that didn't work, he lied. Said if she loved him, truly loved him, she would trust him with this one thing.

And she did love him, she thought. She thought she trusted him.

The rest of the story comes out in sobs, her tear-streaked face illuminated with the light of the fire and the dance of shadows.

The video Jared made, of them, together, for the first time. How he threatened to show her friends, her mom, the entire world.

Nomi and Ori join her, their hands linked, fingers locked tight, and my body itches with the need to be fully part of this thing we've started. But they haven't learned my secrets—ones that put them in the path of a man who nearly killed me.

Ori is next, her voice shaking as she recounts the teacher from school, the one who taught *Huckleberry Finn* every year. Read it aloud. Had students read it aloud. Making sure every Black student listened to all 219 times *that* word appeared. And more often than not, making sure one of those Black students was reading.

Except little Ori, the girl who raises her hand to speak, refused. And started a revolution of student uprisings, parent complaints, and school-board intervention that nearly cost Mr. Valco his job.

But that was two years ago and Valco hasn't really been brought to justice. Now the college reference she needs is reliant on Mr. Valco's recommendation. Her after-school volunteer work at the shelter under his watch.

She tells us the things he whispered in her ear, the comments made just beyond her hearing. She tells us about the fear that one day, his hatred will be too much for him to control. And I'm sick with the knowledge of what I saw yesterday in the hallway—that she had to carry that alone while I stood right there.

She goes quiet then, like only Ori can, until only the heaving of her chest shows through the reach of flames.

My body feels bruised, wrung out, my heart battered. My eyes burn with the flood of tears.

It's too much. Too much to take in. Too much to hold.

I want to set it free, the rumble of fury that builds with every new word. I want to set the world on fire.

They look to me then, the last one, and I promise myself—no secrets here.

I tell the entire story, from the beginning. I tell them about the man who tied me up and threw me into his trunk. I tell them about the letters that have stolen my life. I tell them how there is no part of my life he doesn't see, and that means, though I may be offering to help them, I may be bringing him into their lives too.

The flames color Margot's pale cheeks, and even though it trembles, she holds out her hand. She whispers, "I mean what I said. I'm all in."

Then there are four of us, bonded and linked through our tears and our pain. A sisterhood forged from our promise to balance the weight of men's wrongs.

The fire presses against my back, heat that makes my skin prickle with warning, the stretch of its tongues curling toward the moon.

I shudder with the weight of what they've taken from us. The tiny pieces of each of us, stolen, never able to be replaced. And now those empty spots hold our shame, our fear, our guilt, and our anger.

They're not ours to carry—they belong to *them*. To every person who inflicted the damage and walked from the wreckage they left behind.

I turn to the fire behind me, dragging my fingers through the cooled ashes at the edges, and smudge them along each of our wrists, where our blood flows closest.

This is our blood oath. This is our promise.

We'll give them back the damage they left us with, burden them with the weight of our pain.

We may be forever damaged, eternally broken, but we will leave them charred.

Ashes to ashes.

CHAPTER NINE

Life feels different now.

It's well past curfew by the time I make it home, but the timed lights greet me, kitchen glowing bright.

The alarm sounds its high-pitched appeal for me to enter our security code, and I lock the dead bolt and double-check the garage door is closed before I head to my room.

The thick scent of smoke clings to my clothes and hair, but I don't want to wash it away. It feels like protection. It feels like vengeance.

I'm no longer waiting. No longer alone. We have a plan now, a pact. And none of us will stop until our lives belong to us again.

I toss my bag onto the floor of my room and eye my bed. Collapsing into it is almost too tempting to resist.

But then I see it, a flash of pink through my opened curtains, and that familiar dread crawls into me.

He was at my house. Maybe in my room. Tonight.

I don't open my curtains, not ever, but Dad does. Like if he can let some sliver of light into my bedroom it will chase away the dark things that live here.

Today it brought the dark things *to* me.

I strain for sounds, a clue that will tell me he's still here, and everything in me wants to run to the safety of my closet and hide.

I flip the window lock instead, fingers shaking and fumbling, and shove it open. It's on the other side of the glass, so I have to reach between the bottom ledge and the screen.

I scissor it between my fingers and tug it free, and black soot plumes from the scar I inflict on the envelope, drifting in lazy flutters to coat my carpet.

Ashes. From the fire tonight.

The picture proves it.

It's grainy, taken from far away.

Nomi, Ori, Margot, and me. Our tiny circle, our hands linked. The fire behind me raging high and silhouetting us in edges and shadows.

I won't let him take that from me. I won't let him take anything else from me.

I should be sick with the nearness of him tonight. The implied threat of his presence. I should've known he'd follow me there. But maybe I did.

Dangerous girls.

Margot offered to help. Ori and Nomi too.

I haven't been able to find him—haven't been able to stop him—on my own. But there are four of us now. And everything about tonight has shown me why I can't live by his rules anymore. I can't ask them to confront their fears while I hide from mine.

I need to take back what belongs to me. *I* need to tip the equilibrium.

I scan the room—*my* space, which is supposed to be safe but isn't because he's been here.

I yank the letter from my bag and dial the number he left for me.

It rings, each trill doubling my heart rate until my breathing goes ragged, my hearing muffled.

Then, silence. Not voice mail, just silence. Just *him*.

Waiting.

I find my voice. "I'm ready."

I let the phone drop to the bed and brush the ash from the picture.

Then I center it in my corkboard, stabbing the pin through the tip of the flame at my back.

Let him watch.

CHAPTER TEN

The response is tucked innocently beneath my wiper when I head to school the next morning. The inscription, as always, is the same.

I'll always be the one that got away.

My eyes dart to my house, and I scour the glass for the smudge of a fingerprint, all the strength I felt last night bleeding onto the concrete.

Last night was a mistake. That's what every part of me screams. I should've lain low. I may not have had much of a life, but I was alive. Now our entire agreement is uncertain, all the rules I've come to rely on left in fragments.

My thoughts default to the product of seventy-five times seventy-five, but I shove it all away, replacing it with the thing I need most of all: to know who he is. So I can make him pay.

But there's no sign of him, only the rustle of leaves that have just begun to go brittle at the onset of fall.

It's possible Mrs. Henderson has seen something, but I can't ask her now. Dad's secret spy-on-Cass directive has been revealed, and he might feel guilty enough to tell her to stop watching. If I ask her if she's seen any strange men lurking, there's zero possibility she won't tell him.

After that second letter, Dad was fully prepared to install cameras at every corner of the house and half the street. The only reason he didn't is because the letters "stopped." He still insisted on the alarm. Then he set the passcode as my birthday. So useless.

I can't change the code—Dad would ask why. The company told us to pick a number we'd remember, even when panicked. I couldn't tell him we needed to pick something that meant nothing to either of us, because anything else couldn't protect me. Not when there's no part of my life that's a secret anymore. *He* knows my birthday. Hell, he probably knows my social security number.

Except every night, when the house is quiet and calm, the stillness like a presence, before Dad comes home and things feel alive again, I wish I could've lied better, found the perfect excuses so he'd do what I wanted even if he didn't understand why.

I wish I could've been more like my mother.

I tug the envelope free and tuck it against my body.

I shiver, my skin sick with the nearness of it, but soon . . .

Soon, he'll know what it's like to know fear.

I drive to school with blanched knuckles and the roar of panic threatening to drown the rest of the world, but I make it.

Out of the car, across the lot, into the school.

I make it to the bathroom where I peel open the envelope. Carefully, cleanly.

There's another letter inside. Crisp linen paper with raised fibers that scrape against the pads of my fingers.

FINALLY.

YOU KNOW WHERE.

9PM

• • •

I don't know where.

And the uncertainty of it ratchets that twisted place inside of me, until my hands won't stop shaking and even basic thoughts go muddled.

It's a test and I'm failing. I won't let myself consider what the consequences might be, or how I know there aren't second chances.

I should've gone back inside my house, grabbed the rest of the letters so I could read them again, piece together some clue I missed.

The truth is that I thought about going back inside, when I stood outside my car while the sun shined and the wind sang in gentle breezes, and I couldn't do it.

I couldn't face seeing them all together, reading them all at once. Remembering the entire story.

It still doesn't belong to me. My story still isn't *mine*.

I don't bother changing for gym. Why pretend I'm even thinking about going to class.

I'm doing the one thing I can right now—I'm going to find backup.

Willingly putting myself before the man who kidnapped me is arguably the stupidest thing I've ever done, so I need someone who is arguably no stranger to stupid decisions.

Margot catches me outside the locker room and drags me beneath the bleachers. She scrapes her hair into a ponytail and whispers, "Are you leaving? If yes, can I come?"

I smile, despite the twisted feeling in my guts. "Not leaving. Just have something to do."

She stares at the floor, squeaking her shoe against the glossy surface. "You know you can tell me things, right?"

"I know." I do. We proved that last night. But I don't want to involve Margot until I know what I'm dealing with. "I promise I'll fill you in, okay? No secrets."

I hold out my pinkie, and she loops hers through. "No secrets."

It feels strange to say it—I've been nothing but secrets for months.

Who am I kidding, I've had secrets for years. Easy explanations to complicated questions about my mom, about where she is and why we've moved so many times. That I've had to switch schools more than once because Mom pissed off the wrong person. Or had sex with the wrong person—like my principal.

Not exactly the things you rush to tell your new friends about.

Coach Pheran yells, "Where the hell are Pennington and Adams?" and we both go still. She may not be my coach anymore, but that doesn't mean I'm not conditioned to fear her.

Margot ducks out the side of the bleachers. "I'll distract her. Make a run for it."

I move fast and keep low, and I'm pretty sure Margot is telling Coach I have cramps, which will earn absolutely no sympathy points whatsoever, but I'm grateful for the attempt.

I shove open the door, and the metal clacks as a gust of wind greets me. It's even colder today, summer surrendering to the chill of fall, leaves bleeding from green to red.

I breathe deep, practicing what I'm about to say to Tyler, and head toward the bleachers.

The roar of cars mutes the pound of footsteps on the track, and I scan the grounds.

And there, well behind the rest of the mass of dudes, is Tyler Thorne.

Coach Bulger yells for him to run faster, and Tyler gives him a military salute and picks up his pace. For approximately six seconds.

Then he slows, hands in his pockets, whistling, and Bulger's hands curl into fists.

Tyler's gaze snags on me from across the field, and he smiles, like he's been waiting for me all along.

He holds up a single finger to say "one minute," and before I can nod, he's off. Holy hell is he fast.

Coach Bulger looks like he's about to explode—probably because he's the track coach. Noah doesn't look any happier.

Tyler makes it to my side faster than should be possible. "Hey."

I glance to Bulger, at the vein throbbing in his temple, but it's not Tyler he's staring at. It's me. "I don't want to get you in trouble."

"Nah. Bulger won't give up hoping I'll join track—or baseball. Left-handed batters are universally loved, so he's afraid to be a dick to me."

"He hasn't figured out after three years that it's not gonna happen?"

"We all have dreams, Cassandra Adams, and I am Coach Bulger's."

"Eww."

He laughs, deep and contagious, and I forget all about Bulger. Except he's still staring, and I shift so Tyler eclipses him.

Cowardly, yes, but my nerves are frayed.

Tyler says, "So what's up?"

"I need you to come somewhere with me. I don't know where exactly, but I'll figure that out. Tonight. Did I say that already? I didn't. It's tonight. Somewhere. It might actually be dangerous. No, it *is* dangerous. Jesus, what was I thinking? You know what?" I step away. Far, far away. "Just forget I said anything."

I'm nearly to the gate when he calls, "Cass, wait!"

He flicks his hair from his eyes. "I'm not sure what that was back there, with the talking . . . I think more to yourself than me, actually. But it sounds like maybe you needed a favor."

"It's fine. I'll be fine." I'm such an asshole. I didn't ask Margot or Nomi because I didn't want to put them in danger. Somehow, I didn't think danger applied to Tyler.

Or, I thought danger and Tyler were already so entangled, one night with a potential murderer wouldn't matter. So stupid.

Maybe all of this is stupid. Maybe I should let it go, continue on until I can move to some faraway state for college and leave my kidnapper behind.

It would be better that way. Safer. For all of us.

Tyler steps close, his hand circling my forearm. "I'll come. To wherever. Tonight."

I should say no. A good person would say no.

I say yes.

CHAPTER ELEVEN

Friday, October 8
7 Days Before the End

7:52 p.m.

It's three minutes until Tyler is supposed to pick me up, and I still don't know where we're going.

And I'm terrified of getting it wrong.

If I'm not in the right place at exactly nine o'clock, it'll mean I'm not "ready" like I said I was.

I need him to believe in me. Trust me, even. So I can do what the cops haven't—discover who he is. That's the only way this ends. Once I know *who* he is, the girls and I can find a way to stop him.

But getting it wrong means making him angry. Angry is unpredictable, erratic. Angry is dangerous. To me and everyone around me.

So, I'm making my best guess.

I'm the one that got away, and I'm going back to the spot where I did.

But until then I'm waiting in the Target parking lot, doors locked, cataloging the drivers of every car that passes me—two separate dudes with big trucks that completely ignore the stop sign, at least five mom-looking women in minivans, a guy with a deep scar across his cheek, and two red-shirted employees.

My head knows it's ridiculous to view every one of them as a possible threat, but the rest of me doesn't seem to have gotten that message.

There's a deep, throaty rumble down the street, and seconds later Tyler steers his motorcycle into the lot. I couldn't have Mrs. Henderson watching me leave with some random guy. Dad would stroke out.

A motorcycle. This is not quite what I planned.

He swerves to a stop and pulls his helmet free, shaking his hair to fluff it. "You look terrified."

"Umm." I am. "No. This is just unexpected."

"Is it? I always thought owning a motorcycle was the most cliché thing I could do. Stoneybrook's resident bad boy and his stereotypical motorcycle. There's a reason I don't bring it to school."

"If your reputation bothers you, you could join the track team. Then you'd be a revered student athlete."

"Did Bulger put you up to this?"

I laugh, because oh god, I *wish* this was about track. "Not at all."

"Ah." He wraps his arms around his helmet. "So you're stalling."

"Sort of?" I roll a loose chunk of asphalt beneath my shoe. It's black. Like my jeans, my hoodie, my jacket, my beanie.

"Oookay." He stretches out the word, a smile tugging at his lips. "Let's start small. Where are we going?"

"Stoney Park. Just outside the nature area. Follow route B and a little trail leads you to this clearing with a gravel lot."

"That's very specific. And what are we doing there?"

"That's a little harder to answer. I need to see something—or some*one*. Without them knowing I'm there."

His smile breaks free. "Why, Ms. Adams, are you asking me to help you *stalk* someone?"

A whimper escapes my throat, tangled with a gasp. "It's not like that."

"Hey." He's standing in front of me, ducking to meet my gaze. "It was a joke. A bad joke, apparently. Ask me something."

"What?"

"To even us out. Ask me a question you know I won't want to answer so I won't feel as bad about almost making you cry."

"I wasn't crying."

"I said 'almost.' Now ask."

I should just get on the damn motorcycle instead, but the opportunity to ask the elusive Tyler Thorne a question is too much temptation for a lowly mortal. "Okay. What's with the bad-boy schtick anyway?"

"One: I'm offended you think this is a schtick. I've worked hard to model my very existence off James Dean, thank you." I've barely finished rolling my eyes when he says, "Two: my dad is an asshole. He's made enemies of a majority of the parents in this town. I had maybe two kids at my first-grade birthday party because the other kids' parents wouldn't let them come. Like father, like son."

He shrugs, and it's the saddest thing I've ever seen.

The wind blows my hair into my face, and even once I've scraped it back into place I still don't know what to say. "Tyler—"

"No big deal. I decided to lean into it."

"I'm so sorry."

"Don't be. It taught me what real friends were, saved me a lot of trouble later." He buffs out a smudge on his helmet with his sleeve. "I don't miss him though."

"He's gone?" I cringe at my tone—you're not supposed to sound happy that someone's dad is gone. "Sorry, my mom too. She's gone, I mean. It's better that way, but . . ."

"It still sucks? It makes you mad that it's better that way? You're tired of having to fend off everyone's pity when they find out?"

It's funny because it's true. "Yeah. All of that."

"Guess we have some common ground that doesn't include clandestine Target rendezvous."

"Why did you start sitting at my lunchroom table?" I've wondered, since that very first day. How he knew what I needed even better than I did.

He stares past me, and for the first time, I can see him as the little boy with no one at his birthday party. "I grew up in a big family. Aunts, uncles, cousins—big family business, always people around. And I remember thinking, out of all those people who knew what my dad was like, how none of them ever asked if I was okay, you know? Not when I was little, not when I got older."

I'm struck mute, my chest too tight, and his broad shoulders shrug, like he's Atlas ridding himself of the world.

Then his smile is back, quieter though, haunted. "Anyway, that's why. You reminded me of that—how you can be surrounded by people and still be alone. Now," he says, while freeing the extra helmet from its bungees, "let's go to the park."

I want to hug him. Him and that little boy that no one ever cared enough to ask about. Instead, I climb behind him, wrapping my arms tight around his waist, and whisper a thank-you I'm not sure he hears.

And we head toward the one place I never want to see again.

• • •

We make it to the park too soon. I'm grateful to be pressed into Tyler's shoulder blades, and for the roar of the engine beneath me. I'm grateful my view of the world is blocked and muffled.

I haven't been back here since that night. I can picture every tree branch though. Every spot of bare earth where grass wouldn't grow.

When I lie awake at night, reliving every moment, I can taste the tang of duct tape and hear the squawk of the birds in the trees.

I remember all the things I shouldn't and none of the ones that matter.

I didn't turn around. Didn't catch the license plate or even the type of car. Certainly not the man's height, his hair color. They didn't bring in a police sketch artist because I had nothing to tell them.

Tonight, I'll do better.

We tuck Tyler's motorcycle into the trees, hidden from view of the tiny lot. I tuck myself away even farther into the woods.

Tyler watches while I empty my backpack. Binoculars, camera with zoom lens, a black beanie for Tyler, a blanket. That, I lay on the ground, because spiders live in the woods.

I'm lying on my stomach, elbows bent and binoculars in place when Tyler whispers, "What am I supposed to be doing?"

I press my fingers to my lips, and he lowers next to me.

His voice drops low, quiet. "Cass, if this was something serious—really serious—you'd tell me, right?"

I scan the lot. 8:45. Sixty-one times sixty-one is three thousand seven hundred twenty-one.

Night closes in like a fog, a slow descent into a deep blackness that blurs the curves and lines of the forest. We watch, seconds adding to minutes until time blurs too, as the moon rises, full and bright against an empty sky, forming shadows that grow into living things, moving and swaying with the constant breeze.

It's too quiet—just the chirp of crickets and the scurry of creatures through newly fallen leaves, and I'm numb all over.

I know they're there, the memories of this place, the ghost of the person I was that day. I can feel them, rumbling deep inside me, waiting to rise up, make themselves known until they're too much to hold back. Too much to hold in.

But I won't break down here. Not now. This is my new beginning.

"Cass." Tyler's voice is firmer now, demanding.

I whisper, "It's not serious. There are just some things I need to know first."

"Before . . ."

"Before I decide what to do next."

"So mysterious." He bumps his shoulder into mine. "Hand them over."

I drop the binoculars into his waiting hand and reach for my camera. Photo evidence is more important anyway.

I nearly drop it when my phone goes bright, buzzing in the blanket.

I know the number, recognize it immediately, and I barely hold back the scream lodged in my lungs.

I jump to my feet, slamming my finger to the answer button.

Static greets me, then, "Cassandra."

The voice is distorted, completely unrecognizable, but so calm, the kind that always comes before an eruption.

I force myself to say, "Where are you?" but he's not listening.

"Do you think you need a bodyguard?"

"I didn't—"

"You said you were ready."

I don't know what to say to save this. Don't know how to reassure a man who dragged me off the street, bound me, gagged me, brought me to this place.

The helplessness creeps over me again, weighing me down, clouding all my thoughts until I can't focus on anything but the sweat blooming over my skin, the rawness of my throat.

"I left something for you."

"Where?" I spin, searching for a clue to where I go next. Because this can't be it. I can't leave here empty. Not again.

"And, Cassandra, the next time you say you're ready, you had better mean it."

The line goes dead and Tyler's calling my name, the heat of his fingers burning at my wrist. But I can't focus on anything but *his* voice in my head and the promise of whatever he's left for me.

I spot it then, wedged in the crack of a tree, on the other edge of the clearing.

He's here. He has to be, and this may be my only chance to identify him.

It's stupid to run out to the open ground. Stupid and dangerous.

Dangerous.

That's who I am now.

I run toward the tree, shoving through branches that scrape my hands, my face, over rain-slicked leaves and spongy hills of moss. My foot catches and I go down hard, bruising my knee and scraping my hands, and when Tyler tries to haul me up, I shove him off.

I can't have anyone's hands on me. Can't bear the feel of another person's skin on mine. Then I'm running, sprinting across the clearing until I can yank the envelope free.

I tear it open, a savage rip that shreds it clean down the middle until something slips free from one end, catching the glint of moonlight as it tumbles into the rocky grass below.

I stare at it, recognition taking a moment too long.

A necklace. But not mine. Not this time.

This time it's Margot's.

CHAPTER TWELVE

Saturday, October 9
6 Days Before the End

I scribble a note for Dad that says I'm going to Margot's even though I'm really heading back into the woods to see if there are clues to identify my stalker, when an engine rumbles outside.

I know the difference between a car in my driveway and the neighbor's. I've spent months analyzing every noise this house makes, investigating every sound from outside and cataloging them in my head.

Someone is in my driveway. On a Saturday morning.

I run to the front window, plastering myself to the right of it, where I can peel back the curtain enough to see the driveway.

The driveway that holds Noah Rhoades.

No. Oh no.

Dad worked a double yesterday, so he's passed out, but I *know* he's trained himself on all the sounds around our house as well as I have.

I close my eyes, listen, wait.

The floorboards upstairs creak.

I rush to the door and fling it open before Noah can knock. "Hi. I was just headed out."

He looks me over. "In your socks?"

"No. My shoes are at the garage door. You know how my dad is about shoes in the house."

"Because of the pathogens."

"He'd love you for remembering that. Anyway, I have to go, so—"

"Cass." He scratches the back of his neck. "Can we talk, for a minute? I have this thing I wanted to ask you. A question. I have a question. And I don't want to make you uncomfortable but . . ."

He keeps talking. Rambling. Noah doesn't ramble.

But he's rambling now and the floorboards in Dad's room above us are signaling his immediate approach and I absolutely do *not* want him down here, seeing Noah, talking to Noah, or acknowledging his very existence.

He'll invite him in, and they'll talk about football, and Dad will be ecstatic that I have someone *at the house*, then Noah will leave and there is a distinct possibility Dad will give me a reminder sex-ed lesson and I *cannot*.

Not today, Satan.

I slam the door in Noah's face and sprint to the garage, smashing my palm into the opener even as I scramble into my shoes.

A burst of cold air hits me, crisp, carrying the hint of roasted pumpkins and fireplaces roaring to life.

I'm almost out when Noah peeks around the corner, eyebrow raised.

That's when I fall, tripping on my own half-on shoe.

Noah's there before I hit the pavement, hauling me upward, and he's still very exceptionally sturdy. And warm. With muscles that flex beneath his coat as he sets me upright. I'd forgotten how tall he was, standing this close.

I mumble a thanks and stuff my foot into my traitor shoe.

The garage door squeaks and rattles, and I shove Noah toward his car. "Let's go!"

He starts the engine, but then he freezes. "You're trying to avoid your dad talking to me."

"Yes. So, hurry up."

"*Why* are you trying to avoid your dad talking to me?"

"Because he worked a lot yesterday and he needs to sleep."

"Liar."

I growl at him.

He grins and shifts into reverse but doesn't let off the brake. "Hurry, Cass. Tell the truth. I think I see movement in your front window."

"You are such an asshole." He bursts into laughter, but then there really *is* movement in my living room window and I panic. "Because it will make him happy to think we're friends and then he'll be disappointed when he finds out it's not true."

He pauses, barely a breath. "Right."

The truck rockets out of the driveway, neither of us speaking until we hit a stoplight. He won't stop drumming his fingers against the steering wheel and I hate this.

I hate everything that's gotten so messed up and nothing is the way it should be.

I can't stop my thoughts from racing to opening that letter with Margot's necklace. Holding back the rush of tears, the wave of fury, avoiding Tyler's gaze and ignoring his words.

I'd done all the wrong things. Again.

Then I swallowed all the *fear panic rage* that squirmed beneath my skin and rode home, clutched to Tyler's back.

When I made it to my room, I stood in it and screamed. Then I grabbed the jewelry box that belonged to my mom before it did me and shattered it against the wall, glittering raindrops of glass rotting to a graveyard of ragged shards.

It's something she would've done—rushing out to find him in the woods. And just like her, I put my friends in danger. Even now, it's the same.

But then I close my eyes and remember the four of us around the fire; I remember their hands linked with mine and our stories in the air and the promises in our whispered words.

Ashes to ashes.

I am not like her. I'll never be.

I focus on the blur of the road. "I'm sorry, about what I said earlier."

"Don't say it if you don't mean it."

And that's the problem—Noah always means what he says. And right now, I do too. But I know how little words mean. I listened to my mom's for years. "You can just drop me off somewhere."

"I'm not dropping you off *somewhere*, Cass. Where were you going? Earlier, in your socks."

I scramble for a response. It's not like the girls and I staked our master plan for revenge and destruction to a tree. It's not like I have to admit I'm looking for clues that lead me to my stalker.

I say, "To the woods."

"Ah."

"'Ah' what? Don't be cryptic."

He shoots me an incredulous look that I totally deserve. "I meant 'Ah. You're the reason Margot called at two a.m. offering me her firstborn child for Benadryl.'"

Well shit. I'd forgotten how much mosquitos love Margot. "You and Margot are neighbors."

"Since second grade."

"I forgot."

"Clearly. I assume we're not heading back to the woods for more midnight yoga."

I snort before I can stop myself. I'd also forgotten what a terrible liar Margot is.

We're going to have to practice our stories once we start planning.

My head goes light every time I think about it, the things we're going to do, and I can't tell if I'm scared or thrilled. "Don't tell her what we're doing today, okay?"

He sighs, gaze rocketing between me and the road. "I'm worried about you, Cass. *Have* been. For a long time."

My throat constricts. "I'm fine."

I'm not. Haven't been for a very long time.

I let my finger slide through the fog my breaths have made in the window. "I'm figuring things out."

I stare at the tiny flame my finger crafted before I wipe it away. "It'll be better soon."

. . .

"I didn't come dressed for this." Noah watches as I rope my binoculars around my neck and says, "Is that a magnifying glass?"

"It's your own fault for wearing shorts in October, and yes."

"So we're searching the woods."

"Correct."

"For?"

I trudge into the trail that leads to the campfire, newly fallen leaves crunching beneath my feet. "Things that look out of place. Anything that looks important."

Envelopes that are pink.

I just need a single clue that leads me to *him.* Then I'll find where his weaknesses lie. But I'll do as much as I can alone. Margot's necklace is all the evidence I need that he's a threat to everyone around me.

I don't think my stalker used the same trail as us the other night. Ori would've seen him on her way in, and the picture he took came from a different angle.

Noah pokes at the ground with a stick. "So you and Margot are friends now."

"Did she say that?"

"Not in those words, but if you're hanging in the woods to do *yoga* together, I make assumptions."

I crouch to examine a cluster of leaves, and Noah sighs and shoves his stick into my hand. "Use mine. I'll get another."

He does, the branch cracking so loud it echoes through the thin air. I freeze, because it's the perfect cover for noises the stalker might make, if he's watching right now.

"Cass—"

"Shh." But there's nothing. Just the squawk of birds and the chill of wind blustering off the lake. "I'm sorry. What were you saying?"

"What about gloves?"

"What?"

He points to a mass of black knit. "Gloves."

"Don't touch it." I drop to my knees, wet earth sinking into my jeans, and shrug off my backpack.

I yank a Ziploc free. "Can you hold this open?"

Noah takes the bag, slowly. "What are we doing here, Cass?"

"Bagging the evidence."

"Right. Listen, before things get any weirder, I need to ask you something."

I take my time standing, because it feels like he's about to ask something I want to answer even less than I want to explain why we're bagging evidence.

He lets out a slow breath. "That night, before you—"

He makes a hand motion that can only mean "disappeared from thin air," watching me like if he blinks he'll miss the truth. "Did I *do* something?"

"I don't understand."

"You stopped talking to everyone, and now you're friends with Margot again but we, as you very plainly stated, *are not friends*. So, did I do something? Something that made you uncomfortable? Did I pressure you or—anything? Because I've replayed things so many times, and *you* kissed *me*, Cass. But if you didn't want—"

"Noah, stop." My voice comes out breathless, ragged. "It wasn't you. None of it had anything to do with you, and—"

The weight of it crushes me, that he's spent these months wondering, worrying, that he did something that would make me retreat from the world.

It's my fault, all the suffering, because I wasn't strong enough to tell the truth. I'm not even strong enough to tell the story without pretending it happened to someone else.

Five months later and I'm still making all the wrong decisions.

I grab tight to his arm, like I can show him the truth through force alone. "I'm so sorry. I *never* meant to make you—"

"Hey." He cradles my jaw, forcing me to meet his gaze. "Don't cry."

His thumb brushes over my cheek, and for one stupid moment, I feel almost normal. Like all those horrible memories *do* belong to someone else. Like if I could try hard enough I could banish them from my history.

But I know better. I know what forgetting leads to. It leads to a husband you don't like and a daughter you don't want and a day where you leave everything behind because even the nothing you're heading toward feels better than the life you have.

A branch snaps, too harsh, too loud. I pull Noah's hand away and strain for the next rustle of leaves, crack of wood.

He's here. Of course he's here.

But this time, I *want* him to be.

A flock of birds takes flight, cawing and strewn across the sky and I don't wait for Noah.

I tear through the woods, over fallen trees and through crooked branches, muscles burning and lungs on fire, but I don't stop, don't slow.

For once, I'm the hunter.

A car door slams, engine turns over, and I run faster, pushing toward the sound with every bit of my rage.

Tires slip on rocky gravel and I'm almost there, where I can see his car, where I'll look for things I'm supposed to remember.

I break into the clearing just in time for the crack and screech of metal, the car roaring away, but with a vital piece left behind.

I stutter to a stop, hands bent to knees and my chest heaving.

Noah paces beside me, each footstep sending plumes of dust into the air. "Hey, Cass? What the fuck?"

I rake my hands through my hair, fisting it tight. "You don't want to know."

"No, I do, actually. Because if it wasn't me who made you give up your entire life, then it must've been something pretty goddamn awful. And you don't have to tell me, but chasing after someone who's willing to leave their entire fucking *bumper* behind says you're in some shit you need to get out of."

He scrubs his jaw. "So I say again: What the fuck?"

I can't answer—I'm linked now. Me, Nomi, Margot, Ori. We've put this thing into motion, and telling anyone is a betrayal to all of us.

Telling Noah would be the easiest thing. It would melt his anger and flood it with understanding.

No, with pity. *That's* what I'd see reflected in his eyes—a poor, broken girl who had her life stolen and hasn't figured out how to get it back.

I don't need his pity. And I don't owe him my trauma.

The only things I need are Nomi, Margot, and Ori.

But Noah *is* my friend, and even though he's in this mess because *he* showed up at *my* doorstep, I don't want to lie to him.

But telling him isn't the same. Margot, Ori, and Nomi understood, in a way that only someone who can imagine themselves being lifted from the ground and thrown into someone's trunk can.

I'm not sure Noah could ever understand that.

I'm not ready to give him my whole truth, but maybe I can give him this. "Someone's stalking me."

He blinks, his hands clenching to fists.

I speak before he can unleash the questions forming in his head. "I don't know who, I don't know why. That's what I'm trying to find out."

Then he says it. "Cass, I'm so sorry." He means it. Every single cell in his body screams it.

It's not the *wrong* response—I don't even know what the *right* one is—but I hate the way it leaves me with no replies that feel anything close to honest.

He opens his mouth, and I shake my head. I can't. Not yet.

I head to the bumper, leaves soft beneath my feet, and seeing it lying there, scraped and twisted, erases all the pain from my body. It calms every bit of the indecision lingering beneath my skin.

I did this to him. I made him run.

I made him *scared*.

And I want to do it again.

CHAPTER THIRTEEN

We stand outside the police station, my feet cemented to the steps. I tell myself I shouldn't let him see me here, faltering. I try to recall that feeling, just handfuls of minutes ago, when the rules of power bent in my direction.

I press the edge of the license plate into my palm until it hurts. Fifty-seven times fifty-seven is three thousand two hundred forty-nine.

"I can take it in," Noah says.

His voice is soft, gentled at the sight of me standing here, frozen.

"No." I focus on each contraction of muscle, each flex of tendon, and I move myself toward the front door.

It's just a building. A building where nothing happened. I went back to the *park*, for fuck's sake, to the place I *escaped*.

I can do *this*.

I blink at the glare of fluorescents, breathe in stale coffee and floor cleaner, and the door thumps shut behind me.

"Can I help yous twos?" A gruff voice draws me upright, to the sheriff in front of me.

I hold out the license plate. "We found this in the woods."

He hitches his belt, and the thick leather squeaks. "Found it, huh? Where at?"

Noah fills in the details, leaving out the ones I made him promise not to share—like the bumper in his Jeep right now.

"And what were you doing out there? Necking?"

Necking?

My lips twitch, and suddenly "necking" sounds better than saying we went for a walk like we planned. "That is . . . that is correct."

Noah stiffens, coughing to cover the laugh he's holding in.

I try to use the word "necking" but I can't get my mouth to cooperate. "Anyway, we wanted to see if you could identify the owner?"

"Cass?"

Shit. I know that voice. Detective Michaels was one of the few decent cops I dealt with *that night.*

I don't want to see him now. Or ever.

I wave, and all Noah's repressed laughter dries up. He's staring at me with the same intensity as Detective *Necking.*

Detective Michaels leads us down the hall to his desk, and my shoes squeak because my legs won't work quite right. My fingers circle my wrist, expecting the burn of duct tape but finding only smooth skin instead.

I can't be here.

I can't walk in these hallways and sit in these rooms.

"You know what . . ." The deep rumble of Detective Michaels's voice is a grounding wire, tethering me. "Let's jump on in here."

He steers us to a different office, and all the fight leaves my body in a rush.

I stumble into a chair and grip tight to its arm so I don't float away.

Detective Michaels says, "How've you been, Cass?"

I shrug, because talking feels like an impossibility.

He takes his time assessing me, gaze bouncing between me and Noah, and I shake my head. *No, he doesn't know. No, I don't want him to.*

It's the moment Noah realizes there's more to the story. I know from the way his jaw tightens, the way he stares into Detective Michaels like he's trying to read the story from his eyes.

Detective Michaels is the one who called my dad that night. He has twins a year younger than me. I overheard him talking to them when we left the station.

I drop the license plate into his waiting hand, only shaking a little.

He flips it over, then back. "You have any particular reason for wanting to know who this belongs to?"

I let any emotion drain from my eyes. "No."

"Good thing, then, since you know I can't tell you what this screen's about to say."

"I understand."

He pauses at the hoarseness of my voice, the chair groaning as he settles into it. "Let's see what we got."

The keyboard clicks, the screen flashing as his fingers pause. "You said you just found this?"

I sit straighter. "Yes."

Noah's hand finds my thigh where Michaels can't see it, and the gentle pressure says *too eager, Cass. Way too eager.*

Noah says, "We thought maybe it fell off someone's car"—like that isn't exactly what happened—"and someone might be looking for it."

Michaels stares at me and I can see, so clearly, how the next ten seconds turn out. He's going to say something—a question, a statement—something I won't have an answer to and something I won't be able to explain to Noah.

"Can I talk to you for a second?" The words rush from my mouth, and Michaels blinks in response, just enough time for me to thumb open the camera app on my phone.

I shove the phone onto Noah's knee, trying to telegraph "take a picture of the screen," as Michaels motions me out before him, leaving Noah alone.

I spin the second we get to the hallway, and Noah's still staring at my phone. "I was wondering if there'd been any updates on my case."

He sighs. "Have you spoken with Detective Reed?"

Fuck no. Detective Reed is the one who *suggested* to Dad that I may have made the whole thing up. "I'd rather not."

Noah is still staring at my phone. Not in confusion. I know what his confused face looks like. He's having a morality moment—and I'm going to kill him for it.

Michaels says, "Fair enough," in a tone that tells me he knows Reed is an asshole. "It's not my case, Cass."

Movement flickers behind him, but I refuse to look. "It's not your case, *but . . .*"

He gives me a half smile. "*But* I do keep tabs."

His smile falls, and he can't meet my eyes. "There's nothing new, Cass. If there's anything else you can think of though, *any* clues or things you saw."

He keeps talking, but I tune him out because we've had this conversation before and I'm never having it again. "No. Nothing. But thanks."

It's not surprising, but it *does* prove the only way to end this is to do it myself.

I squeeze past him and into the room, motioning to Noah that it's time to enact Operation Get the Hell Out of Here.

Michaels thanks us for bringing the plate, tells us (me) to call if we (I) need anything, and then he's shuffling us out of the room and out the front doors.

We burst into the soft glow of afternoon sun, clouds lumbering lazily across the sky, and Noah shoves my phone into my hand. "I'm assuming whatever's on that picture is worth something to you."

There's an edge to his voice I don't like. One that makes me feel like I've pushed him over the wrong kind of line.

My mother wouldn't feel guilty about it. "*You can't make people do things they don't already want to do, Cass. Sometimes you just have to give them permission."*

I wish she was here right now. I wish she would've been here five months ago. It's better that she's gone, I know that. But she wouldn't have let Detective Reed suggest I made anything up. Cordelia Adams would've rained hell down upon anyone who dared question me. I may be better off now, but I wasn't that night.

I force myself to look Noah in the eye. "It is. And it's worth a lot that you took it for me."

He nods, just once, and I recognize the look in his eyes, the moment of forgiveness. It may be Noah standing in front of me, but it's Dad's face I see. And that makes me *her*.

Noah says, *"Necking?"* and all those thoughts vanish.

My laughter matches his—easy, comfortable. I'd almost forgotten, the way this feels, the weightlessness of it all. Being *normal*.

Noah pulls me against him, hands gentle, arms open, telling me I can leave anytime I want.

I drop my head to his chest, and it feels like before everything turned sideways. Back when hugs were normal and we both used any excuse to be nearer to one another.

I remember this, how steady his heart beats, how warm he is, how every inhale I take in his presence comes laced with spice and cedar, fresh air and the crisp notes of fall.

His chest rises. "Cass."

I shake my head. I can't tell him what he wants to know.

His exhale tickles the top of my head, his heartbeat now thundering against my forehead.

My body tenses, ready to deflect and avoid, to offer excuses and create redirections, but then all he says is "Okay."

Okay.

"Okay" is exactly what I need.

I pull away, just enough to see my phone screen against the shield of Noah's body.

I scan the page, most of which means nothing to me.

Then I step back, hoping Noah's guilt keeps him from looking at the picture he took.

Because the vehicle owner's name? I sure as hell recognize that.

CHAPTER FOURTEEN

"Coach *Bulger*?!"

Not even my frantic shushing is enough to drown out Margot's words.

I drop my voice low so only the four of us, huddled around the tiny circle table in the corner of Roasted Beans can hear. "I don't know for sure."

He's a coach. At my *school*. It feels impossible to reconcile with the person I know him to be.

"Sure, sure." Nomi drops her mug to the table. "It's a total coincidence that Bulger's dad's car followed you to the woods and the driver wanted to get away so badly they left their fucking bumper behind."

"I know. I *know*. And he'd have access to Margot's necklace at school too. It *all* makes sense that it's him. I just . . . don't want it to be."

Bulger has access to my locker, to so much information about my life.

I try to picture it, Coach Bulger as the man who grabbed me. I try to remember him lifting me from the ground, how many inches I rose. Bulger is tall. He's strong. He could lift me. Easily.

And that trail. My stomach rolls as flashes of memory pelt me. The day of conditioning where I complained about how boring running on a track was and Bulger suggested the trails at Stoney.

He *suggested* the trail I was kidnapped from.

Somehow that's the detail that snaps through my numbness and brings the panic roaring back.

Ori twists a straw wrapper around her finger. "You don't want it to be him because that means he's always so close? Down the hall or around the corner? Because he's a *teacher* and he has all the power and you have none?"

Our situations are nothing alike, but some similarities only the two of us can understand. "Yeah. Exactly like that."

It's a betrayal. Someone I trusted. Respected. And the whole time I was nothing more than a victim in waiting. It means he saw something in me, something broken, something he could exploit. And all these months, when I thought I was so vigilant, I had no idea.

I swallow. "Can we talk about anything but me? Ori, how the hell did Mr. Valco even keep his job after your parents complained?"

Ori rolls her eyes, but it's too flippant a gesture for the anger in them. "He knows the mayor. More specifically, he's done several business deals with the mayor. Real estate contracts for senior living centers."

Nomi mumbles, "Fuck's sake. If we put up one more senior living center in this city they're gonna outnumber the Dollar Generals."

I grab Ori's hand and squeeze. "We'll fix this. I promise."

She nods, swirling her frappuccino—caffeine is a no-no in the Bello household and Ori's still following the rules. Mostly. "So let's find out if it's Bulger. *We'll* watch *him* for once."

And we're back to me. Sigh. "But it's not *Bulger's* car. It's his dad's."

Nomi says, "So Cass and I will watch the dad's house, and Ori and Margot can watch for Bulger watching us. That way everyone is watching everyone else."

Margot says, "Are we really gonna do this? I mean, I know we promised but . . ."

I say, "But sitting in a coffee shop is different than the dark woods?"

In here it's cozy and warm, leafy plants decorating the tables and the rich tastes of chocolate and coffee infusing the air. In here, there are no shadows to hide behind.

Nomi reaches into her bag and tosses a mess of silver chains and dangly charms onto the table.

My fingers brush over the cool metal, and I tug on a charm. A bracelet pulls free, four teardrops roped onto silver links. My voice comes out breathy. "Nomi. What are these?"

"Bracelets."

We all turn to stare at her, and she rolls her eyes. "You asked."

She twists one of the teardrops free, and black powder drifts onto the table.

Everything comes together in a rush. "The ashes from the other night."

She nods. "They're all half-full, enough room for us to fill up after each . . . event."

I blink away tears and drape the bracelet around my wrist, willing my hands not to shake while I fasten the clasp.

Ori's right. I don't want it to be Bulger, because if it's him, it's personal. It was planned and orchestrated. He's held all the power all along, and he still does.

I force confidence into my words. "I'm doing this. I'm in. For whatever we decide and whatever happens."

"*Whatever* happens, Cass?" Margot rolls a charm between two fingers. "I mean, what are we talking about here? Things that could ruin our lives if we get caught? How far are we willing to go?"

"As far as it takes." My confidence isn't forced this time, it flows out of me in a heady rush, every nerve ending tingling. No limits for dangerous girls.

Nomi fastens her clasp. "I have to do this. We promised and I'm not backing down now."

We stare at Ori and Margot, and all the sound and movement in the coffee shop fades. It's just the four of us again, like last night in the woods.

The words I speak don't sound like my own. "I'm tired of being scared, and like Ori said, right now they have all the power, but we can change that. We can take that power away, we can make them pay for what they did to us. No one is coming to save any of us, so we save ourselves."

Ori stretches her arm to Margot, bracelet dangling. "We save ourselves."

Margot pauses, nods, then grasps the bracelet with steady hands as she fastens it at Ori's wrist. "We save ourselves."

Then there's nothing left to discuss. No more hesitation.

I hold out my arm, let it hover over the table, and within seconds Ori is there, then Margot, Nomi last, our bracelets tinkling as they crash into one another.

As far as it takes.

CHAPTER FIFTEEN
CASS ADAMS

The Events of Monday, October 11
4 Days Before the End

I'm telling this part of the story wrong—all out of order, avoiding the parts that are hardest to think about. The things that happened at Nomi's stepdad's house.

So I'll tell the part that doesn't come to me in my nightmares first.

We were all there that Monday night, the night they came for Nomi.

It wasn't the same day I found the license plate with Noah. It was later—early the next week after Nomi's revenge was complete. But when they came, we were ready for them.

Our words prepared and our stories practiced.

This was what we promised.

All of us together, relaxing, having fun. A movie on the screen and popcorn waiting in bowls. Bottles of nail polish scattered across her mother's carpet, our fingers bearing the colors of our efforts. Black for Margot, pink for Nomi, because we weren't ourselves that night. That night, we played the role of innocence.

They knocked politely, brandished their badges. "Just a conversation," they said.

We drove her to the station. Me, Nomi, Ori, and Margot, wearing our bracelets filled with ashes. Filled with their evidence.

Nomi entered their room, the one with the lights blaring bright, with chairs that cut into your flesh, the scuffed and smudged walls.

She answered their questions and delivered her lines.

She told them she was with *us* that night, when her former stepfather's house erupted into flames. No, we hadn't gone to his house that night. None of us had made the voice-scrambled call to 911.

She had no idea where his dog might be. *Her* dog, she clarified. The one she'd had to leave behind the night she and her mom ran away. Her stepfather left the dog outside often. Probably he'd run away.

In the lobby, we sat with heads bowed and voices lowered. So awful, the fire. So tragic. Poor Nomi, we said, as if she'd want our pity for this.

They apologized to her, as they led her from the stark-white room. Just doing their jobs, all bases covered. She understood, didn't she? And would we all mind answering a few questions? To corroborate Nomi's story?

Within these walls, I had a story once too. That one was true.

They led Ori back first. Quiet, shy Ori, who they assumed would crack beneath the slightest pressure. She gave them nothing.

Margot next, then me.

I carried them all with me as I walked those halls again, every footstep an echo of the time before.

I became the someone else they created—*I* created—when being myself felt too much like admitting the truth.

Nomi was with us that night. And where were we? At my home. Surely, Mrs. Henderson could attest to seeing us there, hear our laughter through cracked windows, even as dusk gave way to night.

"Did you know," they asked me, fingers steepled and voices firm, "that her stepfather's home had a dead bolt leading to the basement? That he was trapped down there while the fire raged?"

"No," I lied.

Saturday, October 9
6 Days Before the End

Nomi kicks her legs onto my dashboard, ripped black jeans crossed at the ankles. "I still can't believe Coach Bulger is the guy who's stalking you."

"We don't know for sure."

"Still."

"It's his dad's car, not his." I pull my hoodie strings tighter, until I'm just an oval of face, sitting down the street from Coach Bulger's dad's house, hosting my first-ever stakeout.

All the evidence points to Bulger, but it feels wrong. I just can't trust myself enough to know whether that means anything. I need proof. Something to rule him out or make it impossible to deny.

"Sure." Nomi rolls her head to the side to stare at me, sarcasm written all over her face.

"It's not his car!" I throw my french fry at her, and she tries to catch it in her mouth. "Anyway sit up. You're supposed to be helping me."

"Helping you stare at the same house for another hour? The dude's like ninety-something—"

"He's seventy-seven."

"He's *old.* And not leaving his house. And I have to pee. We should just go knock."

"It's ten p.m."

"Exactly. And we're sitting here waiting for the old dude to leave the house."

She's right. About everything. And we still need to visit her stepdad's house later.

I fiddle with the bracelet at my wrist, letting the charms sweep over the pads of my fingers while I try to summon some of the courage I had in the coffee shop earlier.

Nomi's voice is uncharacteristically quiet. "Do you really like the bracelets?"

"Yes." It's an understatement, no matter how I answer.

No one expected Nomi to buy jewelry for us. Bracelets are not in Nomi's nature.

I whisper, "I love it. And the other girls do too."

She nods at me, eyes closed, like she doesn't care *what* my answer is.

It's the worst kind of reflection—like me when I tell Dad everything is fine, when I go to school and say everything is okay, and pretend I don't have nightmares that shove me from the deepest sleep.

"Screw it." I fling open the car door and the sound of Nomi's "Hell yeah!" bursts into the open air a second later.

Our doors slam in unison, and we jog across the street while the night around us holds still.

Shadows flank the surrounding houses, gentle porch lights fighting against the dark sky, and tendrils of smoke writhe from chimney tops, infusing the air with woodsmoke and pine. The chill cuts through layers and gusts through trees, forcing their leaves to take final flight.

It's an older neighborhood, only forty minutes from my house but generations apart. This used to be the suburbs, before the population spread farther and replaced wooded lots with cookie-cutter, open-concept dream homes with walls in varying shades of beige.

There's history here, but it feels half-forgotten, remnants of the days of booming automotive sales and the ghosts of children who used to roam the neighborhood until the streetlamps blinked on. And now they're all grown-up, with desk jobs and two-point-two kids and a minivan—and they live next door to me.

But here among the cars on blocks and oil-stained driveways, there are tree-lined streets and yards bordered by chain-link fences, actual sidewalks and compact homes with windows topped by metal awnings. A neighborhood stuffed with people born here, raised here, and never leaving.

My footsteps slow as we near the house, and my phone buzzes once, then twice. I shake my head at Nomi when she reaches for hers.

Not here, not when even a single phone light might draw the wrong attention.

We turn up the walkway, and it's only Nomi behind me that stops me from turning back.

I should've brought a weapon. Maybe if I had one that night, things would be different now.

I cling to the railing as I climb the porch steps, letting the cold seep into my palm. My bracelet slides along the railing, the symphony of metal sliding along metal, and when I take my final step to reach the door, I'm steadier.

My knock echoes, thick wood hard against my knuckles, but there are no answering sounds. "Maybe he's asleep?"

Nomi's finger shoves against the doorbell, and it bings loud enough to hear through the brick walls. "Not anymore."

She tucks her phone against her body, blocking the glow. "They say no sign of Bulger."

We ring twice more but there's still no response, and I can't stand another second of standing out here, exposed. "Let's go around the back."

I'm not sure what I'm hoping to find. I doubt seventy-seven-year-old Edward Bulger is doing midnight yoga in the backyard.

The gate creaks, and we slip inside before shutting it again, just in case any neighbors peek out their windows. And if he's out there right now, that squeaking gate may be our only forewarning.

My foot crunches over a bit of broken concrete and we both pause, but there's no sign anyone knows or cares that we're here.

I press my face to the nearest window, nose to frigid glass, but there's only an empty kitchen.

Except . . .

My breath fogs the glass, blurring my vision. "Is that chair knocked over?"

Nomi looks inside, and when she pulls back, I can't tell if it's fear or the wash of moonlight that makes her skin paler. "Maybe we should go, Cass."

She's right about this too, but I need to follow this through.

I need proof.

"You should go. Wait in the car and I'll text if I need you to call 911."

"Cool, cool. You'll just be like, 'Yeah, excuse me, Bulger, dude who kidnapped me and stalked me for five months, could you maybe give me the next thirty seconds to send off this fucking text real quick?'"

The wind gusts, and I scrape my hair from my eyes. "Okay, well then, if you hear me scream—"

The back door shudders as another blast of wind barrels past us, and I skirt around Nomi so I can confirm what I already know.

The door isn't locked. It's not even closed.

All of this is wrong.

Before I talk myself out of it, I grab the handle. The door swings open, and Nomi's hard breaths keep time with my heartbeat as we stand in the open doorway.

I whisper, "Go to the car," but she's not listening, giving me a little shove until I'm over the threshold.

Something sweet and thick coats the air, toppled chair and glass lying silently against the tile floor, the puddle of liquid turned orange and sticky.

There are no sounds save for the rumble of the furnace below us, and the sporadic knock and creak from old boards and settling walls.

We've been standing here too long, waiting for something to happen, and all at once I don't want to be anywhere near here.

I grab my phone and type:

Stay here. Have 911 ready.

Nomi doesn't protest, and I want to cry with relief that she's here.

I'd forgotten, in all these months, what it was like to have someone else.

I heel-toe my way past the tiny bathroom and into the living room. Moonlight streams through the open curtains, cutting through the blanket of black.

The carpet beneath my foot squishes, and my stomach threatens to heave. It's too dark to discern color, and I'm not sure I want to know anyway.

I tug free a few napkins I stuffed in my coat pocket earlier and swipe at the bottom of my shoe, cleaning as best I can, before tossing it to the floor. Later. I'll pick it up later, when I walk out of here calmly because there's nothing awful happening here—the picture frame that's shoved to its side, the series of splotches dotting the carpet and up to the stairs, they're nothing.

A tentative step reveals I'm not leaving footprints all over the floor, so the FBI can't track me down and blame me for—

For *nothing*.

Nothing.

One times one is one. Two times two is four. Three times three is nine.

The stairs creak with every footfall, and I wrap my hoodie around my hand so my fingerprints aren't left behind while I grip the banister, pulling myself higher.

The air feels thicker here, harder to suck in, laced with a musty sweetness I can nearly taste. I move deeper into the hall, following the path of droplets on the carpet.

They lead to a bedroom in the back, the door slightly ajar, and I pause at the doorway, my head so light I have to brace myself against the frame.

My phone buzzes and I swallow a scream, but I can't look at it now. I only need a single excuse to walk away and pretend we were never here.

I nudge open the door, taking in every inch of the room as it's revealed, but there really *is* nothing. Just sparse furnishings and hardwood floors. The curtains are drawn, bathing the room in a blackened fog and a strip of light that imprints my shadow on the bed.

The bed.

It's made, covers pulled high, but beneath the thick covers there's the outline of a body. In all my worst-case scenarios, I didn't imagine walking in on a sleeping Edward Bulger.

Sweat springs over my skin, my blood screaming in my ears.

I should leave. Before he wakes up and calls the cops.

But then, no matter how hard I strain to hear, there are no snores, no deep breaths. There's just silence so thick it wraps me up, stuffing itself into my lungs.

I shudder with every step forward, while I stare, waiting for any sign of movement.

Mr. Bulger's eyes lay closed, arms folded stiffly over his chest, blanket tucked beneath them.

But his face looks *wrong.* Waxy, gray. I stretch my hand above his open mouth, but there's no heat of his breath. No deep sighs of heavy sleep.

There's just . . . nothing.

I let my gaze wander even while trying not to see, but it's impossible to miss the sheets beneath him—the darkened stain, stretching from the outline of his body.

Blood. *His* blood.

A whimper escapes me and I stumble back, nearly tripping over the slippers placed neatly beside his bed.

They're spotted with blood, like the carpet downstairs. The same blood that seeped into the bottom of my shoe.

And that's when the truth of what happened here comes together.

Someone surprised him downstairs, in the middle of his breakfast. And when they were done stabbing him, they brought him up to bed and tucked him in, placing his slippers just so next to his bed.

Someone who then took his car and drove to the woods to spy on me.

My footsteps thunder through the house, stuttering only to avoid the splotches of blood. Down the stairs, through the living room and into the kitchen, where Nomi stands motionless, eyes wide.

I'm nearly to the doorway before I remember the napkin, covered in Edward Bulger's blood, lying in the middle of his living room.

I double back, each footstep into that house harder than the last.

Then the napkin is in my hand and I'm running out the door.

We hop three fences, scurrying through backyards like the criminals we are, until we're far enough from the house to cut to our car.

Nomi grabs my keys, and I don't protest.

I shove off my shoes and curl into my seat, my arms wrapped tight around my knees, and I imagine how nearly I came to being just like Edward Bulger.

How close I came to dying.

CHAPTER SEVENTEEN

Saturday, October 9
6 Days Before the End

"You're sure he's dead?" Margot worries her thumbnail between her teeth, the glaze of tears in her eyes.

"Well. He wasn't breathing, and he was lying in a bed soaked in his own blood, so I'm pretty fucking sure he's dead, yes."

Her head drops and I sigh. We've been hunkered in her finished basement since we left Bulger's dad's house, and we're nowhere near figuring out what to do.

I plop down beside Margot and give her a hug. "I'm sorry. I'm just sorta freaked out."

Ori raises her hand and waits for someone to nod before she speaks. "The posing-him-in-the-bed thing, and the slippers? That's usually a sign of remorse on the part of the killer. Or that they cared for him."

Nomi mumbles, "That's some fucked-up shit," and I couldn't agree more.

I rub my arms because I can't stop shaking. "Okay, so Ori watches too many Netflix murder shows—"

"Well, yes. But I also read a lot of true crime books. Also, there are some great podcasts out there." She stops as we all stare at sweet little Ori, bingeing on serial killers.

She shrugs. "I don't go out much. Lots of free time."

I smile and she returns it, because yeah, that sums up my social life too.

"So that fits though, with the killer being Coach Bulger." I pace the room, running from the images I can't escape.

Margot says, "But why would he kill his dad?"

"Maybe his dad found out what he did to Cass. What he's *been* doing." Ori gives me an apologetic grimace. "If his dad confronted him and threatened to turn him in, it could've set him off."

Margot hugs her knees to her chest. "What does that mean?"

"That Coach Bulger has a rage problem, and an inability to control his actions?"

My mouth goes dry. "Oh, awesome. So he's careful, methodical, smart enough to avoid getting caught, but prone to extreme violence?"

"I mean," Ori whispers, "I'm not an expert. But did it look like a robbery?"

"No. His TV was in the living room. He was—" I try again. "He was still wearing his watch."

"Stabbing someone is . . . personal. You have to get close and *feel* what you're doing. Without a motive like robbery, it usually means it's someone the victim knows. At least—" She ducks her head, and her voice goes quiet. "That's what I've read anyway."

"Okay well perfect." I try to keep my voice light to counteract the panic tearing through me. Was my abduction *personal* too? Because the letters he sends sure as hell feel that way. And now I know exactly what would've happened to me if I hadn't escaped that trunk.

Even if I can prove it's Bulger, what then? How do you fight someone with enough rage to stab his own father?

I blink back my tears and focus, because it's either that or fall apart. "So something went wrong or Bulger . . . went into a rage, and then he kills his dad and somehow switches to feeling bad about it and tries to . . . pretend his dad is just sleeping or something."

The entire room shudders, and Nomi says, "This is next-level creepy, Cass. Maybe we should—"

"Don't finish that sentence. You *know* I can't go to the cops. They think

I made up my own kidnapping, and Noah and I walked in there carrying Bulger's dad's license plate today."

That's just the beginning. We'd be first on the suspect list based on the license plate alone, but I'd have to admit Noah took a pic of Detective Michaels's screen. I'd have to admit exactly how and why we were at the park. I'd have to tell them about all the letters, and how I never stopped receiving them.

But most of all, there's this. "We can't do the things we need to do if the police are watching us."

It's the only way out of this.

Margot nods. "No, Cass is right. We need to keep things quiet. Until we're done."

Quiet oozes through the room, the gravity of this day, of us, of all the things we've promised making it hard to breathe.

We all jump as a door slams upstairs, and Margot's eyes go wide. "Mom's not supposed to be home yet!"

There are at least fifteen seconds where no one moves, like we're caught between the seconds, frozen between the transition from our plans and the normalcy of wanting to avoid Margot's mom.

Nomi snaps from her trance and shrugs on her jacket, but it takes her two tries to get it right. "Is there a closet I can hide in?"

I add, "Same," and Ori winces. "She kind of scares me, Margot."

I am not capable of fielding Melanie Pennington conversation right now.

Margot growls in frustration. "She doesn't hate you guys. She just doesn't know you. And she's not bad—she's just kind of . . . *intense*."

Understatement. Margot's mom lacks an off switch. And assumes no one else has one either. Which is why she expects Margot to get perfect grades (her mom was valedictorian) and be an amazing volleyball player (her mom was slated for the Olympics when a shoulder injury—not to mention accidentally getting pregnant with Margot—derailed her), and have the perfect boyfriend (her mom married the prom king).

But she's been to every one of Margot's games, the loudest parent in the stands, and at least Margot knows where her mom *is*. At least she thinks Margot was worth sticking around for.

Margot grabs my arm. "You have to be here because your car is here. The rest of you can sneak out when Cass and I say hi. We'll pick you up around the corner."

Nomi fist-bumps the air, and Margot squeezes Ori's hand and mouths a "sorry," and I swear a smile tugs at Ori's lips.

Nomi bites her lip until her berry-black lipstick smudges. "We can skip tonight, Cass, if you can't do it."

"No." We were supposed to be watching her stepdad instead of Edward Bulger, but she didn't hesitate to come with me earlier. "We're doing this."

But then Margot is dragging me up the stairs and into her massive kitchen, where her mom is putting away hundreds of bags of assorted leafy things.

"Hey, Mom."

Her mom smothers Margot in a hug, waxing poetic about her leafy things and the community garden.

She grows their vegetables in the community garden because of course she does.

Fewer bugs at night, she says. Then she's asking, "How was your day?" and "How are you?" before she launches in with "How was practice?" even though Margot hasn't answered the first two questions.

Then she sees me.

She takes a step back, eyes blinking. "Oh! Hi, Cass!"

Guarantee my smile is as strained as hers. "Hi, Mrs. Pennington."

"It's so good to see you again, Cass. So what have you been up to? Are you thinking of joining the team again? How—"

"Mom!" Margot gives her a pointed stare that says *stop with the questions*. "We were gonna head out, if that's okay."

Her mom checks her watch, staring at it like Apple's systems must have been hacked because surely we're not asking to go out at eleven thirty at night. "Margot."

"Just a few friends hanging out." She tacks on "Noah will be there" almost too quickly.

I'd forgotten about this, how normal kids needed to check with their parents before going places. I always used to let Dad know when I was going out, back when I actually went places, but the only person more paranoid than him about me turning out like my mom was and is *me*, so I never did anything for him to worry about.

But saying Noah's name seems to be the key to unlocking Margot's mom's approval meter, and minutes later we're out the door, the sound of her voice telling us to be careful and safe drifting over us.

Careful and safe.

If she only knew where we were really headed.

CHAPTER EIGHTEEN
CASS ADAMS

The Events of Saturday, October 9
6 Days Before the End

Nothing was supposed to happen.

Not that night.

We were supposed to watch and wait. Gather information and formulate a plan.

We were *supposed* to be smart, act on reason and not emotion.

We were supposed to do this right.

But there were only two of us thinking with clear minds. Nomi and I were too caught up in that house with the body inside it. The one we left behind.

The four of us parked at the top of the gully, looking down on the house Nomi used to share with her mom and stepdad, and we slid and stumbled through the trees and over the tiny bridge to the backyard.

He'd built it—the bridge—back when she was much smaller, back when things weren't so bad, so she could play in the woods. Climbing trees and settling in their branches to read.

Then the shouts started, and she'd bring headphones to drown them out. That only lasted until she saw one of her mom's bruises.

Nomi's breathing hard by the time our feet touch the grass in the yard that used to belong to her, and all her stories dry up as her eyes go hard.

I recognize it, the look in her eyes. I feel it deep in that part of me that stretched itself wide as I ran through the woods today, chasing the man who chases me.

We should turn around, come back another day when we're not so off-center, but then Nomi looks at me, dark eyes shining in moonlight, and I know how much she needs this.

We keep to the trees at the far edge of the property, running, keeping low, and it feels like hours pass as we advance along the expanse of yard.

The house looms high, pointed roof puncturing a haze of gray clouds. Nomi leads the way, across the yard to the back door. There's no one to see us. No neighbors save for the clusters of trees set far from the house.

Nomi slides in her key, and the lock thunks over. After all these years. Not like the girl and her mother who had to hide, who told no one where they lived, because it wasn't safe. Because *they* weren't safe. From him. From the man who had so little to fear he didn't even change the locks.

The door slams against the wall as Nomi throws it open and stomps inside. The anger roils from her in twisted waves, snaking into the air.

She pauses just inside—me, Ori, and Margot stationed in a row behind. I grab Nomi's hand as Ori's reaches for my other, the tiny jingle of bracelet charms linking us all.

From somewhere deep beneath us, a TV blares, garbled voices and sporadic gunshots, but the rest of the house lies silent.

We didn't plan for this, coming inside. We were supposed to see if the key worked and walk away. But we're in now, and as Nomi takes quiet steps into the marble kitchen, we all know—it's too late to turn back.

We follow her path, into the living room, her steps sure and well-practiced, ours tentative, halting.

She doesn't wait for us as she heads up the stairs. Her footsteps thunder up every step, and my muscles bunch and knot, every fiber alert for the man who didn't hesitate to break bones and spirits.

Ori whispers, "Should we go get her?" and I shake my head.

Some things, a girl has to do alone.

We listen for the creak of wood above us, tracking Nomi's path as she moves through the second floor, and just when my skin itches to run from this place and all the memories within these walls, she reappears.

Pillowcases stuffed with belongings dangle from her hands, and she doesn't even try to wipe away the tracks of tears on her cheeks. She stuffs the pillowcases in our hands and disappears, her shadow trailing behind her like a ghost.

There's a clang of metal, a quiet whimper, before she reappears, a smile lighting her face as the dog in her arms wiggles and squirms.

Something dark and cold climbs over me, a fierce sort of certainty, and I whisper Nomi's name, but she's too far in to hear me. Too far gone to turn back.

She dumps the dog into Ori's arms after giving him one last kiss. "This is Salvador Dogi. We call him Sal. It's time for you all to go."

Ori looks to me, her eyes wide, carrying the same questions as mine.

But we promised. I gave my word, swore I wouldn't let anyone do this alone. As much as it takes.

"I'm not leaving." My voice is clear, certain, even though I don't feel it.

Ori looks ready to protest until Sal lets out a whine. She whispers, "I don't—We don't have a dog and I don't know what it's saying."

I transfer the dog to Margot and stuff my pillowcase into Ori's open hand. "There. Ori and Margot can take the stuff. I stay."

And I do, following Nomi to the basement door, Margot's and Ori's footsteps fading.

A dead bolt sits high, designed to keep things in instead of out, and I shudder at the possibilities Nomi never spoke of.

She flings open the door, and a wave of fumes hit me, enough to make my eyes water—sulfur and ammonia and kerosene. But Nomi tunnels deeper into the darkness as the garbled voices ring clearer, louder, until we're standing in a room lined with tables. They're covered in beakers and burners, bottles of cleaners and solvents.

Nomi stares at me—at me staring at the evidence I don't want to believe.

"Nomi, what is—"

"Meth lab." She scans the room, fingers clenching to fists. "This is when it started getting bad. When he started this."

Nearly too fast to see, the sole of her boot slams into the tabletop, sending it crashing.

It bounces against the floor, throwing its contents in an arc of shattered glass and spilled liquids.

A groan emanates from a doorway, and I stifle my yelp, my legs too wobbly to move.

But then we're standing in the doorway, staring down at Nomi's stepfather.

He doesn't move, doesn't wake at the sound of our voices when I say, "Is he—"

"No. He doesn't use. Doesn't even drink. He kills people while completely sober." Her hand finds mine and grips tight. "We left when he wanted me to sell for him. I was fourteen fucking years old."

She's so calm my mind twists as I try to picture her here in another time. But she's right here when she lifts a lighter from the table.

I'm breathing too hard, the fumes making me light-headed, my throat raw. We're surrounded by chemicals, fire stimulants. The only grace is how remote their house is—no neighbor houses to get caught in the cross fire. "Nomi."

"You don't know, Cass. The things he did to her. The lives he's ruined. You don't know what I've seen. You don't *know*."

She's right. But it isn't him I'm protecting. "You can't take this back."

"I don't want to."

I try to summon my outrage, my remorse. But we promised. We swore we'd go as far as it took.

I move to her stepfather's bedside, let my shadow crawl over his sleeping form, and grab his phone.

I don't want to touch it, but we'll need it.

Nomi joins me, kicking the bed until her stepdad stirs. He's groggy, half-awake, and something jingles as it smacks to his stomach.

Keys. She's giving him a chance to survive. More than he ever gave to anyone else.

We stand in the main room, Nomi surrounded by remnants of a past she'll never escape, and her arm climbs higher, lighter fisted in her hand.

She doesn't flinch. "Ashes to ashes, right?"

"Ashes to ashes."

Her thumb poises on the wheel. "Run."

We do, and a wall of flame gives chase. We're nearly to the top of the stairs when something clamps around my ankle. My body flies forward, chin slamming on the steps so hard my teeth clack together and the taste of coppery blood wars with the sharpness of fumes and fire.

I claw at the carpet, my legs trying to kick free, but I can't even scream because this time it feels like things will end differently. No escape this time. No second chance.

Nomi screams as she thunders down the stairs, a blur of shoes until something thuds above me and my ankle pops free. Her hands band around my wrists, dragging me up, pulling me to the top of the stairs just as the heat feels too thick to breathe through.

We clear the top of the stairs, both of us fighting for air until we can stand upright.

And then it only takes a second, the briefest moment when our eyes meet, and she slams the door shut.

I don't stop her.

CHAPTER NINETEEN

Monday, October 11
4 Days Before the End

Monday morning comes too soon, my body still worn down and wrung out.

We lie low on Sunday, keeping our normal routines, living our average lives.

But normal does not include leaving a dead man to rot or a living man to burn.

Nomi's dad escaped. Not unscathed. He's in the ICU. He won't be able to hurt anyone else for now. And we did what we had to do to escape. To survive. I'm not sure that absolves us of anything.

But maybe I can rectify the other. I just owe it to Noah to warn him beforehand.

Lucky me, he's in my first-period English lit class.

I'm waiting outside the classroom, tucked into a little alcove, where I'll remain until exactly three minutes before the bell.

Five minutes to go.

I scan the halls for Coach Bulger. It feels better, having a name, a face, to set my nightmares to. It feels worse, knowing the things he's capable of. *If* it's him. But right now, I don't see any other options. The license plate in the woods was left by my stalker, and the person that killed Edward Bulger knew him—no one else fits.

Ori jumps into my alcove, eyes panicked. "You didn't text me?"

"Wait, what?"

She locks on to my forearm with an uncomfortably strong grip. "Did you . . . *text me*? After we . . ." She whispers, "Departed Saturday night?"

I check my arm for bruises. "I texted yesterday, and—"

"What did it say?"

"Why are you freaking out?"

"I'm grounded. *Was* grounded, for coming home so late Saturday."

"That sucks. Still not following." Two minutes left.

"They took my phone, Cass. They know the passcode. So *what did your text say?*"

I knew Ori's parents were serious, but no phone for a late curfew is next-level. "Just, like, hope you're doing okay and see you Monday."

Her shoulders sink, a held breath released. "Good. That's good. From now on, don't say anything questionable unless I respond."

"Couldn't your parents pretend to be you though?"

She points at me. "Diabolical. Good thinking. Okay, don't say anything questionable until I say, 'Wakanda forever.'"

"Your safe word is 'Wakanda forever'?"

"It's not—" She hisses, "It's not a *safe word*! It's just a *word!*"

I snicker, then it blooms into a full-blown laugh, and despite being properly scandalized, Ori laughs too.

Then her face falls. "I still have to find Nomi."

"Ori, your freaking out is freaking me out. Did your parents say something?"

This is not the time for parental supervision.

She bites her bottom lip. "They said they don't want to see me hanging out with the wrong crowd."

Not good. We can't have Ori's parents thinking we're the wrong crowd.

"Okay, that doesn't sound terrible. Find Nomi and we'll game-plan. But, Ori, next time, lie if you have to."

She nods, but I don't think Ori's done much lying to her parents. "See you at lunch, Cass."

Then she's off and I'm already a full minute behind schedule.

I force myself across the hall and into the seat next to Noah and blurt out, "There's something I need to tell you."

He scans the packed classroom. "Here?"

"Good a place as any!" My cheer is very false and very obvious. "Something *happened* Saturday night."

He turns and slams his knee into the desk, mumbling about them being sized for second graders. "Are you okay? Did someone—"

"Not to me. It was more like something happened and I didn't say anything. But I should've. *Right* away. But now—"

"Cass." Noah's hand circles my wrist, warm and heavy. "Slow down."

"Right. Okay. I'll do that."

I lean in and he leans closer, until memories of the last time his breath whispered over my cheek flood my thoughts.

"Open your books to chapter twelve!" Ms. Hart's voice breaks us apart, and I don't look to see if Noah's blushing as much as I am.

My textbook opens easily, right to chapter twelve, right to the pink envelope tucked inside.

I smother my mouth with my hand, holding in the scream threatening to erupt from my lungs.

I hate myself for it. For not expecting this. Our truce is shattered, and I'm still expecting him to act like it's not.

It probably wasn't even hard for him to access my locker. There's not a single place that's safe from him. And who would believe me even if I told someone? Beloved teacher. Flawless record. Figurehead of the community.

They didn't believe me when my attacker was nameless.

And now he's everywhere and I'm trapped. Pinned. Bound in the trunk with music roaring in my ears and my screams held fast by the grip of duct tape.

I slam the cover shut and stumble from my seat. Someone says my name, but my blood is too thick in my ears, rushing too fast.

The run to the doors is an eternity, and when I burst through them, I suck in air so fast my lungs burn.

That's when Noah shows up, holding my textbook. "I almost didn't bring this."

"I'd rather you hadn't."

"Yeah, well, I figured if I didn't, you'd tell me I imagined a pink envelope sending you into a panic attack."

"Would that have worked?"

"Cass. Is this about the stalker? Is he—" He stops when he sees the look on my face.

He swallows. "Start easier. What did you need to tell me?"

Right. This is better. Safer.

Sort of.

Not really.

I rub my hands to warm them. Bulger could be watching us, right now. Like he probably did all of last year, all the beginning of this one. In the halls, through classroom doorways, assemblies.

I can't make myself think of how many minutes of my life he's watched, consumed, cataloged.

"Cass. Are you—"

"I'm fine." I am not fine. "You remember the picture you took at the police station?"

"Yes." He says it slow, suspicion building in his voice.

"Well, turns out, the car belongs to Coach Bulger's dad."

"You—" He rubs his jaw. "You didn't think that was relevant?"

"Actually, no, I thought it was really relevant and *that* is why I didn't tell you."

He's mad. Not upset or disappointed and definitely not concerned. Square jaw tensed, flush working its way into his cheeks.

"Got it." He leaves me standing there.

I still haven't told him about Coach Bulger's dad, and he still has my book, and the letter.

I run to catch him, and he almost doesn't stop, even when I grab on to his arm.

He turns to me, his eyes hard, and I can't do it. Not like this. Not when he's already so angry. So I say the only thing I can. "Can you account for Coach Bulger's whereabouts on Tuesday, October fifth at approximately nine p.m.?"

His voice is completely devoid of emotion when he says, "Coaching. Football practice."

I swallow, my throat thick and my mouth dry.

I thought that's what I wanted to hear—that it couldn't have been Bulger on the phone while I was in the woods with Tyler. But the alternative is that it's someone else. Someone unknown and even more unpredictable.

But it could still be Bulger. He could've snuck away.

Noah says, "Is that all?" and I feel his anger with every syllable.

I stare at the grass between us, the droplets of dew clinging to their bent blades. "I need my book back."

He holds it out for me, without hesitation, and it's only then I know how badly I wanted him to resist.

The book's weight drops onto my trembling palms as he says, "I don't play games, Cass. Find me when you're ready to be honest."

Then he's gone, and all the words I want to say go unspoken.

He thinks he wants to know. Thinks he can save me just like Dad thought he could do for Mom.

But Noah has nothing to gain and getting him involved could ruin him. I won't be like my mother, at least not in this.

I clutch the book to my chest, eyes closed, when an engine rumbles in the distance. It's low, throaty. Embedded in my brain and my nightmares.

I sprint toward the sound, as fast as I ran away from it once when my life depended on it. But it's not a car I see when I get there.

My eyes take in the sight while my brain scrambles to form the fragments into a whole.

Bulger, rage pouring out of him as he holds a man against the brick wall, his forearm across the man's throat, words seething from between his lips. The way he ignores how the man claws against his arm, the man's eyes bulging, skin bleeding red to purple.

I blink, willing my vision to clear and leave the space in front of me empty. Because it's not just Bulger, his anger, his violence, it's the man too.

It's the scar down his cheek that I've seen before. In the Target parking lot, driving by me like he wasn't there for me at all.

But now he's here. He's here at my school, locked with a man who I thought was my stalker, but now I'm not sure of anything.

The car engine grumbles again, fading as it speeds down the road, and I'm shocked from my trance, the sound drawing me to a thin tendril of smoke rising from the parking lot. A cigarette. Several of them. Like the person had been here. Waiting.

Not Bulger, not the man with the scar, but a sound I can't forget, and everything feels connected and split apart all at once.

Bulger lets up the tiniest bit, only to shove harder, cracking the man's head against the wall. The thick thud of it makes my stomach turn, my head go light, and for a breath it's *my* head smacking the floor of a trunk, it's Bulger's hand around the knife, plunging it into his father. But it's the scarred man with a blade in his hand, sun glinting off its edge as he slips it back into its handle with quiet *snick*.

A whimper escapes my throat because I don't know what I just interrupted, or what would've happened if I hadn't.

Both their gazes snap to me, and my breathing goes thin and hollow.

Bulger says my name. Not *Cass*. He calls me Cassandra.

I stumble back and Bulger pulls his arm from the man's throat but I don't know which one of them to be more afraid of.

Bulger's mouth opens, seconds from saying something I don't want to hear, and then he takes a step in my direction.

I run.

Like the scared little girl I am.

I don't stop until I'm safely locked in a bathroom stall, my hands shaking so hard I can barely engage the locks.

I drop my head to the metal door, palms pressed flat. I'm not safe here. Not at school. Not at home. Not even the goddamned Target parking lot.

And I don't even know who I'm supposed to run from.

We may have left a man to burn, but this is why.

These are the things we do to survive.

And I won't hide anymore.

I slip the lock free with steady hands, bracelet dangling from my wrist. *As far as it takes.* Dangerous girls don't play games.

CHAPTER TWENTY

Monday, October 11
4 Days Before the End

Despite searching all morning, I haven't spotted Tyler once.

My pink envelope still sits unopened in my backpack, its presence a dagger between my shoulder blades.

But right now, I need Tyler. I need to stop thinking about Edward Bulger's body, his son in the parking lot when he should've been teaching, the man with the scar, and the too-familiar growl of that car.

I need a phone—an in-no-way-traceable-to-me phone—so I can notify the police about Bulger's dad. I owe him that at least.

I settle into the lunch table Tyler joins me at almost daily—still on the other side, always a few seats down—and I wait.

But it's not Tyler I get.

Margot and Ori storm toward me, their hands linked and eyes rimmed red.

Nomi pops in behind them, frantically pointing toward the doors while trying to look nonchalant.

Nomi's telling me to leave, but the closer Margot gets, the faster her tears come, and I'm frozen.

I haven't even told them about the scarred man, and something tells me this isn't about that at all.

Margot and Ori sit in unison and lean across the table, and Margot says, "Did you know he was in the house?"

Nomi slides in beside me and mumbles, "Sorry," while Ori buries her face in her hands.

Her voice trembles. "I didn't agree to—"

Realization creeps in, soft and slow. We didn't tell them about Nomi's stepfather being in the basement, but they know.

I look to Nomi, and she shrugs. "It made the local news." She fakes a newscaster voice. "Meth comes to the suburbs!"

Shit.

My whisper comes out harsh in our little pocket of the cafeteria. "We didn't plan it. I was hoping you'd never—"

"I'm not sorry," Nomi says, not whispering at all. "We saved people that night. The world is better now. Trust me."

Ori and Margot stare in stunned silence, lips parted and faces slack, and Tyler slides in with a "Good afternoon, ladies."

The entire group startles and turns to me, and I'm caught between two incompatible worlds.

Tyler looks over our group and smirks. "Getting a little crowded in here."

"Can I talk to you?" I jump from my seat and rush out of the lunch-room, and I swear the entire cafeteria is watching.

We walk in silence, until I grind to a stop.

Coach Bulger stands straight ahead, deep in conversation with Principal Mason, until his gaze snags on mine. All I see is his arm against that man's throat. The anger radiating from him.

I see all the things he might've done if I hadn't stopped him.

I've got more reason to believe Bulger is responsible than I do some man that drove through a Target parking lot. And that means every moment of the last five months is because of Bulger. Every nightmare and morning coated in a sheen of sweat and twisted sheets is because of what he did. What he turned me into.

Everything I've lost, he's taken from me.

I'm running before I realize what I'm doing, *toward* him this time. But strong arms band about my waist, lifting me from the ground, and my blood goes feral. The way my legs kick and my elbows strike has no order and no intent, but every time they collide with something solid I push harder. I hit harder. And for a minute, I don't know whether I'm in the school hallway or seconds from tumbling into a waiting trunk.

The arms around me disappear and I stumble, nearly slamming into the lockers, and Tyler's apologies come out breathless, hesitant.

It takes four long inhales before I can face him. "Don't—Don't *ever* do that—"

"I punched Lassiter in the face once."

"What?" I scramble to make sense of his confession. "You punched your best friend in the face?"

"He thought it would be funny to sneak up on me and put me in a choke hold."

He stares down the hall. "In my life experience, that particular action was . . . Well, let's just say it wasn't a joke."

"I'm so sorry." I whisper it, because it's a poor excuse for what an admission like that deserves.

He shrugs, smile crooked. "If you ever hear the story about Mark Lassiter, the badass who got in a bar fight at sixteen and walked away with only a black eye, now you know the truth."

"Miss Adams!" Principal Mason echoes down the hallway. "Is Mr. Thorne bothering you?"

I say no because he's not, but when my gaze finds Coach Bulger again, I lose track of everything else. He's fully facing me, his arms crossed, and his head cocks. His eyes narrow, searching, assessing.

I wonder what he sees when he looks at me.

"Careful, Cass." Tyler's voice is the surface of a glassy lake, made for talking people off ledges. "Do you know what happens when you attack teachers in the hallway?"

My nails bite into my palms. "You feel an immense sense of satisfaction?"

"Well, there is that, yes."

Principal Mason calls, "And where are you supposed to be, Mr. Thorne?"

He smiles at her, all teeth, and shouts, "Just headed to lunch!" before his voice drops low again. "People talk, Cass. *That's* what happens when you attack teachers in the hallway."

He waits for me to meet his eyes, ignoring Mason when she tells him he'd better be headed toward the lunch room. "You've done your best to make people forget you exist, so it seems to me, running down that hallway is not what you want right now."

My gaze ricochets between Tyler and Bulger, every bit of me warring between the truth in his words and the blind fury I've waited five months to unleash.

"Stay with me, okay?" Tyler takes a slow step forward, reaching out a hand and leaving it there. Mine to take. Or not.

"You don't understand."

"Yes I do." Another step, and Principal Mason's heels strike the tile. "I'm pretty good at reading people, and I don't think this is what you need. I don't think it's what your friends need either."

It's the exact right thing to say. I can't ruin things for Margot and Ori. I can't drag Nomi into a scandal.

Then Tyler smiles, his blue eyes bright in the sliver of sun through windows. "Or go ahead and beat the shit out of him. He probably deserves it. Then we can Bonnie-and-Clyde the fuck outta here."

A laugh bursts out of me, just in time for Principal Mason to reach us. Bulger hasn't moved.

Principal Mason says, "Is something going—"

"We're fine." I slip my hand into Tyler's, and his fingers thread through mine. Warm, reassuring, like he knows, better than anyone else could.

"I needed Tyler's thoughts on our history project."

I turn and haul ass down the hall, dragging him behind me, but not before he gives Principal Mason a salute.

She is absolutely going to check our schedules. That's unfortunate, because we don't share a single class.

We turn a corner and duck inside an empty classroom. Light ebbs around the covered windows, leaving the room in a muted hush that hangs over the rows of barren tables.

Tyler pulls the door shut. "You need a minute?"

"Several of them." Several minutes, hours, years, until the world stops feeling like it's hurtling me toward an end I don't want to reach.

"Yeah." That's all he says, and somehow, it's enough.

"There's a lot of stuff that people don't know about me."

He widens his eyes in mock surprise. "My little Bonnie, keeping secrets?"

"Shut up." I smile despite myself.

He slides into a chair, his fingers laced behind his head. "We all have secrets, Cass. Some are just better at hiding them."

"Pretty sure I suck at it."

"Oh, I don't know about that." He drops forward, elbows on knees. "You seem to be doing all right."

Tyler Thorne may be many things, but a snitch is not one of them. I could tell him everything I've done, and he'd die with my secrets. He'd never judge me for letting Nomi's stepdad burn.

He nods toward the hall. "Care to tell me what happened out there with Bulger?"

"Not particularly."

"Fair enough."

Though, if Bulger has secrets, Tyler might be the person who'd have heard about them. Right now everything is circumstantial. If I take out my revenge on the wrong person, I'm no better than the man who threw me in that trunk.

His eyebrow raises, waiting.

"Have you, I don't know, ever heard any rumors about him?"

Tyler leans close, his voice dropping low. "Not that I'd condone such activities, but if there's something you're looking for, I happen to know that one Mr. Nathan Bulger comes in early most mornings. Uses the weight room. Runs the track. On Tuesdays, he has to leave his office unlocked for the cleaning crew."

I whisper a thank-you, because I'm just as thrilled with the prospect of getting proof as I am terrified that Tyler can read me so easily.

He shrugs. "No thanks necessary. Just two friends having a little conversation. Let me know when I can do you a real favor."

It's the only thing that gives me the courage to ask. "I need a phone. Like a black-market phone."

It takes two seconds before he busts into full-blown laughter. "A *black-market* phone?"

He's going to make me explain this. "Yeah, like . . . a phone that can't be traced back to me."

He waits, his smile growing, and it takes me way too long to realize he knows exactly *what* I want—it's the term "black-market phone" that's causing him endless amusement.

I say, "Okay, so I'm not exactly up on the lingo of illegal goods but—"

"First lesson: Never use '*lingo*' in the discussion of illegal goods."

"You're making fun of me."

"Absolutely yes."

"Sorry, but if I knew illegal goods lingo, I'd be able to get my own black-market phone."

"Tell me, Cass, what makes you think *I* can get you a black-market phone?"

There's teasing in his tone, but something else too, lurking deeper, sitting darker.

I did the thing he talked about, judging him because of his father, making assumptions about the person he is without any cause. "I'm sorry. I assumed and I shouldn't have and—"

I smother my face with my hands. "Maybe one day, I'll manage to have a single relationship that I don't fuck up."

Something nudges my leg, knocking my elbows from my knees, and when I look up, Tyler says, "Hey. It's cool. Lucky for you, your presumptions are correct. I can get your black-market phone, Cass Adams, on one condition."

"What?" I should sound more grateful, but conditions are promises and lately there are so many I can't keep.

"You tell me if you're into something too deep."

I grasp tight to the charms at my wrist, metal cold against my palm. I've been in too deep from the moment I landed in that trunk. "Easy there, resident bad boy, I just need it for something fun."

"Hmmm." He tips his chair again, tilting himself into a triangle of shadow. "Pranks with your friends, new and old?"

I open my mouth, but all my words feel wrong. I'm out of practice, talking to people, reading between their lines and deciphering their truths. "Something like that."

The front legs of his chair land with a thud, and he swings to standing in one smooth movement. "Be careful, Cass. New friends can't always be trusted, and old ones definitely can't."

"Does that include you?"

He smiles in that way that only reaches half his mouth, filled with all the thoughts he keeps from my ears.

He grabs a sheet of paper, the buckle on his watch clicking against the desk as he scrawls a phone number. "Now you can call me instead of waiting until lunch."

The numbers streak across the page, smudged from his palm. He could've asked for my number, but he gave me his, and it's mine to use or not, without any expectations.

It's only one of the reasons I accept it.

He smiles then, full and earnest, and he runs his thumb over my cheek a second before he's walking toward the door.

He stops, hall light spilling around him and casting him in darkness. "Here's the difference between them and me: You could never fuck up our relationship."

Then he's gone, leaving me to wonder exactly how much Tyler knows, and how much I can trust anyone.

CHAPTER TWENTY-ONE

Monday, October 11
4 Days Before the End

The bowl of popcorn sits in the middle of our circle, untouched. Ori strangles her nail polish bottle in one hand, textbook in the other. She's the only one of us even pretending to summon the concentration for homework.

Margot's notebook sits open, the page blank—she's spent eight entire minutes debating between two shades of red polish.

None of us have spoken, except me and Nomi, with our eyes, telling each other to just start the conversation already, before the cops show up.

We know they're coming, thanks to Nomi's dad. Well, thanks to Nomi overhearing her mom's phone call with her dad. *"They have a two-minute limit of civil conversation before they start fucking screaming at each other"* were the words Nomi chose.

The one thing her parents *do* agree on? They're glad that fucker paid for his sins. Also Nomi's choice of words.

So now we're here, waiting, being normal. If normal is strained silence and intense nail polish debate.

If *normal* is the constant twist in my stomach, the way my veins feel filled with spikes. If *normal* is questioning every decision I've made since we started this and whether I should be allowed to make any others.

We could go to jail. Our lives could all be ruined. We tried to take back what they stole, but I can't shake the panic that the world isn't set up for us. That four girls trying to take back anything means we'll lose twice as much.

I need to tell them what happened today, with Bulger and the man with the scar. But not right now. Not until I fix this.

"I'm sorry." Everyone jumps at the sound of my voice, and Ori's nail polish tumbles to the carpet.

It's closed, but she stares like it exploded.

I twist it open, filling the room with the sharp scent of lacquer, and she takes it from me with shaking hands. I say, "It's not too late to confess," and Nomi responds with an "Absolutely fucking not" before I can form my next words.

"He *attacked* me, Nomi. It was self-defense." It's what I tell myself, every time I close my eyes and see Nomi flipping that lock. Every time the feel of his hands on my ankle takes the place of the duct tape around my wrists in my nightmares. But my words sound empty even to my own ears.

"Right, sure. And was it self-defense that we were there? That we set the house on fire? That we—"

"I know! I know." I take a deep breath. "You're right. They wouldn't understand."

Wouldn't understand. Wouldn't believe us. Wouldn't let us do what we still need to do.

I look to Ori and Margot. "We should've told you."

Margot stares at the bottles in her hand, too long, before she tosses them both in the pile to clink against the others. "You shouldn't have done it."

"Bullshit." Nomi jams the brush back into her open bottle of polish—pale pink and like nothing she'd wear normally. "He kills people—*killed* people—every fucking day, Margot. But their deaths are slow, constant torment. And he doesn't care who he sells to, whether they have kids. He didn't care about my mom, and he didn't care about me either. I can give you the horror stories or you can just fucking *believe me*."

Margot grabs Nomi's token black polish and streaks it across her finger. "We nearly *killed* someone."

"No. *I* nearly killed someone. Cass watched, and you and Ori saved Sal."

Ori says, "And we're not supposed to feel bad about that?"

"Feel however you want, but don't tell me how to."

Silence stretches, and I focus on the brush in my hand. Confidence oozes through my voice, my tone quiet—a flower petal with a razor's edge—and I recognize it, but it's not mine. "Do you think they feel bad?"

I feel their stares, but I don't look up, staining my fingernails a burgundy red, so deep it's almost black. "Do you think Nomi's stepdad *felt bad* when he was hurting her mom? Do you think Mr. Valco *feels bad* every time he harasses you? Every time he assigned you to read in class?"

I move to my ring finger and my hands don't shake, my voice doesn't waver, and I get it, finally, what my mother felt in moments like this, with an audience that was hers to control, to convince.

I accused her once of performing, pretending to be someone else because she hated who she really was.

She laughed, almost sad, and told me that *is* who she really was. She told me one day I'd understand.

Burgundy-red blooms across my pinkie nail as I say, "Margot, do you think it's Jared's overwhelming guilt that made him threaten to show the tape to everyone if you didn't keep fucking him?"

I wait, silent, moving to my other hand to finish what I started. "They *don't* feel bad. That's the point. They think everything they do is justified and warranted. They think we don't *get* a say in any of this. They think we *deserve* this. So we can sit here debating morality, what's too dangerous and too risky, or . . ."

I finish my final nail and hold them up, bloodred tips glistening in the rays of sunlight. "Or we can do what we promised. We can risk everything, go as far as it takes, and we show them that our lives belong to us—and we're the only ones who get to decide our fate. We show them what it's like to feel very, *very* bad."

It shouldn't be this way.

We didn't choose this. They chose it for us.

I meet each of their eyes, and no one speaks, because we all know.

I blow across my fingers, breath tickling against the fresh polish. "Good. Now let's get our stories straight about Saturday before the cops show up."

CHAPTER TWENTY-TWO

Monday, October 11
4 Days Before the End

I'm here, where he said to be.

When he said to be.

By myself, like he insisted in the note he left in my book.

I stood in my living room when I finally opened it.

I left the curtains open. I did not flinch at the sight of his familiar scrawl, telling me to meet him at an abandoned building.

This time, I didn't run.

I just don't know who I'm running toward now. Bulger? The man with the scar? The man driving the car?

Bulger's the only known quantity, but from what I saw today—the rage, the unrestrained violence—I might be more afraid of what I know.

But after I survive this, I'll fix the rest. I'll get the phone from Tyler and call the police to report Edward Bulger's body, and maybe they'll arrest Coach Bulger for killing his dad. They'll do their forensic stuff and agree with Ori about posing Bulger's dad, and that will be the end. Maybe the thing I've been afraid of most for the past five months will disappear. Then we'll finish the rest. Mr. Valco. Jared.

It can't have been just words I said to the girls earlier today—whether they came in my mother's voice or mine—it was *me* that said them. I started this, all of it. I promised them we'd do what needed to be done. I promised I'd risk everything.

I wasn't exactly expecting *my life* to be on the table quite so quickly, but here we are. And now my car sits in an empty lot, surrounded by ragged leaves that tunnel through cracked cement and empty bottles that roll under the force of the wind.

Darkness overtook the sky an hour ago, chasing away dusk and ushering in night.

I have twenty-two unread texts on my phone.

Twenty-two times twenty-two is four hundred eighty-four, and my life feels like it's spinning away from me, too fast to catch. I'm supposed to be texting the girls to check in, but I can't focus on anything but why I'm here.

If he wanted to kill me, he could take me from anywhere. We both know it. We've lived it before.

That's what I tell myself, when the panic threatens to consume me, when the rational part of me resists coming here tonight. But this is where I get answers. This is how I reclaim my life.

I fling open my door and stomp toward the abandoned warehouse. The end of it disappears into the blackness of night, and rows of windows sit empty, their frames vacant in some, the others with sharp edges of glass catching the shred of moonlight. Graffiti travels along the walls, a mix of beauty in deliberate, artful strokes, and hurried scribbles in single tones. It bleeds over the "For Sale" sign bolted to the brick, paint peeling and faded.

I'd bet whoever owns ValPro Real Estate has long since given up hope of making this sale.

Wind whips through the lot, the buildings creating a tunnel that leaves me swiping the hair from my face, straining for every sound that isn't the rustle of trash or the clink of bottles against curbs.

Bits of concrete crunch beneath my feet, and I move faster even though I want to prolong every minute before I walk into this building.

The northeast corner, that's what the note said. The door is chained, but it clearly hasn't stopped countless bodies from moving through it.

It sticks against the cement when I open it, grinding into well-worn grooves. I slip inside, sweat rolling down my spine as I inhale scents of must and rain, and the water-soaked concrete speaks of years of exposure.

A light glows from a far corner, a flickering lantern hanging from a pole that stretches clear to the metal beams above.

I blink against the jostle of shadows, forcing my eyes to see in the darkness.

My footsteps scrape against the floor that's marred with protruding bolts and gaping holes where equipment used to stand. But it's all gone now, just a wide, vast chasm of emptiness.

A phone rings, and I barely stifle my scream as the trill echoes across the space, bouncing off cinder-block walls.

It's for me. I know it is. Maybe this is where the letters stop. Where I prove it's Coach Bulger that's gutted my life or discover it's not. All my evidence points in different directions, leaving me no closer to knowing who to blame for what happened to me than I was five months ago.

But that could change. Here. Tonight.

I don't need the kind of proof the cops need. I just need to know for sure. Then I can do the things they can't.

The phone rings again, and I sprint toward it.

It hits the fourth ring when I grab it from the cardboard box it sits on. The one with the pink envelope with my name scrawled across the front.

I'm breathless, my hello a whisper that carries through the quiet dark.

"Cassandra." His voice is distorted and guttural, speaking my name like it belongs to him. "Why are you here?"

"Because you told me to be?"

"Wrong answer."

"Because I want to be."

"Aren't we beyond lying to each other? We don't play games, do we?"

As if this hasn't all been a game to him. Every letter, every word. Every moment he's spent taunting me and shredding everything left of the girl I once was.

I breathe out, "I know what you did to your dad."

There's a moment's pause. "That was an accident."

I can't stop the tears that blur my vision. Even with the mutated voice, his remorse seeps through the phone.

And that's proof, isn't it? That it's Bulger? "You need to turn yourself in."

Whatever humanity crawled through the cracks in him dries up. "Did you?"

I barely stifle a gasp. "I didn't kill him."

I didn't kill Nomi's stepdad, but I could've. And I didn't kill Bulger's dad, but I didn't report it either.

"We're not so different, you and I."

I nearly killed a man. Left another to rot. Three little charms sit half-empty on my wrist, alive with my promise to fill them full.

I'm surrounded by air. Open, empty nothingness. And I can't breathe.

He pauses, then laughs, a hollow, mocking thing that says he's not Coach Bulger at all. "You think I'm a monster."

Yes. "No."

I scan the blackened room for anything that might tell me where he is. *Who* he is. I need to *see*. I need him to tell me why. Why me. And what he wants next. It's a desperation, clawing through my veins.

"Monsters are rarely what they seem. Look closer."

The line goes dead.

I press the phone to my ear like that might bring him back. But there's only the whistle of wind through broken windows and the scurry of rats.

Just like always. He controls the conversation. The dialogue. Leaving me with more questions than I came with.

He all but admitted he killed his dad—accident or not. But then claimed he's not a monster. That I should *look closer*. Like there's some other part to this I can't see.

A light flicks on at the far end of the room, so faint I blink to make sure it's really there.

I head toward it on shaky legs, the phone nearly slipping from my sweaty hand.

Moonlight leaks through the window, pooling in dust-filled clouds, and I move through the massive room in pockets of shadows.

I focus on the light from beyond a thick steel door, and it's only because of the window set in the top that I can see it at all. But he knows that. Of course he does.

The metal handle is cold against my palm, and I shove inside, musty air tickling my nose as warmth blankets me and noise muffles.

The windows here remain intact, the floors carpeted, the cinder block covered by drywall. Offices line the outside of the space, all of them empty.

A single lantern hangs far across the room, leading me down a hallway, my ragged breathing the only sound now that the howl of wind is cut by the walls that surround me.

They feel too close, too tall. Like if I don't run from this place they might move tight, squeezing until I can't move.

It's the light that keeps me moving, flickering toward a hallway sunken deep into the heart of the building.

Not even the lantern can pierce it, not even my phone when I thumb on the flashlight, sweeping it over the worn carpet and up the beige walls.

But *there*, at the end, taped to a door with no windows, with a thick dead bolt like Nomi's stepdad's, is the slightest glimmer of pink.

That door feels significant in its similarities, like it carries some clue I haven't divined.

Every part of me screams to run back. To escape.

I tug the note free. *To the One That Got Away*. But maybe not this time.

A faint slam filters into the hall, an echo of heavy metal doors, far away.

But not far enough. Not when I'm hemmed in, stuck in a narrow hallway with no way out, the door behind me locked tight.

I run.

Down the hall and through the office, back to the only place with a path to freedom.

I burst into the warehouse just as a beam of light sweeps over the far wall.

It swings my way the moment I step inside and I plaster myself to the cinder block at my back, keeping in the shadows.

A voice shouts, "Who's there?"

It's not him—he wouldn't have to ask who was here.

I want to be relieved. This is not the day I die.

But that other part of me, the flicker of fire waiting to be set free, *wants* it to be him.

Footsteps advance, swift and sure, and I sprint along the back wall, where there are no windows, no moonlight to give me away.

The steps come faster, thundering through the open space as he heads toward the office door. It saves me, gives me just enough space to dart from my corner and toward the door I came in.

I slam into the doors at full speed, but instead of them flinging open, my head cracks against the surface.

Everything goes dizzy, spots flickering in my vision like the particles of dust, and even though my hearing's gone dim, his shouts still register. Then his footsteps stampeding closer.

I shove against the door again, because it's too late to do anything else, and they fling open, chain rattling against the metal.

I sprint toward my car, and he bursts from the building the second I jam my keys into the ignition.

My tires slip and squeal as I reverse through the lot, too quick for him to catch.

I don't stop until I'm out of the complex and well past any sight of it. And then I stop, pulling over into another empty lot so I can peel my fingers from the steering wheel, force oxygen into my lungs. So I can blink away the stars that still coat my vision.

I wince as I prod at the bump on my head, but my fingers don't come away sticky with blood. I could flip over my visor and let the lights show me the bleed of purple beneath my skin—but I don't. I'm too afraid to meet my own eyes.

I'm not like him.

We are *nothing* alike.

I grab the phone he left me and dial the number I've had memorized since Saturday night.

A voice answers, "Crime Stoppers," and I rattle off Edward Bulger's address from that same spot in my memory. I hang up before she can ask questions.

I hope they tie it to him. I hope this phone is registered to his name. I hope he pays for what he's done.

I trade the phone for my envelope. I wonder if he has a stack of them in his house, full of pictures or letters or whatever the fuck he's too much of a coward to say to my face.

I rip it open, and a picture floats free. But it's not of me this time, even though so many of the features match.

My mother stares up at me, smiling in that way that hid all the tears she never let anyone see. And on the back, scrawled in his handwriting:

LOOK CLOSER.

CHAPTER TWENTY-THREE

Monday, October 11
4 Days Before the End

I'm feeling douchier by the second.

Also of note: When Noah Rhoades says something, he means it.

I knew that already—it's one of my favorite things about Noah. It *used* to be anyway.

But now, standing outside his house while he refuses to answer my phone calls, it's actually my least favorite thing about Noah.

My head throbs from the unfortunate run-in with the door earlier, and I should go home, lie down, go to bed. But I can't.

My stalker knows something about my mother.

He claimed monsters are rarely what they seem, that I needed to look closer. Then he gifted me a picture of my mother.

Bulger has no *reason* to even know who she is. *No one* in my life does, save for my dad. And yet, the proof sits in my hand, in a picture of her I've never seen.

As soon as I'm sure it's Bulger, there's another reason to believe it's not.

Tomorrow, I go to his office. Tyler claims it'll be unlocked. Getting caught will mean suspension at best, expulsion more likely. But I have to know. I need to see his handwriting and compare it to the letter in my hand.

But tonight, I need to warn Noah the cops might come questioning about Bulger's dad; then I need to find my mother. Because her involvement complicates everything. And everything I thought I understood feels unknown.

It feels like that car in the school parking lot *was* there for me. Like there's meaning behind that man with the scar. It feels like everything is for nothing.

I grope through the ground beneath the shrubs at the back of Noah's house until I find a handful of pebbles. They're smooth and cold in my hands, made for skipping across placid lakes.

I heave one at Noah's window, and it plinks against the glass.

He's up. His light is on. None of the others are.

Wet grass tickles my ankles, an earthy mix of soil and rain-soaked trees rising through the air. Everything feels cleansed, renewed. I am anything but.

I weigh another pebble in my palm and fling it skyward, a little harder this time.

The blinds shift, a slow tilt that reveals a shadow that is *not* Noah's. I want to tunnel into the ground and stay there until they plant a tree over it in my honor.

A second shadow joins the first, and I drop the rest of my pebbles at my feet—the feet that are moving me as quickly toward my car as I can without running.

I do have some pride.

I'm halfway there when the front door swings open, and I pretend not to hear when he yells my name.

Soft footfalls follow me, and I'm nearly to the street when he spins me to face him. "Cass."

This . . . is a mistake.

He cringes as his gaze lands on my forehead, and his fingers follow, whisper-light. "What happened? Did—"

"I'm sorry. I interrupted you with your . . ." I make useless hand motions because I don't want to say the word "girlfriend."

I shouldn't be surprised. Noah and I shared one kiss. It's been five months. He's still very sturdy, and his facial features are still put together in a very aesthetically pleasing fashion.

"It's not like that."

"Sure. I have lots of boys over at"—I check my watch—"eleven p.m."

"I thought you didn't have *anyone* over anymore."

"That's not—I'm gonna go . . . now. Right now, actually, and you can get back to . . . whatever you're not doing."

I pull free, but it turns out the thing I hate second most about Noah is his persistence.

He jogs into my path. "Come inside. Shelly was about to leave anyway."

"Ugh, Shelly?" It slips free, and I instantly regret it. Even more when she appears on the porch three seconds later. Maybe I'll threaten to take her spot on the team again so she'll leave.

I mumble, "She hates me."

"No, she—Okay, yeah, she does. Give me one sec."

They have some murmured conversation, and Shelly spends as much time glaring at me as she does making kiss-me eyes at Noah.

He doesn't though. Not even a hug. He waits until she's seated inside her car and waves while she drives off.

Then he turns back to me, and I'm not sure I can handle Noah's one-on-one attention right now. "Come inside."

"No thanks."

"Cass—"

"Coach Bulger's dad is dead. I found him. Dead. I think he was stabbed, and I think Coach did it. Maybe? The cops know now. That's what I came here to tell you. Just in case they question you because, well, you handed them the man's license plate and claimed to have found it in the woods. Which is my fault too, so I'm . . . terribly sorry for, maybe, potentially, incriminating you in a murder investigation."

His parted lips draw shut, only to fall open again. "Cass. Get inside."

He marches toward the door, and while I *should* follow, I just really don't want to, so I head in the opposite direction.

I barely make it two steps, like he knew exactly what I'd do, and his hand is at my elbow, steering me back toward his house. "Start with finding Coach Bulger's dad."

I give him a CliffsNotes version, leaving out that the girls were with me. Also why I think Coach killed his dad, also why I was there in the first place. Basically I leave out everything.

We don't speak once we're inside his house, where even the shush of our clothing feels too loud. He leaves his shoes by the door, and his feet are bare.

He rushed out the door to stop me, which has me feeling all kinds of ways.

He nods toward the stairs like I don't know the way to his room, like I don't still think about how sometimes, when his mom would greet me with a hug, I'd pretend it was normal instead of something I only wished to have at home.

We move through his bedroom and into the bathroom attached to it, and he pats the sink. "Jump up."

I don't jump anywhere, and he rummages through the closet, filling his hands with cotton balls and some kind of antiseptic spray. I say, "It's just a bump."

"You're bleeding."

My hands fly to my forehead against my wishes. "I am?"

He nods to the sink again, and I guess if I let him do this it saves me from having to look at it myself.

The marble is cold against the back of my legs, and I drum my fingers against the counter.

"Why do you think Coach did it?"

"His dad was in his bed. Sort of *staged*. Ori said that's a sign of remorse." Also I talked to Maybe-Coach and he said it was an accident. Non-CliffsNotes version.

"Close your eyes."

The second I do, he sprays something cold against my forehead and a line of fire zips over my skin.

I whisper-yell, "That stings!" because I don't need his parents finding us in a locked bathroom.

"No it doesn't."

"Is it your forehead?"

"It says it on the bottle." He holds the evidence in front of me. "'No sting.'"

"The bottle lies."

"Imagine that." He spritzes me again. "Wouldn't want to risk infection."

He nudges my knee with his hip, sliding between my legs to wipe at the drips of his devil spray.

I don't look at him. "Is this"—I gesture at his current position—"absolutely necessary?"

He smiles, and it's just like I remember. "Not at all."

Things I Hate About Noah, Volume 3: Even his flirting is honest and direct.

He says, "It does have the added benefit of making it harder for you to run away though. Since when did *Ori* join the ranks of FBI profiler?"

My head throbs. "It's just something she knows."

"So you've convicted Coach of killing his own father based on 'just something Ori knows'?"

"No."

He tosses the cotton ball in the trash, and then his hand lands on my thigh, fingers scorching my skin, and when his thumb strokes over me, goose bumps rise in a rush.

He says, "You're lying to me, Cass. I can always tell. I meant what I said about not playing games."

Just like the stalker said earlier. Except only one of them means it.

There's no winning here. No way I can tell him the things I know, the things that have happened, without twisting him into this any further.

So I kiss him instead.

It's stupid. Unfair. Irresponsible.

It's something my mother would do.

Not even that stops me.

And when his half second of shock slips away and his fingers tangle in my hair, my nape tingling from the force of his grip, I pull myself closer, locking my legs around his waist.

His shoulders are strong and wide beneath my palms, his arms roped around me—solid, unyielding.

He doesn't give even an inch, just like the first time when he held me up, kept me standing. But this kiss isn't like that one. It's not soft or slow. I'm not the girl I was then.

Something inside me breaks free, like all the past months of seclusion have bottled up, waiting to come alive again. And I could, just for now, let him help me forget.

I let the heat of his hands wash over me, lose myself in the feel of his lips. I could let him carry me from this sink and into his room and all of the last months would be a lie, a nightmare buried and forgotten.

A knock sounds at the door—too loud and too insistent to have been the first one—and Noah's mom calls his name.

He drops his head to my shoulder and mumbles a curse I was already thinking.

He clears his throat. "Yeah, Mom. In here."

I mouth, "Clearly," and he flips me off as she says, "We heard voices."

We.

Oh god. Noah's parents are sitting outside his bathroom door listening to me groping their son.

He lets out a deep breath before grabbing the ice pack and sticking it on my head, and I jump from the sink a second before he opens the door. By some small mercy, it's only his mom.

Her gaze darts to Noah, then me, up to the ice pack I'm holding on my forehead. It's very obvious there are too many possibilities swimming through her head to land on one that fits.

But then her grin stretches wide and it *is* like the last five months never happened.

She smothers me in a hug. "It's so good to see you!"

I squeeze her back and blink away my tears. "You too. Sorry, about showing up here—"

"Don't be, honey. Now let me see." She pulls the ice pack away and winces. "You should have your dad look at that."

"I'll definitely do that." I will definitely *not* be doing that.

I slip past her and into Noah's room. "Anyway, I should be going, so thank you, very much for the . . . ice pack."

I don't have a chance to move before Noah points out how late it is, that I'll be going home to an empty house.

That's all it takes.

It doesn't matter that my car is two houses down, or that I sleep in that empty house nearly every night.

Mrs. Rhoades's mind is made up.

Noah will drive me home. He will pick me up for school in the morning and drive me back here after so I can collect my car. End of discussion.

And that's exactly how Noah ends up playing chauffeur while I set out to find my mom for the first time in over a year.

CHAPTER TWENTY-FOUR

Monday, October 11
4 Days Before the End

Noah does not drive me home like he promised his mom. That is, of course, completely my fault.

The motel's neon "Open" sign flickers, casting Noah's car in a series of pink strobe flashes.

He nods toward the sign proclaiming this fine establishment to be the Wander Inn. "Rent by the month *or* the hour. Wide range of services."

"You could've just let me take my car."

"I could've. And when my mom woke me up in the middle of the night when she checked to make sure it was still there, I'd be sure to send her to you."

"You wouldn't."

"I would. Now . . ." He rubs his hands together. "Start by explaining why, if you're so convinced Coach *killed his dad*, that you haven't gone to the cops."

Because I've been there, done that, and the cops didn't believe me. Because *I'm* not even convinced it's him that's stalking me. Because something in this is related to my mother, and if I involve the cops, she'll run.

Look closer. The man who kidnapped me claims he's not a monster, but he knows me well enough to use my mother—the one person I promised to forget but can't seem to let go of.

And if it's not Bulger, my mother is the closest link to finding out who it really is.

I doubt those are answers Noah will accept.

I slip from the car. "Evidence."

"What evidence?"

"Exactly. I have none. Do you see room two-oh-seven?"

Noah pauses, scans the face of the run-down motel—the rusted balcony, ocean-blue paint peeling to review the mottled gray beneath.

The carpeted walkway outside the doors has long since lost its pattern, worn thin in spots and bare in others, cigarette burns and stains marring anything that's left.

It's not the first time I've found my mother in a place like this.

Noah says, "Half the doors are missing numbers," as he jogs up the metal stairs that squeak and groan beneath his weight.

We traverse the open hall with only moonlight to replace the vacant lights, and stale cigarette smoke drifts from beneath doorways. "I think we're on the even side."

The even side, it turns out, does not connect to the odd side, which means more time for Noah to question me. "Why do you think your mom is here?"

"I don't. This is just the last address I have for her. She tends to leave an impression."

Noah nods because he knows *some* things about my mother, but he doesn't know specifics. Specifics aren't the things you tell new friends. Specifics let them picture you doing those same things to them. Genetic poisoning.

Door 2-empty-space-7 comes into view, and my footsteps slow until I'm standing in front of it, reliving every time I've waited in front of doors like this, my dad behind me, ready to take her back, ready to try again at making her into something she'd never be.

She came back so many times because of me, I'm old enough to recognize that now. She *tried*, even when she knew she shouldn't. Some people aren't meant to stand still.

The door rattles beneath the force of my knuckles, the wood paper-thin, and someone inside shuffles toward it.

I don't see who it is when the door swings open—the gun in my face is sort of distracting.

My hands fly into the air while Noah's wrap around my waist like he can pull me to safety faster than the bullet would enter my brain.

I talk slow and even. "I'm looking for someone."

The man glares at me with bloodshot eyes, but his hand doesn't waiver. "Who?"

"I could give you a name, but it probably wouldn't be the one you know her by. I have a picture though, in my pocket."

"Which one?"

"Jacket. Right side."

He leans in, the alcohol on his breath sour, and tugs the picture free.

He holds it up, leaving the slanted black handwriting, harsh and bold like the author carved the page rather than laid ink to it, directly in my view. And Noah's.

The man grunts. "Don't know her."

"Her hair might be shorter, longer, a different color." Anything to reinvent yourself, to play a different role and forget the one you were born with.

"Still don't know her." He looks me over, Noah behind me, and his arms drop. "If yous were smart, you'd get out of here."

"Yes, sir, thank you."

The door slams in my face, and Noah says, "Front office?"

"Absolutely."

The "front office" sits nearest to the road, at the end of a bend in the building, and a small TV blares from behind a peeling counter.

Noah walks beside me, questions written in every glance. "I don't get it, Cass."

There are any number of things he could be referring to, and it's very likely I don't want to explain any of them.

He continues. "Your dad is—"

"Smart. Handsome. Educated. A great guy. A *doctor*. So *why* would he end up with a woman like this."

Like me.

"This is what he does, Noah. He *fixes* people."

But not her. Cordelia Adams, née Wilson, has always been his biggest failure. *The one who got away.*

"It's my fault, that he tried for so long. When it was just the two of them, she was this wounded little bird that he thought he could fix up and make better. Except she was more like a wounded little snake that needed a chance to grow its fangs in."

"That's not your fault."

"I'm not done. He'd have been like any of the guys before him. Or after. Probably *during*, but I try not to think of my parents' sex lives."

"Solid coping mechanism."

"I have a few. But here's my point. My existence . . . cemented them together. For always. And she tried, at first, to be a mom. Sometimes it was really great—her love is big and consuming, and when you have it, it's addicting. But it flares out because fire needs oxygen and no *one person* can give her enough. But he wouldn't give up. For me. *Because* of me."

His hand cradles my jaw, his eyes dark in the glare of flickering light. "That's on them."

I shrug. "And yet, here I am."

Chasing her, filled with questions she won't want to answer. Just like always.

I swipe at the single escaped tear and march toward the office, where bullet holes speckle the glass into webs of cracks.

A man clicks off the TV as we enter, his free hand dropping beneath the counter.

Cigar smoke tumbles from his bearded mouth, rising toward the tobacco-stained ceiling. His gaze snags on Noah's hand at my waist. "For an hour then?"

I say "no" while Noah says "maybe," and though I try not to, I smile.

"We don't need a room. I'm looking for someone." I hold out my mom's picture. "Her hair might—"

"That bitch."

Sounds about right.

He charges the counter, but I stop him using the voice my dad always does. I've always wondered if he perfected it from the families he gave the worst news to, or for my mom. "Listen. I'm not here to cause trouble. She's my mom, and—"

His meaty hands fist. "Then you don't want to fucking find her."

"Trust me, I'm not looking for a happy reunion."

He waits without asking, but we both know I have to give something to get something, even if it's just a little piece of myself.

This is what Dad did too. Ripped himself open again and again to untold strangers so they could *see*. Until they believed enough to give him answers.

Until they *pitied* him enough.

I'd rather they all held guns to my head.

"Something happened to me. Something bad." Behind me, Noah's body snaps taut, his breath hot against the back of my neck. "Someone told me that she might be involved. That's why I need to find her. And I promise, if I do, I'll tell you where she is."

Dad always promised that too. But I mean it.

The man's fists unfurl, but his scowl doesn't. He rips a paper from the wall and slams it onto the counter.

The edges are yellowed, curled on the sides, clearly not created by the police because it's typed in Comic Sans. No self-respecting officer types wanted posters in Comic Sans.

Two pictures grace the page, grainy, out of focus, but I'd recognize her anywhere. I spent years searching for her in crowds, along the street, from countless school stages.

But it's the man that leaves me struggling for air, that sends my hand reaching for Noah's.

The scar stands in sharp relief to the rest of his picture, a line that connects multiple dots but I don't know how.

I blink and the vision of Bulger, with his forearm locked across the scarred man's neck, crowds my brain. I strain to remember the details— if they said anything, did anything, that could tell me how they fit together.

The manager says, "He went by Ronnie," in a way that shows he knows how shaken I am.

I nod because I only have enough for my next words. "He drove by me in a parking lot last week, and then I saw him at my school."

Noah squeezes my hand, and it's more confirmation than comfort. *Ronnie*. It could be him as easily as Bulger. Some scary man who found me through my mother.

It's not hard to imagine someone trying to get revenge on her through me. Or someone who might use her to lure me in. It's not hard to imagine a mess of her making that I'm paying the price for. Just like always.

Thoughts swirl in my head. Bulger admitting he killed his dad. Ronnie following me to Target, coming to my school. Maybe Bulger was protecting me from him. Or maybe he was angry about someone else trying to terrorize me the way he does. And in the middle of all of it, my mother.

This is worse. This moment, of knowing nothing but also too much, is worse than before. It's worse than hiding in my closet, worse than waiting for the next letter, even worse than holding the next pink envelope, breath held in fear of what waited inside its folds.

This is *my* fault. I started this, pushed for this. I said I was ready, and I brought him further into my life—into my friends' lives—without a plan. With nothing but my own hubris and desperation.

And now it's too late to stop this, no matter what answers wait for me. No matter what kind of end this leads me to.

I thank the manager for his time—and for hating my mother enough to pay such close attention to her—and he sends me off with the hope I turn out better than she did.

But when we hit the parking lot and Noah smothers me into a hug, whispering apologies into my hair, I don't do any of the right things and confide in him, put my trust into the hands of someone who hasn't betrayed me.

I drag him to the car, my mouth on his. I use my hands beneath his shirt to erase his protests, his concern.

I pull him through the car's back door, neither of us belonging here, neither of us safe.

My blood hums, my body on fire, the outside world a haze and a rush surging through my veins.

I know he wants this. Wants me.

But it's only his pity I feel.

I smother it in the darkness of his back seat.

CHAPTER TWENTY-FIVE

I wake up hungover.

Not from alcohol. That would mean I had some excuse for what happened last night.

Instead I'm drowning in a flood of rejection-induced shame and embarrassment.

My first text is to Noah, to say Margot is driving me to school. The second is to Margot, begging her to drive me to school. *Early.* I truly don't deserve her.

But I will walk before I face Noah again. Or explain that I need to go in early so I can go through Bulger's office because I'm no closer to confirming the identity of my stalker than I was the night I escaped his trunk.

I will walk before I have to sit in Noah's car.

The one I made a fool of myself in last night.

I don't even read his response.

Margot is late because she's Margot, and that means Dad is shuffling through the door as I'm walking out.

He's too tired to notice I'm headed in early, or the lump on my head.

Dad gives me a hug, holds on longer than he needs to, like always, and I duck away before he sees the guilt threatening to explode from me.

I promised him, the day we vowed we were done with Mom for good, that I'd never try to look for her.

I pinkie swore and so did he. It bonded us—we had a pact that existed outside of her, the two of us on the same team without her in the middle to force sides.

"Cassie."

His mouth slips open like he's going to say something real, something too big for this moment. But all that comes out is "Everything okay?"

I force a smile. "Yeah. For sure."

"Okay good." His gaze falls. "I know things have been hard, and I'm not here enough with the new job schedule, but—"

"I know." I blink to cover my tears, because I don't know how we got to this. From being on the same team to feeling worlds apart.

"You can tell me anything, you know that, right?"

I have two pictures of my mother in my backpack, and it feels like he knows. Some weird parental intuition telling him I've broken our agreement. But he won't just ask. He won't say what he wants to say. He won't be honest.

He's not in scrubs, that's what hits me as I stare at him, tucked inside our home while I stand on the outside. It's not totally unusual—sometimes he showers at the hospital so he doesn't bring germs home. And yet, it feels like another thing he's not telling me.

I know what secrets look like, and there's only one person who can get the Good Doctor Adams to keep them.

He clears his throat. "I love you, Cassie. More than anything or anyone. I don't tell you that enough."

The tears come too fast for blinking this time, and I mean it when I tell him I love him too. More than anyone.

That's *why* I don't tell him everything.

I close the door between us, wiping my tears on the way to Margot's car.

She raises an eyebrow. "You okay?"

I flop into the seat. "Yeah. Dad stuff."

"Is he okay?"

I hope so. "Yeah, he's fine."

"Cool. Now that that's settled."

I let my head drop back. "Don't."

"Sooooo what were you up to last night?"

"What did Noah tell you?"

"That it wasn't my business."

"It's annoying, right? All his honesty and being-a-decent-person bullshit. I can't be the only one who thinks so."

The car rocks as she backs out of the driveway. "Wow. This sounds like a hell of a night."

It's barely there, but her voice wavers.

I sit up straighter. "Margot. What happened?"

"So why the early arrival?"

"It's Bulger's open office day, remember?" She remembers. She's avoiding. "Margot. *What happened?*"

She waves me off, then rolls her eyes and tosses me her phone. "I know we're not supposed to do the Jared thing until Saturday but—"

I think she's crying, but I can't tear my eyes from the text exchange between her and Jared. "A date?"

That's the summary—blackmailing her into seeing him tomorrow.

"Not a *date* date, Cass. Not candlelit dinner and conversation."

"So sex via extortion? That fucker belongs in jail."

"Yeah, if only my mom wouldn't disown me and the whole school wouldn't decide I'm a slut ten minutes after I went to the police."

I capture her hand in mine. "I wasn't saying you should do that. Promise."

She squeezes back. "We're not ready."

We're not. Not even close. We were supposed to have this entire week to plan.

We were supposed to avoid all the things that went wrong with Nomi's. And now there's this thing with *Ronnie*. Another potential suspect. Tonight was supposed to be for finding my mom, unraveling the mystery laid out in that pink envelope, not for planning the Jared revenge.

The second her car rolls to a stop at the light, she bursts into tears. "I can't do it, Cass. I can't even be near him. An entire night?"

"We do it tomorrow then."

She guns it when the light turns, streetlights swimming by. "We're not ready."

"No. We're not. We'll just have to take some risks with getting the supplies."

After the cops interviewed us about Nomi's stepdad, we decided to be more careful. Spend the week collecting the gasoline in small containers, paying with cash. Nomi borrowing her dad's handcuffs.

Then there's Ori's parents. We just got out of "Wakanda Forever" text mode, and now she'll be out late tomorrow. "Ori's going to need an excuse. Something that won't raise suspicion with her parents. If Ori's mom starts asking around, this could all fall apart."

She salutes me. "Yes, Captain, my captain."

I shove her, and she swerves out of her lane. "Is this plan B? You get us both killed so Jared gets no extortion sex?"

I laugh because it's either that or cry. "This is so fucked up."

"Yup."

"You can handle Ori?"

Her cheeks shade pink. "I can handle Ori." It's the exact moment the subtext of her words becomes clear, when their little looks and touches and wordless conversations make total sense.

I'm an idiot for not seeing it earlier, but Ori is not Margot's usual type. She's quiet, sweet, an introvert even. Margot's type is the loudest person in the room.

They're probably perfect for each other, but this is a wrinkle. And Nomi won't like it. I'm not sure *I* like it.

The ice we're treading is so thin it bends beneath our weight, laced with webs of sharp cracks, and the slightest shift could drown us all.

"Margot, this—"

"I know." She lets out a breath. "It's too soon, and it could all end horribly, but—" She pauses. "This isn't casual, Cass. At least not for me."

There's no way to miss the joy in her eyes, even with the mess we're in. And Ori, the girl who said nothing and held me while I sobbed in the stairway that day, she deserves all of this. She deserves happy and so does Margot, and if it falls apart, we'll deal with it then. Like everything else.

I say, "You're gonna miss practice if we do this thing with Jared tomorrow night."

I hate that I remember the practice schedule, that it's one of the first places my head travels. I miss the locker room noise and the way the world quiets right before the first serve. I miss the exhaustion and the bruises that remind me I accomplished something. I miss the *winning*. And every memory is a reminder of where I should be. Where I *would* be, if I could erase the last five months.

"I know."

"Your mom's gonna lose her shit."

"Yep. Know that too. I'll tell her it's my anniversary. Jared might be the one thing she loves more than volleyball."

My mom was never the type I confided things in, but Margot used to be that way with her mom. To have that, and have it taken away, I can't imagine the hole it must've carved from Margot's life.

"I'm sorry."

She waves me off and slides into the school's parking lot. Security lights cut through the darkness, bathing the empty lot in a soft haze. The whole building looks quiet, only a handful of rooms illuminated.

Margot cuts the engine. "What about Nomi?"

"Let me take care of Nomi."

The Events of Tuesday, October 12
3 Days Before the End

There are some people who never leave us. Even when we want them to.

We can cut them out of our lives and tell ourselves we've exorcised them from our souls, but memories have roots. There are always pieces left behind.

That's what it felt like, walking through the dimly lit school hallways on the way to Bulger's office that morning. Like Mom had taken root in my heart again, like I'd let her grow there without realizing I'd neglected to scrape every bit of her out when we said goodbye that last time.

She'd have encouraged this—sneaking through the halls, my footsteps so light they don't make a sound, peering around darkened corners and plastering myself to walls.

She'd have looked at the flush in my cheeks, taken my hands to feel the adrenaline surging through me, and she'd have smiled. *This is what it's like to feel alive, Cassie!*

A life without risk is a life wasted. That's the seed she planted, way back when I was too little to understand. Most days, I'm too afraid to admit how scared I am that if I lose that piece of myself, I'll never feel alive again.

The wheels on the cleaning cart squeak as it rolls down the hall, the janitor trudging behind in no particular hurry. The vacuum's cord scrapes the scuffed floor, and I hold my breath, waiting to see which office he'll start with.

Bulger's is at the south end, punctuating a long line of administrative personnel's, and my joy at seeing the janitor head north vanishes the second he pulls out a ring of keys.

Of course he has keys. So why would Bulger need to leave his office unlocked?

The answer stares at me in cold steel when I sprint down the hall and stand before his door.

Two locks. One of them a dead bolt none of the other offices have.

I duck into an alcove and text Margot. She responds immediately, like she's waiting to hear from me.

Theft. Bulger claimed someone broke into his office and stole expensive equipment.

I wonder if it's really equipment he's trying to protect.

Margot texts, "hold tight," and then her voice wipes out the silence down the hall. "Hey, Mr. John! I spilled some water and I don't want anyone to slip."

The janitor—Mr. John—smiles, following her toward whatever mess she's made and I truly, *truly* do not deserve her.

I rush toward the keys Mr. John left in the door and slip them free. My lungs burn as I race toward Bulger's office to unlock it, back down the hall to replace the key. Then, finally, I'm alone in Bulger's office.

The room sits dark, only a quiet stream of light from the hall spilling inside, and I flick on my phone's flashlight.

Bulger is neat, fastidiously so, and the office smells of lemon furniture polish and his peppermint gum.

My entire body shakes as I lower into his chair and pull his letter from my pocket. I don't need it. I'd recognize the handwriting anywhere. But my head is all over the place. The nearness of him, the access he has to my life, it makes my stomach hollow, sends panic raking over my skin.

But if it's not him, then it's someone I know nothing about, and they still know *everything* about me.

Bulger's desktop holds only a few photos, one of his dad. I flip it facedown.

Two times two is four. Three times three is nine.

I yank open a drawer, then another, before I find something with Bulger's writing, and it's nothing like my letters.

It's blocky and short, nothing like the harsh slants I've committed to memory.

My stomach rolls because that can't be right. He *admitted* he killed his dad by accident. But then there was that laugh. And Bulger was coaching when I got the phone call with Tyler. And then there's Ronnie.

I want to scream, shove everything from Bulger's orderly desk and trash the rest. I was an idiot for thinking I could do anything the right way.

I want this to be *done*. I've spent month after month being afraid, locked out of my own life. And now it feels so close to changing, like I could almost live again. I could be free. I could set my own rules, on my terms. And I could walk into that police station, and watch as they all realized they were wrong.

Wrong to doubt me. Wrong to have picked apart the stories of everyone like me, until "doing their job" meant protecting the wrong person.

I yank open other drawers. People can change handwriting if they want to. If they practice. What kind of idiot would write stalking notes in their own handwriting?

Not Bulger.

I can *feel* him in this office, where everything is just so. Organized. Precise. Every millimeter under his control and locked up tight behind his dead bolt with only one key.

He writes the narrative. Always. Here and everywhere else.

I grab the next drawer, and my fingers rip free as I pull. Locked.

I shine my phone light onto the drawer and metal glints from the small gap at the top. It's a simple lock—a metal tab that slides into a slot. But it's not fully engaged.

I ignore the squeaks of Mr. John's cart as he inches closer, and jam Bulger's letter opener through the gap. I bring my heel down across the length of it, and it only takes two kicks before the lock inches down.

It's filled with hanging files, stuffed so tight they barely move. Each folder with a tab, all in his block handwriting. Student names with disciplinary records. Manuals. Staff meeting notes.

I scan, searching for my name, but there's nothing. There's not enough time to search through each file, but if I don't, this was all for nothing.

I yank the first group, wiggling them against the pressure until they pop free and scatter.

Shit shit shit.

He *will* notice this. Maybe he'll even know it was me.

But then it doesn't matter, because there, at the bottom, is the faintest smudge of blue on manilla. I shove the remaining files back and pull it free, pausing before flipping it open.

Pictures of me. Grainy, clear, color, black and white. Taken at night. In the morning. From every angle.

And at the back of each, written in the handwriting I'd remember anywhere, is the date, the time, the location.

My vision goes fuzzy as pictures slide through my fingers, one by one, my life documented through Bulger's eyes.

I don't know what he sees when he looks at these, what story he tells himself about the broken and empty girl in front of the lens.

I nearly don't recognize myself. It's like the life has been drained from the girl I used to be. My cheeks hollow, eyes haunted. And this is why Dad is always so worried. It's this image of me he sees every day.

A small key slips from the pile and I stare, transfixed. It means something. It has to.

I curl my fingers around it and let my mind wander. It's too small for a door, too nondescript to be for anything special.

The answer comes in a rush, and my body stands like I no longer control it, the pictures fluttering to the floor.

It's for the lockers. The *gym* lockers.

We're not allowed to have removable locks, but mine broke last year and Bulger gave me a replacement while we waited for maintenance.

"Consider yourself special, Adams." That's what he said as he dropped the key into my palm.

I grab a handful of photos and shove them in the waist of my jeans. Then I cram each hanging file back into the drawer.

Alive alive alive.

That's what I feel as I set Bulger's office right, as I slip into the dark hallway, as I slip past Mr. John and down the quiet path that will lead me to the locker rooms.

I am not that empty girl in the photos. I am alive.

Bulger has pictures of me, in his office, in the right handwriting, but if I stop now, I'll never know the truth about my mother's involvement. And that's not a thing I can live with.

I burst through the girls' locker room and run through the aisles, but there aren't any hanging locks. But then, the key isn't something he intended me to find. This key is for *him*.

A hush runs through the boys' locker room, scents of lemon cleaner and spicy body washes mingling in the air.

But it's empty, the lockers cold beneath my trailing fingertips as I search them for a lock.

A shower surges to life deep in the room, and I jump, scanning faster, my breaths coming quicker. I've gone through nearly all of them before I spot it amid a sea of lockers with their doors ajar.

My hands are steady as I slip the key inside, letting the patter of water against tile drown the sound of the lock clicking over, the clang of metal as the door wobbles open.

Bulger's jacket hangs from one hook, his work clothes from another. I don't want to touch the things that are this close to him.

But then the shower squeaks off, and I paw through the entire locker for the things he doesn't want me to find. I feel the empty top shelf, turn over his shoes at the bottom, shove into the pockets of his clothes.

I tap his phone screen, and it flares bright. One missed call. Behind it, a nondescript nature picture. Only, I recognize those woods, that park. It's not the same trail, but it doesn't need to be.

I shove it back, sweat rolling down my spine, and grab his wallet. The leather opens easily, just as wet footsteps slap against the floor, and I grab whatever fills the billfold section and click the locker shut.

I stuff myself into the one next door seconds before Bulger turns the corner.

I try not to breathe, every muscle locked, and I'm terrified the door trembles where I hold it slightly ajar, just like I found it.

My eyes fall shut, my ears tuned to the slightest sounds. The slide of a key into a lock, the click of a door opening, the shush of fabric as he dresses.

My legs cramp and my stomach rolls, but I will not move. I will not give in. This is me standing at the service line with the ball in my hands and the winning point waiting for me.

For a moment, there is no sound, and I let my mind go blank, let my hand press flat to the wall I share with him, where the metal feels warmer than it should, and I ask him to go. I tell him he was right—I'm not ready yet.

Then his voice echoes through the room. "This is Nathan Bulger. I had a missed call from this number."

The only sounds are him emptying his locker, zipping a bag, shrugging on his coat, and then he's gone.

I wonder if this is what he feels as he watches me. This rush of knowing things the other doesn't. Of seeing them, knowing the pieces of their lives that aren't meant to be seen.

My fingers uncurl from the papers in my hand. A twenty-dollar bill. Two tens and a single. Then a picture of me. From before. My name on the back in the handwriting he reserves for me.

Behind it, a picture of my mother.

I looked closer and found another link to her. Her picture next to mine. Maybe we're mirror images in this. Bulger stalking her just like he is me. I have to swallow past the thickness in my throat and the burn of tears in my eyes. Maybe she's out there, hiding in her closet, too afraid to go outside.

No. That's never been who she is. Maybe she's already saved herself and just forgot to wonder if she needed to save me too.

And what I hate, more than anything, is that in this moment, I understand my mother better than I ever have.

The adrenaline rush of being here, a place I don't belong, doing the last thing I should, and paying no consequence.

In this moment, I belong to no one, answer to no one. There is no part of me that is not mine.

I am Cassandra Adams, and I am *alive*.

CHAPTER TWENTY-SEVEN

Tuesday, October 12
3 Days Before the End

"Are you fucking kidding me, Adams?"

I'm not doing a very good job fulfilling my promise to Margot to take care of Nomi. I'm too unfocused, still riding the high from this morning even though it's been hours. After five months, I have a face for my enemy.

I'm no less terrified by what Bulger might do next, no less worried about how Ronnie fits into this, no less panicked that I've got this all wrong, but I'm not helpless anymore. I'm not standing still.

I keep my voice low. "I am *not* fucking kidding, Tanaka. Jared needs to be resolved. Like . . . now."

"Hey, remember that one time, when you were all at my house and the cops came and I had to go to jail—"

"You didn't go to jail."

"I *could've* gone to jail."

I stop cold, forcing the throngs of students to part around us. "You didn't. Because we were there. Because we lied for you. All of us."

She sighs, holding up her wrist so I can knock my matching bracelet into hers.

The charms tinkle as they connect, and she whispers, "Ashes to ashes," and just like that, I don't care if we're ready anymore. I don't care if the cops show up on my doorstep.

Confessions are for the guilty.

We head toward my locker, bouncing between the throngs of students, and I whisper, "So listen, I need a favor."

"Does it involve finding more dead people? Because I'll pass on that."

"No. I mean, probably not." I shuffle through my locker combination, drawing out the last spin to buy myself courage. "This would be a good time to tell you I called Crime Stoppers about that particular incident."

"Did you? That's great. You should call them back and report your own murder, courtesy of your friend Nomi."

The metal door wobbles as I fling it open, and everything goes quiet.

It's just me and the pink envelope dangling from a pretty polka-dot ribbon.

I rip it free as Nomi whispers, "Oh shit."

This could be it. The next clue that will put all the pieces together. Definitive proof of how Bulger, Ronnie, and my mother fit into this tangled mess.

It's not a clue I get though.

It's another picture.

My image, a shadow that looms over Noah's, my hands cradling his jaw, my mouth on his. The words on the back press through to the front, written with such vitriol it nearly tears through.

Sickening heat roils through me—the violation of this moment stolen by *him*, and all the moments that came after. Like the way Noah captured my wrist as I reached down, the way he pulled away, his breathing heavy. "Cass, stop."

"Cass." Noah's voice hits my ears—here, *now*, not last night—and I startle so hard I nearly drop the photo.

I turn, tucking the picture behind my back, jagged rise of the letters pressing against the pads of my fingers.

I can't look at him, not without reliving the way he rejected me.

He whispers, "So remember the phone call you made . . . to the people that . . ." He gives Nomi a worried glance, like he's not sure she should be hearing this.

I say, "I remember," in a way that's intended to say "you mean the phone call I made to Crime Stoppers about Bulger's dad being dead?" Hard to forget.

"Right. Well, Coach isn't here today."

"Yes he is." Shouldn't have said that out loud.

"No," Noah says with far too much suspicion, "he's not."

He must've left right after the locker room then. But the letter wasn't there when I switched out books second period.

Noah says, "There's something else. The day we found the license plate, that wasn't Bulger. I did some checking and he was at a conference—"

"No, he—"

"Cass, he was gone, the whole day."

"No." No no *no*, because there are pictures of me in his desk and in his *wallet*, and there was finally proof. I didn't stand in a room with a dead man and implicate myself *and* Noah in his murder for *no reason*.

"Cass." Noah looks pissed. "What are you not saying?"

That I'm still lost. That every time I think I understand, that I've figured *something* out, I learn how wrong I've been.

I'm not saying that this is the most terrified I've ever been—two different men as threats and no way to know which I'm supposed to fear most.

Nomi mumbles that she's calling a group meeting, and like she summoned them, Ori and Margot turn the corner.

The three of them stare at me while Noah and I stare at each other and I try to smother the scream building in my chest, try to forget the way he splintered my heart and drowned all the pieces in his kindness—in his *pity*.

There are no limits to the things my mom didn't do well, but I'd guarantee she never had anyone turn *her* down. She'd never have waited this long for her revenge. She took what she wanted. She belonged to no one.

I turn from all of them, stuffing the picture into my bag, the harsh slashes of letter staring back at me.

This is NOT who you are.

Except, maybe it should be.

. . .

Detective Michaels doesn't look happy to see me.

He leads me to a conference room, arms crossed over his chest, and I'm filled with the delusional compulsion to lay out all my evidence against Bulger. All the things that prove he did it and the ones that didn't, and have him tell me which is right so I can get rid of this writhing in my gut.

I want to tell him about Ronnie. How he showed up to my school with a *knife* and I don't know whether he meant to use it on Bulger, or me.

I want to hand this entire mess over to him and let him fix it for me, keep my friends out of danger and keep me safe. But I tried that once, and I'm still standing here with no answers.

Detective Michaels looks at his watch, back to me, to the watch again. Right. Because it's a school day and this is lowest on the list of acceptable places to visit when actively truant.

"It's for a good reason."

He frowns. "It better be."

"I need to find my mom."

"That ain't it."

I try to focus on something other than him, but there's just taupe walls and path-worn carpet, a fake-wood table stained with rings of coffee mugs that overstayed their welcome.

I hate that he knows about her. I hate that Dad told him so much. It was one of their questions, the night I was abducted. If I had any enemies.

The cops dismissed the idea of my mother as an enemy immediately. Of course they did.

But she's your mom! She loves you! It's the national anthem of people who make excuses for shitty mothers.

Maybe they should have asked for a list of *her* enemies. They wouldn't have lacked for suspects.

I try again. "I have a lead, and—"

"Your dad know about this?"

"No." I did not think any of this through. "This has nothing to do with him. There are just . . . things I need to know."

He shakes his head, but it's there, a crack in his resolve. "Cass, listen. You've been through a lot. You want something that feels normal when there's lots that doesn't, but—"

"Please." My hands twist, fingers numb from the force. "I haven't asked for anything. Not even when . . ."

I let my voice trail off, let his guilt fill in the words I don't provide.

She would've done the same.

He rises wordlessly, and minutes later, I leave with the information I came for.

CHAPTER TWENTY-EIGHT

Tuesday, October 12
3 Days Before the End

I avoid looking at the spot where Noah's car sat last night.

I absolutely, 100 percent, do not need the reminder. But unlike last night, I'm armed with the picture of Coach Bulger, ripped from my yearbook.

The picture of me and Noah could only have been taken from the front of the motel. It's the only way to see the angle through the front seat and into the back.

He *had* to have been here.

He is *not* at school. Our group text is filled with speculation about whether he's gone on regular old bereavement or a you-have-the-right-to-remain-silent sort of leave, but right now, either seems possible because nothing makes sense.

He admitted he killed his dad. He has pictures of me in his desk, but he couldn't have been there that day in the woods.

That license plate, that car, it was my direct connection between the person stalking me in the woods and Bulger. And that means I can't assume he's my stalker anymore. That means, right now Ronnie is the closest thing I have to a suspect. But that doesn't mean I'm not going to show the motel manager this picture of Bulger while I have the chance.

I tread over fallen cigarettes and bits of discarded trash as I scan the ground for some sort of clue. The manager from last night stares at me through the window, and I doubt he's going to be any happier to see me today.

It's quiet, an uneasy sort of stillness, perched on the edge of something dangerous, unpredictable.

I can see her here, picture her laughing as she stumbles through the chipped parking lot after having one too many drinks.

But she always knew when to stop, where those things were concerned. My mom never gave anyone or anything control.

Control was the thing *she* craved. The thing she'd do anything to have, push any limit just a touch beyond. A path of destruction left behind and not even a thought of looking back.

"Thought I told you all to leave."

I can't see his face but I remember his voice, and technically he said I could come back with information about my mom, which I *do* have but *am not* willing to share. Not yet.

I turn, and he looks the exact same, down to the cigar dangling from his lips. "Could you maybe look at one more photo for me?"

"I look like some kind of missing persons Rolodex?"

No idea what that means. "Well, the thing is, he isn't missing. He was here, last night, at the same time as me. He—" Heat floods my cheeks. "He took pictures."

He takes a long drag of his cigar, smoke billowing from between his thick lips. "How old are you?"

"Seventeen." That's when I realize I may be seconds from explaining all this to the cops if he decides to report it. "They weren't like"—I whisper—"pornographic or anything."

His eyes narrow, and I can't stop my mouth from moving. "Nothing happened, is what I'm saying." *Because Noah pities me too much to let me touch him, but you, sir, do not need that detail.* "But there *were* pictures! Of the nothing . . . happening."

I stare at his feet, because they can't see my humiliation.

But then my breath catches at what sits behind him, tangled in a plastic bag.

"There!" He jumps out of my way as I charge forward. "See that ribbon? It's proof."

I bend to grab it and he says, "I wouldn't touch that, darlin'," and he's got a very good point, so I reach for the crumpled napkin beside it and he says, "Not that either."

Dammit! I yank a tissue from my pocket so I can pull the ribbon free.

The bag comes with it, puffing and twirling with the force of the wind.

Up close, I'm even more convinced. It's the same ribbon that held the letter in my locker earlier.

Red and white. Stoneybrook High colors.

Manager Guy follows me as I rummage through the rest of the trash, kicking piles with the toe of my shoe while holding the ribbon as far from me as possible. But there's nothing else here.

Then he grimaces as I put my newfound evidence in my back seat. I know what he's thinking—the trunk would be a much better choice.

For obvious reasons, I never use the trunk.

I hand him the picture. "Do you remember seeing this guy here last night?"

He studies it, like he's actually trying to remember. "Sorry, kid."

"It's okay. Was anyone else here last night? Anyone who looked out of place?"

"Besides you?" His mouth twitches into a smile I can't help but return.

A phone chirps, not a ringtone I recognize, and he looks at me, eyebrows raised.

It's coming from my pocket. The phone from the warehouse.

My hands shake as I claw through my pockets, trying to catch it before the ringing stops, before I find out what happens if the ringing stops.

I rip it free, my "hello" breathless and strained.

"Cassandra, where are you?"

Even with the voice changing, the tone is impossible to miss. Like staring down the barrel of a gun. Like being poised on the edge, waiting to see which way the wind decides to blow.

He asks where I am again, each word measured, emphasized, the anger in it oozing from every syllable and the threat of it like the cold metal of a blade down my spine.

I hug myself across my middle, but I can't stop the shaking in my voice. "I left school."

"Do you *think*, Cassandra, that I don't know that? Do you think there is anything about you, any place you have been, anything you have done, that I don't fucking know?"

I know that he knows. The pile of photos proves it. But this doesn't feel like Bulger, with his just-so desk. This feels like a man unhinged.

"I'm sorry." I pace the lot, the manager watching my every move.

"Are you with him?"

I spin to look at the only "him" in the vicinity, and then I get it, what he's really asking. Me and Noah and the back seat of his Jeep. *This is not who you are.*

"I'm not. I promise I'm not." I shove all my pleading into my voice, begging him to hear the truth. Begging him to not be mad.

"Then where is he?"

"I—I don't know." My mind whirls. Noah was at school, not even an hour ago.

He sighs, flipping to calm like the world just tipped upside down. "I believe you."

"It's the truth." The manager's eyes on me spurs me to say things I probably shouldn't. "What are you trying to tell me, about my mom?"

He makes a "tsk, tsk" noise, followed by a garbled laugh that sounds barely human. "Some things, you have to discover on your own."

"I can't find her." That's a lie. I have her address in my pocket, courtesy of one Detective Michaels, but there have to be some things he doesn't know. There *have to be*. Because I can't live with the alternative.

"Try harder."

Tears fill my eyes. "She's my *mother*. Why do you want me to find her? What do you want with her?"

I hate that even now I still need to protect her.

"One day, you'll learn what real love feels like. And it won't come from her."

I double over, phone pressed tight to my ear because I can't stop listening. I need to hear this. Remember it.

No matter how much he helps me. No matter what secrets he guides me to uncover. He will always—forever—be the man who makes me want to turn myself inside out.

The man who taught me I'm not safe anywhere. All I wanted was to go for a fucking run that night. I just wanted to *live*, to *exist*, to do something as mundane as a fucking jog through the trails.

His voice slides through the phone's speaker, quiet now, a knife snicking free of its sheath. "What you did with him in his back seat last night. It won't happen again."

I swallow, fighting down the nausea. "It won't. I promise."

"You won't see him again, Cassandra. Don't make me hurt him."

CHAPTER TWENTY-NINE

Tuesday, October 12
3 Days Before the End

I lie on the coach at Margot's house, my face smushed into the cushion.

A hand that's too gentle to be anyone's but Ori's rubs over my back. "How did he sound? Do you think he would hurt you or Noah? Or . . . anyone else?"

I know what she's thinking because I'm thinking it too. He took Margot's necklace.

I flop over. "Well, when he was asking where I was, he sounded like he wanted to throw me back in his trunk and slit my throat. By the end, he just sounded like he wanted to keep me in his basement for a few years."

She grimaces. "I'm so sorry."

"I don't think he's going to hurt Margot though. He's never even brought her up, but he had no problem threatening Noah."

It's me he wants, and in this game, he'll say whatever he can to keep me off-balance. First, Margot's necklace. Then threatening Noah.

They're just the bait—I'm the end game.

"Hmm." Ori pauses to consult her serial killer facts database. "He's threatening the person he thinks you're closest to at that moment."

"Awesome. So my friendship comes equipped with a danger clause."

My throat tightens. "I'll understand, if any of you want to, you know, walk away from me."

Margot says, "Shut up," and Nomi follows with "What she said."

Ori gives me a smile. "I wish I could say something or do something or—"

I grasp her hand, and she squeezes back. "You are. It helps to just not keep everything in my head."

Nomi pops a chip in her mouth. "You know what would really help? Killing him."

"Nomi!" Margot tosses a pillow at Nomi's face, voice dropping to a hissed whisper. "We can't *kill* all of them."

"Not true."

"Did you forget getting called into the police station for *almost* killing someone?"

"It happened yesterday, so no."

"Okay, exactly."

"Exactly. They let us go, and my dad says they're not really pursuing it."

"Nomi," I say. "For fuck's sake. You didn't think that was maybe something worth sharing with the group?"

"Why? Were you worried? He lived in a *meth lab*, Cass. The place could've blown up from breathing wrong in it."

"But they know the door was locked. He *saw* us there. That's not suspicious?"

"Yes? Drug dealing and lots of enemies are kind of a package deal. And he saw *you* there, not me. Anyway investigating is a waste of police resources."

"So . . . that's it?"

She shrugs. "So that's it."

That's it. It's that easy to nearly kill a man and get away with it.

That easy to abduct a girl and not have a single person looking for you.

Maybe you're never held responsible as long as you pick the right victims.

Margot crosses her arms. "Well, I'm not killing Jared."

Ori mumbles, "That's a shame," and when everyone turns to her in shock, she bursts into giggles.

Nomi's arms shoot into the air. "Two votes for killing Jared! C'mon, Cass. Don't let me down."

I chuck a pretzel at her, and she catches it in her mouth, laughing so hard she nearly chokes. "Okay, fine. Can we at least kill Valco?"

Ori says, "I don't want to kill Mr. Valco either. I just want to humiliate and destroy him. Like a slow-motion vengeance scene. Villain being taken away in handcuffs while an awesome score plays in the background."

Nomi's smile starts small, stretching into a full grin. "I like you even more than I thought I would, Bello."

Ori's head drops, but her smile doesn't. "Same, *Tanaka*."

I drag my laptop onto my thighs. "Give me the rundown again. What do we have on Valco so far?"

Nomi says, "He's a douche," at the same time as Margot's "We hate him," and I stare at them both until Ori raises her hand.

I glare at her until she lowers it and whispers, "Sorry. Habit. Anyway we don't have much. All his social media is school stuff. Pictures of him and his wife."

Everyone has something to hide. Some weakness to exploit. And a guy like Valco, who puts his racism on display for an entire classroom, so emboldened he can make comments directly to Ori, there's bound to be more there.

"Has he friended the fake profiles yet?" We created two fake profiles and sent Valco requests—both with just enough dog-whistle racist bullshit that we thought he might accept.

Margot shakes her head. "There are a few Twitter friends that are sketchy as hell. 4chan links and QAnon-type stuff, so you can tell they're racist fucks without them outright admitting it. A few with ties to the Three Percenters or Proud Boys. But nothing that can be directly tied to him."

"What about an image search?"

"Trust me, I've been staring at his stupid face for hours." Ori pretends to gag. "Pictures of him at pep rallies. Running in the local school district half marathon. With his mom at Christmas and his brother outside his real estate office. On vacation with his wife in Ohio."

Nomi says, "Who the fuck goes to Ohio for vacation?"

My head flops back. "There has to be *something*. What he's doing to you, Ori, is so . . ."

Everyone's voices jump in with "Sadistic?" "Evil?" and "Totally fucked up."

"Yes. To all of those. There's more. I guarantee it. And if we can't find it online, we follow him. After Jared. Clear your Thursday night."

Ori tucks her hands into her lap. "My parents, they're going to start asking questions."

I pop a pretzel in my mouth, and the salt turns sour. "Yours and mine both." Only, that's not really true. Dad hasn't asked any questions of me. Not lately.

I went from virtual hermit to plans every night, and I don't think he's noticed.

That's the way it started with my mother too. We didn't skip right to abandonment. It came on slowly, the spark into an inferno.

We coddled it like Dad and I are doing now. Absences that grew longer until they were more expected than togetherness. Conversations that grew shorter until even a handful of words were too hard to find.

We let it grow, watched it char the line between us until it became a wall neither of us were willing to walk through.

And now every step I take toward finishing what we started drives me further away from him. Closer to the day he walks away too.

I say, "That's even more reason why you shouldn't come with me tonight, Ori. Why none of you should."

Margot rolls her eyes. "The last time you went alone you ended up with a bowling ball on your forehead."

I touch the lump on reflex. "It's not even close to that big."

Nomi's voice is all sweetness, but it's a big, fat lie. "Tell us again, what the motel manager told you when he gave you this location earlier?"

I never should have admitted this. I never should have told them I went back to the motel earlier.

But it turns out, pity has its uses.

Things it will not get you: any sexual interest from Noah Rhoades.

Things it will: the name of a "business" where I might be able to find information on my mom.

Manager Guy at the motel gave it to me after he witnessed me generally falling apart after the phone call.

The Wander Inn giveth, and the Wander Inn taketh away.

Nomi stares at me, and I mumble, "He said it's dangerous and I shouldn't go."

"Yeah, so now you want to go to a place that the manager of a motel that rents by the hour considers dangerous, and you want to go alone. You're not stupid, Cass. Don't be stupid."

"Fine."

"Good. Now let Auntie Nomi fix the next problem. Ori, what kind of cover will your parents buy for Thursday?"

Ori says, "A school project with one of you?"

"Do you have a single class that isn't advanced level?"

"No. Oh! Physical education!" She mumbles, "I hate it."

I rub my eyes. "Okay, so tell them Margot is helping you with the volleyball unit."

"Won't work. I used Margot as an excuse for tonight. Tomorrow night too."

"Let's hope your parents don't talk to Margot's parents then because *she's* supposed to be with Jared tomorrow."

"I *know*!" Her eyes go glassy. "Three nights in a row with Margot will mean she has to come over. Family dinner. Third-degree questioning."

Nomi tips the chip bag upside down, emptying the crumbs into her open mouth. "We don't have time for that shit."

She's right. The longer this stretches, the greater chance of getting caught. And our schedule feels more dangerous by the day. Tonight, the scary place. Tomorrow, Jared. Thursday, researching Valco. And that's if nothing goes wrong.

I say, "Use me then. Tell them you're with me."

"They'll want to talk to your dad." Ori rolls her eyes, but she doesn't mean it, not fully. There's safety in knowing someone stands behind you, surveying the path ahead.

"That can be arranged." It just won't be my dad they're talking to.

She breathes out a thank-you, then says, "What about you, Cass? Do you want your kidnapper dead?"

I have to reorient my brain, switch from harmless parent talk to murder, and for a moment, I want to call off everything, tell them all to walk away before things go too far.

But we're already past that, from the moment in the woods when we pledged allegiance to each other.

I used to want my stalker dead, more than anything. But now . . . "I don't get it."

Nomi says, "What's not to get?"

"I mean I don't get it, what he's trying to do. If he wanted to re-kidnap me, he could've. He's been in my *bedroom*. But he never even tried. So maybe he just gets off on tormenting me."

Nomi murmurs, "Fucker," and the room nods in agreement.

"But that's not it. At least not anymore. He's literally giving me clues to the other people involved. Why? Why now? What's changed?"

Margot says, "Your mom."

"She's the missing piece. Bulger has pictures of me, which is fucking terrifying. But he's not the one who was stalking me in the woods that day."

Nomi says, "So you think it's this Ronnie dude?"

I shrug, because that's how confident I feel. "He's clearly been following me. And he showed up at our school with a knife. And he's clearly trying to lead me to my mom. That tracks if he's using me to get to her. But I still can't *prove* anything."

"Maybe it's Noah."

"No." Margot's head shakes. "I've lived next to Noah since second grade. He couldn't do that."

Ori cringes. "Generally speaking, the 'nice guy no one ever expected' thing is exactly what people say about serial killers."

"Really, Ori?"

"Sorry, but it's true."

I say, "It's not Noah. He was in the picture in that note. There's no way he could've taken it."

Nomi nods. "Fair point. Tyler?"

"He was literally right next to me when I got the phone call."

Nomi fidgets, which can only mean bad things. "I hope it's Bulger." She breathes deep before continuing. "If it's not him, Cass, it's someone dangerous enough to kidnap you, someone unhinged enough to stalk you, but someone smart enough—diabolical enough—to either involve Bulger or set him up. Maybe your mom too. That's fucking *scary*."

I refuse to acknowledge how terrified I am that she's right, because I'm not sure I can do this anymore if she is. "Or maybe my mother has a bigger role in this than I think."

Margot gathers her hair, twisting it into a bun. That's what she does when she's afraid she's going to upset someone. "Here's the thing, Cass. I absolutely think we follow whatever leads we have."

"But."

"But. He knows you probably better than I do at this point." She blinks back tears, and it's like every moment of the last five months will haunt me forever. "So, he knows what a sore spot your mom is. I think—"

She pauses, and the way Ori's rubbing my arm a little too earnestly tells me they've discussed this already. "I think it would be good if you could keep yourself open to the possibility that this has nothing to do with your mom at all. Maybe it's all like you said. He gets off on tormenting you."

My whole body goes so stiff Ori slides off the couch to sit across the room.

Sweat breaks out over my skin as what I truly want, what I've truly been hoping for, becomes clearer. Some sad, pathetic part of me that hoped for a connection, no matter how terrible the reason.

I can barely speak around the lump in my throat. "Yeah. You're right. Simplest explanation is usually the best one, right?"

She speaks to the floor when she whispers, "I'm so sorry, Cass."

"It's okay."

It's not okay. She knows it. So do Ori and Nomi.

But it's better this way, that I put it out of my head now. Bury all those fantasies about him helping me in some way or there being a bigger motivation than just me making the wrong choice to go running, at the wrong time, the wrong place, and near the wrong people.

Maybe all the clues are so he can watch me struggle, chasing after something I can never hope to catch. The picture of my mom in the warehouse letter, the same picture in his wallet. The leads that track to Bulger. Maybe it was all staged. Another mind game.

But then.

I go still, memories of the warehouse slamming into my brain. And while maybe everything he said about my mom is just his sick game, he *is* giving me clues. It's too coincidental to be anything but.

Valco knowing the mayor. The senior-living-center real estate deals. Valco with his brother outside the family office.

Nomi says, "Spill it, Adams."

"I know where to find what we need on Mr. Valco. We're gonna need a crowbar."

CHAPTER THIRTY

Tuesday, October 12
3 Days Before the End

Nomi's palm taps the steering wheel. "Tell me how dangerous the shitty motel manager said it would be to come here?"

"Here" is downtown's west side, a forty-minute drive through gradually declining neighborhoods and increasingly potholed roads, deep in the old industrial district. "Here" is the business where I might be able to find my mother.

Here is also not far from where we'll be Thursday night when we recon Valco, thanks to the clues at the warehouse where I got the *bowling ball–sized* lump on my head. The note. Taped to the *locked* door. Hence, the crowbar.

*Val*Pro real estate. That's what the "For Sale" sign on the building said. Ori said Valco escaped getting fired because of his connection with the mayor, forged through his family's real estate dealings. That has to be why my stalker led me there. But none of us can risk stumbling into Valco, or worse, if we go charging into the warehouse tonight. Hence, the recon.

Nomi says, "Adams. How dangerous?"

She's trying to convince me to leave the mom thing alone again. But I didn't stop her when she flipped that lock, just like she won't stop me now.

I pull my hair into a pony and yank my beanie on. "Very? He said I shouldn't come."

Ori glances up from texting her parents. "I don't understand why the shitty motel manager—"

"Bill. Uncle Bill is actually what he said." I wish she'd have stayed home, where it's safe. Margot and Nomi too. Instead, we're all here, in Nomi's car, right down the alley from whatever this place is.

"Why would *Uncle Bill* give you this address if he truly didn't want you to go there?"

I flip down my visor and smear black body paint over my face, ignoring Nomi's snicker. "I'm trying to blend in! Be unnoticeable."

"You missed a spot."

I smear a streak down her cheek before she can stop me. "Uncle Bill told me because—"

"This is going to make me break out." She scrubs at her face with a napkin. "You are such a bitch."

"That is *not* why he told me. He told me because of pity."

Margot lays her head on Ori's shoulder, trying to read her texts without reading her texts. "I don't get it."

"He thought I was talking to my boyfriend when I got threatened about ever seeing Noah again. My possessive, abusive boyfriend. That, coupled with the whole missing-mother thing, was enough to tip him into guilt caused by—"

"Pity."

"Exactly. In a plot twist, he did give me a very insightful talk about gaslighting, emotional manipulation, and toxic masculinity. So that was . . . refreshing."

The car goes quiet, and I zip my coat, transformation to secret agent nearly complete. "Anyway, I promised him I'd dump my abusive boyfriend, and Uncle Bill says if I ever need backup to let him know."

It feels good to have Uncle Bill standing behind me.

"Okay, gotta go." I'm fully out the door before Nomi calls my name, and when I turn, she says, "Just . . . don't get killed, okay?"

"Roger that. Ten-four."

I slam the door as she whisper-yells, "You are *not a spy*!"

I mouth, "Secret agent," before sliding into the alley.

Dumpsters line the sides, trash spilling from their crooked lids. A lone streetlight flickers at the mouth on the opposite end, leaving mine awash in darkness.

Rats scurry across the concrete, their claws scraping, their bodies rustling bags and cartons as the sour scent of rot fills the air. Shadows advance and retreat, cutting human figures into the blinking beams of the streetlamp.

I keep close to the wall, my jacket snagging on the rough brick, and voices float closer. They sound male, all of them.

Something bangs and I stifle my yelp, but it's just a garage door clunking into place, until the pool of light cuts off completely.

I shake out my hands. Remind myself that seventy-two times seventy-two is five thousand one hundred eighty-four, and I take another step.

Glass crunches beneath my feet, and a side door swings open, ushering out a shadow form of a man.

His lighter flares, and I squeeze my eyes shut to drown the memory of standing across from Nomi, waiting for her to set the basement on fire.

His cigarette glows red, a pinpoint of light in the darkness.

He stops, turns, stares in my direction. I go painfully still, every muscle frozen until he starts in the other direction.

This is stupid. Any place that's too dangerous for Uncle Bill is certainly too dangerous for me.

But I've spent the last five months with life slipping by while I refused to move, and *this*, this could be what unravels everything.

I've survived dangerous before. I've *been* surviving it.

I inch forward, until I can hear every hitch of his inhale, every soft sigh as smoke billows from his lips.

I keep low, slipping through shadows and the reach of the light, and when the streetlamp flickers in a flare of brightness, every inch of him is highlighted in sharp relief.

There's something so familiar about him, almost a memory, but none that I can place.

A screech of metal jumps through the walls, followed by a staccato rhythm of something I can't name. The man knocks on the door once, then twice, and when it opens, a shower of sparks burst forth, slipping into the alley and dying in the dark.

A man inside laughs, but the boy in front of me does not, and when he shoves his way inside, I move too, cramming the only thing in my pocket—a pack of gum—into the door's corner.

The cigarette's smoke rises from the ground and I breathe in the sweetness of tobacco and the sharpness of mint and all at once my feet are being lifted from the ground, a hand over my mouth, those same scents invading my airways, stifling my screams.

My knees buckle, my shoulder crashing into the brick as my heart pummels my ribs. But then the door shifts, my gum not enough to resist the heavy metal.

It's just a cigarette. It's not proof of anything. And if I fall apart now, everything I've done is for nothing.

I force my body to move, reach for the door, open it, just a crack.

I need something to disguise my entrance, and it comes in a rampage. Metal screeching, tools whirring, men shouting loud enough to be heard over it all, and I slip inside.

Light assaults me, bright and fluorescent and completely unsuitable for hiding in.

But no one is looking *for* me or *at* me, and I slide to the floor and army-crawl behind one of the cars strewn throughout the room.

The tires are stripped clean, its engine sitting lamely on a pallet near its front bumper.

Electrical wires crisscross the floor, some dangling from metal rafters in the ceilings. Cinder-block walls turn from black to gray halfway up, and a mix of burned rubber, gasoline, and oil clings to the air.

The symphony of power tools comes to life again and I move faster toward I don't know where—someplace less open, someplace I can hide.

I sprint behind another car, balancing on the balls of my feet so I can peek through the side window.

Four other cars sit in differing states of decomposition, all their pieces slowly peeled away by the men across the room.

None of this is legal, I'd bet my life on that. Which I'm probably doing because I'm sure none of them would appreciate having a witness to a chop shop.

Somehow, my mom is connected to this place. She was always wild, stupid, and impulsive. She hated rules and loved breaking them. But this?

But *this* is the only lead I have. This might tell me who Ronnie is, why he's following me. And the pathetic part of me that must come from my dad's genetic contribution needs to know that she's okay, that feels compelled to protect her from living my fate.

Movement flickers in the far corner, an office set high from the floor with only a single set of metal stairs to reach it, and I know—I *know*—that's the only place my mom would belong in a place like this.

I dash toward the stairs, ears ringing from the barrage of grinding and shrieking, and the metal treads bite into my shoes but I keep my footsteps light. It doesn't stop the stairwell from shaking beneath my feet, rattling against the bolts that hold it firm.

There's barely a walkway at the top, just a small strip that stops after less than four feet. Voices filter through the door though, gruff and angry, and I crouch beside it, my ear to the crack that's giving up none of its secrets.

Then, for the second time in two days, a door swings open, and there's a gun to my head.

CHAPTER THIRTY-ONE

Tuesday, October 12
3 Days Before the End

He dangles a baby wipe above my head. "Wipe that off your face."

I do, because I can't exactly refuse a man whose henchman has a gun to my head.

The wipe comes away streaked with black, and he hands me another, then a third, until whatever job I've done satisfies him.

He doesn't look like a stolen-car dealer, from his short-cropped hair with just the right touch of gray to his perfectly tailored suit. His cuff links catch the light and spin it back as he tugs down his sleeves, lowering into the chair behind a massive desk. "That face is much too pretty to cover."

My flesh threatens to shrink in on itself, shriveling until I'm swallowed whole. I don't want him to think I'm pretty. I don't want a man who has a henchman with a gun to my head to think anything about me at all.

He says, "Who are you?" in a way that expects more than just my name, but it's the only thing I've got.

"Cassandra Adams."

His pencil taps the desktop, drawing out each second until I'm sure the next one will be where everything goes blank. "Why are you in my shop, Cassandra Adams?"

"I'm looking for someone."

"Who?"

Fuck it. Might as well go all in. "My mother."

"Your mother." He has a vicious smile, one that speaks of promises no one wants held.

He presses a button on his desk phone and holds a finger to his lips. "If you say a single word, I'll fucking kill you."

He nods to the man with the gun and his arm falls, but it doesn't stop my body from trembling as Nomi's words about what type of man might be responsible for my kidnapping ring through my ears.

Beeps echo through the room as he dials, too practiced to be from anything but memory.

She answers on the third ring.

Thirteen months. That's how long it's been since I've heard her voice.

Thirteen times thirteen is the sound of my heart ripping open, my blood spilling from my chest.

"What do you have for me, Scarlet?"

Scarlet. That's not even her real name. She ran so far she left even her identity behind.

"I don't have *anything*, Bruce, because I told you, I'm out."

His voice goes quiet, a snake through placid water. "I told you, there *is* no out."

His eyes never leave mine, his message for me as much as her.

She says, "You can't hold this over me forever."

"I can though, can't I? Unless you want her to know what you did."

"I didn't—" She goes silent, but I remember her voice, every inflection. I studied it my entire life, trying to pry the secrets from her head, to predict the things she wanted so I could give them before she thought to ask.

I did everything I could to make her stay.

That's the only reason I know she's crying right now, tears coming as fast as mine.

Bruce may not have had years to study her, but I'd swear he knows it too.

"I could find her." He winks at me, his face blurred through my tears. "I could tell her what you did."

The "her" is me. And I already know what she did.

All the pieces snap together into the picture I was too afraid to see. Too blinded to even *consider*.

I am so fucking stupid.

I was worried about her. I thought we might be suffering the same, that she might be as scared as me, that in some twisted way, we were enduring the same fate. I wanted to *protect* her.

I'm no different than Dad, following her from one motel room to the next. Searching for my scared baby bird to fix up and make better.

And now I've found her and I've discovered what I should've known all along.

I'm here because of her.

She's not a victim in this mess; she's a cause. Maybe not all of it. Maybe this is another time she's caught up in the consequences of her actions and dragging me into the center of them.

But she did *something*. Something she's so ashamed of, she's terrified I'll find out. And that's how I know just how much I don't want to know what she's done. I can't hear it. Not now. Not here. Not when there's still some stupid, pathetic part of me that's so desperate to have something— *anything*—from her, I'd take even this.

I don't want to believe my mom had me kidnapped. But I don't want to believe she abandoned me even more.

And some twisted place inside me would rather have her be the source of my torment than for her to care so little that I'm not worthy of her time at all.

She says something else, but I can't hear it, not when every word she speaks is like her hand inside my chest, twisting my insides until I can't breathe, can't move.

I press my hands to my stomach, and my charms jingle, blocking out the sound of Bruce's voice. Of *hers*.

Nomi, Ori, Margot. They're sitting in an alley where they shouldn't be, and if I don't make it out of here, they won't leave.

I won't do to them what my mother did to me. I won't drag them into danger and leave them to save themselves.

I won't end up like her.

I scrub away my tears and shove her voice from my head. I won't listen to another word. I don't care how sorry she is, and her tears are not for me.

And I won't pay another price for her decisions. Starting, right now.

Bruce kicks his feet onto the desk, toying with my mother on the other end of the line, and the henchman's eyes are trained on him, not me.

It's not a wide office.

I plant my feet and lunge.

My shoulder slams into the door, and I crank the handle so hard it comes free in my hand.

I whirl and rifle the doorknob at the henchman's face.

It bounces off his nose, blood spurting in a waterfall, and I jump onto the rail, riding it down until it shakes beneath me, as Bruce's voice thunders through the shop.

But they can't hear him down below, buffered by the chaos.

The staircase rumbles, and I tumble over the side, my fingers barely catching on the step.

The metal treads cut into my fingers, and I let go, bracing for the impact before it comes. I hit the ground and roll into the fall, but it's not enough to stop the pain that spears up to my knees.

A pop jolts through the building, and the concrete next to me erupts in a spray of dust and jagged chunks.

Too late, I make the connection.

Another bullet buries itself to my left, and I sprint across the room, dodging sections of vehicles and piles of metal debris, until I hit the door with the sound of footsteps on my heels.

I run, muscles burning, lungs heaving, but the street sits quiet, empty, not a single place to hide. A car barrels toward me, headlights off—I know exactly who sent it.

I can't outrun them, and it's too dangerous to bring the girls into this now.

I duck into an alley too narrow for the car to follow, and puddles splash at my feet, patches of moonlight illuminating the ground in pockets.

Tires squeal behind me, boots smack the pavement, but I'm still faster than them, quieter, and secret agent or not, I'm cloaked in black that matches the starless night.

I wait, quietly, patiently, keeping my breaths slow and light so not even my lungs move.

The world goes still, holding its breath, and I let myself believe, just for a second, that I made it out easy.

But then something smothers my mouth and my head slams against the brick. My legs kick but don't land, because I'm frozen by the sliver of cold—the bite of a blade—along the side of my neck.

The side. Home to the carotid artery, which pumps about 10 percent of my blood at any given minute, which means I will be dead before I could even try to call for help.

"Shhh." He presses harder, and I focus on the man in front of me, the feel of his breath over my face, the scent of gasoline that coats the fingers pressed tight to my mouth, the scar that runs a jagged length down his cheek.

His gruff voice cuts through the silence. "I've waited a very long time for this."

My tears pool on the edge of his palm, my body shaking so hard the brick cuts into my scalp where it's pressed tight, every swallow threatening to split my skin against his blade. Still as helpless as the first time.

My body screams to yell, to fight, to *not let this happen again*, but he will kill me if I move. I know this, as sure as I know anything.

He says, "Where is she?" and I don't have to ask who.

He followed me here because of her. Because of something she did, I ended up in the trunk. I ended up here, with a hand over my mouth and a knife at my throat.

I mumble that I don't know where she is but I'm not sure he's even listening, and then there's a flash of light. Twin beams of light that barrel into the alley, and someone shouts. The knife eases, just enough, and I bring my knee slamming into his balls.

He folds over just as car doors swing open and boots hit pavement and I run, from all of them, adrenaline blurring everything but the end of the alley and freedom.

The alley opens, the empty service drive and overpass straight ahead, and I dart across the service road and over the metal fence that runs alongside it, slipping on the wet grass as it slopes downhill to the freeway. I tumble the rest of the way, skidding to a stop in the buildup of gravel and debris at the bottom.

Shouts ring out above me, but they're distant, muffled, just far away enough to give me time to hide. I scramble under the overpass, climbing until I reach the small ledge of cement.

My feet tangle in something soft—a blanket, sleeping bag—someone's home. I crouch low, deep into the dark, cold cement pressed against my side, and I listen.

There's just the whistle of wind carried on the backs of vehicles as they rush down the freeway.

I fish my phone from my pocket, my hands shaking so hard I have to try three times before I can thumb down the screen's brightness until it's barely a glow. I dial the only person who has any chance of knowing how to navigate a mess this big.

He answers on the second ring, and I whisper, "Remember when you asked me to tell you if I got in too deep?"

CHAPTER THIRTY-TWO

Tyler leans against his bike, shaking out his hair. "So I got you that black-market phone you wanted."

I can't find words. The only thing I've managed was texting the girls to tell them to get the hell out of there.

Tyler says, "What? No 'thank you'?"

"I just got *shot at*! I had a man hold a *knife* to my *throat*! And you're talking about a phone?"

I stomp through the empty lot, scanning for Ronnie, for Bruce's people. I can barely track the people I need to be afraid of.

The lot is set back, surrounded by buildings, with a little grassy area and picnic table. The faint scent of bonfires and summer nights clings to the air, like if we closed our eyes we could pretend to be somewhere else.

It's secluded here, safe, and too perfect to be random.

Tyler pulls a flask from his pocket, the metal matte-black, so dark it blends with the space surrounding us. "But you *didn't* die, and I figured you'd appreciate talking about your black-market phone before the other conversation we're going to have, where you tell me exactly what I rescued you *from*."

He takes a long drink and holds it out for me. "It'll help."

I blink at him, rubbing my arms to stop them from shaking. "How'd you get here so fast?"

"Ah, there's the Cass I know. Deflection and misdirection. You would have preferred I leave you stranded beneath an overpass? Because you're a very competent girl, Cass Adams, but it doesn't seem like you had things handled."

"I wasn't—" I grab the flask and swallow twice, wincing as the liquid burns down my throat. "I wasn't accusing you of anything. And I'm *really* grateful you didn't leave me there. I guess I feel like I can't trust anyone right now."

Even as I say the words, the alcohol floods my veins, a wave of hushed warmth that blurs all the sharp edges of tonight's memories. The ones I know I'll be begging to forget. I can still feel the heat of Ronnie's palm against my lips.

Tyler steps closer, rubbing his palms down my arms. "C'mon."

His fingers circle my wrist, tugging me toward the picnic table, where a slice of light from a security lamp cuts a path through the darkness.

The bench creaks as he sits, pulling me next to him. He takes another drink, and maybe it's the buzz of adrenaline or the slow burn of alcohol, but I watch his lips as they close over the bottle, the way his throat works as he swallows.

He says, "I'm here because you asked me for a favor," and holds out his hand, where a phone rests in his palm.

I don't have the heart to tell him I don't need it anymore—Bulger's phone from the warehouse did the job—but I take it anyway.

"What do I owe you?"

"How about the truth?"

I cup the phone in my hands, let the warmth heat my skin. "I was following a lead."

"Ah." He leans back, fingers laced over his flat stomach. "What kind of lead?"

I've trusted all the people I care to with the full story, but this one part of it, I sort of owe him. "One that leads to my mother."

"That is not the answer I expected. Bit of advice?"

"I feel like you're going to give it anyway, so . . . sure."

"Don't."

"It's not that simple."

"Nothing ever is."

He turns, straddling the bench and caging me between his legs. "And the guys who were chasing you?"

"From a chop shop, a few blocks east of where you picked me up."

"Yeah." He grasps my hands. "I know them. Them and every other asshole out this way, stealing for a living, giving their great big 'fuck you' to the world without realizing they're stuck at the bottom of it. What about the guy from the alley?"

"Ronnie. He knows my mother. Turns out, she may be the reason all of this started."

He drops my hands, and his gaze gets lost in a place far from here. "I said I was glad I don't have contact with my dad anymore—I didn't feel that way the first time I kicked him out of my life. Or even the second. Trust me on this, Cass. People don't change, and the reasons you wanted them gone in the first place don't disappear."

A breeze rustles the trees, sending the hair that's come loose from my ponytail to tickle my face. "This is it. The last time with my mom. I won't need a third time, but—"

I blink away tears, banish the sound of her voice again. "I have questions, and I need her answers." But that little voice inside whispers that, after what I heard today, maybe it's not just answers I'm looking for anymore. Maybe this time it's payback.

He nods like he understands, even if he doesn't agree. But he doesn't try to talk me out of it. Doesn't ask questions he knows I won't answer.

We both have our secrets, closets filled with skeletons that keep coming to life. The bones of our bad decisions strung together.

He says, "You have any other leads? Maybe ones that won't get us shot."

I laugh, even though my ears still ring with the sound of those gunshots. "I know where she lives. I got her address from a cop. No promises on the not getting shot."

He doesn't flinch.

He doesn't lecture me about my safety, warn me that my actions are erratic and unreasonable even though they are. Even though I can feel things slipping out of my grasp, all the parts of me that have kept me safe the last five months shredding.

He's not scared though. He isn't braced for that moment I turn into her, when I stop caring about any of the rules and start living by my will.

There is no pity in his eyes.

I cross the space between us, and he smiles against my lips before he kisses me back. Slow, languid, like the flicker of streetlights are the twinkle of stars and the ground beneath us a bed of sand.

He tastes like whiskey and all the things I should be running from.

He lets me lead, even as he pulls me against him, and I know in that moment he'd never stop me.

Tyler would never push me away.

And somehow, it breaks the heavy press of my despair into ragged pieces.

I break free, our heavy breaths mingling as I drop my forehead to his.

He whispers, "I should've asked for that as payment for the phone."

My mouth drops open. Then I slug him in the arm.

He holds up a single finger. "One: What kind of sexual favors would an iPad get me?"

I hit him again, and he says, "Laptop?" capturing my fist in his hand before it makes contact.

His smile falls, and he meets my eyes. "Next time some douchebag tries to hurt you, Cass, if there's nothing else, use this."

He lets his hand open until mine rests on his palm. "Left hook, right to the jaw. Don't tuck your thumb though, unless you want it to break."

He plants a kiss on it, then another on my lips. When he pulls away, I'd swear he murmurs that it was about damn time.

"I threw a doorknob at someone's face. I think I broke his nose."

"That's my girl."

I stand, and when he asks where I'm headed, I turn, walking backward toward the bike that a week ago, I was afraid to ride. "Want to meet my mom?"

CHAPTER THIRTY-THREE

Tuesday, October 12
3 Days Before the End

A winding path of pavers sits at my feet. It leads to a cozy front porch that leads to a door that may be the only thing standing between me and my mother.

Wind gusts and I pull my jacket tighter, but the cold seeps through the fibers and leaches the warmth from my skin.

Heat washes over my back as Tyler steps closer, leaning to whisper, "Not quite what I expected."

The flask appears in front of me, and I don't hesitate, whiskey blooming in my stomach until I feel quieter, my thoughts clear.

I hand it back and head toward the door, letting all the anger I've gathered over a lifetime build and broil.

Thirty minutes. That's how long the drive was to my mother's home. Thirty minutes from downtown and all of it headed toward home, making her less than twenty minutes from me.

Twenty times twenty is four hundred and thirty times thirty is all the fucking minutes I've spent wondering where she was, worrying whether she was safe.

She's been here long enough to have gotten a ticket—speeding, of course, seventy-five in a forty-mile-per-hour zone, according to Detective Michaels—and this was the address on her license.

She's been here long enough to have an accurate address on her license.

I didn't believe it while standing in the police station. A real home. A stable address. But now that I'm here, it's too real to ignore.

Tyler slides next to me as I pound on the door, but no lights flicker on, no footsteps filter through the walls.

I raise my arm again, but Tyler blocks my path. "Hear me out. How about we"—he wraps his hand around mine—"put the fists away and find a solution that doesn't end up with the cops here."

"Right." She's not home, but that doesn't mean we have to leave. "Go kick rocks."

"Are you telling me to fuck off using the slang of an eighty-year-old?"

"No. Literally. Kick the rocks." I kneel and peek beneath a little trio of flowerpots. "My mother is an *infant* who can't be counted on to remember a fucking house key."

I slam the third pot, and a crack crawls up the side, spilling its soil over the cement. Let her clean it up.

Tyler sends a rock skittering through the mulch. "So there's a spare."

"At least one. Probably two because she'll have taken the first one inside and lost it or left it on the kitchen counter or *in* the fucking door because it's too much to expect she'd be even the slightest bit fucking responsible."

The welcome mat comes up empty, so I drag my fingers along the top of the doorframe. I'm nearly to the end when something hard and cold touches my fingers, and I knock it free until it pings against the porch.

"Guess you were right." He holds a fake rock in one hand, a key in the other.

We try them both, but the lock doesn't move. This doesn't surprise me either.

I point around the back. "Occasionally, she loses her keys, and all the spare keys, then you get new locks."

The gate squeals as I swing it open, pushing through to a tiny backyard with a patch of manicured grass and a pergola. Exposed string lights crisscross over a small patio set.

It's the same set we used to have, before Dad upgraded this summer.

Like she drove by the house and came back here to create her own version of it, without the parts she didn't want. Namely, me.

But then I remember. Dad's weird hours lately. How distracted he's been. Coming home wearing normal clothes instead of scrubs, and now a patio set that looks like *our* old patio set is in *her fucking backyard*, and everything feels sideways.

I jam the key in the lock, and it thunks over easily, door yawning wide.

We step inside, and Tyler says nothing as I take it all in. The tasteful decorations, the dishes piled in the sink because, just like the keys, some things never change.

But it *feels* like her—frenetic and chaotic linked with an invisible pull that draws people to her, until they're so caught in her orbit they can't break free.

I move deeper, fingers trailing over the walls, the furniture, soaking in every inch. They come to rest on a picture frame—heavy, with gems at the corners, and inside, a photo of ghosts.

Me, my dad, my mom, snuggled close, smiling like we knew where she'd spent the night prior.

The glass shatters the first time I slam it into the buffet. It spills over the floor the second.

I pry the picture free, shredding it into pieces small enough she won't be able to put them back together.

I glide down the hall on unsteady legs, the whiskey mercifully muddling my thoughts.

Tyler slips inside her bedroom and thumbs on his phone's flashlight, letting the beam roam over the room. "What are we hoping to find? Aside from these of course?"

He holds up several bundles of cash, formed into tight rolls, and that proves everything.

The voice on the phone was hers. She's working for a man who shot at me. She was staying at a motel with the man who just held a knife to my throat. There was a picture of her in Bulger's wallet too.

Maybe Bruce sent the guy with the menthol cigarettes to kidnap me because of her, and Bruce doesn't know or care that he's been terrorizing me the last five months. If that's true, I was so close to him today. In the same building.

I float into the room, my mind like a bruise, too battered to touch. "When you kicked your dad out of your life, did he try to get you back?"

"He didn't have to."

I meet his eyes, and he shrugs. "One of the biggest lies the world teaches us is that every parent loves their kid. So we keep going back, hoping they're going to be the person we need this time."

He opens the closet, and his brows raise. "So I kept going back, all on my own, until I finally realized the difference between people you fight for and people you fight to leave behind."

He pulls out one of Mom's wigs, lofted high. "Care to explain?"

"She's always had them. I assumed it was her escape from the whole 'mom and housewife' life she felt trapped in."

"Kinky."

"Gross. And no. I mean, maybe? But again, gross. She'd wear them wherever. The grocery store or the bank. The backyard. It never seemed to matter where."

She just wanted freedom. Change. The chance to be someone else. Someone who didn't live the things she'd lived.

If only it were that easy—different hair, different places, and all the bad things cease to exist. I want to hate her for it, but I can't.

It's not evil that drives her. It's desperation.

Tyler's smile grows more wicked with each step, until he spins me so we both face the mirror on my mother's dresser.

Smudges of black paint still streak my face, and my eyes look hollow, tired. Haunted.

He lowers the wig onto my head, tucking my hair inside and tugging the cap down just right.

The sharp cut ends just below my chin, the color deep black, severe, nothing like mine.

He whispers into my ear, "And what about you, Cass? Are you ready to escape? Be someone else?"

His hands leave a trail of heat over my hips, my stomach, his mouth trailing down my neck.

I look like her. All the features I always thought were my dad's belong to her now. In this moment, I am more of her than I am of myself.

The alcohol makes my thoughts blur at the edges, and my voice escapes so quiet I barely hear my own words. "Every day for the last five months, I've wanted to escape. Be someone else."

I swallow as Tyler's hands climb higher. "We tried, when we came here. That's *why* we came here. To run away from the latest mess she made."

But it never works. All those new beginnings, and I'm still where we started.

This is the closest I've been to her in so long. All those months, and I forgot so much. It's better when she's gone. It's *better*, for all of us. But I still can't make myself leave.

Tyler pulls me to the bed, and when he lowers on top of me, sinking me into soft fabrics with the weight of his body, I can almost forget where I am. I can almost forget how much I hate every part of who I am right now.

He says, "You didn't run far enough."

I'm afraid that will always be true. "Have you?"

He brushes a strand of black hair from my cheek. "Offer still stands, Bonnie. You and me, we set this place on fire and run."

Strong hands capture my wrists, holding them tight above my head with my bracelet caught between them, and the room swirls as his tongue meets mine.

Set this place on fire.

My mind whirls, spiraling with possibilities. Weighing the possibility that Tyler knows. Everything. And he's still here.

But there's no running. There's no place I can go where *he* won't follow. Where he won't find me. He's studied me, watched me, learned everything.

But even more, I promised I'd see this through. Get the answers I need about why I landed in that trunk, no matter how hard they are to hear. And then I'll do what my mother never did—I'll pay the consequences.

Light slices through the part in the curtains, and Tyler's in front of them before my fuzzy head can process he's gone.

"Fuck." He almost sounds scared.

I scramble from the bed, my body gone cold. "What is it?"

"We need to leave."

He grabs my hand as he runs past. "We head out the back. The bushes in the corner of the yard—hide in them until I come for you."

"Where are you going?" I stumble behind him, into the living room, where the sound of footsteps scuffling on the front porch bleeds through the door.

"To get my bike. I'll go out the back and come around the side."

The door rattles and creaks as something very strong and very heavy hits it from the outside.

We sprint out the back, and I run toward the bushes while Tyler launches over the fence in a single jump.

A man cuts into his path, and I don't even have time to scream before Tyler lays him out. A right hook that sends the man wobbling back before he slumps to the grass.

Wind cuts through my thin clothing, numbing my skin—then I'm running and Tyler is too, until I lose him in the darkness of heavy clouds that drape over the moon, muting its sliver of light.

I dive into the bushes and branches scrape my skin, poke through my clothes, but I force myself still. Listening, waiting.

That's when I see it.

The pink envelope, taped to the door.

It wasn't there when we entered. I unlocked it myself, and Tyler was right behind.

That means my stalker is out here somewhere, watching and waiting, just like always.

I can't leave the letter there. For my mom to find. For Bruce to find.

I need to know what it says.

I burst from my hiding spot and sprint to the door. The envelope pops free, and I'm stuffing it into my pocket when a voice grumbles that I shouldn't move.

I ball my hands into fists, thumbs out like Tyler taught me, and turn slowly.

He's a huge white dude, leather jacket stretched tight across his shoulders, with a jaw that looks far too solid for punching.

His gun—if he has one, and I'm betting he does—isn't pointed at me for once.

I drop my head into my hands, faking scared sobs while I peek at him through my fingers.

He creeps closer, and I draw on every bit of whiskey-infused courage to punch him as hard as I can.

He stumbles, probably more from surprise than pain, but I don't wait to find out.

I fly through the open fence just in time to hear the rev of a motorcycle.

Tyler skids to a stop at the end of the driveway, and I fling myself onto the seat behind him, speeding away from the people trying to kill me for the second time tonight.

CHAPTER THIRTY-FOUR

Tuesday, October 12
3 Days Before the End

I stand in my bedroom, my hands still shaking despite all my assurances to Tyler that I'm all right. Despite three separate phone calls to Nomi, Margot, and Ori to convince them of the same.

I don't have to convince my dad since, while he's supposed to be home tonight, he's not waiting up for me. He's not here at all. Picked up an extra shift, according to his note.

The glue pops free as the envelope opens, and two photos sit nestled inside.

There's no note this time. Not a single message anywhere.

But then, the pictures are enough.

The first is my mother, standing across from my father on the door-step of the house I just fled from.

In the second, she's standing across from Noah. Outside somewhere. I don't know where. Don't *care* where.

I adjust her wig on my head so it fits just right, so if I stare, just long enough, I can convince myself I'm her.

Then I crawl into bed with the pictures tucked beneath my pillow, and I dream of her, surrounded by flames.

CHAPTER THIRTY-FIVE
CASS ADAMS

The Events of Wednesday, October 13
2 Days Before the End

With Jared, we went in with a plan. Choreographed our movements and synchronized our decisions.

This time, there would be no surprises. No locked dead bolts or news reports. This time, no one would get hurt. We'd do things right.

Because this night, there would be a witness.

We drove into the woods and waited, me and Ori.

Nomi stayed with Margot, hiding in a closet where she wouldn't be seen, holding the camera Jared wouldn't know was there. Recording his confession. Streaming it to us to record too, just in case.

Ori and I watched every second through the live feed, the need to close our eyes a constant battle with the promise to be there with Margot, however we could.

Together. We promised to do this together.

We watched as she ripped her soul open, told him all the things she'd barely told us. We watched as he argued through her tears, denied all the things he'd done.

Ori grabbed my hand, crushing it so hard my bones ground against themselves, and just when we thought she wouldn't go on, Margot went deeper.

Until he couldn't deny it.

His apologies weren't real. They weren't meant to be—an empty gesture made to appease rather than repair.

He didn't feel sorry. Not truly.

Until Nomi stepped from the hallway and showed him everything she'd captured.

They loaded him into the car then, the promise to send the video to the world enough. Enough to let them blindfold him and bring him here, where Ori and I have prepared for his arrival, tucked deep into the woods and far from witnesses.

There's a chair in the middle of the clearing now, the extra length of its pub-style legs buried deep. Around it, rings of gasoline soaked into the frozen grass, a path just wide enough for Margot to walk through, to watch as the flames get closer to where Jared will sit.

The ground outside the rings are soaked through—gallons of water closing the ring in a barrier that will be the first line of defense against any errant flames. The extinguishers beside me the second.

But Jared doesn't know any of that.

A confession would never have been enough.

Ashes to ashes.

The fumes sit thick in the air, even with the crisp breeze, and my palms are sore with the threat of blisters.

Ori glances to my hands, the bump on my head. She wants to know if I'm okay.

But those questions, I don't have answers for.

Margot's tires signal her arrival, the pop and crunch of branches giving way beneath them, and Ori's hand shakes in mine.

Jared stumbles into the clearing, Nomi shoving him from behind.

Margot's eyes meet mine and fill with tears. She scrubs them away, the charms at her wrist twinkling in the light through the canopy of trees.

I want to smother her in a hug. I want to fall to the ground and sob alongside her, for all the things she's lost and for all the things she was forced to live.

Instead, we nod. Resolute. Our wounds scabbed and scarred, but no longer open.

We're stronger now, in ways we shouldn't have to be.

Nomi says, "Surprise, motherfucker," and gives Jared another shove toward the chair he can't see.

I hear his voice but not his words, and I can't stop wondering if that's what it was like for my kidnapper while I screamed against the tape over my mouth. If he shut himself off from all my pain.

"We're not so different, you and I."

Not so different than him. Not so different than the mother that spiraled out and left everyone behind.

Maybe he's right. Maybe that's who I am. My mother's daughter. Maybe that's always who I was meant to be.

I move before I'm supposed to, leaving Ori to catch up.

The handcuffs Nomi "borrowed" from her dad jingle, dangling from my hand, metal warmed from the heat of my body.

I wonder, if Jared is feeling the helplessness yet.

If his thoughts come too fast to see through to their end, his body so alive it hurts and his mind so constrained it suffocates.

I wonder if he still thinks this will end in his favor.

Margot says, "Sit down," and she's not crying anymore. Her voice doesn't even waver.

Jared feels for the chair behind him, arms waving aimlessly until he brushes against the seat and stumbles into it.

Ori and I move in unison, advancing at his back with our handcuffs ready.

This is the closest Jared will get to paying for what he's done.

We hit the ground together, Ori's hand and mine reaching to close the cuff around Jared's ankles.

The cuffs click against my palm as they ratchet tighter, and while Ori has the other around the chair's leg a moment later, I freeze, memories of my hands bound, my mouth covered, roaring through my head.

Jared kicks his leg and rips the cuff free from my hand, and I blink, back to our place in the woods again instead of in that trunk.

It's a breath too late.

Jared throws himself forward, but his left cuff holds firm, sending him tumbling to the ground, only inches from the rings of gasoline. His voice sinks into the grass. "What the fuck *is* this, Margot?"

I grasp his ankle, and he kicks harder, squirming and fighting, just like I did.

Then Nomi's there, both hands wrapped tight to his leg, dragging him within range of the cuff. I scramble for it, wet heat of my skin fogging the shiny metal, and when she gets him close enough, I don't freeze.

The teeth catch and I shove, tightening, click by click, while Jared shouts.

His blindfold inches up, and before it can come completely free, Nomi and I grab his shoulders, forcing him from the ground and back into the seat.

My hands burn—gasoline-soaked skin raw and tender—and I wipe them against my jeans.

This wasn't part of the plan. We're barely minutes into this, and I've already messed up. All my decisions are still the wrong ones.

Jared's voice filters in, yelling Margot's name as we slip the rope around his chest, winch it into a tight knot.

Margot approaches, her movements slow, methodical, and she pulls his blindfold free.

She doesn't wait to see his face, doesn't bother answering his questions. None of us do.

We move back, outside the ring of gasoline, away from the reach of the flames that will soon flare bright.

Margot reaches the outer rings, and the scrape of the match in her hand travels the space like an explosion. The flame reaches and flares, traveling the length of the wood until it nears her fingers.

Jared goes quiet, his breathing ragged, and we leave him there. Handcuffed, tied. Helpless. "Margot, listen to me. Margot—"

The match tumbles end over end, a haze of red against the dark woods—then the ground blazes.

The fire follows the path we've laid for it, cold air turning hot as it brushes past us and back to Margot. Then it's just her. Red glow traipsing over her skin, lighting her dark hair in a halo of flame, and Ori's breath catches at the sight of her.

Margot takes another step, lights another match and lets it fall.

It moves faster than the first, grows taller, and smoke clouds the sky, spiraling toward the stars.

"Every time," she says. "Every time I said no and you didn't listen, this is how it felt."

"Margot, please. You don't have to do this. This isn't you."

She smiles then, and the third match strikes. "Oh, this is me, Jared."

The third ring lights, a brutal path that ends at her side, reflects in the dark of her eyes. "This is how it felt, being with you."

She scrapes the fourth match so hard it cracks, tip tumbling from her fingers and catching before it hits the ground. "This is how it *felt*, discovering what you did, listening to you defend your actions. This is how it felt with every text you sent, every phone call, every moment in your presence."

The fifth ring has no path for Margot to walk through—nothing but a solid wall of flame that will surround Jared and lick at his shoes, heat the air that sinks into his lungs.

He's crying now, heaving sobs and muddled apologies, and he feels it, the helplessness.

Just like she did. Just like every minute she endured where he pressured and manipulated until he stole what she didn't want to give. Every moment that came after, when he used her actions to silence her, control her, use her. Every second where she cried, worried, forced herself to live through the panic of his threats to ruin her life.

Just like every hour of this night would have been for Margot, if it had gone the way Jared expected.

She waits, staring at him like all those thoughts are flooding her mind too. "Fuck you, Jared."

She lights the last match and tosses it into the air. It takes flight, flipping high and flaring higher on the way down. And then it hits.

A circle of fire surrounds him, raging, impervious to his regret, to his fear, and indignation.

And so are we, the four of us. We are every edge of the flame, we are the heat that fills the air, we are the destruction that edges nearer, creeps higher.

We are dangerous girls, and we have lost all our mercy.

CHAPTER THIRTY-SIX

Thursday, October 14
1 Day Before the End

It takes longer than I anticipate for the next envelope to come. It wasn't waiting in my car Wednesday morning, or in my locker. Not in my bedroom that evening, when my car was still covered in dirt from the woods and ashes from the fire we made around Jared.

Everything has gone quiet. Even Noah.

That's not so surprising, since he's a traitorous asshole who's hopefully wallowing in the deepest depths of shame and guilt for associating with my mother and not telling me.

Either that, or he hasn't gotten my note yet. But I prefer to think he missed school yesterday because he was crying about the shame-and-guilt thing.

I turn the envelope over in my hand. Bulger's still not at school either. Hasn't been since news of his dad broke.

So he would have to go out of his way to bring this here. But it could explain the delay. But Bulger didn't try to kill me in an alley, so my current bet is on Ronnie.

Even if Bulger admitted to killing his dad. And the proof he's been stalking me was in his desk and his *wallet*. But then there's Bruce, my mother, the boy at the door and his cigarettes. I thought I was making progress, but instead I just reached another layer.

They're all connected. Somehow. And I need to find out how.

I drop my head against the stall door and my forehead throbs from the impact. I let myself feel it, let the pain center me.

Tonight, we go to the warehouse. And if my suspicions are correct, we'll find something on Valco there. *Look closer.*

The door where the note was taped in the warehouse felt purposeful because it *was*. He swore he wasn't a monster, and I think this is his way of trying to prove it. By helping me.

There is not enough pain to force my brain into making sense of this. Any of it.

I wish I could blame all of this on my mother—even if she had me kidnapped, I don't think she'd have me *killed*.

It would be safer if she orchestrated this.

But then I think of that phone call when I was at the motel. The violence with which he scrawled the words on the picture of me with Noah. Whoever he is, this part isn't faked, even if I wish it were.

And then there are those pictures of her with Dad and Noah.

I'm a hypocrite for being mad at Dad. For feeling betrayed that he saw her again after we agreed not to. I *did* visit her house two nights ago.

But Dad was the one solid thing I had, and now he's as adrift as me. Like the only constant in my life is chaos and there's nothing I can do to ground it.

Like the one person I counted on unconditionally chose her instead of me.

And that's why I didn't feel bad about having Tyler impersonate him when calling to cancel my therapy appointment. Or when calling Ori's parents to say we'd be hanging out together.

I rip open the envelope as voices fill the bathroom, echoing off the tile.

Another picture this time. Of Tyler but not with me. He stands next to his motorcycle, his gaze to the sun.

Except, the version of Tyler in this picture isn't seeing anything with his eyes scratched out.

The scratches go clear to the back, the photo paper flimsier than the others.

"Cass, I know you're in here."

It takes a minute to recognize the voice, and when recollection hits, it's too late to climb onto the toilet and pretend I'm not here.

Shelly sighs, miserable and long-suffering as always. "Noah sent me in here."

Fuck. I mean—Whatever. I hate him. "Well I'm sending you out."

I flip the photo over, and there's a single word: NO.

I guess that's clear then. Apparently I can't date anyone. Maybe tonight I can look forward to another ranting phone call.

"He said if you don't come out, then he's going to come in."

Giggles erupt, and it's obvious none of these girls would mind a visit from Noah in the bathroom.

"Since when did you become Noah's personal messenger? Do you carry his backpack for him? Do his homework? Does he always send you home immediately after?"

A hush settles over the room, and I almost feel bad when Shelly says, "You're such an enormous bitch, Cass," because she's not wrong.

But then she adds, "Just like your mom."

I fling open the stall door, because I've spent enough of my life hiding from the things people say about my mother.

Karen Neelly says, "Wait, I thought she lived with just her dad," like I'm not standing right in front of them.

Shelly smiles, all teeth and venom. "Oh, she does. But that's because her mom is a whore who was cheating on her dad with the principal and got caught on video by some kids filming a senior prank. Whoopsie-daisy. Poor Cass has to find *yet another* new school."

I will the tears away, force the mask onto my face. You can never run far enough from anything when the internet exists.

"Hey, Shelly?"

"Yes, Cass?" She coats her voice in sugar and sunshine.

"You're a shit defensive specialist, and Coach almost benched you last year." I shove past them and send an SOS text to the girls before I have to face Noah.

That backstabbing, lying, piece-of-shit motherfucker.

I'm still crafting derogatory adjectives for him when we're standing face-to-face, and he holds up the picture I left for him.

The picture of him and my mom. I left it in his locker—stalker-style—with a note on the back.

So much for not playing games.

His jaw flexes. "What the fuck is this?"

"Funny, that's what I said too."

I storm down the hall, and he shoulders people out of the way to walk in step with me.

He keeps his voice low, the timbre of it wavering with the force of what he's holding back. "I deserve an explanation."

I stop short. "*You* deserve an explanation? I think that's my line."

He scrubs his hand over the stubble he didn't shave this morning, and below the eyes that look sunken, tired. "I wasn't mad, Cass, when you stopped talking to me. And I didn't ask questions. When you asked for help, I gave it. And even—"

His eyes glaze a second before it disappears. "Even when I sat in a *police station* yesterday, answering questions about a license plate and a *dead man*, I didn't rat you out."

Faces pass in a blur, some of them slowing, heads turned. We should stop this. Move somewhere private. But nothing feels solid, like the floor slides farther out from under me with every heartbeat.

"None of that changes what you did." That photo of him, talking to *her* hits me again, a punch to the chest.

My voice thickens, and no amount of blinking stops the tears from burning in my eyes. "I'm learning there is *no* end to the things people are capable of, Noah, but that"—I point to the picture in his hand, the one crumpled into his fist—"I didn't see that coming."

"No. See, *that* is *my* line. Imagine my surprise when your Detective Michaels launched into questions about your relationship with Tyler Thorne."

"I don't have to explain myself to you."

"No. You don't. And good for you, Cass, because you don't like to explain anything, do you?"

"Because when you trust people, they betray you!"

He steps closer, voice dangerously lowered. "Except you never fucking bothered to trust me."

"He locked me in a fucking trunk!"

The world stops, every voice quieted and every pair of eyes centered on me, on the secret I've fought for months to protect, only to deliver to every waiting ear.

Noah's spine shoots straight, and he's seconds from a response when Nomi shoves past him.

For once, he's unsteady.

Nomi shouts, "Move along, assholes! Go back to living your boring, pathetic lives!"

Ori and Margot are right behind, and seconds later two hands slip into mine, until we're all standing against him.

He looks to each of us, pausing at Margot because they're friends, before I was with either of them. She shakes her head, squeezing my hand in case I don't understand.

She chooses me.

All of them have.

He whispers, "Cass—"

"Did you know it was my mother you were talking to?"

It's the one shard of hope I've clung to since seeing that picture—that he didn't know.

He shatters it with a single word. "Yes."

The salt of my tears slips against my lips. "When?"

"The day after."

The day after. The thought that's teased at the darkest corners of my mind shoves to the forefront, and if not for the girls at my side, I wouldn't be standing. "Did she say she wanted to be part of my life again?"

He nods in response, and it's all I need, because I know my mother. I knew two days ago when I asked Tyler if his dad had ever tried to win him back. Maybe I even knew the minute Bruce threatened to tell me what she'd done that night in the warehouse.

She did this. Tried to wreck me so she could build me back up. She may not have planned for it to end with stalking, but she set it in motion.

There was only one way this could've ended—the way it always does. My heart bleeding and her holding the knife.

I'm nearly past Noah, almost to the ring of bystanders when he says, "I knew, because she looks just like you. But whether you turn into her, Cass, that's *your* choice."

CHAPTER THIRTY-SEVEN

CASS ADAMS

The Events of Thursday, October 14
1 Day Before the End

We didn't know what waited for us, behind the bolted door that held Mr. Valco's secrets. We only knew we were led there for a reason. *I* was led there for a reason.

But this was for Ori. And we were almost done.

The building still stretched beyond sight, buried in fog this time, like even the gods were on our side.

I don't have to convince myself to go in this time. I don't sit in my car, hoping for a reason to wait.

This time, I've run out of things to lose.

The crowbar sits heavy in my hand, metal cold and hard, and Ori walks next to me, her jaw set as we creep along the length of the structure.

Our car is parked out of sight. Hidden from the security guard who found me last time.

He drives through every twenty-eight minutes. We'll wait for him to pass; then we'll have less than half an hour.

Ori's voice barely carries in the rush of wind. "Thank you for this, Cass."

I stop dead. "You don't need—"

"Yes I do. So do Margot and Nomi. You started this. You brought us together."

"Ori—"

"No." I barely recognize the command in her tone—sweet Ori filled with brutal edges. "The things we've done. They're not things I wanted. I don't know how I'm going to reconcile them."

She scrubs away tears. "But I don't regret them. We did what we had to do. But without you, I'd be playing Trivial Pursuit with my parents right now, just *imagining* doing something to Valco, so . . . thank you."

I smother her in a hug. "I don't believe you'd have done nothing. You did it before and you'd do it again this time."

We both go still as headlights pass, the car leaving a trail of exhaust that burns in my throat. But then the headlights fade, disappearing into the hazy night that clings to my skin, cold and damp.

Ori rolls her eyes and steps back. "Okay, maybe that's true. But this way is more fun."

"More illegal. More dangerous. More likely to end with imprisonment or death?"

She winces but charges forward anyway. "Let's do our best to avoid all those things."

We creep along the side of the building, keeping tight to the pockets of shadow, until we reach the door.

There's no one to leave it open for us this time.

Twenty-four minutes left.

She heaves the bolt cutters, and it takes two of us to slice it through, sharp tang of metal springing into the air. The chain rattles as it falls, and I scoop it up, wind it around my arm.

I've already been locked in here once. I won't repeat it.

We're through the warehouse in minutes, through the offices in less, and to the door where the picture of my mother was taped.

Look closer.

If I'm right about what's behind this locked door, it's proof he meant to look closer here too. It's proof he's trying to help me.

Margot and Nomi arrive, filling the small hallway with the scent of gasoline.

Just in case.

The first lock breaks easier than the second, and by the time they're both free, long strips of metal twisted into jagged points, we're all covered in a sheen of sweat.

Ori pulls the door open, and fresh air greets us, laced with the sweetness of tobacco and something darker, caustic.

I click on my flashlight, shining it into the shroud of darkness, over to the small loveseat and side tables set inside the door.

It's bigger, wider, than I imagined. Windowless and stretching so far my flashlight can't hope to penetrate the length of it.

I step inside, scanning the wall for a light switch, and when I find it, I wish I hadn't.

Ori goes still, and Nomi whispers a curse.

Pictures line the walls, looming over the room. Men in white hoods. Men in salute. Flags of hate tacked high above rows of guns.

The room is filled with it, stocked full.

A desk. A conference table with enough room for twenty men, and I can picture them here—picture Valco here—their sickness shared and revered.

Monsters, living in this world like kings.

I want to be sick.

I want to raze this place to the ground.

"Ori," Margot whispers, but Ori steps farther into the room, until she stands in the center of it, spinning to take it all in.

Her voice wavers, but it's firm, loud enough to reach to each corner of the room. "Burn it."

"It's evidence." Nomi speaks gently, but the flush in her cheeks shows how badly she wants to leave this place in wreckage. "You said you wanted to destroy Valco. If you burn everything, you'll destroy any hope of that."

Ori turns, eyes hard and hands fisted. "I've spent my whole life letting things go. Being *polite*. I've ignored the looks when I walk into stores, getting seated at the back of the expensive restaurants and never in the front windows."

She travels the room, voice rising higher with each word. "I've spent a *lifetime politely* declining when white women ask to touch my hair and *politely* slipping out of their reach when they don't bother to ask. I watched those same women clutch their purses and cops clutch their guns when my daddy walks past. Watched them make excuses when a cop kills another Black man, call us thugs when we take protests to the streets. I've politely watched the world wait for Black women to do all the work only to stay at the bottom of everyone's priorities. And now this."

She stops in front of the picture that centers the far wall. It's three times her size, framed in gilded wood, and the men's eyes watch. "Now my entire *future* gets put in the hands of a man like this."

She reaches high, muscles straining beneath the weight of the frame; then she heaves it up and sends it crashing down.

Glass shatters in a waterfall of ragged slivers, spilling onto the floor and dusting over her feet. She shakes them clean. "I'm tired of altering my *existence* for these people. I'm tired of them deciding my future. I am *tired* of being polite."

She hisses through the end, her face blurring through the tears in mine.

I point across the room. "We could save the computer. And files if they have any. For evidence. We should see if we can copy the hard drive too—for us to keep. Just in case. I have flash drives in my backpack."

Nomi says, "And the guns. The cops can destroy them, but a fire might not."

Ori nods, all the permission we need, and Margot speaks for the first time. "We can't leave them lying around outside. What if the wrong people find them. Like one of *them*."

Nomi adds, "Or the security guard," and we all check our watches.

Fourteen minutes.

"I'll turn it in. Directly. There's a detective I know."

Everyone stares at me and Ori whispers my name, because we all know what I'm really offering.

I'm the scapegoat. The face they'll hang all of this on if—*when*—they put it together.

I'm the sacrifice.

Thirteen minutes.

Ori nods. "Burn it."

We're a torrent of rage, our hands destroying, demolishing, tearing apart. We leave nothing unbroken. Nothing unmarred. My fingers bleed from the cut of glass, burn from the sting of gasoline that slips into my lungs, lightens my head.

My legs ache, my throat gone raw, but we clear the walls, overturn anything unbreakable.

We match the evil in this room with our own. We are a symphony of screams and cries as we leave this room nothing like we found it.

They'll know, even after the last embers go silent. They will know we were here.

Ori turns to me, lungs heaving, face streaked with tears, and her gaze travels to my hands.

They're bare, my gloves removed. If there's enough left to fingerprint, it's mine they'll find, and no one else's.

Four minutes.

I shake my head to buy Ori's silence and say, "We need to take the evidence to the car and get the rest of the gasoline."

"The *rest*?" Margot's eyes widen. "The place is drenched, Cass. I don't think we need it."

We need it. There's no part of this place that should remain standing.

We gather the computer, the files, and cram the guns that will fit into their duffels. The others fill my hands.

My hands. My fingerprints. And the rest of the gasoline, locked in my trunk, where Nomi loaded it earlier. I haven't opened it in five months.

I kick over the last of the containers, letting the fuel leak into the carpet below, spreading in a dark stain across muted blocks of color.

We hurry through the offices and to the massive door that leads to the warehouse when a flicker of light stops me cold.

He's early.

Already through the warehouse.

I sling the duffels over Nomi's shoulder, until she's so bogged down she can't carry even another ounce. I grab the gun that looks most vicious and drag it from the bag.

It's heavy, cool beneath my touch, its metal smooth, malignant.

Nomi whispers, "Do you even know how to use that thing?"

"No. I'm going to pretend. Wait here. I'm going to distract him."

She mutters a string of curses, but then I'm sprinting through the warehouse, the guard's voice echoing through the empty space.

I block out the words, the undeniable threat in them until I'm clear to the other side, far from the door. Until I can turn toward him, the gun I don't know how to use pointed in his direction.

His is drawn, held chest high, and that fear—the one that spikes in my veins every time I've stared down a barrel—is gone.

He steps forward, slow, smooth. We're nothing but shadows here. No way to look each other in the eye.

I wish he could. I wish he could see the things mine would say.

Another step and he says, "Do you even know how to use that thing?"

"Yes."

I cradle it to my shoulder, center him in the sharp line of the sight.

It's convincing enough for him to pause, and Nomi travels along the other side of the building, out of his sight.

Her steps grow slower, the awkward weight hampering her, but she's almost there, and I dare not track her progress with my eyes.

"Put it down."

"Do you know who you're working for? Do you know what you're protecting? Because if you do, it'll make this a lot easier for me."

A boom bounces off the walls of the warehouse as the metal door slams open, and the guard spins in time to see Nomi run out.

He fires, a single shot that assaults my ears and leaves them ringing, and before he can turn back to me, I close the distance between us and bring the massive gun down over the back of his head.

His knees buckle, and he stumbles through a shaky step before he tilts and crashes to the floor.

I barely make it in time to catch his head, and as I lay it down gently, a wave of sickness rolls through my stomach.

Nomi bursts back in, barely pausing before she sprints to my side, panting. "I'm so out of shape. That fucker *shot at me.*"

"Yeah, it's not a great feeling. We have to get him out of here."

"He weighs five hundred pounds."

"He does not weigh five—"

"Hyperbole, Cass. He's muscly and fucking heavy."

"Wait here."

I'm off before I can hear her protests, and I don't slow through the office or even into the room where Ori stands, next to Margot, waiting, a match in her hand.

I grab the rolling office chair, and then we're all running, pushing it in front of us until we skid to a stop at the guard's body.

Ori's eyes fill with tears, and Margot starts on a refrain of "oh my god oh my god oh my god."

But there isn't time for regret, and compassion and sympathy died just beyond the doors of this building.

It takes all four of us, heaving, out of breath, sweat clinging to skin, until he's safely outside, tucked into the corner of the lot where the police will find him.

When I call them.

We carry the evidence to my car, where the girls wait as my hand stills over the trunk. My eyes burn and my body shakes and I remember . . .

I remember every second of that night.

The trunk pops open, fumes heavy and thick, and we remove the things we need and replace them with the ones I promised to deliver—the evidence that will ruin Mr. Valco for good.

We don't run back through the building. We walk, all of us in a line. Margot's hand in mine on the right, the heavy container of gasoline on my left.

We enter the room somber and quiet, surrounded by the wreckage forged with our hands and our bodies, and as Ori strikes the match, letting the flame climb higher, blackening the wood beneath it, she whispers, "Ashes to ashes."

CHAPTER THIRTY-EIGHT

Thursday, October 14
1 Day Before the End

The moon's reflection ripples across the surface of the lake as I drag myself through the park's empty lot, my vision blurry and my throat ravaged from the fire at the warehouse.

Detective Michaels was not happy to see me. Even less happy to let me go.

It's an amazing source of leverage, the guilt he feels for leaving me unavenged. And the pity he feels for me over the mother that left me behind.

It's the only reason I walked away from the police station instead of being stuck there in handcuffs. It won't work again. Even pity has its limitations. Even guilt fades as time erodes the memory.

But we're almost done. Only one act of retribution left.

I float down the park's walkway, high on the visions of flame climbing higher, of all the things we removed from the world tonight.

I called from the phone Tyler gave me, waited until we were sure the fire had turned it all to dust.

We watched as sirens grew louder, until lights flashed in swirls of red and blue over the white-brick walls. We watched as the roof collapsed and the firefighters let it.

There was nothing inside to save.

And as the fire slipped away, its job done, it was Ori who snuck close, scooping water-soaked ashes into her palm.

They're streaked across my wrist, my fingers black, and traces run through my hair. I left them there for Michaels to see. I dared him to ask why.

He led me out the back door instead.

Crickets chirp in the grass, cicadas singing beneath the clear sky, and three figures wait for me along the edge of the lake.

My feet shift as the sidewalk gives way to sand, and I kick off my shoes, rolling my leggings until my calves are bare.

The beach is cold, tiny grains drifting over my toes as the wind tousles the girls' hair against the backdrop of water behind them.

I want to capture this moment. I want to hold on to it forever.

Ori turns and holds her hand out to me, and it's only a few steps before mine is linked in hers.

Her hair is wet, lavender-scented, her clothes clean. Margot and Nomi too. They showered in the changing rooms, probably shivering in the frigid cold, with only the cinder-block walls to block the wind, the ceiling open to the sky.

Their clothes are strewn throughout the park, shoved into trash cans and beneath discarded food and used picnic tablecloths. Their clothes are evidence, and now they're gone.

I whisper, "You okay?"

Ori nods. "Yes? No? I will be?" She laughs through tears before her smile drops again, her gaze directed at the stillness of the lake. "I hate him. *So much*. I hate all of them."

Nomi says, "You should."

"No." Tears track down her soot-smudged cheeks. "I mean yes. I should hate them because *their* hate makes them ugly. It makes them cruel and awful and I'm *happy* about what we did tonight. I'm *happy* that we destroyed that place and everything in it."

Her hand shakes, and Margot's arm wraps around her, whispering things too soft for me to hear.

Whatever she says, it works, Ori's grip going softer but her voice stronger when she continues. "But I hate that I have to be angry. I hate that *I* have to do things I don't want to because of who they are. I'm seventeen. I shouldn't have to be this tired already."

"You're right. You shouldn't." It's the lamest sort of affirmation—one without solution or suggestion.

Ori stares at the sand. "I don't know if I can do this anymore."

"Well that's bullshit." Nomi breaks from the chain of our hands. "So . . . what? Now that our issues are taken care of, you're both just going to ditch Cass?"

Ori's eyes go wide, her head shaking while Margot says, "No one should have to sell their soul, Nomi."

"Real fucking convenient that she gets worried about her soul *right after* her shit gets taken care of."

Ori's hand falls from mine, her whispered "Stop it" lost to the wind.

I don't want this. I've never wanted this. This doesn't feel like the thing we started two weeks ago.

Margot spins to face Nomi. "We've both been worried about our souls from the moment we nearly *killed a man*, then *lied about it*. All our lives could be ruined because of that."

"Again with this? *You* didn't kill anyone. I sent you away because I fucking knew you couldn't handle it."

"Couldn't *handle it*? You say that like it's an insult, like it should be something we all accept as no big deal because *you said so*."

"I told you, Margot, feel however the fuck you want, but stop trying to make *me* feel guilty for something that had to be done. Should I have let him drag Cass into the basement with him? I didn't see you vacillating when we had Jared in the woods."

"Exactly. In the woods. And we didn't fucking kill—"

"Shut up!" Ori is breathing hard, her chest heaving, and she rubs her arms as she paces. "Margot, I can speak for myself. And, Nomi, stop acting like what you did doesn't bother you, because maybe it was the right thing but that doesn't make it easy. And, Cass . . ."

I shake my head and smoke still sticks to my hair, soot still streaks my face. Every breath still tastes like the thick fog of smoke.

But Ori, Margot, and Nomi, they're clean. Their names are clear.

"Cass." Ori slips into my line of sight, brown eyes bright in the rays of moonlight. "No one is going to leave you to finish this alone."

She holds up her wrist, the bracelet circling it waiting for mine to crash against.

I step back instead. "You should."

Nomi mutters, "Oh fuck all of you," and Margot buries her head in her hands.

I focus on the water at their backs, the reflection of the stars, the way the wind bites at my skin through my thin jacket. "I wouldn't be mad. And I still don't even know who I'm supposed to be targeting."

Ori steps forward, just an inch. "That's not the point. We agreed."

"We did. But now I'm letting you out. None of this has gone the way we expected. When I walked up and saw you all standing here, I wasn't thinking about Ronnie or Bulger or Bruce or my mom or what I was going to do next. I didn't start this to solve my problems. Honestly, I started it to avoid my problems."

I laugh, joining everyone else, and wipe a rogue tear from my cheek. "When I walked up here, I felt . . . grateful. Relieved. Vindicated. *Content.* My friends were okay, and that's all that mattered."

Nomi's voice is strangely soft. "Well you're my friend, and you're not okay, and that matters to me."

My heart lodges in my throat, tears flooding my eyes, and I sink to the sand, lowering until I'm lying on my back, flat beneath the open sky.

The beach cradles my head, cool against my skin, and if I close my eyes, I can almost conjure the scents of summer before all of this happened. "No, I'm not okay. And I can't stop what I started—I don't *want* to. I want my life back. I want to stop being afraid to live. And that means I have to see this through, but it doesn't mean you have to do it with me."

It feels like a repeat of the last time we talked like this, turned upside down. I'm not talking them into it anymore. I'm talking them out. And the voice feels like mine.

Nomi lowers beside me, our shoulders touching as she nestles into the sand. "You didn't leave me. I'm not leaving you."

Margot joins my other side, Ori next to her, until we're lined in a row, water lapping just below our feet.

Ori says, "As far as it takes. I don't go back on my promises," and beside me, Margot's breaths keep time with her tears.

She whispers, "You're my best friend, Cass. I don't know how this ends. I don't know if any of us will ever be totally okay with what we've done. But I won't leave you."

Her hand rises, a slash across the moon, her bracelet rolling down her arm until it finally comes to rest. Nomi's meets hers, then Ori's reaches to join the others as Margot mutters, "Oh my god, Ori, get off me. Your arm's crushing my tits."

My laughter rings through the night even as tears roll down my temples, and I raise my hand to meet the others.

I want to hold this moment forever too.

• • •

I kick off my shoes and leave them outside. I'd rather not explain to my dad why they're coated in sand and reek of gasoline.

Though that would require him to notice. That would require him to step free from her vortex and see the world around him. But he's not here, even though he's supposed to be. His car absent and not even a note takes its place.

The floor above me creaks, and every nerve springs alert.

Maybe this is where it ends. I don't even know who I expect to see.

I slip into the kitchen, avoiding all the spots that groan and crack, and slip the butcher knife free from the block.

I hit a man with an assault rifle today. I can stab the man who destroyed me.

I keep tight to the wall, keeping my breathing even, and something thumps to the floor.

In my room.

It's not his first visit there. I stopped thinking of it as safe the moment the first letter came. I stopped getting dressed in there the same day.

I slide down the hallway as something crashes to the ground, papers tear, and bedding flops across the room.

This isn't how he works. He's calculating, precise, silent and methodical. Items moved just a fraction, to let me know he was there.

I step into the doorway, and the knife slips from my hand, clattering to the hardwood, where it lands only inches from my feet.

Dad watches it fall, his face stricken, all color drained.

His doctor shoes lie piled on my rug, surrounded by a patchwork sea of pink envelopes and the photos I stole from Bulger's office.

The cold creep of anger slithers down my spine, all the joy and comfort from the moments on the beach erased. "Those aren't yours."

His jaw falls and a letter slips from his hand, fluttering to the floor where he sits. "Are they *yours*, Cassie?"

He gathers a stack of them, lets them fall like he can't bear to hold them. "How long?"

"They weren't yours to open. They're *mine*, and I—"

"How long?" He's off the floor, his voice booming.

"They never stopped."

He rocks on his heels, just as off-balance as that first night, when he walked into a hospital room and found me lying there, my skin raw and bruised.

The bed squeaks as he drops onto it, head in hands. "Why didn't you—"

"I did. The first one, and the second, and it didn't *help*. It made it worse, listening to them tell me the things I should've said and should've done and all the ways I fucked everything up and they still didn't catch him. They never even *believed* me."

"If you'd given them these, then—"

"Then what? Something would've changed? I gave them the first two, and all that got me was more letters. But sure. I could've kept handing them over, and maybe that would've earned me another lecture on how I opened them? How I held them? Whether I breathed on them wrong and hindered their entire investigation?"

"They were just trying to cover every angle."

"The only angle they covered was all the things I did wrong. The things I didn't do. The things I didn't look for. Their failure to find him was all my fault."

"Cassie—"

"I heard him, Dad. I heard Detective Reed say I made it up. So don't tell me they were committed to finding out what really happened."

He winces. "I never believed that was true."

"But you didn't say that to him! You *never* stood up for me!"

It's a thing I didn't know was true until the words were there, yelled from someplace inside I never looked.

I swipe away tears, my hand coming away smudged with dirt and ash.

He never stood up for me. Never defended me. Never told them I made the best decisions I could. Never said to *them* how brave I was.

He left me to fight alone.

In a battle *she* started.

Then he chose her. He gave her our patio set, and they played house and left me.

His tears match mine, but I can't bear to see them. I've never been able to see him cry.

Except this time, the anger pushes the rest away, drowns it deep.

Tears don't help me now.

His voice hoarse, he whispers, "I'm so sorry, Cass. I didn't—"

He shakes his head. "I just wanted to find the man who did this to you, and so did they. Everyone was—"

"Don't." My body shakes so hard the charms on my wrist chime, and it's only because I know what tomorrow night holds that I can finish this conversation. "Don't you dare defend them. Don't you *dare* make this my fault too."

"Look at you, Cassie." He stands, the space between us like eternities. "Your face, your hair, your clothes. You came in here holding a knife for god's sake!"

"Good thing I recognized you."

"You—you think this is a joke?"

"No. I think this has consumed every moment of my life for the last five months and I'm not letting it anymore."

He may never understand, but I have friends who do. And that will have to be enough.

Three broad steps and I reach the line of pink envelopes, the letters inside them, the photographs, scattered at my feet.

"Detective Michaels called. He said—" He scrubs his hands over his face. "He said he thinks you have been starting these fires. I told him he was wrong."

"And you came up here to prove him right? You went through my things and—"

"You're covered in ashes and reeking of fire. Margot's mom said you girls have been out every night. *Every night.* Two weeks ago I couldn't get you out of the house!"

Two weeks is fourteen days and fourteen times fourteen is . . . fuck it, I don't know.

I *do* know what this moment feels like. It feels like standing in the midst of the flames, watching them devour the walls around me, until everything that's left comes crashing down.

We're so close. The bracelet at my wrist nearly full.

One more day. Two. We just need to hold on.

Dad says, "I talked to your friend Ori's parents tonight—you had someone *impersonate* me?"

This is bad. Ori can't be implicated in any of this. "What did you say to them?"

"That's between us. The parents. The grown-ups who realize the gravity of what you girls are doing."

"None of this is Ori's fault. She wasn't involved. She—"

"This isn't some kind of game. This is *dangerous*, Cassie." He holds out the picture of the four of us, standing before the fire on that first night when we put all of this in motion.

I snatch it from his hand, and he flinches like I slapped him. "You are throwing away your life for—"

"I don't have a life!" I point to the graveyard of my existence. "This! This is what I'm throwing away. Waiting to see what he's taken from my room, what pictures he's snapped of me in my two-minute walk to school. Steeling myself for what secret he's pulled out of my head and what parts of me he knows that *no one* else does because he is *always* there."

I drop to my knees, gather them up, one by one, stacked in a neat pile. They're mine. They're every minute I've lived since the moment he stole me from that trail. And I'm going to burn them alongside him.

Then I'll carry his ashes at my wrist. Let the blood in my veins flow past them in the life I'll live when his is gone.

Dad crouches in front of me and tips my chin to meet his eyes. "I'm worried about you, Cassie. I am *so goddamned worried* about you."

I whisper, "Say it."

We sit there, until my knees go numb, neither of us willing to admit what we're both thinking.

He drops his head. "Your mother—"

"*Say* it. Say you're afraid I'm just like her. That you haven't been waiting, watching out of the corner of your eye because you didn't want to face the truth. Say you've *always* been afraid of who I am."

"You are my daughter. You are *not* your mother. And I love you, Cassie. No matter what you've done. I will *always* love you. And that means keeping you safe."

"No."

"We leave tonight, Cass."

"No." I'm off the floor, paper clutched to my chest. "We're not running again."

The wind whips through my open window, sending the curtains snapping against the air.

I don't leave the window open. Not ever.

"It doesn't have to be permanent, but you need some distance—"

"We're not finished yet." The words slip free, the lick of a flame as it crawls up a matchstick, devouring it. The fire always wins.

His face goes stricken, twisted with worry and fear.

I see it, the moment he decides it *does* have to be permanent. Another life left behind. A fresh start.

But it never has been. We've always ended back here. In my mother's galaxy, caught in her orbit.

Except this time, I've made my own.

"Cassie." Desperation clings to his voice, and when he grabs my hand, his fingers solid and warm, he squeezes too tight. Too afraid to let go. "We'll take these to Detective Michaels. We'll get you an attorney, and we'll figure this out. But I cannot allow you to continue like this. You've lied to me. Snuck around and done god knows what. You could've been injured or killed or . . ."

He trails off as I pull my hand free, and his silence grows as I reach into my pillowcase. I tug the picture free, the one of him, standing with her, on her doorstep.

I stare at it, imagining all the things they must've said to one another, thinking of all the times he wasn't here because he was *there*. Wondering what it was that broke him, made him destroy the vow we made that she was gone for good.

I turn to him. "This is her fault. You know that, right? She's the one who had me abducted?"

His face goes slack, mouth moving but not forming words until "Your mother has many faults, but she would never want you hurt like that."

"Ask her."

I don't give him a chance to shatter my heart into smaller shards as he claims he doesn't know where she is.

I hold out the photo so he has to reach to tug it from my fingertips, and as he takes in the evidence of his betrayal, the proof that he's as much a liar as me, I leave my room, then my home, with no intentions of coming back.

CHAPTER THIRTY-NINE

Friday, October 15
Zero Days Before the End

"No intentions of coming back" may have been a bit hasty.

I had no *intention* of going back home, but then I slid into my car and remembered I was filthy, the gasoline seeped into my clothes was giving me a headache, my socks still had sand in them, and I had nothing else to wear.

So I waited in Mrs. Henderson's old tree house, where I had a view of the front of my house. Where I could watch as the sun dipped lower only to rise again, flipping shadows on their heads and ushering a wave of clouds into the sky.

I listened as the chorus of coyotes howling at the burst of stars gave way to the chirp of birds, the quiet bend and crack of branches as squirrels heeded their wake-up call.

And I froze my ass off waiting for Dad to leave.

Except, Dad had visitors.

I nearly set the tree house on fire with my rage as the first one loped up the driveway, all fucking sturdy and supportive as he hugged my dad.

Hugged him.

Traitor. Backstabbing, mother-meeting, dad-supporting traitor.

I should've drowned Noah in his bathtub instead of kissing him.

I'm sure he tried to call me. I'm sure Dad has tried to call me too. My phone is in Mrs. Henderson's mailbox, turned off. That way, if Dad tries to get Detective Michaels to hunt me down, it'll lead them nowhere but right in front of our house.

I sent texts to the girls—I didn't even wait for Ori's "Wakanda

Forever"—but I kept it vague. Just enough to let them know I'm alive—for now—and won't be available.

It's honestly the best thing I know to do for them.

Noah stays in my house, being supportive, for twenty-four minutes, and as he leaves, I try to telepathically maim him.

But then.

Then the real proof arrives.

Her hair is shorter now. Her frame thinner.

I knew it was her before she even got to the house.

She always drove too fast, no matter where she was headed and no matter how much time she had.

Sunlight glances off the windows, shadows of tree branches crisscrossing her face as she waits for something I can't see.

Her fingers flex on the wheel. Open and shut. Grasp and release.

I've never seen her nervous. Angry, frustrated, impatient. Annoyed and furious.

But never nervous.

The front door swings open, and Dad stands in the frame, waiting.

I can't watch this.

This was why we promised. Why we removed her from our lives and made a pact to never go back.

It's like nothing has changed, even when everything has.

He's still watching her, his life on hold while he waits for her next move. His eyes tracking over the car she can't possibly afford, wondering, too scared to ask all the questions she won't answer anyway.

I roll onto my back, let the tears trickle over my temple and drown themselves in the tangles of my hair. I watch the clouds float overhead and birds flutter from branch to branch, never settling.

I close my eyes and wait for them both to leave so I won't do all the things that growing fire inside me tells me I should.

CHAPTER FORTY
CASS ADAMS

The Events of Friday, October 15
The Morning of the End

It was only me when the cops came to my house that Friday, two days after we took Jared into the woods, one day after the warehouse. No Nomi, Ori, or Margot to lie for me or corroborate my story.

Detective Michaels didn't come to talk about Jared. Jared was the one revenge we never had to answer for. His silence was the price for keeping the video of his confession a secret.

Detective Michaels came for everything else. He showed up at my doorstep with nothing but suspicion in his eyes.

He asked about the license plate from Edward Bulger's car. The one I found, alongside Noah, in the woods.

Funny coincidence, he says, finding a license plate that belonged to a dead man whose son worked at my school.

"Coincidence" is not the word I'd use, but I keep those thoughts to myself. I tell him how much I wish I could help, but then, I've never been very good at getting things right, have I?

He asks where I was, two nights ago, on a Wednesday night where someone set a fire in the woods.

The smoke, he says, drew the attention of several park rangers. The scene, they said, didn't appear to be a normal campfire. And why, he asks, have I been captured on camera buying so many gallons of gasoline. So many fire extinguishers at the nearby hardware stores.

We weren't ready. I knew that. I knew we'd have to take risks, and I took them.

We were halfway there, and I refused to turn back.

He says my name that way adults do, in the moment the decision in front of them becomes clear.

He has every reason to ask these questions at the station. Every right to question my whereabouts for the night of Jared and the night of Mr. Valco.

Especially the night of Mr. Valco.

I gave up pretending last night, when I brought Detective Michaels the evidence that will fulfill Ori's request to see Mr. Valco humiliated and destroyed. I showed up on Michaels's doorstep, my clothes still reeking of smoke and gasoline, my face still smudged with soot, and I laid waste to the idea I could escape this unscathed.

It's the only way I summon the courage to stand there, my arms braced on the doorframe beside me, charms twinkling in the rays of sun. Three of them full. One more waiting.

"Cass," he says again, harder this time. "It's well past time I tell your father about *all* of this. I can't ignore you coming to the station yesterday."

I close my eyes, just long enough to see myself standing in my mother's skin, to pour her essence into mine so I can do what needs to be done. "I don't want you to ignore it. It's evidence."

I look him in the eyes, mine holding guilt for nothing, regret for less. "I want you to go through all of it, and I want you to find every person responsible or involved."

"You left an unconscious man in the middle of the parking lot."

"Incorrect. He was . . . off to the side. In the grass."

He blinks. "Guns, Cass. You brought assault rifles into the station."

"I know." Duffel bags filled with them, the straps cutting into my shoulder and numbing my arms. My fingers clenched around the computer in my other hand.

I stood in the entrance, every set of eyes on me and every hand poised over a gun, and I asked for Detective Michaels.

Then I dropped them all at his feet.

"This path you're on," Detective Michaels says, "it's dangerous. This does not end well for you."

I drop my arms and my charms jingle on the way down, and as I close the door in his face, I reply, "I think you're wrong about that."

CHAPTER FORTY-ONE

Friday, October 15
Zero Days Before the End

My phone is still in Mrs. Henderson's mailbox, but I am showered, fed, and armed with a duffel bag filled with the necessities.

I am also sitting outside the home of Coach Bulger's father.

The visit I got from Detective Michaels is proof that I'm running out of time, and I still need answers to how Ronnie, my mom, and Bulger fit together. I can't trust my mother to tell me the truth, and I have no idea where to find Ronnie, so Bulger it is. And I'm armed with the pictures of me from his desk and wallet. I *will* get answers about those. Or die trying. The last time I walked through that door, I found a man soaked in his own blood.

I breathe deep, let the twisting in my stomach calm, and I relax my fingers from the steering wheel.

I'm supposed to wait for the girls for this. But it's a school day, Margot's and Ori's parents are sure to be watching everything they do, and this isn't the final act. It's better that I do this alone anyway—the truth, where my mother is concerned, has never been pretty.

Bulger isn't watching me. He's loading things into the dumpster beside the house, carrying boxes to his truck, directing the guys that came to load up some shiny vintage car onto a flatbed.

The kind of car Bruce and his chop shop would pay excellent money for—and another connection to my mother falls into place. That means what happened to Edward Bulger is partially her fault too.

His funeral is Sunday, according to Margot's text. Bulger's father hasn't even been laid to rest, and he's already throwing away his things.

I hold tight to my anger, twist it around itself until it's in a knot that can't be undone.

I hold my bracelet to my chest and remember.

We're almost done.

I fling open my car door and head across the street, straight to the back door.

It's propped open, a rock crammed in the corner of the frame, and I slip into a soundless house.

Boxes sit strewn over the room, overflowing with pots, pans, bundles of kitchen towels.

The breeze tunnels through the back door and ruffles the calendar tacked to the wall, the string of thick black Xs through the dates giving way to empty boxes instead.

I need Bulger to be on this level, not upstairs. I don't know that I can climb those steps again.

I step forward, linoleum squeaking beneath my shoes, and grab a knife from the block that lies in one of the boxes.

The metal glints in the rays of the midday sun, the blade sharp and wicked.

I don't know if I can stab a man.

A crash explodes in the air, and my feet leave the floor, my head cracking against the wall.

I try to scream, but there's no air, only the crush of pressure against my throat. Just like he did to Ronnie.

I don't want to die. That's all I know to think.

"Cass?"

The pressure eases, the heat of his fingers seared into my skin, and I blink to clear the blur from my vision.

"Cass Adams?"

He says it like he's not sure. Like maybe I'm some other girl he hoards creepy pictures of.

He steps back, giving me room. "I'm sorry. I'm so sorry." He pauses. "I guess I'm a little on edge, being here."

I force myself to speak, my voice gravelly as I edge out of his reach. "Bad memories? Like the time you stabbed your own father?"

His face blanches, his eyes stricken. "I what?"

"What about the pictures of me in your locked office drawer? Or in your fucking wallet. The—"

"Stop." He runs his hands through his hair, and his mouth works like he doesn't know the words he needs. "Cass, I don't—"

"Shut up!" My voice is hysterical, even to my ears, betraying just how lost I am, about everything. I need answers but can't even get the questions to form right.

I grab the pictures and throw them at his feet. "I know everything."

I know nothing.

I inch toward the door, my back pressed hard to the wall. "But I need you to admit she had me kidnapped. I need the truth."

And *that's* why I'm here. I couldn't admit it before, but now I can't deny it.

A tear tracks down my cheek, and I hate that I'm crying in front of him.

His gaze bounces between me and the floor, and he drops to his knees. His hands hover over the photos, like he's afraid to touch them.

He whispers, "My god," as tears fill his eyes. "Cass, I'm so sorry. I had no idea—about any of this."

If Bulger was my stalker, he'd be telling me it shows how much he loves me, that he's proud of me for putting it all together. That we're the same, both of us, hiding our secrets and breaking all the rules.

He may not have thrown me in that trunk, but that doesn't mean he's free from guilt.

"I found those *in your desk*. I found *these* in your wallet." I shove the pictures in front of me.

His face cycles through too many emotions to catalog, then he sighs.

He clears a box from the chair and motions me toward it with one hand, the other patting his pockets. "You can have a seat right there and give me a second, okay?"

He scans the room, until his gaze snags on his phone, and he's two steps toward it when he kicks the knife that *used* to be in my hand, sending it spinning across the room.

Guess that answers the question about whether I can kill a man face-to-face. I can't even hang on to the knife.

But I am *not* stupid enough to have a seat—1 inch closer to the door.

He holds out his hands, like he's trying to calm a cornered animal. "I don't even know where to start."

"Start with the truth."

"I didn't kill my father, Cass."

"Liar. You *admitted* it. You told me you did." I replay that whole conversation, trying to make sense of it, but my head is too jumbled, like all the *fear uncertainty frustration rage* are pouring out of me with no way to stop them.

He heads toward his phone, his eyes never leaving me, and it hits me then—he thinks I'm the dangerous one.

He reaches the phone and holds it up. "See this? I'm supposed to be calling either the school or 911 right now."

"Then why aren't you?"

"Because you've had a rough five months. And because whatever you *think* you have figured out is wrong. I didn't kill my dad. I did not take those pictures. I'm very sorry, Cass, that someone did those things to you, and I hope the police are searching for whoever did, but it was *not* me. And because if you know something about the fucker who killed my dad, I want to hear it firsthand, not through those asshole detectives."

The room tilts, everything sideways and inside out. I didn't know how much I wanted this all to be him until this very moment. Bulger alone, a straight connection that started with me and him on a trail in the woods. An obsession with me that led to my mother too. I've been wanting to believe it all along.

But it's not. It's not Bulger. And that means it started with her. It means the real stalker is just as dangerous as Nomi said. Someone as dangerous as Ronnie, who held a knife to my throat without blinking. She sent a man like that after me.

I've tried not to believe it. Not truly believe it. But now it's real, and every part of me is twisted and torn apart.

"That day at the school, why were you attacking Ronnie?"

"Shit." He holds out his hand, palm up. "I saw him pull into the school that day, and I . . . made him tell me why he was there, and he said he was looking for you."

My blood goes hot and cold at the same time. Ronnie was there for me that day, with his knife, just like in the alley, and if Bulger hadn't stopped him—

But something else slots into place. "You weren't just defending *me* that day, were you?"

He was way too angry over some random dude that did nothing more than ask for me. That fight between him and Ronnie was personal.

I say, "And how do you know what I've been through the last five months? First you said you didn't know anything, then you said I'd had a rough five months."

He rubs the back of his neck, and even through the hazy shade of dusk in the unlit kitchen, a blush rises in his cheeks. "I, uhhh. Well . . ."

"My mother."

It always comes back to her. She didn't just ruin my life, she dragged Bulger into this too. He thought he was protecting her from Ronnie. He thought he could save her, because he's just as much of an idiot as me and Dad.

That's what kept him away from me in the hallway that day, why he defended me when Ronnie came, why he pushed to get me back to conditioning—not guilt for what he'd done to me. Embarrassment for knowing what he knew. His *pity*.

Bulger says, "We sort of dated, for a bit."

"Until?"

There's a flash of anger, the kind only my mother can elicit, but it gets swallowed by something else. "My old man, he restores old cars. *Restored* old cars."

He clears his throat and wipes away a tear. "Anyway, didn't take too long for me to figure out it wasn't me she was interested in."

"She wanted the cars."

"Yeah." The blush is unmistakable now, a bright red that's spread to his neck and beneath his sweat-dampened shirt, and I'd bet anything he's lying about one thing—it took him plenty long to figure it out. And he hasn't put together that it's the reason he's clearing out his father's house.

"And Ronnie?"

"They were together, before we were." He mumbles, "Or maybe during," and he's probably not wrong.

"Don't feel bad. This is sort of what she does. I'm her own daughter, and she had me kidnapped."

He shoves an empty box to the floor and nearly crumples into the chair. "I can't believe that's true."

I rest my head against the wall and breathe in the mix of crisp fall air and the cloying scent of bleach. "Then you're not trying hard enough. My whole life, people always dismissed the things she did just because she was my mother. They're not all fit for Hallmark cards, you know?"

His gaze travels the length of the room, like it's all starting to make sense, like through the haze of grief and shock, the real picture has started to take form.

"Cass." His voice is gravel. "Do you know who killed my old man?"

God do I wish I could say yes. I wish I was sure about anything. "I told him—who I thought was you—that I knew he killed his dad, and he said it was an accident."

His mouth stutters open. "You talked to him on the phone? Do you have the number? If we could get the cops to trace it, we could find him."

Tears well in his eyes, and I wish I could feed his hope rather than snuff it out. But this is no fairy tale and there are no happy endings here. "I'm sorry. He called me on a phone he left for me, and there was no caller ID. And even if there was, I'm sure it's untraceable."

He curses under his breath. "You said you found these photos in my desk? In my wallet?" He blinks, and his eyes fill with suspicion.

My face heats, because it feels a lot like I majorly invaded the privacy of someone whose worst sin was dating my mother. "I was looking for proof. I *found* proof."

"*When* and *how* did you find these?"

I don't answer. Won't answer. I went through his things. I hid in the locker room. *We're not so different, you and I.*

"Cass, this has gone long enough. I'm calling the cops."

"No!" The words leave my mouth with a confidence I don't feel. "If my mother meant anything to you, you won't. She'd want you to help me."

She wouldn't. She'd only tell him not to call to save herself, but he doesn't know that.

"I can't—"

"I'll tell them I think it was you."

He straightens, the full impact of what I'm saying settling into his bones.

Her picture, the one from the warehouse, stares up at me, and I do what she would've done.

I don't stop until it's finished. "I'll tell them what I found. Where I found it. I'll show them the other pictures and all the letters, and I'll tell them about how you've been watching me. Or, you can let me handle this."

He looks sick, his skin sallow, and when he stumbles back into the chair he cleared off for me, my resolve nearly crumbles.

It's not just the guilt. It's the way he looks at me. I know what he's seeing right now—he sees *her*.

He looks away first, his gaze falling to the picture of my mother that lies between us.

And that's when the world stops, because for the first time, I recognize exactly where that picture was taken.

Margot's backyard.

CHAPTER FORTY-TWO

Friday, October 15
Zero Days Before the End

Another layer.

Bulger is not my stalker, Ronnie was looking for me because of my mother, and she was a visitor at Margot's house.

He wanted me to know it. He told me to look closer.

I don't want to believe Margot had anything to do with this. That she would betray me. That she could've hugged me as I recounted what happened if she'd known everything. That she didn't *pretend* while I told her about the time I thought I was going to die, and all the moments after when I wondered if it would have been a blessing to.

I don't want to believe, but the clue that led us to Valco was legit, and I need to prove whether this one is too.

But without my phone, I'm cut off from the world. My dad could have an entire search party set to turn me in the second anyone spots me, and the girls' parents are sure to be on high alert.

That leaves me with one person who would know the gossip, who has a view of Margot's house, and who—loath as I am to admit its usefulness—will never lie to me.

Except I'm not talking to Noah right now. Or ever.

I drum my fingers against the steering wheel, willing the universe to give me another way. Because calling Noah is admitting I have his number memorized. Permanently engraved in my brain cells from the nights spent staring at it, daring myself to call and tell him I didn't want to be just friends anymore.

But now I don't want to be friends *at all* because he's a traitor and I'd rather die on this hill of pettiness.

Only, I got shot at yesterday and today isn't looking great either, so maybe I need to rethink the petty dying thing.

Fuck it.

I pick up the phone Tyler gave me and dial.

It barely makes it past the first ring.

"Cass?"

"Does my name show on your caller ID? This phone is from the black market. It's supposed to be untraceable."

I pull the phone from my ear to check the screen, but Noah's voice makes it to me anyway. "*That's* the first thing you say? Are you fucking kidding me?"

Followed by "Wait. Don't hang up. I didn't mean that." A pause. "Yes I did. I've called you twenty times today."

"My phone is in a mailbox."

"Of course it is." He sucks in a breath like he's about to say something else and thinks better of it. "Cass, are you okay?"

I shove from the car and pace the gravel lot, kicking up tiny clouds of dirt that settle into my socks and shoes. "Physically or emotionally? I think it's the same for both. Bulger's not my stalker, FYI. It might be this guy named Ronnie, who held a knife to my throat once, and it's very possible my mom sent him to? So that's how my day has gone."

"I—"

"Don't. Don't say you're sorry, or any of the things you want to say."

He pauses, like it's taking everything in him to do what I'm asking, and then he says, "Okay," and I whisper a thank-you.

Then I completely and obviously change the subject. "For real though, did my name show up on your screen?"

He sighs so loudly I nearly pull the phone away again, until he finally says, "No. Your name doesn't show up. I was just hoping it was you, since everything is going to *shit* today, and your dad is just waiting on paperwork to make you an official missing person."

I do not need cops right now. But if he's waiting on paperwork, I have time.

I force my voice even, infuse it with calm. "Do you know where Margot is?"

"Why'd you say it like that?"

"I didn't say it like anything. My voice is infused with calm."

"For fuck's sake, Cass."

"Okay, fine. Hold on." I snap a photo of the picture of my mom, then text it. "Where is she in this picture?"

The line goes quiet for a half second while he opens the text, and he must recognize it immediately because he mutters, "Shit."

"Yeah. I need you to look next door and tell me if Margot or her mom are home."

"So you can break in?"

"No. I have a key. Margot gave it to me last year."

He pauses, undoubtedly gathering his patience, while the sun drifts just a bit lower in the sky. "They're not home. Margot's at practice, and her mom is probably at the school so she can criticize every play Margot makes while missing none of the gossip."

My lungs go hollow. "What gossip?"

"The shit about Mr. Valco. He's a white-supremacist Nazi. I mean that literally. Not just that he's a racist shitbag. We've known that for years."

I put on my movie poker face even though he can't see me, focus on the distance where the swings that used to hold children now rock listlessly in the wind.

There's no way Detective Michaels worked that fast. Rumors, maybe.

But anything official would require an investigation, and he's barely had time to start one. "Oh. Wow. How do you know?"

"I know your voice, Cass, and your lack of surprise is noted. There are pictures of him in his full douchefuck costume with all his shitfuck friends on every social media platform, including the official Stoneybrook Facebook page. They took it down, but screenshots are forever."

I should act natural. Say things in a way that mimics normal human behavior. "Any idea who posted them?"

"No one knows." He pauses. "Or no one is saying. They posted it under the initials 'W.F.'"

It takes a second, but then I get it, and not even my poker face practice is enough to stop the snort that escapes my mouth.

Wakanda Forever. Ori is a treasure that should be protected from all evil in this world.

He sighs again, like he's too tired to fight that battle right now, and the deep baritone of his voice hits my ear. "Cass, where are you?"

"I can't tell you that. What did you mean when you said everything's going to shit?"

"I can't tell you that. Where are you?"

"I hate you, Noah. I really do."

"Hate me all you want. I have information. You need it."

"I'm leaving soon anyway."

"Fine, then name the time and place."

I do, because he *does* have information and I *do* need it.

But first, I have a house to not break into.

CHAPTER FORTY-THREE

Friday, October 15
Zero Days Before the End

I tear apart every inch of Margot's room, looking for something, *anything* to prove her guilt or her innocence.

Then I move to the den, the living room, the spare bedroom and even her parents' room, searching for some sliver of proof.

Then I make it to the basement, past the area where we spent hours talking, where we developed our plans and swore to each other, and into the craft room, where I finally find what I'm looking for.

The ribbon. A half-full spool that matches the one I found at the motel and the note hanging in my locker. Same pattern. Same colors.

Now they're all stuffed in my bag. One of them dirty, another looped into a bow, the knot still wound tight. And now I need Margot. I need to show her what I found, watch for her reaction—the one thing that will tell me if our friendship really exists.

Someone planted evidence on Bulger, but he couldn't plant my mother in Margot's backyard.

My tires screech to a halt outside Stoneybrook High School, kicking up bits of asphalt and blooming a cloud of burnt rubber.

Kids I don't know clear from my path, even as their gazes stay locked across the lot. I follow them to the woman wearing sensible heels and sporting expertly coiffed hair—and the man with the enormous camera beside her.

Video camera. Currently live. Camera light trained right on my face.

Excellent. I've made the six o'clock news. My dad and Detective Michaels will know where I am within the hour.

I sprint up the sidewalk, beating the reporter and her heels by a mile, except the door is locked.

I slam my fist into it, praying there's someone on the other side to hear it. School security never did me a bit of good over the last five months, nice to know it's majorly fucking me over now.

"Excuse me, miss?"

I pound so hard my wrist aches, but no one comes to my rescue.

"We're with WKDV Channel 4, and we're following up on a story about a teacher here."

I turn and do my best to avoid being that person that stares at the camera while the reporter says, "We've received reports that claim a Mr. Valco may be linked to a local white-supremacists group in the area, and various pictures have been posted on social media sites and even emailed to several school board members."

I couldn't be prouder of Ori right now.

I also know if people find out she's the one who exposed Valco and all his friends, it will destroy her life.

Luckily, I've got one that's already a mess.

The cameraman steps in closer, blinding me with his light, and the reporter's voice takes on an edge of desperation. "Are you a student here?"

"Yes."

"And what's your name?"

"Wanda Ferris." Great work, Cass. Wanda was an excellent choice. Very hip.

"Okay . . . Wanda. Care to comment?"

"I would!" The door behind me swings open, and some poor freshman goes blank at the sight of a camera. I shove him inside and prop the door with my foot. "Mr. Valco is a piece of shit, and everything people are saying is true. I hope he's fired. I hope he's arrested, and I hope he's put on trial for hate crimes. You can quote me. Wanda Ferris."

I jump inside and slam the door shut, blocking out the bomb I've just set off in what's left of my future.

The halls are empty. It's always been weird to walk them at night, an expectant sort of hush blanketing the surface.

Like we didn't quite belong there, like we were breaking some sort of rule, free to destroy a handful more if we wanted.

It was just like this, last year with Noah, on *that* night.

Only then it was the birth of spring, when everything felt alive, on the verge of days spent lying in grass and leisurely trips to the lake. It felt filled with promise.

That's why I kissed him. I let myself believe there were good things ahead.

My therapist says I'm allowed to hope for things. She says it's okay to enjoy the positives without waiting for the negatives. I hope she's right.

I slam open the gym door, the clack of metal exploding through the room, and my entire volleyball team spins to face me.

Well, not my team anymore. Not since that night.

Lights glare off the shiny floor, its surface scuffed with a thousand shoe marks from students living their ordinary lives.

It feels like something I can never belong to again. I wonder if it was like that for my mom, if that's why she could never live the way we needed her to. She didn't know how.

The volleyball dribbles from Margot's hand, and Coach Pheran yells, "Adams! Suit up or get out."

Shelly screeches, "She's not even *on* the team anymore!" but I ignore her and Coach, all my attention on Margot.

I yell across the gym, "Did you know?"

Margot widens her eyes and gives the smallest jerk of her head. "Cass! We've been so worried about you!"

She runs toward me, wrapping me in a hug. Her smile is still plastered to her face when she hisses, "Where in the hell have you been?"

I stumble as she releases me and turns to the group. "Hey, great news, everyone! Cass is fine. She's not missing. So we should probably all just stop . . . spreading rumors and—"

"Margot!"

She lets out a little squeak and mutters, "Oh shit," as her mom walks into the gym.

I don't care who's here to witness this. I don't care who hears or what rumors they start.

I need to know who I can trust, and I need to know if my best friend was truly part of this.

I say, "Were you involved?"

Her brows knit, ruby-red lips moving but forming no sounds. "Involved in what?"

"In having me kidnapped. Yanked from the trails and hands bound and tape on my mouth to muffle my screams. *Were you involved?*"

I yank the ribbons from my bag and hold them all up. "One of these is how the stalker hung his note in my locker. One is from the motel where he followed me when I went looking for my mom. And the last one, Margot, is from your house."

I can't look at the faces surrounding me, all my teammates' reactions to questions they've been asking for the last five months.

None of them have moved, the whole room locked in collective shock.

"Say no." Tears burn in my eyes and my voice wobbles. "Please say no."

After that night, the four of us in the woods, hands clasped, after last night on the beach, my wrist pressed to hers, after everything, I need her to be the person I thought she was. I need to believe it was real.

"No, Cass. Oh my god, no." She nearly tackles me into a hug, whispering so fast I can't make out the words, and sobs rack through me so hard my entire body shakes.

I'm crushing her, squeezing too hard like she's doing to me, but I can't let go. I need her to hear the words I'm barely stringing together—that I'm sorry, so sorry, that I had to ask, and she shushes me, whispering that it's okay.

Then someone behind her clears their throat, and we both go still.

I'm going to kill Shelly if she says even one word.

She doesn't. She just darts her eyes across the gym.

To Margot's mom.

I've never seen Mrs. Pennington so still, her face so devoid of color. The hand that holds the phone to her ear shakes.

She's terrified. Bone-deep, life-altering terrified, and there can only be one reason.

It was never Margot involved in my kidnapping. It was her mom.

If she conspired with my mother to have someone kidnap me, there is only *one* person she'd be calling right now.

And considering how he shot at me the last time, I'd rather Bruce not know where to find me.

I grab a ball from Lola's hands and toss it high, two steps, jump, and I serve it into Mrs. Pennington's face.

She screams as it slams into her, snapping her head back and sending her phone sliding across the floor.

Mrs. Pennington stumbles, and Margot's voice cuts the silence, a yell amid the gasps and whispers. "What did you do? What the fuck did you do? Mom!"

I run to the phone and the initials "B.T." display above a call timer that ticks upward, Bruce's voice calling to Mrs. Pennington from the speaker.

I put it to my ear as he falls silent, and despite my total certainty that it's the wrong thing to do, I say, "Bruce. It's Cass. And I know everything."

The gym doors fly open and Detective Michaels storms through them, and I am majorly, royally fucked because he's blocking the path to my car.

He says, "C'mon now, Cass. I told you how this ends."

I take a step back as he moves forward, past where Margot looms over her mother, who whimpers, "I did it for you, baby," and the gym erupts as Margot tackles her the rest of the way to the ground.

The team rushes forward, a mass of bodies trying to separate them or secure a front-row seat.

Detective Michaels calls my name, and I'm debating whether to take my chances of outrunning him when hands wrap around my wrist and something cold presses against my palm.

Shelly hisses, "South lot. Red Jeep," and shoves me toward the locker room.

Of all people, Shelly was not the person I expected to save me.

I sprint through the locker room to the sound of Detective Michaels yelling my name, but he won't follow. Not through here. But there's something that snags in my brain, something I can't quite pinpoint.

I jam the panic button on Shelly's keys so many times I'll probably owe her a new one, and when I finally burst through the south-lot doors, her lights are flashing, horn honking.

Three jumped curbs later, I swing out onto the road on my way to Noah, and that's when it hits me, the thing my mind refused to process and refused to forget.

The initials on Mrs. Pennington's phone.

CHAPTER FORTY-FOUR

Friday, October 15
Zero Days Before the End

This is the park where I last spoke to my mother. Where we sat across from the picnic table, Dad's hand wrapped so tight in mine my fingers crushed together, and we told her what we'd decided.

This was the end, we said.

She cried, but by then her tears had become a cloud of breath on the dawn of winter. All the weight floating away like they'd never been.

I'd given up crying for her long before.

I sit at the picnic bench, on her side, the paint more worn, wood more warped, and I watch the sun drown in the horizon.

Notes of fresh-cut grass and bonfires lace air that's thinned from fall's approach. Laughter drifts from across the hill, where kids slip down slides and fly on swings, all of them bundled in thick coats and warm sweatshirts.

It's a night made for lying on blankets in the grass, watching the stars track the path of the moon.

It's a night for held hands and whispered secrets. But I've had too many of both.

Noah sits across from me, and his hands flex and release, blood vessels straining beneath his skin, the set of his jaw tighter with every passing second.

His forearms, planted against the picnic table, cage the pink envelopes, the letters, the pictures, the tokens taken from my room and gifted back to me.

It's all there, everything my life has been reduced to, laid out in a circle small enough to fit in someone's arms.

B.T.

Those are Bruce's initials.

I don't know his last name, but I can guess, and if I'm right, a million other connections snap into place.

A direct connection to Bruce. To Bulger. And to me.

It was never Ronnie—he never had any reason to care about me at all, and certainly not enough to attempt to help me find the truth about my mother. He's just another of her victims, seeking revenge through any means possible, including me.

It's not Bulger and it's not Ronnie. It's the one person who knew when I'd be looking through Bulger's office. The one person who *suggested* the exact day and time to be there.

I scan through every moment of that morning, replaying every slice of memory. The partially unlocked drawer, just enough so I could force it open. The file folder lying at the bottom of the rest—manilla with a blue smudge.

Memories click into place. Tyler scrawling out his phone number, his watch sliding across the desk, the ink smudging across the paper.

His watch. On his left hand. People wear watches on their nondominant hand.

Tyler, punching that guy at my mom's house. With his right hand.

"Noah." My voice breaks the silence, jolting him from his trance. "Tyler said Bulger wanted him on the baseball team because he's a left-hand hitter."

He blinks, pausing while his mind reorients. "Tyler is a switch hitter. He's—"

"Ambidextrous." I finish it for him.

I was right, that time I theorized my stalker became a different version of himself. Different personality. Different handwriting. Switch flipped.

He set me up to find that evidence, to give him time to get closer to me, pull me in deeper. He sent me looking in the wrong direction so I wouldn't look in his.

Noah says my name, but he can't compete with the roar in my head.

Tyler has access to school.

He has connections to the same people as my mother and access to a phone that's untraceable.

He knows everything about me.

He knew what to say and when to say it because he's studied all the things to cut to the softest part of me.

I kissed him. Let him touch me. In truth, I barely know him. A handful of conversations. Lunches where we sat near each other but never really talked.

But when we did, I never had to explain. He *knew*, in a way only people who've been through the same things can know. He knew what to say because he'd helped himself to part of my life I never granted him access to.

He terrorized me to keep me off-balance, to give me a reason to need him, tried to make me question my friends and their loyalty. I told him things, pieces of me I didn't trust with the rest of the world. But every bit of that trust was another weapon for him, another weak spot for him to sink himself into, to twist and carve out until, one day, all of me would be replaced with all of him.

He created a world I couldn't live with, then offered me a way to escape it. With him.

"Offer still stands, Bonnie. You and me, we set this place on fire and run."

CHAPTER FORTY-FIVE

Friday, October 15
Zero Days Before the End

I don't know how long I stand there, my fingertips gouging the wood of the picnic table, seeing all those letters, all those photos, with new eyes.

Noah waits, says nothing, while my mind struggles to see Tyler in the place of a nameless threat.

Tyler said his dad was gone. *Gone* is not a forty-minute drive away.

Of course, I said my mother was gone too.

But that night at her house doesn't fit—me, hiding in the bushes, finding the next letter taped to the door.

Tyler could *not* have put it there. Not even with some magician-level sleight of hand. We walked in at the same time. There was no place he could've stashed a pink envelope that I wouldn't have seen it. I literally plastered myself to him the entire ride.

But to pull it free, tape it, and stick it to the door? No way. Not even a single chance. Maybe I'm as wrong about him as I was about Bulger.

I scour every note. Every photo. Searching every corner and each word until my fingers go numb.

Only the last photo is different. The paper thinner. Only one word scrawled on the back. The picture of Tyler.

He could've taken his own photo and scratched out his own eyes. Theoretically.

There's been no jealously homicidal screaming phone call like with Noah. But then, everything that happened with Tyler was inside the walls of my mother's bedroom. There was no way to see in there. Not like with Noah.

And that day in the woods, he was *right next* to me when I got the phone call.

"Cass." I startle at the sound of Noah's voice, and he squeezes our linked hands. "What are you thinking?"

I pull free so I can pace. "I'm missing something. So my mother accosts you and Margot's mom. Somehow she ends up at her house. My mother and Bruce and maybe even Ronnie are all involved in having me kidnapped, roping Margot's mom into the whole mess because that's what she does. Then Bruce sent Tyler and touched off a string of pink letters. That's all the pieces but no answers. And that's not good enough."

Noah nods, easing from the picnic bench. "Cool. You find your answers. I'm going to go kill Tyler now."

I'm blocking his path before he can take his first step, and I poke him in the chest. "One: I don't even know it's him. Two: If it *is* him, it should be me that kills him. And three: You owe me information."

He lowers his voice, too gravelly for a whisper. "I told you that day in chem that you should avoid him. I've known him a lot longer, and I don't fucking trust him. Never have."

"Because he's automatically just like his dad, right?"

"No, because sometimes people earn their reputations all on their own. Even if he didn't do all this, Cass"—he points to the mess of papers on the table—"can you honestly say he wants what's best for you? Or does he just want you for himself?"

"I'm not stupid, Noah."

I didn't let Tyler keep me from my friends. I didn't stop trusting them. I didn't take his opinion as truth on anything. But then, there were moments where he offered a way out, a way to leave all this behind and I wanted to take it.

"I know you're not. That's my point. You want to self-destruct? Fine.

Your choice. But don't expect me to help. Find someone else to pull the pin."

He stares at me, gives time for his words to sink in as he points again toward the pile of letters only feet from us. "But I guess you already have."

I hope he doesn't know how right he is. I hope he never finds out.

Because Tyler's always been the one with the finger on the grenade. The match strike beside the pool of gasoline.

We'd burn together. Bonnie and Clyde. *Set the world on fire.*

Dangerous. That's the word they use when they talk about the four of us. About the things we've done and the things we still have planned.

But it's me they should be afraid of. I'm my mother's daughter. A trail of destruction everywhere we go.

I may not want to set the world on fire with Tyler, but I won't burn Noah like my mother did to Dad.

I back away, far enough he can't reach me again. "Tell me."

He nods, just once, and it says everything he needs it to. "You're officially missing. You have a lawyer now. Maybe you should give him a ring on your *black-market phone.*"

"You've just been waiting for the chance to bring that up—"

"From the moment you told me, yes." He smiles, and I roll my eyes.

"What's going on with the girls?"

He sighs. "Nomi wasn't at school. Word is she's hunkered down at the police station with her dad."

"Shit. Ori?"

"On lockdown."

My heart stutters, and I focus on the leaves swaying in the wind. If Ori's in trouble, I'll find a way to fix it.

Noah whispers my name, staring down at me, and I know what he's going to say even though he promised he wouldn't.

That was the deal. I'd tell him the truth, and he promised no pity. No "I'm so sorry" or "I had no idea." No platitudes about how strong I am or sad, puppy-dog eyes that make me feel damaged.

He threads his fingers through my hair and forces me to look him in the eye, which I've done an excellent job of avoiding so far. "One: Fuck your rules. I'm sorry this happened to you. Two: You can kill him first, and I'll make sure he's dead by killing him again. Three: I don't *pity* you, Cass."

"Right." I pull free, night air cold against my skin where the heat of his hands belongs. "That's why in your car at the motel—"

I stop because I can't bring myself to say the rest. Because I hate myself for saying the beginning.

"I didn't stop you because I pitied you. I stopped you because you were sad."

"Angry."

"Fine, both. But you sure as fuck weren't happy."

"Next time I'll be sure to wear a mood ring, and we can end the problem before it starts!"

Noah tips his chin toward the space over my shoulder, and I turn to see an elderly couple, openly staring. If they were hoping to voyeur on some teen romance, they've definitely come to the wrong picnic table.

I rub my temples—this is not the time for an emotional meltdown.

I have one goal. Put the picture together. Discover who deserves my vengeance. "Why didn't you ever tell me about my mom visiting you?"

"Is that a serious question?"

"Okay, fair." I *did* fake laryngitis to get out of speaking to him about something as mundane as chemistry.

"Maybe she didn't know." He won't look at me when he says it, like he doesn't trust himself to make it convincing.

I rub my arms against the chill that seeps deeper into my bones with every passing minute.

I'm running out of time for all the things I need to do.

"Yeah, sure. That's why she admitted, on speakerphone, that she did stuff she didn't want me to know about. Speaking of, I need your phone."

"Not a chance."

"Fine. Have fun when the cops call you in for questioning and you can't say you don't know anything. I need you to google something."

"Well now, that's sad." He makes a show of pulling his phone from his pocket. "Two black-market phones and no Google."

I mouth, "Hate you," and the bastard not only notices but smiles in return.

"I need Bruce Thorne's address."

Noah moves in slow motion, letting his phone drop back into his pocket. "Yeah, we're done here."

Then he's charging toward his car without so much as a pause when I call his name.

I cram all my letters and pictures together into a pile and run after him—past him—over the paths and through the grass that tickles my ankles.

By the time I throw all my evidence into my car, he's opening the door to his, and I block his path just in time, wedging myself inside the triangle of space. "Noah, I need you to move."

It takes only the smallest glance to see there's no reasoning that will appease him. Clemency for Tyler hinged on only one thing—me behaving with some measure of common sense and staying as far from the Thorne family as possible.

I shouldn't have let him read the letters. I shouldn't have told him about Tyler. I shouldn't have involved him in any of this.

After everything, I'm still making the wrong decisions.

"Noah." My palm presses into his chest, and his muscles go taut but don't yield. "I'm the one that gets to kill him."

For a moment, I think it might work. That stable, sturdy, rational, practical Noah will listen to reason and walk away.

For a moment, I think he might save himself.

Instead, he says, "Not if I get to him first."

CHAPTER FORTY-SIX
CASS ADAMS

The Events of Friday, October 15, Evening
The End

THIS IS THE END.

THIS IS THE BEGINNING.

That's what the note read. The final note. The one that would spiral us toward all the answers I'd been searching for.

All the answers I'd soon discover would tear everything apart. The end and the beginning, and I needed both.

In some ways, that night is like the one when he grabbed me from the trail in the woods—a thing I have to view in bits and pieces so I can handle facing the whole. A thing I've blocked out in moments of blurry vagueness that compete with memories imprinted in excruciating detail.

But this I remember: He knew I'd go. At the time he said. To the location he said. Deep in the city, one of the dark areas of downtown, where we'd be alone, unbothered.

The street held more vacant lots than houses, and those that still stood bore no trace of triumph.

Their roofs caved, windows left jagged, porches limping and falling away. Grass swayed tall, bristling with the kiss of wind.

Streetlights stood tall but empty, their lights long since gone out, only moonlight to replace them.

But in the house, the one he told me to find, a flame flickers in the highest window, perched beneath a slanted roof and above the skeletons of the floors below.

His shadow stretches to the ceiling only to fall beyond sight.

He's not alone up there. I hear voices, cries.

When they get too loud, the flames flicker against the flurry of movement and all is quiet again.

I thought I faced death before. I thought I survived it.

But that was just the start—the prologue to a saga that ends here.

I float to the front steps on legs that don't feel like my own, closer to the end that's always been there, waiting.

I have all the answers now. All the strings knotted together, all the connections met. Tyler, Bruce, Ronnie, my mom, and Margot's too.

It doesn't feel like I thought it would, *knowing*. I thought it would all make sense.

I thought it would quiet the screams in my head. I thought it would make me whole.

The charms at my wrist scatter moonlight against the door as it squeaks open, and darkness smothers me when I step inside.

Droplets of blood form a breadcrumb trail for me—through the vacant living room to the stairs at the far end.

I take them one at a time, slowly, listening for anything that might prepare me for the next few seconds, minutes.

Anything that might prepare me for the end.

Wind whistles through jagged windowpanes, tunneling through the vacant home and sending bundles of dust to dance in the shards of moonlight.

It's quiet now. They're waiting for me.

The thin gasoline vapors hit me halfway up the second floor, so familiar now it's almost comforting.

Except fire, in this place, is a death sentence.

But then, that's why we're here.

I creep up the last set of stairs, to the door at the top, where the handle is warm to the touch, the room beyond it silent.

It opens, and he's waiting for me. Knife in one hand, flame in the other, smile stretched wide.

This is the end.

CHAPTER FORTY-SEVEN

Friday, October 15
The End

I shouldn't have been able to get through the gates to Bruce Thorne's house so easily.

That's what I tell myself as I navigate his winding drive, past stone statues and wide oak trees turned the colors of flames, wrought-iron lamps that flood the paved concrete in a soft glow.

The main road veers left, so I go right, deeper into the cover of trees and the crunch of fallen leaves beneath my tires.

My headlights cut paths into the blackness, the drive becoming narrower the farther I travel. Then the house comes into sight, looming high and lit with heavy sconces that highlight the thick ropes of ivy, and I tuck my car into a little gravel-covered square next to a large shed.

The engine knocks and pings, and I press the door shut, not bothering to lock it.

I crouch low, keeping to the trees until I can't anymore, and shuffle toward the side door. It's locked, of course, and no matter how many rocks I kick, there are no spare keys.

The next two doors around the back are no better. Neither are the windows.

I shouldn't be here.

I should be talking to Dad, to Detective Michaels. I should be pointing them both in Tyler's direction—and in Margot's mom's—and I should let them follow this through.

I've spent five months hoping for an end to this, waiting for the day I didn't live by the days on a calendar. For a time when I looked forward instead of back.

And now it's here. So close.

I need to make sure this ends. Not like last time. Not when I trusted the people I was *supposed* to trust, when I put it all in their hands. Doing that brought me here. It left me questioning all my decisions. One big circle where they still have none of the answers and I'm still the one paying the price.

Bruce Thorne has been evading prosecution for decades if I believe what Shelly claims. Handing this over to the police won't mean justice for me. I have no evidence, no proof, nothing but my word.

It's too late to trust them now. I've discovered more in two weeks than they have in five months. I can't wait around, hoping they do better this time, *believe me* this time.

Never again. This fight is mine. The answers are *mine*.

Light flickers in the distance, a curtain flapping in the wind far down the house. From an open balcony door. It feels like a sign.

I miss the balcony the first time, my hands stinging as they rip from the floor. But on the second try my fingers grip tight to the edge, concrete pressed into my skin as I pull myself up, hooking my leg onto the ledge.

Then I'm over the metal railing and standing before an open door, with no idea what I'm walking into.

I pull the curtain aside, just enough to glimpse the room beyond. A den of sorts, leather armchairs and book-lined shelves. A bar in the corner and etched-glass tumblers, empty and waiting.

The phone on the end table is the only sign of life.

But phones are not things people do without for long, and if I can't get through this room, I'll never find what I need.

I ease inside, glossy wood floor holding my hazy reflection, and I head toward the phone.

A quick tap to the screen flares light into the dim room, but there are no message previews, not even a background picture.

I don't remember if Tyler's parents are divorced. If his dad is remarried. I don't even know who he lives with or where. He never told me, and even if he had, I couldn't trust it now.

I can still feel his hands on my skin, taste the whiskey on his tongue. I hear his voice in my ear, and it's only the other Tyler I can hear now. The one from the warehouse, the one from the parking lot. The one I'm afraid of.

I push forward, hurrying through the room and into the hall.

It's just as empty, stretching deep in both directions until darkness envelops it. Gilded mirrors hang over buffets, ornate picture frames on opposing walls, and a stone banister leads the curving staircase to the lower floor.

I could search this house the entire night and still not find the evidence I'm looking for, or even the room I might find it in.

Light glows from below, pooling onto the lowest steps before spreading over the marble tile beneath them.

Wherever the people are is where I want to be least, so I pick a direction and head in it.

I choose wrong.

Bedrooms, bathrooms, a game room, closets. All of them deceptively perfect—bedding pulled taut, marble gleaming, rooms frozen in time and waiting for use.

I head in the other direction, skipping past rooms that look like duplicates of the others, until the view of the driveway gives way to the woods and the hallway bends.

These doors are closed. All of them.

I move quieter, grasping each door handle and turning them, only to find nearly all of them locked.

I'm to the fifth before it turns, the angled glass knob pressed hard into my palm, and then the smallest of clicks as the door opens.

I inch it open, my eyes straining in the darkness, my hearing muffled by the thrum of blood in my ears.

A triangle of illumination spreads wider as I ease the door farther. The walls are bare, comforter plush and pulled tight, pillows piled high. A row of windows lines the opposing wall, dark curtains cloaking them straight to the floor, a sitting area stationed before them. To the left of it, a desk.

I head toward it, slipping open drawers and pawing through them, searching for pink envelopes and thick paper, for ribbons and photos.

But there's nothing of that here. Only the roll of pencils across the expanse of drawers, the flutter of blank pages beneath the pads of my fingers.

In this home, Tyler is a ghost too.

I slide open the last drawer, and it's the first proof he was ever here, sleeping, thinking, *living* in this room. The knife lies there like it's waiting for me.

Ronnie's knife, with the marble inlay handle he nearly stabbed Bulger with, that he held to my throat. The relief of knowing Ronnie doesn't have it gets engulfed by the thick dread that comes with its presence *here*.

Beneath it lies a single sheet of the cardstock that's so familiar I know the feel of it even without touching. The thickness of it, the way the papery nubs and valleys feel against my fingers. The weight of it, slipped inside a pink envelope.

The front bears my name in the slash of handwriting I've memorized too. The back reads only: I'M SORRY.

This, of all of them, is the message he chose to leave unsent.

I tear it straight down the middle, letting both pieces sink to the floor.

There's nothing else here for me, nothing in the other open rooms, only one of them lived in—and it only takes a glance at the pictures lining the dresser in it to recognize the face. The man from the chop shop, who looked so familiar though I couldn't place how, the scent of menthol lingering behind him. Tyler's brother. One of the men who chased me down. One of the people Tyler helped me escape from.

I need a minute before I can move, before I can stop the cold crawl of fear that spreads through me. So many people, and all of them a part of this. Each of them responsible for me, in this moment, standing here with *my* life on the line. And in another breath the fear gives way to anger. To a need to make them all see what they've done.

The far end of the hall holds two doors but only one of them is unlocked, and the lights spring to life the second I enter.

A massive desk looms in the center of the room, bookshelves flanking the stained-glass window behind it, the bar to the right stocked full, whiskey stones poised in a single glass.

I close the door behind me, turning over the lock with a thunk that echoes in my ears.

My footsteps click against the wood floor, then mute in the plushness of the carpet, and I ease around the love seat and chairs at the front of the room as I head for the desk.

There's only one drawer locked, and if any of them have answers, it's bound to be this one. Just like Tyler set things up in Bulger's office.

I jam the scissors into the brass lock, shoving and twisting until my fingers ache, and then, finally, it glides open.

It's empty save for a hard drive not much bigger than a deck of cards. But if it's worth locking up, it's worth taking.

"Find what you're looking for?"

The deep voice rumbles to my left, and the only thing that stifles my scream is the terror that has me locked in place, my heart on hold and my body gone still.

I locked the door. I'm staring at the *locked door.*

"Get out of my seat, please, Ms. Adams. And leave the drive where you found it."

I obey without question, but this time, I keep my weapon in my hand.

I'm not sure me and a pair of scissors can compete with Bruce Thorne and the gun in his hand, but I'll die trying to find out.

"Sit." He motions toward the armchairs in front of his desk with a flick of his wrist, his shirtsleeves rolled to the elbow to reveal tattoos that crawl toward his wrists.

I stumble into the chair, shoving the scissors deep into the cushion, and stare at the open space where a bookshelf used to be, now shifted to the side to reveal a small hallway.

A secret entrance, and me, trapped behind a locked door.

He smiles. "You don't look happy to see me."

I'm not. But I'm not *not* happy either. I came here for this. Somewhere deep inside me knows this might be it. Maybe Bruce makes me disappear and no one ever knows to look for me.

But I won't go easy. I won't sit back like I have been for five fucking months, suffocating while everyone else breathed my air.

"Well, the last time I saw you, I found out my mom had me kidnapped and then you shot at me. It's not what I'd call a fond memory."

"Hmm." He drops the gun to the desk, barrel aimed at me. "You've made some incorrect assumptions, Ms. Adams, and I'll let you decide if you'd like me to correct them."

"I want the truth." And any evidence of it that I can take to the police, thanks.

"The truth. So noble. So absolute. If only the world worked that way." He slides open a drawer, and with one quick downward press, something clicks. A laptop appears in his hand a moment later.

Secret passageways and trick drawers—definitely the kind of guy who views the truth as a gray area.

He plugs in the drive and clicks a few buttons before spinning it around to me, and Margot's mom fills the screen.

From the angle, it's clear she didn't know she was being filmed, and her eyes look panicked.

"Your mother found me when you and your father kicked her out of your lives."

"Is that what she told you? Poor—What did she say her name was? *Scarlet?*"

"She told me her name was Cordelia." He knows he's right, his smirk shows it.

I hate that he knows her—any part of the real her. That was the one thing she was supposed to save for us—for me and Dad. There was supposed to be *some* part of her that was true for us and no one else.

I press my palm into the cushion just to feel the hard edge of the scissors' blade close at hand. "We kicked her out of our lives because she was never really in them. And we got tired of being the place that only existed to her when she fell. We got *tired* of being the people she used and manipulated and called it love."

"Your father stifled her."

"He tried to keep her out of prison—unlike you."

"She's free to make her own choices."

"As long as they don't involve leaving, right?"

He steeples his fingers and leans closer. "As I'm sure Tyler's told you, there is no way out of this family."

"She's not your family, and the only thing Tyler's told me about you is that you ruined his childhood and you were gone now."

He laughs, husky and baritone. "You see, Ms. Adams, the truth is only true to the person telling it. Everyone else has their own version. And because I like you, I'll tell you mine."

He leaves the gun where it lies, sauntering to the bar to pour himself a drink while I calculate my odds of grabbing the gun and shooting him before he can tackle me.

They're not good.

The rocks clink against the glass as he takes a long sip and offers it to me.

He grins when I don't respond. "I understand, what my son sees in you. You have a way about you—not unlike your mother. It's a shame I'm going to have to kill you."

I don't move. Not a single muscle. I swear the blood seizes in my veins. I'm going to die here.

"I do appreciate you making it easy for me though. A man has the right to defend his property when someone trespasses and scales a balcony. I clearly thought I was being robbed."

He led me into this. Into the front gates. Into the house through the second floor. He left a trail of breadcrumbs straight to the wolf and I followed them. I ignored that voice inside me that screamed for me to listen.

I force my voice steady. "Are you going to miss like last time?"

His eyes crinkle over the top of his glass as he drinks. "If I'd wanted to kill you, I would've. I'm not a monster. I was trying to scare you enough to run back to Daddy and live your safe, happy life. But I'm afraid you've become a problem for me, what with your . . . *extracurricular activities* drawing attention to yourself, and by extension, to *me*. I'm not the kind of man who wants attention."

I refuse to acknowledge more than 90 percent of the bullshit he just spewed out. Plus, if I'm going to die, I at least want to achieve what I came here for. "Why did my mother have me kidnapped?"

"I never said she did." He breezes past me, not the least bit worried or intimidated, and presses play on his laptop.

The screen jumps to life, Margot's mom stumbling through her words, hands twisting the straps of the handbag clutched in her lap.

It's at the chop shop, which means he clearly picked the location that would make her most uncomfortable.

But then her words start to make sense, bits and pieces of them stitched together to weave a cloth. There's a "complication in her daughter's life." Margot has "worked so hard to get where she is"; then there was a "setback" that she feared would "interfere with her future."

Her "future" means volleyball, and that setback, the complication, is *me*.

Before I can stop myself, I'm on my feet. "Volleyball? This was about fucking *volleyball*?"

Margot's mom has always been intense, always wanted all the things for Margot she didn't have for herself, but *this*? I could kill her myself, right this very instant.

He leans back in his chair, an ankle across his knee. "Ms. Pennington was a former volleyball player."

"State champs three out of four years in high school. Slated to play in the '96 Olympics before she suffered a catastrophic shoulder injury making her unable to spike or serve without surgery. Hasn't been able to let it go since then and instead tries to push her dreams onto her daughter. Yeah. I know. She had me *kidnapped*?"

"To be fair, she requested something that would scar you enough you could no longer play, thereby giving Margot back her rightful spot on the team. You should thank me, Ms. Adams. She had . . . *alternative suggestions*." He mimes someone swinging an object to the side. "I let you keep your knee."

I blink at him, fire building inside my rib cage, and I don't care about dying as long as I can bring her with me. "She wanted to maim me over fucking *volleyball* and you compromised with PTSD and I should *thank you*?"

"You would've preferred the former?"

"Yes." I don't realize how true the words are until they break free. But injuries I could heal from, even if I was never the same. Even if I could never step onto a court again.

But *this*. This life I'm left with. This is worse.

"I have spent every day—every *minute* of my life over the past five months just *waiting* for your son to finish what he started. There is no place that's safe for me. Not my school. My car. My house. My *room*. I've given up everything that mattered to me. So *fuck* you."

He raises a brow. "Well now you really sound like your mother."

"Fuck her too. What was in it for you?"

"Money."

"Like you don't have enough?"

"I'm afraid 'enough' doesn't exist, but since you asked, no, it wasn't just money. In my . . . line of work, sometimes you need the right people in your debt."

Of course. Margot's mom has no shortage of connections. No lack of dinner parties with the city's finest lawyers, and the local chief of police is her neighbor. "So Melanie Pennington was your get-out-of-jail-free card."

He smiles, the same crooked grin his son gives. "So you see, your mother didn't have you kidnapped."

"No, she just set the whole thing up, right?" I pace the carpet, watching the barrel of the gun for the moment it leaves the table and sits level with my forehead. "She was already stuck with you and trying to claw herself back into my life by accosting all my friends and their families, then Margot's mom asked for a connection and my own mother led her right to you."

"You're leaving out a few of the details, but all in all, a very accurate summary. You're smart, Ms. Adams." He spins the gun, lets it wobble on its side before coming to a halt, pointing directly at me. "I could spare your life if you'd like a place in my family."

"I pick death, thanks."

He shrugs as he stands. "Very well."

"Wait. What about Ronnie?"

"Ronnie." He rolls his eyes. "One of your mother's more unfortunate choices. And none of my concern."

And that confirms that. Just another unfortunate choice that I paid for.

I say, "Did my mother know? At any point. Even after it was over. Did she know why Margot's mom came to you?"

He doesn't pause, and his voice holds no pity. "Yes."

It happens so fast I barely see it. A sickening crack fills the room, and Bruce crumples where he stands, a trail of blood oozing over his forehead.

Tyler drops the candlestick to the carpet and lowers his dad to the chair, dropping his head onto the leather blotter. Then Tyler turns to me, smiling wider than I've ever seen him.

I can't smile back. I can't even move as he heads closer, can't speak, not even when his hand slips around my waist and his mouth finds mine.

I can't breathe.

He brushes my hair from my head with bloody knuckles. "Hey, baby. I've missed you so much."

CHAPTER FORTY-EIGHT

Friday, October 15
The End

I'm transfixed by the blood as it twists in rivulets of crimson, following the angles of Bruce's face before pooling on his desk.

His body jerks as Tyler yanks him up from the desk, slipping a thick zip tie around his wrists.

He smiles. "We make the best fucking team. You don't know how long I've been trying to get close enough to do that."

He saved my life. I'm sure of it. But he ruined it too. I'm not sure he realizes that.

The gun scrapes against the desk as he tucks it into his waistband with practiced ease, and I send a silent plea to let Bruce wake up. Right fucking now.

I'm not ready for this. For Tyler. I *know* who Bruce is. He's greedy, power-hungry, controlling, manipulative, and a whole host of other horrifying adjectives, and I have no doubt he destroyed whatever spirit his son had, but Tyler . . .

I don't know who he is. But I know what he's capable of.

Edward Bulger's blood pooled into his mattress. Me, screaming into my pillow with another letter clutched in my fist.

Tyler squats behind the desk, out of sight, and another *zip* tells me Bruce's ankles are now bound too.

My voice comes out hoarse. "What are you going to do with him?"

Tyler pops up, brushing his hands together like he's ridding himself of something dirty, and his brow furrows. "Kill him."

The oxygen flees my lungs, my head dizzy. "Tyler. I can't be part of this."

Not like this.

Genuine surprise flits across his face, replaced by a slow burn of anger. "You could've killed Nomi's stepdad."

"That was—" That was what? I locked him in a basement to burn. "Different."

He leans against the desk, ankles crossed, and sighs. "C'mere."

My mind holds my body in a vise. I can't be near him. I can't touch him. I can't let him touch me.

He destroyed me, and now he's standing here like it was salvation.

I'm in that trunk again. The world dark, tape burned into my wrists as I twist them free, breathing too hard and threatening to choke because my mouth is covered and I can't get enough air . . .

I step forward, and my body doesn't belong to me anymore.

I watch myself move toward him, watch his arms band around me and his lips press into my forehead.

He whispers, "The first kill is always the hardest. It'll be easier next time. Trust me."

I snap back into myself and break from his cage. "You lied to me. About . . . everything. You framed Bulger. You—"

"You weren't ready. You said you were ready, but you weren't. And after you flipped out about finding Bulger's dad, I knew you'd never forgive me for that even though it wasn't my fault. Your mom told my dad he would be an easy mark and instead the fucker was home *and* fought back. So I pinned it on Bulger and gave you someone else to hate. But you, Cass, had to keep digging. You should've let it go."

And that's how he sees all of this. My fault. My hang-ups. None of this is on him—an innocent man is dead, another nearly framed for kidnapping, and Tyler has no regret for any of it.

I swallow hard so I don't get sick all over the floor. "You said your dad was gone. You acted like my friend when you were stalking me—"

"Hey!" The vitriol in his voice sends me stumbling back, bracing myself for a blow.

Instead, he goes quiet. "I did it for us. For *you*. If it weren't for me, you'd still be going to parties with Margot and fucking Noah Rhoades, pretending you were like them. You'd be running from Ronnie Kida and hoping the cops showed up in time to save you."

Oh god.

My voice is barely a whisper. "You killed him."

"He threatened you. I took care of it." He reaches for me, cups my jaw in his callused hand, and I want to burn my flesh from my bones.

His thumb brushes over my cheek. "I saved you, Cass. I showed you who you really were."

No. He showed me the worst side of myself. The one who lived through fear and ran from hope. He showed me terror.

He snuffed out all the parts of myself I loved most.

But I want to live. I don't want to die in this house, no matter who pulls the trigger.

I force my hand to his wrist and pull it free. Gently. Reverently. "We can't kill your dad. There will be consequences."

"Bonnie and Clyde, remember?"

"Tyler, they died. Horribly. Lots of bullets."

"I know, Cass. And I don't appreciate you questioning my intelligence."

"I wasn't. I—"

He slices through my words with a quick jerk of his hand. "Do you think I haven't thought this out? It's the only thing I've thought about. From the moment you showed up at school."

He circles around the back of Bruce's chair and wheels him to the wall, his hand fisted in Bruce's hair to keep him upright.

It's my only chance, maybe the only time his back will be to me. My only opportunity to run.

But I don't know what's waiting for me in that tunnel, and if I survive this, I want it all to have been for something.

So I don't run. I grab the hard drive instead, tucking it inside my jacket pocket and zipping it closed.

Tyler shoves his dad into a spot beneath an ornate family photo. "We're the same, you and I. All that bullshit your mom put you through and all the bullshit this asshole put *me* through. We understand each other. Better than any of them ever could. Now help me with him."

A frame on the wall swings wide as he presses it, revealing a safe buried deep in the studs. It beeps, glowing soft red.

Tyler bends to drag Bruce upward, letting his head loll against his shoulder as he peels open Bruce's eye. "Get his hand."

Bruce's wrists slip from my grasp the first time, my hands too shaky to work right. I force them steady and raise his finger to the second scanner.

Tyler says, "Count of three," and presses a button, sending the scanners flaring to life.

A robotic voice calls out, "Authentication successful," and Tyler drops Bruce so hard I have to catch him before he topples.

He's too heavy, all dead weight, and it takes everything in me to ease him into the chair. My hair comes away sticky with his blood.

Tyler drags a duffel from the safe, its contents shifting and cracking together. He fills the empty space with guns, bound piles of cash, bags filled with things I can't see.

He's so distracted, so enthralled by the treasure he's captured for himself, he doesn't notice me. Crouched low, slipping the knife from Bruce's ankle holster and into my pocket.

I left my scissors behind. Stuffed in the cushion, where they're useless. Like the knife I dropped at Coach Bulger's feet.

I won't make that mistake again. Any of them. If I survive this, I won't give anyone a single choice to question. Not even one decision to second-guess.

When I survive this.

"Are you going to ask me?"

I startle at the sound of his voice, but when I look to him, he shows no signs of having seen the knife. "Ask you what?"

"Whether we were supposed to kill you that night?"

We. I'm back in that moment on the trail, when my feet left the ground. His hands felt like they were everywhere. Holding my arms, forcing the tape across my mouth, binding my wrists. "Your brother helped, didn't he?"

"Dad thought I should be able to handle it myself, but I told him you'd be a two-man job. I told him you'd fight."

A cold sweat covers my skin, my mouth going sour. I hate the pride in his voice. The admiration.

I couldn't even tell the police it was two men. I couldn't even get that part right.

I say what he wants to hear. "You wouldn't have let them kill me."

A smile lights his face, pulls a flush to his cheeks. "You know I wouldn't have." He fans a stack of fifty-dollar bills. "Killing you was never part of the plan though. Melanie Pennington is a goddamn coward. You should've seen her. She could barely say what she wanted done to you."

He says it like we're discussing dinner plans. Like it's normal that my best friend's mother hired a man to kidnap me to get her daughter's spot on the volleyball team back.

He says it like it's okay he was there. That he listened to that conversation and didn't warn me. He listened and threw me in his trunk, and he calls that love.

He kisses me again, too hard, resting his thumb against my bottom lip when he's done. "It was my idea to stop at the park, see if you'd escape on your own so it would seem more authentic. I knew you wouldn't disappoint me."

He heaves the duffel over his shoulder. "Now. Let's load him up."

"We should—" I swallow. "We shouldn't kill him here. We both broke in. We could be suspects."

He tucks my bloody hair behind my ear. "That's my girl. No. We'll take him by the shop. Do it there. Your dad's at home. He called off tonight. That will make things easier."

My hand goes to the knife in my pocket, fingers clenched around the hilt, and I imagine plunging it deep into Tyler's gut. I force myself to feel it—the resistance of his flesh, the rush of warm blood over my hand.

I live every second of it so I don't hesitate when it's real. If he tries to kill my father, it will be.

My voice wobbles, tears burning. "No. We leave him alone. He won't—"

"He won't stop looking for you. That's what he won't do. He has to go. I'll do it for you, if you can't. Now give me your phones."

He knows I have two. Of course he does. He gave them both to me. And I put my actual phone in Mrs. Henderson's mailbox. He probably knows that too.

I pull them from my hoodie, and I'm sealing Dad's death. I have no way to warn him, and for all Tyler's talk of doing it himself, there's no way to tell if he'll get someone to do it for him. His brother could be there right now.

I drop them into his waiting hand. "Please, Tyler. I'll leave with you right now. I'll go anywhere. Just leave him out of this. Let him—"

"I love you, Cass. I have since the moment we met."

He pockets the phones and drops one of the duffel's straps onto my shoulder, weighing me down so it'll be harder to run.

Then he heaves his father's limp body over his shoulder. "But if you don't shut the fuck up, I'm going to have to hurt you. Don't make me."

CHAPTER FORTY-NINE

Friday, October 15
The End

The secret passageway leads to a garage. Of course it does. What good is a secret passage unless it helps you escape?

Only, it's not the regular garage. It's an underground cellar, carved into the ground, damp and earthy. Moss coats boulders that pile high to form the walls, thick and cold as I pass by them, Tyler on my heels.

He's carried one of the duffels and his father the whole way, his breathing never laboring.

I can't run from him—I've seen his speed. Can't overpower him or reason with him.

He'll use me as bait for my dad. Then he'll kill him.

We move deeper into the cavern, the light from the passageway slicing a triangle into the muddy darkness.

Tyler says, "Keys are in the car. Get in and start it. Driver's side. And pop the trunk."

I feel my way around the car, cold metal greeting my palms, and I'm not even around the front bumper when he makes it to the back of the car. He doesn't need light. Doesn't need to feel his way. He knows exactly where everything is.

I yank open the door and slip inside, soft leather seat cushioning me. The keys aren't in sight, but this car doesn't need them. I press the brake and stab the start button, and the engine turns over, but the car stays dark, all interior lights disabled.

"Trunk, Cass!"

My hand hovers over the gearshift. One second. Maybe two. That's all it would take to throw it in reverse, pin him to the door behind him, run him into the ground.

One second would be all it takes for him to jump out of the way too. Then he'd know. He'd know I'm willing to die before I leave with him.

I work all but my car key free from my key ring and stuff it into the tiny pocket in my leggings, and pray the Bluetooth in the console is actually connected.

I press the button for the garage door, and it rumbles as I hit the button for the trunk. It pops open, giving me the only window I'm likely to get.

I rifle my keys toward the open doorway that leads back to the house just as the car bounces under the force of Bruce landing in the trunk.

"Cass!"

Tyler shouts my name a moment before I hit the ground, rolling beneath the car and onto my stomach, the ground beneath my palms slippery with wet earth.

His feet pivot, a half second where he considers and discards the idea I could've made it past him and out the garage. He charges toward the open door and everything in me says to run, take my chances with whatever waits for me through the exit.

Instead, I do the last thing anyone who knows me would expect. I head toward the one place he'd never think to look for me.

I crawl toward the trunk.

Tyler calls my name again, but it's quieter, coming from farther in the house, and I push harder, until my elbows flare with cuts and bruises and my knees feel raw.

Then I jump in.

I press myself to the back of the seats, behind Bruce, but if Tyler looks, he'll find me. I just need him not to look. I need him to know me so well he doesn't think to.

"Cass! You fucking bitch!"

Closer now, and my whole body shakes, my breathing choked because there's not enough air. Tape on my mouth and my wrists bound tight, and I'm going to die. This is the day I die.

"Shut up."

The voice shocks me from my panic, because it's not Tyler's.

The passageway door slams, and I'd bet my life it's locked now.

"Don't make me hurt you, Cass!" Tyler's footsteps sound next to the car, past the trunk, until they carry him farther away.

Bruce whispers, "There's another gate," and I get it then, what he's trying to say. There's another gate at the end of the secret exit. I'm trapped in here. With the two of them.

My nails gouge the carpet, cold sweat blooming on every inch of skin, and my head goes dizzy from lack of air.

I hear words, but I can't make them out, can't open my eyes to see what's happening around me.

Bruce shouts Tyler's name, and everything crashes back in. Every sound amplified, every sight in too-clear focus.

Bruce lies right next to me, pinning me in, the heat of his body pressing against me.

He laughs, without an ounce of kindness. "I taught you better than this."

It's not until Tyler shoots back, "Shut up," that I realize Bruce isn't talking to me. That he isn't pinning me in this trunk.

He's shielding me.

He says, "She's just a girl, Ty, and *you* let her get away."

Tyler's footsteps pound closer, and Bruce laughs again, louder now. "Getting colder!"

Each of Tyler's steps hit the ground like an explosion. "I told you to shut the fuck up!"

The trunk slams shut and for a moment I'm gone again, but I reel myself back, force my breathing even.

I'm not there. I'm *here*.

I'm here I'm here I'm here.

The car lurches, rolling me farther into Bruce, then him into me as we start the incline that leads aboveground.

My hands roam over the back of the seat, searching for the plastic handle that will fold it down.

I just need Tyler to stop the car. I need him to need me badly enough he can't leave without me.

Bruce groans as his head bounces against the floor. "He'll head toward your car."

I owe him nothing, but I'm not Tyler, and I can't hold another death on my hands.

I whisper, "He's going to kill you," and Bruce's breathy chuckle rumbles against my ear.

"If he does, I suppose he's earned it. I didn't see this coming."

The ground beneath us shakes, and Bruce says, "Second door."

"Where are the car keys?"

"Middle console." I swear he sounds amused.

My fingers land on the plastic seat lever, and I hook them beneath it, holding tight while the car shifts and sways through winding roads.

Everything about this has to go right, or I'll die knowing my dad is next.

I scrub away a tear with my shoulder and work my car key from my waistband.

I'm not sure I want the answer, but I ask anyway. "Why are you doing this?"

He pauses before responding, his voice gravelly, and I'm not sure I can fully process what he says.

But then the car skids to a stop and Tyler screams my name again.

I ease the lever up until it clicks, and the weight of the seat back pulls against my fingertips.

I lower it slowly, straining for the direction and strength of Tyler's voice when he yells, "You will not leave here without me!"

The seat drops the rest of the way, and I shove myself through to the back seat, where the spill of moonlight threatens to expose me.

I wiggle between the front seat, the console biting into my middle and scraping my skin as I slide into the front seat and down to the floorboards, cool wind rushing over me through the open door.

Keeping as low as I can, I reach into the console until my fingers land on metal and plastic.

Outside, Tyler paces, moving from shadow to shadow under the trees.

It takes one glance to know plan A is ruined. Tyler parked the car sideways, perpendicular to the road, hemmed in by trees at the front and back, which means I can't just gun it and drive both me and Bruce out the front gates.

Too much maneuvering, not enough time.

I do the next best thing.

My finger stabs the trunk button, and it pops a second before I cut the engine.

Tyler rushes toward the trunk, and I throw myself into the woods.

I can't hear their conversation, can't pinpoint the cause of Bruce's laughter or the words that spill from Tyler's mouth in response. But it gives me time to creep closer to my car, until it's only steps away.

It's a narrow road—two seconds to the door, another to open it. A fourth to slide inside. Five is the key in the ignition. Six to turn it. Seven and eight to shift into drive and hit the gas.

He's too fast. Eight seconds is too many.

Eight seconds. Eight times eight is sixty-four, and if I don't do this, my dad dies.

I grasp the charms at my wrist. I promised the girls. We promised each other. We're not done. One more to go.

I fly from my hiding spot, and eight seconds feels like forever and no time at all.

I'm barely into the car when he yells my name.

He's close.

So close.

I slam the door. Lock them. Two more seconds and his hand closes around the handle, yanking so hard I brace for it to break free and then he'll be inside, dragging me onto the ground.

Ignition, turn, shift, gas.

The car rockets forward, tires spinning, and the acrid smoke of burnt rubber clouds my lungs. But then they catch, sending the car rocketing down the drive with Tyler's voice filling my head as the handle finally rips free of his grasp.

I don't slow, not even when the road bends too sharply, when the trees scrape along the side of my car.

I don't breathe until I break free and onto a road that does not belong to Bruce Thorne.

Then it's his voice I hear, telling me he's not a monster.

I hear him, whispering in the back seat, the heat of his breath hot against my scalp when I asked him why he was helping me. *"If my son doesn't kill you both first, tell your mother I saved you."*

CHAPTER FIFTY

Friday, October 15
The End

My phone isn't in Mrs. Henderson's mailbox anymore.

I broke every speed limit and road rule in existence, and my phone isn't in her mailbox because Tyler took it. Of course he did.

And that means he was here.

Mrs. Henderson's door flings open, and she calls out, "Cass! Oh, thank the good Lord."

"Where's Dad?"

"Well, he's been everywhere looking for you!" She settles her hand on her hip, her face pinched in reproach.

"Today. Right now. Where is he?"

"Last I saw him was when he was letting that boy in the house—the one who's been hanging around here—"

I don't hear the rest. The world blurs as I race to the front door, panic stealing every ounce of air from my lungs.

I'm too late. I didn't tell him about Tyler, about anything, and now I'm too late and I fucked everything up again.

I slam into the front door, but it's locked and my keys are in Tyler's house. The side door is locked too, but lastly, finally, the back door swings open.

I recognize the smell immediately.

Thick. Metallic.

But this isn't Edward Bulger's house. It's mine.

I make it to the living room before the first drops appear. Droplets of red soaked into carpet fibers, pools of it at the bottom of the stairs, so red it's nearly black, crawling into the cracks and crevices of the wood floorboards.

I buckle at the knees, my stomach revolting until I'm retching with nothing left, my legs too shaky to get me back to standing.

Dad could still be alive.

He's a doctor. He'd know how to save himself. He'd know how to stop himself from bleeding out.

People can survive traumatic blood loss. He told me.

I grab tight to the banister, pulling myself hand over hand until I'm on my feet.

I take the stairs two at a time, my shoes sliding in blood-drenched carpet as I run toward Dad's room, steeling myself to see him.

Lifeless. Unmoving.

I don't see him at all.

Not in his room or mine or the guest bed or any of the bathrooms.

The front door rattles in the frame, and I hold myself up using the sink, waiting.

Waiting to hear Tyler's voice. Waiting for him to tell me where I can find Dad's body.

But it's Mrs. Henderson instead.

I fly down the stairs, sliding through the last five of them and streaking my shoes and clothes with blood.

Dad's blood.

I fling open the door, and Mrs. Henderson goes pale, her eyes wide. Her mouth moves, but no sound comes out.

I snap my fingers in her face. "I need you to call 911. Tell them my father is missing and Tyler Thorne took him. Can you do that?"

She blinks once, twice, and shakes her head while whispering, "Oh my god!"

"Marcia!"

She startles at the sound of her first name coming from my mouth, and I speak slowly for the rest. *"Can you do that?"*

"Of course! Yes! But . . ."

I'm poised to shove her out of the way and sprint across the street to her phone so I can call them myself when she holds it out to me.

Her hand shakes. "There's someone who wants to speak to you."

I hold it to my ear, too scared to do anything but say hello.

"Baby?" my mom says, tears bleeding through her words. "I'm so, so sorry."

• • •

She's sorry. For what, she won't say.

Bringing Ronnie into my life, aiding in my kidnapping, telling no one before or after, setting all of this in motion.

She struck the match that left Dad dead.

She can keep her tears, swallow her apology.

But that's not why she calls—she calls because she has to.

Because she's with Tyler.

And when she tells me where to go, I do.

I go alone, because she says that too. She *doesn't* say not to tell anyone, and that's why I call Nomi.

She listens in shocked silence, witnesses everything I have to say. Only, I can't say it. Not out loud. I can't speak the words to tell her Dad is dead. Murdered. Because of me.

And Nomi—*Nomi*—hangs on the edge of tears, begging me to tell her where I'm headed.

"We're supposed to do this together. All of us, Cass. That was the deal."

Except, no one has heard from Ori. Not since her parents discovered she'd been hiding a relationship with Margot—no secrets allowed in the Bello household. Especially not since they discovered the man they spoke to was *not* my dad, and Ori was definitely not practicing volleyball the other night.

Ori is locked in her room and Nomi is locked in her father's police station—only a city away but it might as well be thousands—and Margot is locked in a hell of her mother's making.

Margot hasn't stopped sobbing, Nomi tells me, since the moment I left the gym. Since the moment she realized what her mother did.

Margot's mom is missing. Nomi tells me that too.

Only, she's not missing. I know where she is.

She's with my mom, and they're both with Tyler.

He has them all.

He has everyone that's wronged me, and everyone that's wronged him. I said that's what I wanted.

This is the end.

That's what his note tells me when I find it, a knife stabbed through the heart of it, pinned to a tree along the path he abducted me from.

This was our beginning, and soon, we'll meet our end.

CHAPTER FIFTY-ONE

Friday, October 15
The End

No cops. That's what I said to Nomi before leaving Mrs. Henderson's house.

But now that I'm here, climbing the stairs through the house Tyler summoned me to, I'm regretting it. No one's coming to my rescue—this is the part of downtown you come to when you don't want to be helped. Don't want to be found. The only things bearing witness in this neighborhood are the rotted bones of houses that used to be beautiful.

But I keep moving anyway. I may not be able to forgive my mother, or Margot's, or Bruce, but I don't want to be the thing that stands between Tyler and their deaths either.

But for the first time since leaving that police station five months ago, I'm trusting my instincts. I'm doing the things that buried-deep part of me keeps nudging me toward.

I know Tyler, maybe as well as he knows me. I know what he wants. Almost as if all this time, all those letters, I've been studying him through his words. Learning him. So when this day came, I'd be ready.

And here's what I know: He'll kill us all.

Before he gives up, before he surrenders, before he lets even one sliver of this plan for us to leave here fail, he'll kill us all. Without hesitation.

He'd kill Nomi too. Margot. Ori.

This isn't what they agreed to.

I may not be finished, but they are. My bracelet lies in Mrs. Henderson's hands, so if things go very wrong tonight, they'll be able to do what we promised.

I climb the last flight of stairs, my head dizzy from the fumes, from what I'm about to witness.

I reach the door at the top, where the handle is warm to the touch, the room beyond it silent, and it opens wide.

He's waiting for me. Knife in one hand, flame in the other, smile stretched wide.

A smile. Even though I ran from him. Left him stranded with a father I tried to help escape.

None of that seems to matter.

In so many ways, he's still that unloved little boy that no one thought to ask about. That no one cared about. And now he doesn't know what love is. He thinks it's this—this twisted fairy tale he's created for the two of us. He thinks he's found what he's always searched for. He thinks we're meant to be together, no matter what we do to one another. No matter what happens now, he'll never stop believing that.

And part of me still wants to hug him—go back in time and fix all the bad parts that made him into this—but I am not Dad and I know not everyone can be saved. I know Tyler is not mine to redeem and his choices are his alone.

Two metal gas cans scatter the floor, perched on uneven planks, the wood gone gray with age and neglect.

The center of the room holds three chairs, three captives, their arms and legs bound.

They face the front of the house, only their backs visible, but there is no mystery here.

Bruce, my mother, and Margot's.

In the corner, the sheet covering him wet with gasoline, lies my dad.

My hand covers my mouth to smother my scream, my sob.

I don't even remember the last words I said to him. I've tried. I've tried to play it all back in my head, bit by bit, until that very last moment.

The moment I last saw him alive.

But I can't, and that's why I'm certain my last words weren't "I love you." It wasn't anything that told him how much he means to me or all the ways he's saved me over the last five months and all the years before it. He was always there. Safe, practical. The Good Doctor Adams, who kept me on solid ground even when my mother upended my world time and time again.

That's how I know the last thing he'll remember of me is everything I want to take back.

My tears splash onto my hand, and I barely manage a strangled "Can I see him?"

Tyler's hand is around my neck before I take my next breath.

Fingers dig into muscle, his palm against my throat so tight I gag.

He pulls me in, until the heat of his breath tickles against my ear as he whispers, "No."

He releases me, and saliva pools in my mouth—then my head snaps back as his fist tangles in my hair, dragging me to stand before his line of victims.

Bruce inclines his head—probably the closest to a thank-you I'll get for trying to give him a chance at freedom. But then, I didn't exactly fight for him. I left him, bound and in the trunk.

I left him to die.

Margot's mom sobs, stuttering apologies and promises I don't need. Fighting for forgiveness I can't give.

But there's only one place my gaze rests, and she stares back, eyes red and tear-filled.

Thirteen months and everything about her looks the same. Thirteen months and I can't look at her without remembering all the things she's done, without reliving all the times I waited for her to be different, to be the person she swore she could be.

She mouths, "I'm sorry," and I look away because she may think she is, but those words lost meaning for her long ago.

Knowing that does nothing to ease the pain in my head, my heart. It does nothing to make me wish, any less, that her apologies are real.

I've spent so long worrying I'd turn out like her. I cut myself off from everyone, everything, five months ago because I couldn't bear to face what happened to me, because I was afraid they'd confirm what the police told me—that I really had done everything wrong that night. But deep down, there was always the fear I'd hurt them the way she's hurt me. But I know now, standing across from her in the crumbling attic, that I was never like her.

I never will be.

I'm messy, guilty, complicated, and all sorts of damaged. I locked a man in a basement to burn and I left another in a trunk to die.

Maybe there's no forgiveness for those things. Maybe everything I've done—all the things Detective Michaels knows about and even more of the things he doesn't—maybe I'll pay for those in ways I haven't even imagined.

But I won't run. I won't pretend to be someone else and leave the wreckage behind for someone else to pay for.

Margot, Ori, Nomi, and even Noah aren't here right now. Promise or no promise, I'll protect them.

My promise is this: I'll keep the people I love safe.

That means this last thing I do alone.

This is what I wanted. All the people who wronged me, lined up, ready to be turned to ash. And I don't want any of it anymore.

Tyler's grip loosens, and his body presses into mine from behind, his chin tucked into the curve of my neck. "I did this for you, Cass. *All* of this is for you."

"I don't want this."

I don't. No matter how badly anyone in this room has hurt me, I don't want to watch them die.

And if I can save them, maybe I can tip the scales. It's not that simple: a life for a life. I know it's not. But it can be a start.

The candle in the window gutters, sinking shadows into the floorboards, and Tyler pulls a match from his jacket, setting the flame alive again.

He crosses the room and grabs a fourth chair, a ragged wooden thing, tucked beneath a boarded window. "You're wrong about that. You *do* want this. I've seen you, Cass. I've seen the things you've done. I've *watched*."

He slams the chair into the floor, and it vibrates beneath my feet a second before he throws me into it.

Pain flares in my stomach, sharp and burning, as the edge of the knife in my hoodie bites into my skin.

Just a scratch. Just a reminder it's still there. This time, I didn't drop it.

This time, I did it right.

My arms wrench backward, Tyler's fingers wrapped around my wrists, and then, the rip of duct tape.

I flinch, all those memories like the roar of a flame I can't escape, and Tyler whispers, "I *am* sorry for this. I know you don't like it."

He threads my arms through the back, so I'm attached to the chair. I can stand—my chair isn't bolted to the ground—but there's nowhere to go.

"Let them go, Tyler. You and me, Bonnie and Clyde, right? We'll leave everything behind."

He curls around me, and the flash of knife spins moonlight through the room. "Now, now. Maybe before—before you *left me*—before you *ran away from me*, I might've believed you. But it's not good enough anymore. You need to see."

Margot's mom sobs harder, her prayers nearly drowning out Tyler's footsteps as he prowls the room, the glow of candlelight stretching and shrinking into the farthest corners.

Tyler spreads his arms wide. "*Look* at what I've done for you, Cass! You won't have to worry about Ronnie ever again. Look at all of them here, waiting for us. And the best part is that I didn't even have to try."

He pauses, tapping the knife's blade against his lips. "Well, killing your dad wasn't easy. He put up a great fight, Cass. You should be proud. You've got his spirit."

My stomach heaves, cold sweat covering every inch of skin, and all the things I should say—all the things I need to say—are gone.

Tyler taps the knife against Mom's temple. "But the rest of them, do you want to know how I got them here?"

I shake my head because I still can't speak, and Tyler answers, "I called them. That easy. Two little phone calls from Dad's phone, and they both came running. Sometimes the best plans are the simplest ones, don't you think?"

Bruce says, "Tyler, this has gone far enough," but Tyler doesn't even respond, and for the first time, I see fear in Bruce's eyes.

It leaves me cold, a line of ice through my veins and a sick sort of certainty burrowing itself deep.

"If my son doesn't kill you both first." That's what Bruce said to me. No mention of Tyler killing *him*.

But now, here in this room where the fumes thicken the air, where the candle's flame flickers in the breeze, I wonder if he sees things differently.

I wonder if he knows how this ends for him too.

I work at the duct tape holding my wrists, twisting them until my bones ache and my skin burns.

Something slices into my wrist, and I smother my wince, feeling for the source while keeping my movements small.

My finger catches on it—a crack in the wood, splintered deep.

I pull the tape tight against the point, pulling until it punctures.

I try again and miss, slicing my wrist, and my skin throbs. "If you kill them, the cops will know. They'll never stop hunting you. What kind of life will that be for us?"

He smiles then, wild and wicked. "The best kind. Free of all of them. They've done nothing but hurt us, and they've *always* gotten away with it."

He grabs tight to Bruce's hair, knife ready in the other hand, and I *know*. I see it happen seconds before he moves, and I can't get free. My hands are still bound, my eyes still open, and words stream from my mouth but none of them matter.

None of them can stop this.

None of them reach Tyler's ears as he holds the knife to Bruce's throat and says, "But not this time."

The blade slices clean, a strip of crimson blooming beneath its edge.

A scream rips free from my throat, and Melanie lets out a wail so loud it pierces my ears.

She shoves backward, scrambling so hard to get away she tips her chair and lands to the floor with a thud that rattles the room.

Blood pours over Bruce's neck, soaking his shirt and spreading as the fibers soak it in, and I watch as his eyes go empty.

My stomach heaves, and I force it down, shutting out the sounds of my mother's cries.

"If my son doesn't kill you both first, tell your mother I saved you."

Tyler points the knife at me. "Sit, or I'll kill the loud one next."

I have no memory of standing, but the weight of the chair dangles from my wrists, wrenching my shoulders back.

I let the chair crash down, falling into it as hard as I can, praying the splinter becomes a full break so I can cut through the last of the tape.

Tyler's boots slam into one of the gas cans, and the fuel leaks free, a river bubbling into the floor and spreading through the dried wood. The candle on the window ledge flickers, reaching for the thing that can give it life, let it spread and rage.

That's who Tyler and I are together—fire and fuel. A toxic mix that ends in scars and wreckage.

It didn't seem that way, not at first. Not when he sat at my table to keep me company when I'd run from everyone else. Not when he told me things weren't my fault, that I wasn't an awful person, that the things my mom did to me were wrong.

But all of that was a lie. This is Tyler's truth.

He takes a heaving breath, arms stretched wide, and points the bloodied knife in my direction. "I know you, Cass. They don't. I understand you in ways they never could. I *saved* you."

He slips closer, his boots leaving prints on the warped wood floor. "You were wasted on them. *Margot Pennington* and *Noah Rhoades*. Volleyball and teammates. You see what that got you. How they betrayed you."

The knife points at Melanie, and she's not screaming anymore. She's barely moving, too far in shock to feel much of anything.

I lick my lips, trying to calm the tremor in my voice as my wrist gouges against the splinter of wood again. "You're right. They did. They never cared about me, not like you. But if you love me, Tyler. If you love me anywhere near as much as you claim, you need to stop this—"

"There is no stopping this!" His voice booms through the room, his shadow stretched to the ceiling as the candle's flame jumps higher. "This is what you wanted! And I helped you! You want me to prove my love? I did. *I* was the one to show you where Valco's secret was. *I* was the one to save you when that security guard locked you in. *I* let you admit how you felt about your mom—I supported you. *Me*, Cass, *I* did those things. And now, it's your turn to do something for me."

He lays the knife in my lap, and it smears Bruce's blood across my leggings as it jumps with the force of my trembling.

I recoil, as much from genuine horror as cover for the next puncture of the tape at my wrists. One more, and I'll be able to tear it free. Just one more and I can end this.

He circles my chair, his hand gliding down the length of my arm, until it pauses at the tape I've nearly broken through.

I still, waiting. Waiting for the knife to slice through my throat next.

He laughs instead, the force ruffling the hair at the back of my head. "That's my girl."

He finishes the job I started, and when my arms fall free, they prickle as blood rushes back through.

I stare at the knife in my lap, the curve of the blade and the streaks of blood.

He says, "Pick it up."

I do, gripping it tight in my hand, the weight steady in my palm. I can do this.

I can kill him and save us all.

He breezes past me, and my chance disappears. I can't kill him if he sees me coming. He's spent a lifetime learning to survive, and I've never stabbed anyone before.

"Now." He grabs hold of Mom's hair, jerking her head to the side, a clear path to her throat. "Your turn."

"No."

Tears stream from her eyes, but her voice is firm. "It's okay, Cass. Do what he says. This is all my fault."

"No." Her form blurs with the tears I can't stop from falling.

It's not all her fault. I'd like to lay it all at her feet. I'd like, for once, to make her feel the weight of the mess she left behind. But Tyler, Bruce, Melanie, and even me—we all share this blame.

Her voice wobbles, words forced between gasping breaths. "I was just trying to be a part of your life again, show you how things could be different for us. I wanted to be like a normal mom. Show you I could make friends. Then Melanie asked for a favor, and I had no idea she was going to ask Bruce to hurt you. You have to believe me."

"Not at first, right?" I grip the knife tighter. "I believe you didn't know what she wanted when you introduced them. But after? When you *knew* what they were going to do? What about then?"

She can't look me in the eyes, confirming everything Bruce said. "It was too late by then, baby. The deal was already in place, and Bruce promised they wouldn't hurt you—"

"You thought—" I swallow, my throat burning. "You thought I wouldn't be hurt by what they did?"

She flinches, and it's the only way I realize I've taken a step closer, the knife raised higher, and Tyler's smile grows.

She tries to shake her head, but Tyler's grip holds firm and she blinks away tears. "You're so strong—you've always been. And *believe me*, Cassie. I never meant for you to end up in this mess. But then there was nothing I could do! I tried to get out so I could be the mom you needed, but you know what Bruce says: There is no out. If I warned you, he would've killed me."

"Don't." The knife shakes in my hand. She *knew*. She knew and she saved herself instead. "Don't blame him for this. For once. For *once*. Admit what you did. Did you know your friend Ronnie nearly slit my throat? Because of *you*. *Admit* what you did and fucking stick around to pay the price for it."

Tyler laughs, deep and rumbling. "I don't mean to point out the obvious here, Cass, but"—he waves over my mom, bound to the chair beneath her—"I think she's sticking around."

He leans in close, until his lips hover near her ear and his eyes set on mine, and he whispers, "And I think she's ready to pay the price."

Her eyes squeeze shut, new tears tracking over her cheeks. "Just do it quick. Do it, Cassie. And I'm sorry. I'm so, so sorry."

"Listen to your mother, Cass." Tyler shakes Mom's head like she's a puppet. "This is for us. We don't need any of them. No one loves you more than I do. Certainly not *her*."

He grips tighter, yanking her head farther back. "I'm not a monster. Neither are you. We're survivors, you and me. But you have to prove yourself to me. Prove you're with me. I don't want to kill you, Cass, but you're *mine*."

I step forward, knife dangling at my side while the floorboards creak beneath my feet.

She's not sorry. Not really. Not when she'd make the same decisions all over again. Not when I've listened to her admit she left me to suffer.

My mind scrambles, recalling and discarding all the conversations I've had with Dad about his ER patients. The ones that lived and the ones that didn't.

Because it's the *where* that matters. A millimeter in either direction means the difference between a few stitches and bleeding out in minutes. Survival means missing the vital organs, the arteries.

It means doing everything just right.

I don't know if I have that in me.

I close my eyes, conjure Dad's voice in my head, all those nights he'd talk about gunshots and stabbings, poisonings and accidents. All while chopping vegetables for dinner while little Cass urged him on with a thousand questions. Before my mother told me to stop asking. Too much trauma for the dinner table.

Look at us now.

The knife shakes in my hand, and I squeeze my eyes tighter, blocking out the sounds of her cries and replacing them with his voice.

"The upper-right quadrant holds the liver, plus veins from the rest of the body.

Upper left is the spleen and abdominal arteries. If you ever get stabbed, Cassie, you'd better hope it's just below the belly button, lateral to midline."

Mom's eyes fall shut, an endless litany of apologies and permissions, and Tyler above her.

This is what he's wanted, all along. Me, alone. My last true connection to this life just a foot away. No mom, no dad. I'd be his because I couldn't be anyone else's.

I'd be his to control, to manipulate.

I'd be his to own.

I raise the knife, step closer, and I whisper that I'm sorry.

Then I turn the blade and plunge it into my stomach.

CHAPTER FIFTY-TWO

Friday, October 15
The End

I expect pain. A deep, flaring burn. A sharp sting.

But there is none of that. Only a nauseating sort of pressure that leaves me stuck, immobile, too afraid to breathe deep when all I want is to hyperventilate.

This was not part of the plan.

I didn't go deep—less chance of organ puncture—but that doesn't mean I didn't clip something vital. Something that will leave me in a puddle of my own blood while my soul lifts from me, floating free like Bruce's did.

The world slams back into focus. Mom screaming, Tyler as still as me, his mouth dropped open, all his plans unraveling, thread by thread.

But I need him to *move*. I need him close, and every step toward him could drive the knife deeper, lower, a millimeter away from dying.

I slide my trembling hand along the blade, steadying it, gritting my teeth to resist pulling it free, force it from my body.

Heat flushes through me, hot and sick, and I stumble back.

Tyler springs forward just as I tumble to the ground, pressure in my gut twinging harder.

One millimeter.

I want pain. *Something* to tell me what I hurt, how much damage I've inflicted. I want something to tell me if these are my last breaths.

Tyler hovers over me, tears welling in his eyes. "It's okay, Cass. I can fix this. We'll get you out of here. I know people who can fix you."

I shake my head, swallow hard, and whisper, too soft for him to hear.

He leans closer, the heat of his tears trailing down my neck. "You'll be okay. Don't die."

The catch in his voice undoes me, and I hate what I feel—pity.

Pity for this sad, desperate boy who never learned what actual love is. Pity, because he tried to ruin me, and I can't give him forgiveness.

Pity, for what I'm about to do.

I clutch at his jacket, pull him closer, and slip my hand into his pocket, let my fingers close around the tiny matchstick. "I'm so sorry."

"No, baby." He brushes my hair, slick and sweat-soaked, from my temple. "We don't say sorry."

I drag the match against the ground, waiting for the crackle of the flame given life, and when heat floods my fingertips, I launch it free.

It ignites in the river of gasoline, snaking across the floor and branching into the weather-worn wood. The flame reaches toward the spout, yearning to catch on the fuel trapped inside.

He looks to it, his whole face alight, and it's the only chance I'll get.

I pull the knife from the pocket of my hoodie, aching fingers clenched around the hilt, and drive it into him.

Deep, aiming for every vital organ, every artery.

He gasps, and I wrap my other hand around the hilt, twist.

His eyes lock on mine, stunned and shocked. Devastated.

The flames breach the walls, crawling high, spreading across the floor.

Sobs rack through my body, but I don't let go, not even when his hands cover mine and the ceiling above us bleeds fire.

Heat soaks into my lungs, clogging them, making every inhale thinner.

He yanks the knife free, his scream low and guttural, and his blood pours over our linked hands, hot and thick.

He stares at me, his hands pressed to his stomach, stained red, and I can barely hear over the crackle of flames. "You and me, Cass, we're the same. And you'll always be mine."

His voice goes strained and breathy. "Say it."

I swallow, my mouth too dry, too raw, to form words. "I was never yours."

"Now that—" He smiles, and all the color drains from his face. "Is the wrong answer."

He rips the blade from my stomach, and pain roars through me, all my insides churning. He sways, choking, a trail of blood leaking from the corner of his lips.

I don't move in time.

His body topples onto mine, pinning me beneath him as the fire draws closer and the house groans.

I dig in my heels, shoving with my legs, my arms locked tight as I heave him free. It takes too long. Longer than I have left, and the house shudders.

I roll to my stomach, one arm clutched to my abdomen as I drag myself closer to my mom.

Her chair is toppled now too, just like Melanie's. But where Mom is talking, crying, Melanie hasn't moved, even as the flames creep closer.

The uneven wood scrapes through my leggings and ravages my knees, my elbows, but I can't let them die here. Not after all this.

Mom's chair scratches against the floor as she kicks against it, spinning herself so her arms draw closer to me. So I don't have to drag myself as far.

That, maybe, scares me more than anything.

Heat pushes down on me, the fire spreading to a second wall, and gray-black smoke curls above us in vicious clouds.

My hands shake as I raise the knife, and it takes every bit of my willpower to slice through the ties at her wrists.

The plastic snaps apart, and the knife drops from my hands.

I don't listen to what she's saying, don't care about anything but *finally* doing something right.

I drop the knife into her hands, and my voice croaks as I say, "Cut the ties on your legs, then get Melanie out."

I can't think about whether those will be my final words to her, whether she'll spend the rest of her life trying to play back this moment, forcing her mind to show her the things she doesn't want to see.

The house groans again, a long, slow wail that shifts the floor beneath me as a *crack* blasts through the air.

A corner of the roof crashes to the ground, kicking off a wave of dust that gives way to an avalanche of flame.

It's too hot to breathe, the air too thin, but I drag myself anyway, through the only path that leads to Dad, and just as I reach him, my fingers brushing over his cold body, the world goes black.

• • •

"If you die, I will kill you." Nomi's voice rings against my ears, and I blink, the world fuzzy.

Flames still jump toward the sky, a world of reds and yellows dancing among the black canvas, and I don't feel pain anymore. I feel nothing but quiet.

Nomi mumbles, "You stupid bitch. You stupid, stupid bitch."

By the time she gets past the third reference to my stupidity, her voice is thick with tears.

She grasps tight to my arms, dragging me, but I kick and fight, clawing closer to Dad.

"It's not him!" Noah now, his hands scooping me against him. "It's not your dad, Cass."

And that's how I know life is cruel, even in death. To give me the one thing I want more than any other, while letting me remember it for a lie.

I reach out, my fingers grazing something shiny, something that crinkles beneath my touch, and Noah rasps, "Fire-retardant blanket. This is going to hurt."

He hoists me higher, pain flaring through my middle until I can't think. A blanket covers us both, and he's running through a wall of fire, stumbling through the end as we reach the steps.

We crash down, down, down until he catches himself against the stairway wall, jerking me back to his chest, and just when I think I can't stand a second more, we burst into the starry night sky.

Air floods my lungs and the wail of sirens bellows while Dad's voice calls to me, his hands cradling my head. I hear him, shouting directions—where to apply pressure, what supplies he needs next—I feel the cool flow of oxygen pressed to my lips, but it all feels too much a dream to be real.

A myriad of voices join him—Margot, Ori, Noah.

So this is what it's like to die. To dream of the things you'll leave behind. All the things you want most, forever out of reach. Caught in a space where you don't know living from death.

I whisper that I love him anyway. This time, I do it right.

The house rattles again, smoke billowing from the gouged roof to twist toward the moon, and the top floor explodes in a pillar of flames.

Ashes to ashes.

CHAPTER FIFTY-THREE

Saturday, October 30
15 Days After the End

We walk together through the cemetery, hand in hand, like it always will be.

Me, Nomi, Ori, and Margot.

Ori squeezes my hand. "My car's over there. I'll be ready. You know the code word."

We all know the code word. Some things stay the same.

Some things are a surprise. Like the way Ori—tiny, quiet Ori—kicked down a boarded-up door so Noah and Nomi could come save me from the burning house that night.

Turns out, she was a little bit superhero all along.

And Valco, he lost his job, and his wife. Every part of his life is under investigation, and maybe, this time, justice won't have to come from the victim.

Ori kisses Margot before she leaves, and after everything—the time I've spent in the hospital, the recovery, and all the nightmares that have come after—seeing them happy has been a spark of light.

I'm not sure Margot would've survived these last few weeks without her.

Margot's hand slips into mine, squeezing so tight my bones crush. We've promised to stop apologizing to each other. To start believing we're not responsible for the things our mothers have done.

It works better in theory.

Her mom is out on bond, awaiting trial for arranging my kidnapping. Her lawyer's suggesting a plea bargain. Video evidence is hard to defend—even harder when your motivation for having someone abducted is volleyball.

I didn't take that evidence—the hard drive that held her mom's confession—to Detective Michaels.

Margot did.

She says she doesn't regret it.

As a girl who agreed to cooperate with the police in exchange for immunity from several breaking-and-entering charges and tampering with a crime scene, I don't believe her.

My testimony is part of the case that will put my mom in jail. For her role in my kidnapping, for all the things she's done for Bruce. I told her to pay for the things she's done, and I guess I'm helping her do just that.

Daughter of the year.

I'm trying to summon the sadness I should be feeling about where we've ended up, but there's only numbness there. A bruise that hurts to press but that ceased its throbbing long ago.

My therapist calls it a coping mechanism, and I'm sure she's right. What she doesn't tell me is if it's a good thing—if I should feel guilty for finally breaking free.

But maybe, finally, I don't care what any of the world thinks about me, about her, about our relationship. Maybe, finally, I'm learning to move on. Outside her orbit. Free. Forever.

My dad though, he keeps telling me I did the right things. He tells me I made the right decisions because I did the best I could. He tells me he loves me too. That he's sorry.

He *was* seeing my mom again, but not the way I thought.

She wanted back into our lives. She swore things were different now. For once, he didn't believe her. Didn't fall back into her orbit and get swept away. He set ground rules, and they talked, like real grown-ups who know how to use their words.

It didn't take him long to realize nothing much had truly changed with her, and that's why he didn't tell me. Why he didn't tangle me in their ongoing mess. He shielded me.

Like he's done every day since—through the police questionings and the lawyer discussions. Through it all, he's been there, *right there*, standing up for me. And listening to all the apologies I've given back to him. We both made the best decisions we could, and the ones that didn't work out as well as we hoped—those, we're trying to learn from.

The trees creak, wind screeching through branches and sending fresh batches of leaves tumbling to the grass, where they collect against headstones.

Margot smothers me in a hug—careful to avoid my stomach—and our necklaces clink together.

Our bracelets are gone—the final part of our pact in the woods complete—replaced by necklaces holding ashes from a different fire.

She finally lets me go, scrubbing at the tears she promised she'd try to stop shedding every time she looks at me. "Okay. I'll be behind the Scripps mausoleum, and if you need—"

"Jesus, she knows!" Nomi shoos her away. "Take your guilt and get your ass into position."

Margot glares at her, flips her off in case she might not have gotten the full message, and jogs off.

Nomi and I turn onto the path that will lead me where I'm headed—to *whom* I'm headed.

She says, "You sure about this?"

"Yes?"

"Your confidence is very reassuring."

"Well, I *am* a stupid bitch."

She sighs, like she does every time I remind her. "You're not a stupid bitch, Cass. You're a stupid, stupid, stupid bitch."

She's laughing before she gets to the second "stupid" and I am too, clutching my stomach because I'm still irrationally worried about all my insides spilling onto my feet with the slightest movement.

But I'm alive. I'm alive because of Dad. Because he was there to save me the second Noah carried me from that house.

Ironically, I'm alive thanks to Tyler too. The fire inspector said the only thing that saved us from a massive explosion and a fire big enough to engulf us all was Bruce Thorne's choice of gas can—the expensive kind with a flame arrester. Somehow, I doubt Tyler knew about their safety features when he pulled them from his dad's garage. But I passed Bruce's message to my mom—I told her he saved me, twice. Maybe he doesn't deserve it, but maybe that's what mercy is.

Nomi smiles, and for once, she doesn't try to hide her tears. "We did it, Cass."

I smile back, because we did.

Well, almost. But that's why we're here.

She taps the toe of her boot against the concrete, sending a pile of leaves skittering. "You scared me. When I saw the upper floor go up in flames, I was so scared."

I whisper, "Me too."

"I know I promised no cops. And I tried to let you do things your way like you did for me, but . . . I'm not sorry."

I hug her hard, or as hard as I'm willing to hug anyone. "Dad said with the limited supplies he had things could've gotten bad for me in seconds. I'm glad you called them, Nomi. I mean it. Plus you sort of saved my life, so it's hard to complain."

"True. We're even, then. Actually, fuck that, you owe me."

"Don't test me, Tanaka. Unless you want me to tell Detective Michaels the story of how you got your dog back."

She gasps. "Oh my god, you *are* a bitch!"

It feels entirely wrong to joke about any of this, utterly sick to find humor in what we did that night.

But we paid the price for it too. All of us, carrying the scars forever.

But I wouldn't change it. We survived. We did what we had to.

It's messy, gray, lost somewhere in the space where right and wrong blend.

We did what we had to.

Nomi's phone chimes. "She's on her way. Your prince awaits."

She glances down the path to where Noah leans against a headstone, and he nods in our direction.

We haven't talked, not really. Dad didn't leave my side at first, and then . . .

Let's just say some old habits die hard and I may have been inflicted with a very brutal case of laryngitis.

Nomi takes a few steps back, pulling the camera from her bag. "You know, he might've been more scared than me."

I don't know what to say to that, so I don't, and she rolls her eyes. "I can't believe I'm saying this, but be nice to him, Adams. He's a good guy. And it was very cinematic, the way he carried you from that burning building."

"Really?"

"No, you were half-dead and he looked ridiculous in that fire-retardant blanket cape. It was fucking horrifying. But feel free to imagine it as awesome."

She winks and struts away, leaving me with nowhere to go but my next stop.

He waits for me to walk to him, never moving from his spot on a headstone, until he tosses me something I catch on instinct.

I hold up the bottle of antibacterial spray with "No Sting!" plastered over its front. "Is this what you recommend for my gaping wound? You can keep your lying bottle of spray."

I don't throw it back though. Stupid or not, I'm keeping it.

"One," he says, "I tried it on a scrape I got from dragging your ass from a burning building, and it didn't sting."

"Now you're a liar too."

"Two: Your wound is no longer gaping. Your dad says you made a remarkable recovery. Shame, about your laryngitis flaring up again."

I hug myself to ward off the chill. "Thank you, for everything you did. For being there when I needed you, and—"

I hate how much I mean what I'm about to say, because it will delight him endlessly.

So I mumble, "For never lying to me."

"I'm sorry, what?" He leans closer. "I'm not sure I heard because you were kind of quiet, and a little mumbly—"

"I was *not* mumbly."

"There was a definite mumble."

I yell, "Thank you for never lying to me," and his smile grows wider with every syllable.

"I hate you, Noah, I really do."

I throw myself into him, for once, not caring at all about my gaping wound, and his arms close around me, hands threading through my hair and his breath hot against the top of my head.

And just like the first time, he holds me up.

We stay that way, for longer than I mean to, and when I finally let go, all the cold he kept at bay rushes in again.

He rubs at the back of his neck. "I need to say something, so don't interrupt."

"I—"

"That's interrupting." He pinches my lips together, turning me into a duck, before I swat him away. "Did I make it worse, threatening to go after Tyler at the park?"

I blink at him. "*None* of what happened was your fault."

"That wasn't the question."

I think, examining every angle, because he deserves an honest answer. "No. I would've done everything the same, even if you weren't trying to find him. That's the truth, Noah."

He only nods in response, but his whole body softens. A weight lifted.

"You didn't even go after him anyway."

"Oh no, I did." Everything in him goes tight again, his languid lean against the headstone replaced by rigid shoulders and curled fists. "I looked, and I was ready to put him in the fucking hospital—and that was only if I could hold back."

I believe him. And part of me wishes he had. But not all. Not the biggest part. That part knows it was always my battle to face.

I stare beyond him, at the figure moving closer to the freshly made grave. "You couldn't find him?"

"I stopped looking."

He paces, like he's still questioning every decision, still wondering if he did everything wrong. "I decided I could spend the whole night searching all over town, or I could trust you to handle it the way you needed to."

Something in me eases, a knot that formed that first night at the police station, when I decided trusting myself was my biggest mistake. "So what did you do?"

"I decided to protect what meant the most to you."

Dad. He went to warn my dad. "You got him out of the house, before Tyler came."

His cheeks flush. "It took some convincing. He was afraid you'd come back and he wouldn't be there."

I shudder, remembering how I *did* come back—to blood-soaked carpet and absolute certainty I'd lost my dad forever.

They tested the blood—animal, not human. It's still something I try not to think too hard on.

"We left a note. Clearly, Tyler made sure that disappeared."

"How'd you know he'd go after Dad?"

He shrugs, but it comes with a wince. "I've known guys like Tyler. He wanted you for himself, Cass. That wasn't going to happen as long as your dad was still around."

He's right. Dad was always my anchor. But he wasn't the only one.

I grasp the charm on my necklace. Ori, Margot, Nomi. And on the days I'm not too scared to admit it, Noah. They all hold me here too.

I step closer and rest my hand against his chest, let the steady beat of his heart against my palm calm me. "I really want to kiss you, Noah. If that's okay with you."

He grins, running his thumb over my cheek to whisk away the tears. "Who could blame you? I'm a fucking delight."

Before I have a chance to argue, he kisses me. Soft, slow. Steady. Like the world waits for us. Like neither of us are scared anymore.

My phone buzzes, and I jump so hard Noah has to stop me from stumbling to the ground.

I've developed a bit of an aversion to phone calls. I'll hate the color pink for eternity.

But I know who this text is from before I even look.

Can we hit the fucking pause button on the make-out session? The eagle has landed.

I hold out the screen for him. "Nomi says hi."

He laughs, low and deep. "Guess I'd better get to my post then."

He makes two wide strides toward the headstone where he's stashed his baseball bat.

The sound cracks through the air as he smacks it into his palm. "I won't blame you if you can't, but I'd appreciate if you kept the violence to a minimum."

"Is this where you get all chivalrous and say it's against your moral code to hit a girl?"

"No. My moral code makes exceptions for this one."

And maybe *that's* the problem.

Because mine does too.

• • •

The wind tosses Shelly's hair in every direction, creating a halo above her head as she stands at Tyler's grave.

I stare past her, to the glossy marble that bears his name. The date of his death etched into the solid stone.

I did this.

No matter what came before, it was me that stuck that knife into his stomach. My hands that twisted the blade to inflict the most damage.

Messy. Gray. Me.

With a scar that matches the one he went to the grave with.

I breathe out. Slow. Steady. "It took me a few days to figure it out."

She startles at the sound of my voice, surprise giving way to a smile as she turns and sees me. "Oh my god, Cass! I'm so glad you're okay!"

Liar.

"It was the photo paper, you know? Such a stupid little thing, but I couldn't let it go. Well, that and the phone call I got while Tyler was next to me. I ruled him out because of that at first. But then I realized it was just like the actual kidnapping. Tyler had a partner in that too."

It takes her a few tries before she can form words. "I'm sorry, but I have no idea what you're talking about."

She scans the cemetery, her brow furrowed. "Are you okay? Are you even allowed to be here?"

"I mean, why would he use two different kinds of photo paper? Sure, he could've run out—no time to go to the store while he was stalking

314

me or plotting to kill my family—but then, something still seemed off."

I step closer and pull out the picture in question. The one of Tyler on the front, the scrawled "No" on the back. The one I found in my locker, hanging from the ribbon that led me to Melanie Pennington.

It's a copy, of course. The real one doesn't belong to me anymore. It's police evidence.

They all are.

I hold it up for her, make her stare at Tyler's face. "I mean, the ribbon seemed so obvious at first—direct line to Melanie, right? That was pretty convenient, the way it was lying out in plain view for me. And Margot's necklace, that would've been easy to grab at one of the team meetings Margot always had at her house. Tyler didn't have easy access, but you sure did."

"Are you serious? Ribbons and necklaces?" She holds out her arms, wrists together. "Open-and-shut case—arrest me now. I mean, what do those even have to do with the picture?"

"Right. See, when I got the note about kissing Noah, it was a picture of both of us. But the Tyler one, that was just him. Makes sense, right? I mean, if Tyler's stalking me, he can't exactly take a picture of *himself* with me. Only, it was just that one little word on the back. 'No.' Doesn't have much energy behind it, does it? Not like the note I got for Noah. *Nothing* like the phone call I got about it later."

Her eyes flare in surprise and she crosses her arms. "Cass, honestly. This sounds like stuff you should be telling the cops, not me."

"Oh, don't worry, I did. Or, *do* worry I guess."

We stare in silence, until her lips settle into a flat line. "I don't know what you're getting at here, because it sounds like you're saying I had something to do with this."

"See, Shelly, that's because I am."

She laughs, until it echoes off the headstones and fills the open air. "Okay, now I know you're not okay. Did Tyler hit your head or—"

"Nope." I pull up my shirt to reveal the jagged pucker of my wound. "Stabbed myself. Mental facilities still intact."

Her face pales, and she stumbles until her thighs hit Tyler's headstone. "I have to go."

"You have to stay. Until I'm finished. You'll want to wait for the end."

She scans the grounds again, like she knows there's not a single direction she could run where someone wouldn't be waiting for her.

I drop my shirt, shivering as warmth covers my stomach again. "I was actually grateful to you, that day in the gym when you helped me escape. I thought—for a second anyway—that maybe I had you wrong. That you didn't hate me. But then Noah said you did, and Noah doesn't lie."

"So, what? You think I helped you because I hate you?"

"No. I think you helped me because you hate my mom."

Her face goes slack and colorless, her voice thin. "You're crazy. You know that?"

"I did stab myself, so it's possible you're not wrong."

A couple walks by, their mouths open and stares completely obvious. They think I'm crazy too. The kind of person who doesn't think about consequences. The kind of person who'd leave her family behind and stay silent, knowing her daughter was about to be abducted.

The kind of person who'd kill his own father in a quest to conquer the person he believes he loves.

It used to be the thing I feared most, being like them. Being one of them.

In my nightmares, it's Tyler's voice I hear most. *"You and me, Cass, we're the same."*

I'm not though. I never was.

I move closer, pinning Shelly to Tyler's headstone. "See, the more I thought about it, the less it made sense. On one hand, Tyler was giving me these notes to help me solve my kidnapping. Leading me directly to my mom's involvement. Melanie Pennington's too. And I figured, in his head, he was isolating me. Showing me how the people who were supposed to love me had actually betrayed me. Setting me up for being completely dependent on him."

I slip my hands into my pockets, and she watches them, her breaths coming harder as I take another step. "And really, that's exactly what he was doing. But then it switched focus. His clues were helping me, leading me to ways that would help me find some . . . other things I was looking for."

"Oh, you mean your crazy revenge escapades? Do you think no one knows about those?" Her eyes narrow, lip curls. For the first time, I see the real Shelly. The one that used Tyler to meet her own ends.

The one that let him stalk me, terrorize me. *Encouraged* him to do those things, all for her own gains.

Her shoulders set. "Careful, Cass. If I did the things you're saying, it means I know things that could make life *very* difficult for you."

That, she's also not wrong about. But the only thing the cops don't know about is Jared.

But then, we knew that, the four of us, and we paid him a little visit. Just to make sure our deal was still in place.

Jared Bedford had no plans to go public with anything, not with his confession saved on each of our hard drives. And a few backups.

Messy. Gray. All of us.

I smile at her, and the smirk melts from her face. "Do you want to know where you messed up, Shelly? It was that day in the bathroom, when Noah sent you in to ask me to come out, and you were so determined to humiliate me you forgot not to give yourself away. And you couldn't help bringing up my mom and how those kids caught her on camera with the principal."

She rolls her eyes. "*That's* your smoking gun? Seriously, that wasn't hard to find, Cass. Google exists. The video of your mom is all over the internet if you search for it."

"True, but that's not what gave it away. You talked about me switching schools so many times, and there's no easy-to-find video for that."

It was always different reasons—because Mom had an affair with the principal, because she got a little too comfortable and decided to trust people with her secrets. Because so few of those secrets ever stayed with the people she trusted them with.

Over and over, I paid the price. The looks from the other kids. The rescinded birthday party invites. The canceled play dates, and when I got older, the rumors that I was just like her.

This time though, we're weathering the storm. This time, Dad and I are doing things right.

She pushes past me, clipping my shoulder. "We're done here."

"I'm sorry. For what she did." I say it to her back, and it draws her up straight, stops her where she stands.

She turns, slowly. "You're *sorry*? Fuck you, Cass Adams. You don't even know what I went through."

"Yes I do." I did my research on Shelly too. How she switched to Stoneybrook two years ago, after her dad got busted with weed in his car. He had a woman with him. Discovering her identity did not yield any surprises.

She hisses her words. "My dad was a *pastor*, Cass. A married man of God who preached to a congregation of thousands. I had friends at school, almost my entire family went to that church. That fucking bitch took everything from us."

I've been here before. My head bowed. Stomach twisted. Absorbing all the vitriol, all the anger, for sins I didn't commit.

All the guilt too.

But I can't do that anymore. My therapist says it's not healthy, holding myself responsible for anyone else's actions. Not Dad's, not Tyler's, not my mother's either.

I say, "No offense, but your dad made some decisions there too."

She shakes her head, tears streaming down her cheeks. "Just like her. You are *just* fucking like her. I knew it. I always knew it, from the day you transferred to Stoneybrook. You didn't even know who I was. Your mother ruined my life, and you didn't even know my name."

Somehow, I doubt pointing out I don't know the majority of people whose lives my mother's disrupted will be helpful. Besides, what I really need is for Shelly to keep talking.

So I stay silent, and she does. All the things she's been building inside rush to the surface.

"It was her pot. He took the fall because she told him she'd just gotten busted a month before. He thought he loved her, but she was using him. Just like you did to Noah. Because you're a fucking *whore* just like your mom. And your dad is a desperate, pathetic twat."

My hand fists, and I want to hit her. Punch her in her stupid face. But that's not what we're here for.

"Too much truth for you, Cass? Well, how about this? Tyler was a psycho, and you liked him because he's the only person crazier than you. I didn't *make* him stalk you. I didn't make him kidnap you either. I just nudged him in the right directions. I was just smart enough to recognize an opportunity to ruin her life—and yours—like she did mine."

She turns to leave but stops herself, pivoting back. "And you know what? I'm not sorry. I hope she rots in prison for the rest of her life. The only thing I'd do differently is make sure Tyler killed you both."

A slow clap starts to my left, then my right, until Nomi, Ori, Margot, and Noah all creep from their hiding places.

Nomi says, "Well that's a wrap," and turns off the video camera she used to record the entire conversation, and Shelly's panicked gaze bounces between each of them, her skin growing paler by the second.

She stares at Noah, the pleading in her eyes nearly desperate, but a head shake is all he gives her, even as his grip on the bat tightens.

Ori drops her phone into her pocket—backup video—and says, "A-plus villain monologue, by the way. Next time you might want to get a little bigger picture with it though. Frame your vendetta against the human condition. Our faults and struggles? Humans are selfish and flawed and not worth saving? Things like that. Classic villain-type stuff."

Margot rolls her eyes, but she's smiling as she drags Ori away.

I double-check to make sure all the cameras are off, including the one I'm wearing. "You got everything?"

"All of it!" Nomi blows a kiss in Shelly's direction. "The girls and I will take it to my dad. We figured you've seen enough of the inside of police stations."

"Amen."

"I want to watch though, so hurry up."

I do as she asks.

My fist connects with Shelly's jaw, and no matter how much pain flares through my knuckles, it's worth it to watch her land in the grass at the foot of Tyler's grave.

She didn't force him to do anything. She's right about that, and only Tyler is responsible for the decisions he made. But she used him, weaponized him, without a single regard for anyone who got hurt in the cross fire.

I stare down at her, all the messy parts of me. "That's for what you said about my dad."

Now, finally, we're done.

We leave her there, the three of us following the path to Ori's car, Nomi's arm around my waist and Noah's hand wrapped around my throbbing one.

He raises it, pressing the softest of kisses against my skin. "You probably need first aid. You should come home with me."

"I have my own Very Stingy spray now. I don't need you."

Nomi gives me a final squeeze. "Your alternative is the police station. Or we could leave you here with Shelly."

I flip her off, and her head tips toward the sky as she laughs.

I yell, "I don't need any of you!" to her retreating back.

Noah goes quiet, his face serious, and he's still not lying when he says, "Yes you do."

CHAPTER FIFTY-FOUR
CASS ADAMS

The Events of Friday, October 27
The New Beginning

We had one last promise to uphold. One final part of the agreement we made that first night in the woods.

And this is it. Our pens to this paper. Our written confessions.

The fire between us crackles and hisses, flaring heat that battles the night's chill.

After each new chapter I finish, I stare through the flames to Ori, her head bent in concentration, end of her pen chewed.

To Margot, sketching lines and circles in the corners, sneaking glances in Ori's direction, smiling without realizing.

And to Nomi, her knee bouncing with all the vulnerability of putting her deepest thoughts on display.

But she continues. We all do. Our words a final testament to the things we did to survive. To the thoughts and fears that shadowed our choices. To the lives we took back for ourselves.

It takes hours, the sound of our tears mingling with the chirp of crickets. Each filled page another step toward forgiveness. Toward absolution.

We stoke the flames, smoke seeping into our hair, our clothes, branding us with the memory of this night and all the ones before it.

And when we've finally finished, we share our souls.

Each of our words, passed through each set of waiting hands, so we can finally see. So we can understand all the things we didn't say. All the things we're brave enough to speak now.

And when the last page is read, all of us, our faces tearstained, our bodies drained but more whole than they'd been before, we feed our confessions to the fire.

The pages curl and blacken, every new ounce of ash setting us free. Releasing us from the bonds of our guilt.

Our bracelets follow, metal melting beneath the force of the flame, dripping deep into the soil where it will become something else. Something new. Ashes to fill the charms around our necks.

We stay there, shoulders pressed against shoulders, until the sun climbs into the sky and the fire gives its last gasping breath.

We're all that's left.

Ashes to ashes.

And all of us, born from the fire.

ACKNOWLEDGMENTS

I owe immeasurable thanks to every person who helped this book become a reality. Writing may be a solitary venture, but shaping those words into the pages that lie in readers' hands is most definitely not.

First and foremost, my eternal thanks to my agent, Sarah Davies, for being a fierce and determined advocate whose dedication and honesty are an absolute benchmark. Your advice and guidance are a lifeline and I am so very lucky to have you in my corner!

To my editor, Mallory Kass, for her brilliant wisdom and enthusiastic support. You've helped make this book the best version of itself, and managed to make it painless and maybe even fun? (Is that possible?) Working with you has been an absolute joy, and I'm so incredibly grateful to have the opportunity.

To the entire Scholastic team, who've been so wonderful to collaborate with. Maeve Norton for the perfect cover and interior page design. To Janell Harris, production editor. To my copy editor, Jackie Hornberger, for taking on the unenviable task of making sure my timeline made sense, and to Susan Hom, Genevieve Kim, and Lara Kennedy for their proofreading prowess.

I would never have made it to this point without the constant support, encouragement, and sometimes commiseration from writing friends.

To the best found family: Sonia Hartl, Annette Christie, Auriane Desombre, Kelsey Rodkey, Susan Lee, and Rachel Solomon. This book would not exist without your love and support. I am eternally grateful for every single conversation, for sharing your joys and sorrows, your accomplishments and frustrations, and for making even the worst days brighter. You all have my heart forever.

To all the wonderful friends Pitch Wars has brought me. Rajani LaRocca and Emily Thiede, I cannot wait for the day I get to hug you both again. Thank you for always being there, for your constant support, for letting me celebrate alongside you during all our successes. I love you both!

And to Kylie Schachte, Anna Mercier, and Kristin Lambert for still being there to talk and celebrate all these years later! I'm so glad to have all of you in my life.

To my fairy godmother, Elle Cosimano. Your support means the absolute world to me and I remain in awe of your generosity and talent. I'm so grateful my journey led me into yours.

To my wonderful Pitch Wars mentees, LL Madrid, Elora Ditton, and Erinn Salge, who've taught me as much as I've (hopefully) taught them. Thank you all for being wonderful, for cheering me on, and always, for letting me be part of your journey.

To my first and forever writing friend, Claribel Ortega, whose talent, humor, and compassion still inspire me. I will always feel blessed to call you a friend. All my love.

To my personality twin, Roselle Lim. You are one of the kindest, most talented people I know, and I'm so grateful to always be only a text away. Love you!

So many thanks to Susan Gray Foster, the very first reader of this book and so many more. Thank you for always making time for me, and for your support and wonderful critique!

To my friends and family, who continue to have the faith in me I sometimes lack in myself.

And most importantly, to Eva and Joei, my reason for everything.

ABOUT THE AUTHOR

Andrea Contos is a writer of young adult mysteries and thrillers, and an International Thriller Award nominee. She harbors deep obsessions with true crime, angry girls, and morally gray characters. Andrea grew up in Detroit and currently lives outside the city with her daughters, her husband, and their very fluffy dog, Winston. Andrea is a Pitch Wars mentor and the author of *Throwaway Girls*. Follow at @Andrea_Contos on Twitter and at @andreaacontos on Instagram, or visit andreacontos.com.